MIDNIGH

A thought took him ... e
stood gazing down at her, ... r
innocence. She slept on her side, her cheek resting ... e hand. Her hair was spread across the pillow like a splash of sunlight, tempting his touch.

She stirred as he sat down beside her.

"Sleep, sweet Rhianna," he murmured. "Dream your young girl's dreams." He brushed a lock of hair away from her neck, placed his hands lightly on her shoulders. "Rest well, you have nothing to fear."

Slowly, he bent his head toward her, his tongue stroking the warmth of her neck. She moaned softly as his teeth grazed her throat.

"Sleep, little one," he murmured. "You have nothing to fear, it's only a dream..."

Other *Love Spell* books by Madeline Baker
writing as Amanda Ashley:
SUNLIGHT, MOONLIGHT
DEEPER THAN THE NIGHT
EMBRACE THE NIGHT

A Darker Dream

Amanda Ashley

LOVE SPELL BOOKS NEW YORK CITY

For JAMES BARBOUR

L.A.'s fabulous "Beast"
Who brought my favorite
Disney character to life
and reaffirmed my belief in magic
and happy endings.

LOVE SPELL®
July 1997
Published by

Dorchester Publishing Co., Inc.
276 Fifth Avenue
New York, NY 10001

Printed in the United States of America.

HEART OF DARKNESS

In the darkness of the full moon,
his spirit has wandered for centuries,
lost and alone,
never sharing the light
of a new day,
always in the midnight hours
he has walked.

Darkness claims his troubled soul,
the past haunts his waking hours;
Then, like a glimmer of sunlight,
she came to claim him,
touching places long dead,
reviving hope, promising love.

If only he dared believe,
if only he dared reach out,
and take that which he needs.
Within the sadness, the emptiness,
if just for tonight,
her warm hand and gentle ways
could dispel the endless night.

Could love break this darkness
he lives in?
Believe, my Lord Rayven, only believe
and love, happiness, and peace
will find you.

—Mary Lou Von Meter

A Darker Dream

Part One

Prologue

He had always loved the night. His favorite pastimes—drinking, gambling, the pursuit of a beautiful woman—were best accomplished in the hours of darkness.

The best times of his life had been spent in dimly lit saloons and smoky gambling dens, or in lush candlelit bedrooms. But that had been long ago.

Only now did he fully understand what he had lost when the light had been taken from him. Because she was like the sunlight—bright, warm, beautiful.

And, like the sun, she could never be his.

Chapter One

I hide in the shadows
and lust for the light
For I am Vampyre
forever imprisoned by the night.

Millbrae Valley, 1843

Rayven sat back in his chair, trying unsuccessfully to mask his disgust as he watched Vincent McLeod attempt to auction off the eldest of his five daughters.

Head down, hands limp at her sides, the girl stood mute, like a beast bound for slaughter. Her hair, a dull dirty blond, tumbled over her shoulders, hiding her face as effectively as the shapeless gray dress hid the body beneath.

"See here, Rayven," Montroy complained. "Can't we have a little more light?"

Rayven shook his head. The room was dark, and he liked it that way—dark wood paneled the walls, a dark green carpet covered the floor, matching draperies hung at the windows, the lamps were turned low, as always. Anyone who shared the back room of Cotyer's Tavern with him knew he avoided bright light. It was one of his many quirks, one the rich young men of the town endured for the sake of being in his rather questionable company.

"Well, if we can't turn up the lamps, then have the girl disrobe," Lord Tewksbury called from the back of the room. "I refuse to bid on a pig in a poke."

"Aye," Nevel Jackson agreed. "Tell the girl to peel off those rags so we can see what we're buying."

The call was taken up around the room. Vincent McLeod hesitated, then whispered something to the girl. Head still bowed, she began to unlace the bodice of her dress.

Rayven watched through narrowed eyes, noticing the way the girl's hands trembled as she unfastened the shabby frock. Though he could not see her face, he knew her cheeks were flushed with embarrassment, knew her heart was pounding like that of a fawn caught in the jaws of a wolf.

"Enough." Just one word, softly spoken, but it carried throughout the room.

"See here, Rayven," Tewksbury protested. "I think . . ."

Rayven silenced him with a quelling glance. "The girl is mine," he declared, having decided, in that moment, to buy her, though he still had not seen her face.

"Seeking a new mistress?" Lord Montroy inquired.

"No."

"A housemaid, perhaps?"

Rayven met Montroy's gaze. Dallon Montroy was a tall, good-looking man, almost as wealthy as Rayven himself. Of all the men Rayven gambled with, Montroy came closest to being a friend.

Ignoring the viscount's question, Rayven waved to the old man. "Bring her here."

"Aye, milord." Hastily, Vincent McLeod grabbed his daughter by the arm and dragged her across the room. "You won't be disappointed, milord. She'll serve you well."

"Yes," Rayven murmured. "She will, indeed."

Reaching into his pocket, Rayven brought out a handful of bank notes and thrust them at the other man. "Has she a name?"

"Of course, milord. It's Rhianna, but she'll answer to anything you wish to call her."

"You know where I live?"

"Aye, sir." Everyone knew of Rayven's castle. Located at the top of Devil Tree Mountain, it stood like a sentinel over the town, tall, dark, and mysterious, like its master.

"Take her there. My man will look after her."

"Aye, milord."

Rayven waved his hand in a gesture of dismissal. Turning back to the game, he picked up his cards. "You lose again, Montroy," he drawled softly, and spread his hand on the table.

Dallon Montroy tossed his cards into the pot. "Seems to be your lucky night," he remarked good-naturedly.

Rayven grunted softly. "Perhaps you're right,"

he mused as he watched the girl follow old man McLeod out the door. "Perhaps you're right."

Rhianna huddled on the narrow wagon seat beside her father, unable to control her body's trembling, or to accept the fact that her father had sold her to a man like Lord Rayven, a man who was rumored to have many strange and unusual habits.

The spires of Castle Rayven loomed in the distance, a dark shape rising out of the smoky gray mist that shrouded Devil Tree Mountain both summer and winter.

With each passing mile, her trepidation increased. She thought briefly of jumping out of the wagon and taking her chances with the wild animals that lurked in the woods.

She was gathering her courage, deciding death would be preferable to a life of servitude to the mysterious Lord Rayven, when she felt her father's hand close around her arm.

"Rayven paid me a handsome sum for ye," McLeod said, his mild tone at odds with his vicelike grip. "Ye'll stay with him so long as he wants ye, and do whatever he asks without question. Do ye ken my meaning?"

"Aye, father."

McLeod nodded. A short time later, he parked the wagon in front of the castle. "Go on, girl."

Rhianna slid a glance at her father, trying not to hate him for what he was doing, trying to feel some sense of satisfaction in knowing that the money her father had received would buy food for her mother and younger sisters.

"There was no other way, lass," Vincent McLeod said in gruff apology.

Rhianna nodded. Most likely, she would never see her father again. She had lived in Millbrae Valley all her life. She was not ignorant of the tales told of Castle Rayven's dark lord.

"Good-bye, Da."

"Good-bye, lass." McLeod met her gaze briefly, then looked away. He knew some would condemn him for selling his own flesh and blood, but she would be better off with Rayven. At least she would have enough to eat. "Ye've always made me proud, Rhianna," he said brusquely. "Go on with ye now."

Blinking back tears, Rhianna alighted from the wagon. Squaring her shoulders, she walked up the narrow stone steps to the wide double doors, took a deep breath, and lifted the heavy brass knocker.

Moments later, the door creaked open, and Rhianna found herself staring into a pair of hooded brown eyes.

"Miss McLeod, I presume."

"Y . . . yes," she stammered, startled that the stranger knew her name, that he had been expecting her. How had he known she was coming?

"I am Bevins."

The man stepped back, gesturing for her to enter. He was a tall man, with wavy gray hair, a rather sharp nose, and thin lips. He wore a pair of tan trousers, a white shirt, and a dark tweed jacket. He looked as if he was at least as old as her father.

Feeling abandoned and very much alone, Rhianna stepped over the threshold. The entryway was cold and dark. She shivered as Bevins closed the heavy door behind her.

"I have a bath prepared for you, miss."

"Thank you."

"This way."

Pulse racing with apprehension, she followed him down a long narrow hallway, up a steep flight of stairs, into a large room that was lit by a single fat white candle.

"You will find the tub in there," Bevins said, pointing to a door across the room. "Please leave your clothes out here, on the floor. I have been instructed to burn them."

"Burn them! But they're all I have."

"No doubt Lord Rayven will provide you with suitable attire, miss. There are clean sheets on the bed. The bellpull is there, should you have need of me during the night."

Too stunned to speak, Rhianna nodded.

"Good night, miss. Sleep well."

She waited until he left the room, then went to the door and closed it. Undressing, she dropped her clothes on the floor, then went into the other room. The light from a dozen candles revealed a large tub of hot water, a bar of scented soap, and a length of heavy toweling.

She stared at the steaming water. Never in all her life had she had a bath drawn for her and her alone. At home, baths were infrequent. In the summer, she bathed in the river. Only in the winter did they bathe indoors, and then she had to wait her turn. Usually, by the time she got in, the water was cool. And dirty.

She stepped carefully into the tub and sat down, a contented sigh escaping her lips as the blissfully hot water closed around her. Perhaps living here would not be so bad. The two rooms she had been given were larger than the hut she shared with her parents and sisters.

She washed her hair three times, her body twice, and still she sat in the water, basking in its warmth, until the water grew cool.

Stepping out of the tub, she dried off, then wrapped herself in the towel and went into the bedroom. The first thing she noticed was that her clothes were gone. And then she saw the nightgown. It lay on the bed like a splash of white paint against the blue coverlet. Unable to resist, she ran her hand over the material. Dropping the towel, she lifted the gown over her head, sighing with pleasure as the garment slithered over her bare skin.

She glanced around the room, hoping to find a mirror, curious to see how she looked in such a costly gown, but to no avail.

Crossing the floor, she drew the heavy draperies away from the window and peered at her reflection in the glass. The material clung to her like a second skin, outlining her breasts, the curve of her hip.

"Silk," she murmured, running one hand over the gown in disbelief. "It feels like silk."

"And so it is."

Releasing the curtains, Rhianna whirled around, her arms crossed over her breasts in an age-old feminine gesture. "My lord, I didn't hear you come in."

"Do you like the gown?"

"Y . . . yes," she stammered. "V . . . very much."

Rayven regarded her through narrowed eyes.

Cleaned up, with her hair falling in damp waves down her back, she was quite the loveliest thing he had ever seen.

He took a step forward, his hand reaching to touch a smooth, peach-colored cheek.

With a little cry, she backed against the wall.

Immediately, Rayven lowered his hand. "I will not hurt you," he said quietly.

Rhianna swallowed hard, mesmerized by his voice. It was deep and soft, yet strangely compelling, as were his eyes. Fathomless black eyes that looked old beyond their years. Eyes that seemed able to look into her and through her at the same time.

Moving slowly, he closed the distance between them, stopping when he was only a breath away. She had not realized how tall he was. He loomed over her, his long black hair framing his face like a dark cloud. He was dressed all in black save for his shirt and a blood-red cravat loosely knotted at his throat. A thin white scar bisected his left cheek. His nose was straight and aristocratic, his lips full and sensual. She guessed him to be in his early thirties.

Like a mouse mesmerized by a snake, she watched his hand move toward her, felt his fingertips stroke her cheek. His skin was smooth and cool.

"How old are you, girl?"

"Fifteen, my lord."

Rayven swore under his breath. He knew many girls her age were already married and had borne children. Still, he had not thought her quite so young. Not that it mattered. He had no designs upon her flesh, soft and smooth though it might be.

"Shall I . . . shall I get into bed, my lord?"

"If you wish."

He watched a blush stain her cheeks as she slid a glance at the bed.

"Should I . . ." She gulped, the blush in her cheeks spreading down her neck. "Should I disrobe?"

Rayven raised one brow, then shook his head. "I've no intention of bedding you, girl."

"No?"

The relief in her voice caused a sharp pain in the nether regions of a heart he had thought long past feeling. "No."

"Then why . . ." Her cheeks grew redder. "I thought . . ."

"I bought you for reasons of my own, sweet Rhianna," he replied, his voice as silky as the gown she wore.

"Might I ask what those reasons are?"

"No." He turned away from her, his hands clenching at his sides. "You may have the run of the castle, save for the rooms in the east tower. You are never to go there."

"Yes, my lord."

"Bevins will supply anything you wish. You have only to ask him."

"Anything?" she asked.

"Anything. If you desire to paint, he will provide canvas and brushes. If you wish to play the pianoforte, he will instruct you. If you wish to pass your days reading, I have a rather extensive library."

"I don't know how to paint or play the pianoforte or read, my lord." She lowered her gaze. "I don't know how to do anything."

He swung around to face her, a curious light in his eyes. "Would you like to learn?"

"Yes, my lord," she said eagerly, "very much."

"Bevins will teach you whatever you wish."

"Thank you, my lord."

Rayven stared down at the girl. Her eyes were blue, like a summer sky, like the lake in the village where he had spent his youth. Deep blue eyes, filled with excitement. And fear.

She was afraid of him. The thought cut deep, though he could not fault her for it.

"Bevins will take you shopping tomorrow. Buy whatever you need."

"You are most generous, my lord."

"Not at all, sweet Rhianna, for the price will be dear."

Her eyes widened at the veiled threat in his voice. She clasped her hands together, hands that trembled violently.

"You have nothing to fear from me," he said. "After tonight, you will not see me again."

The fear in her eyes turned to bewilderment. "My lord?"

"Go to bed, girl."

Rhianna scrambled into bed, her heart pounding wildly as he drew the covers up to her chin. She stared up at him, frightened and confused, yet fascinated by him at the same time. What a strange man he was. She had the oddest feeling that he had bought her simply to save her the embarrassment of disrobing before a roomful of half-drunken men. He was soft spoken and well mannered, yet she sensed a hint of carefully controlled violence lurking beneath the smooth facade, and beneath that smoldered an emotion more dangerous, more deadly, something she could not define. It was that which frightened her the most.

"Rest well, sweet Rhianna," Rayven murmured.

He blew out the candle, and then he was gone.

Chapter Two

The moon is my sun,
the night is my day,
Blood is my life,
and you are my prey.

Rhianna woke slowly, and even as she opened her eyes, she thought she must still be dreaming.

She sat up, plumping the pillows behind her. Last night, she had not given any heed to her surroundings. Now, she gazed around in breathless wonder. Blue-and-white striped wallpaper adorned the walls. Heavy blue damask drapes covered the windows; a matching counterpane was folded on the foot of the bed. There was a thick rug on the floor, woven in shades of blue.

She was about to get out of bed when she heard a knock at the door.

"Miss Rhianna?"

"Yes, come in."

She drew the covers over her breasts as the door opened and Bevins stepped into the room.

"Lord Rayven instructed me to take you shopping this morning after breakfast."

Rhianna nodded. "Yes, he told me."

"I've brought you something to wear," he said, placing a large parcel on top of the table beside the bed. "When you are dressed, please come down to breakfast."

"I will, thank you."

"Is there anything you prefer?"

Rhianna shook her head.

"Very well, miss. I shall expect you in, say, half an hour?"

"That will be fine."

"Unless you wish to have breakfast in bed."

"In bed? I'm not sick."

A slight smile flickered over his lips. "Half an hour then, miss," he said, and left the room, quietly closing the door behind him.

"Breakfast in bed," Rhianna mused, smiling. "Imagine that."

Rising, she opened the box, marveling at the bounty within. The dress was of orange and brown taffeta, with a square neck and long fitted sleeves. A bouquet of yellow silk flowers adorned the bustle. She ran her hands over the undergarments, unable to believe the finery of it all. Everything was edged with delicate lace and tiny pink bows, so pretty she wished she could wear it on the outside. Never had she owned anything so fine in all her life.

She dressed slowly, inspecting each item. She glanced around the room again, wishing for a mirror. At home, a looking glass was considered a luxury beyond their reach, but surely Lord Rayven could afford a hundred mirrors.

Odd, she thought as she made her way down the narrow staircase. But then, rumors of strange doings at Rayven Castle were rampant in town. Some said the place was haunted; others said that they knew of women who had gone there and had never been seen or heard from again. But they were only rumors, and she had never given much credence to idle gossip. After all, people said her father drank too much and that he beat his wife and children, and Rhianna knew that wasn't true. Vincent McLeod might not be the kindest, most affectionate father in the town, but he wasn't a monster, either.

When she reached the main floor, she wandered from room to room. Vaulted ceilings. Dark wood. Heavy draperies at the windows. Costly paintings and tapestries on the walls. Numerous statues and figurines and carvings made of silver and pewter and wood. Crossed swords above a massive stone fireplace. Expensive rugs imported from exotic places. But not a single mirror. She frowned. There were no clocks in the house, either.

The dining room, like the other rooms in the house, was large and dark and expensively furnished.

A lace cloth covered the long trestle table. A pair of silver candelabra stood in the center of the table. Long white tapers filled the room with a soft glow. Dark green velvet draperies covered the windows. There was a painting of a hunting scene on one wall, a painting of a sunset done in bold shades of pink and crimson on another.

There was only one place setting on the table. The plate was china rimmed with gold, the water glass was of fine crystal, the flatware was gold. Stunned by such opulence, she sat down.

Moments later, Bevins entered the room, a covered tray in his hands. As he uncovered it, a variety of rich aromas filled the room. There was sliced ham, poached eggs, fluffy biscuits, pats of butter, a jar of quince jam, a bowl of porridge, fresh strawberries and cream, sliced peaches, a pot of tea.

"I hope this is satisfactory, miss," he said.

"Oh, yes." She had never seen such a variety of food at one time. "Will . . . will Lord Rayven be joining me for breakfast?"

"No, miss."

She should have been relieved. Instead, she felt a wave of disappointment.

"Will there be anything else, miss?"

"No, thank you."

"Very well, miss. I'll bring the coach round when you're ready to go."

Rhianna nodded, overwhelmed by the richness of her surroundings, the bounty spread before her.

Certain she couldn't eat it all, she sampled everything, and when she sat back twenty minutes later, she was amazed to see there was nothing left. She had eaten every bite.

She spent the rest of the morning at Madame Sofia's. At a loss to know what fabrics and styles to pick for herself, Rhianna gave herself over to the modiste, who, after taking her measurements, sent Rhianna on her way with the promise of three day dresses to be delivered the following afternoon, and the rest within the week, along with all the necessary undergarments, hats, shoes, gloves, and parasols a lady required.

Rhianna's head was spinning by the time they returned to the castle.

Bevins prepared a lavish midday meal, graciously accepted her thanks, then suggested Rhianna take a nap.

Rhianna smiled. A nap in the middle of the day! She had never had that luxury before. But, tempting as it sounded, she wasn't tired.

"Would it be all right if I looked around?"

"Of course, miss. This is your home now. You may explore at your leisure. All the rooms are at your disposal save those in the east tower."

"Thank you, Bevins."

"What time would you like supper, miss?"

"I don't know. What time does Lord Rayven usually dine?"

"Lord Rayven rarely dines at home."

"Oh." She felt a wave of disappointment as she recalled that Lord Rayven had told her she would not see him again. Even though he frightened her, she thought him the most fascinating man she had ever met.

"Seven o'clock, miss?"

"What? Oh, yes, that will be fine. Thank you."

She spent the rest of the day exploring the castle, certain she would never find her way around. So many rooms and stairways and passages.

She bypassed the first story, where, in olden times, the granaries had been located, as well as the boxes and barrels and casks that had held household supplies.

The second floor housed the dwelling and common rooms for the inhabitants of the castle. Bevins's kitchen was here, adjoining a large, well-stocked pantry.

A passageway led to a dormitory where the castle's ladies-in-waiting had once slept. It occurred to Rhianna that her chamber, which was the largest room she had seen, must have been the sleeping quarters for the lord and lady of the castle. Knowing that made her wonder anew where Lord Rayven's chamber was.

She turned down another corridor, glad she had thought to bring a lamp with her, for the hallways were dark. She had never been given to flights of fancy and she wasn't about to start now, although, if one were going to believe in ghosts and goblins, she supposed the castle at Devil Tree Mountain would be the perfect place to start.

She paused now and then, admiring the paintings and rich tapestries that hung on the walls.

The first room she came to was a library filled with more books than could be read in a lifetime. Rhianna ran her fingers over the spines. She lifted a heavy volume from another shelf and opened it, staring in wonder at the fine spidery script. Gilt edged each page. She saw beautiful drawings of cherubs and winged horses.

Turning the pages, she found drawings of wolves and ravens and bats, a skeletal figure in a long black cloak, a dark angel who held a skull in one hand and a silver chalice in the other.

Disturbed by the images, she closed the book and put it back on the shelf.

She entered the great hall next. This room, where the family had once dined, was furnished with a long trestle table and a single high-backed chair made of black wood. Looking closely, she saw that the back of the chair was carved in the shape of a raven with its wings folded. Weapons of every kind imaginable decorated the walls.

A solarium located in the eastern corner of the house was filled with plants gone wild.

Caught up in exploring the wonders of the castle, an hour became two, three.

She spent a few minutes in the music room, running her fingers over the yellowed keys of a small pianoforte. She had often wished she could play, but there had been no time to learn, and no one to teach her. She smiled as she remembered that Lord Rayven had promised her lessons. A rather elegant-looking harp stood in the far corner of the room. She found a violin resting in a dusty case atop an equally dusty table.

On the third floor, she counted twelve rooms that she assumed had once been bedrooms for the master's children and servants. All were empty, the floors covered with a thick layer of dust.

She climbed another flight of stairs and found herself in a round tower room that overlooked the river and the forest beyond.

She went down several narrow, twisting flights of stairs and found herself in a dungeon. Wrinkling her nose against the damp, musty smell, she held her lamp higher and took a few steps inside, her footsteps muffled on the hard-packed earthen floor. Long rows of iron-barred cells lined both sides of the corridor.

Standing there, she felt a sudden sense of evil.

Men had died here. She could almost hear their screams echoing off the gray stone walls, taste their fear as they met violent death. . . .

With a squeal of fright, she turned and ran out of the dungeon. She took the stairs two at a time, her heart pounding as ghostly images rose up in her mind—grotesque images of blood and horror, of men being tortured, of terror and pain beyond bearing.

She was gasping for breath when she reached her room. Inside, she slammed the door, turned the key in the lock. She blew out the candle, then fell across the bed, willing her heart to stop pounding, her pulse to stop racing.

There was nothing evil in the dungeon, nothing to fear. It was only the fact that she had never been away from home before coupled with a vivid imagination that had her running scared. She was lucky to be here, in this place. For the first time in her life, she had a room of her own, food enough to eat, a beautiful dress. And, if Rayven was to be believed, anything else she wanted was hers simply for the asking.

Comforted by that thought, she fell asleep.

Rayven sat in front of the huge fireplace that dominated his bedroom, his elbows braced on the arms of his chair, his chin resting on his folded hands. He stared into the flames, but it was the girl's image that filled his vision. Vivid blue eyes deeper than any ocean. Beautiful blue eyes wide with fear. Pale pink lips. Skin the color of wild honey. Golden blond hair that reminded him of the sunlight he had not seen in four centuries.

She had cleaned up well, he mused. Perhaps too

well. Never before had he brought home one so young or so innocent or so lovely. For a moment, he contemplated sending her away. But only for a moment.

He glanced out the window, judging the time. She would be asleep by now.

He licked his lips as he rose from the chair.

A thought took him to her bedside. For a moment, he stood gazing down at her, bewitched by her beauty, her innocence. She slept on her side, her cheek resting on one hand. Her hair was spread across the pillow like a splash of sunlight, tempting his touch.

Moving slowly, he lifted a lock of her hair. Soft, he mused, so soft. He let the fine strands trickle through his fingers and then, unable to help himself, he stroked her cheek, let his fingertips slide down the length of her slender neck to rest lightly on the pulse throbbing slow and steady in her throat. Heat rushed through his fingertips. Ah, yes, he would have to be extremely careful with this one. She aroused far more than his accursed hunger.

Muttering an oath, he withdrew his hand.

She stirred on the bed as he sat down beside her.

"Sleep, sweet Rhianna," he murmured. "Dream your young girl's dreams." He brushed a lock of hair away from her neck, placed his hands lightly on her shoulders. "Rest well. You have nothing to fear."

Slowly, he bent his head toward her, his tongue stroking the warmth of her skin. She moaned softly as his teeth grazed her throat.

"Sleep, little one," he murmured. "You have nothing to fear. It's only a dream . . ."

In the morning, Rhianna woke feeling hungry and oddly lethargic after a good night's sleep. Recalling that she had missed supper, she decided that accounted for her hunger as well as her lassitude.

Sitting up, she felt faintly dizzy. "Too much sleep and not enough food," she muttered as she slid her legs over the edge of the bed and stood up.

She looked at the bellpull, hesitant to summon Bevins, wondering if she would ever get used to the idea of having someone ready to fulfill her every desire.

"No time like the present to start getting used to it," she reasoned, and tugged on the cord.

Minutes later, Bevins knocked on the door.

"Come in."

"Good morning, miss." His gaze moved over her, and Rhianna thought she saw a look of pity in his eyes, but it was quickly gone, and she decided she had been mistaken.

"Could I . . . that is, I'd like a bath, please."

"Right away, miss. The water is heating." He left the room, only to reappear a moment later, a tray in his hands. "I thought you might like to take breakfast in your room this morning."

"Why, yes, I would, thank you."

"Is there anything else, miss?"

Rhianna shook her head, wondering if he was some kind of mind reader.

"Your bath will be ready shortly, miss."

"Thank you, Bevins." She paused, frowning. "How did you get in here?"

"Through the door, of course."

"But I . . . It was locked, wasn't it?" She glanced at the door. "I'm certain I locked it last night."

"You must be mistaken."

Rhianna shook her head. "No, I'm sure it was locked when I went to bed."

"Will there be anything else, miss?"

"No, thank you."

Feeling somewhat dazed, Rhianna carried the tray to bed. She'd been tired last night. Maybe she hadn't locked the door. With a shake of her head, she put the thought from her mind.

Making herself comfortable, she ate a leisurely breakfast, took a long soak in the tub, then spent an hour trying on her new clothes, wishing there was a mirror in the house so she could see how she looked.

Later that day, she asked Bevins if he would find one for her.

"I'm sorry, miss," Bevins said, his expression impassive, "his lordship refuses to have them in the house."

Rhianna frowned. "But why?"

"I'm sorry, miss. I'm afraid that's something you must discuss with Lord Rayven."

"How can I, when I never see him?"

"I am sorry, miss. Is there anything else I can do for you?"

"Lord Rayven said you would teach me to play the pianoforte and to read."

"I should be pleased to help you, miss."

Rhianna smiled at him. "Thank you, Bevins. I

should like to begin this afternoon, if you don't mind."

"It will be my pleasure, miss. Shall we meet in the library at three?"

In the weeks that followed, Rhianna's days fell into a pleasant routine.

She spent her mornings wandering about the grounds when the weather permitted; if it was raining, she struggled with a bit of fine needlework. Like all girls, she had learned early how to sew a seam or mend a tear, but she'd never had the time to sit and do what her mother called "fancy work."

She ate a late dinner, took a nap, and then spent the rest of the afternoon under Bevins's tutelage. He taught her to play the pianoforte; he taught her to read, and to write. She almost squealed with delight the first time she wrote her name without any help. *Rhianna McLeod. Miss Rhianna McLeod. R. McLeod.* She wrote it over and over again, thinking how grand it looked, how wonderful it was to be able to write her own name. After supper, she spent a quiet hour going over her lessons, and then she retired for the night.

One evening before going to bed, she told Bevins she wished she could plant a garden; the next day, she found a variety of seeds and seedlings on a bench in the side yard.

As the days passed, she came to realize that Bevins was quite a remarkable man. There were no other servants in the castle. Bevins was cook, butler, valet, and housekeeper, all rolled into one. In addition, he did the shopping and the laundry, looked after the grounds, and tended the horses.

He never intruded on her privacy, yet he was always there when needed. Truly, a most amazing man, she mused.

She had been at the castle several weeks when the nightmares began—dark dreams filled with a sense of impending doom, horrid dreams filled with death and hideous fangs stained with blood. Other nights, she awoke feeling cherished and desired, her heart beating fast as she recalled a phantom hand gently stroking her cheek, the touch strangely erotic. And always, after such dreams, she woke up feeling tired and hungry.

She voiced her concern to Bevins, wondering if she needed to see a doctor, but he assured her that she was perfectly fine, that it was only the change in diet and atmosphere causing her distress, and that she would soon adapt. There was pity in his eyes when he said this, and he refused to meet her gaze.

"Is something wrong?" she had asked. "Something you're not telling me?"

"I'm being as honest with you as I can, miss."

"Will I ever see Lord Rayven again?"

"I don't know, miss. I hope not," he had replied, and left the room.

Chapter Three

I long for what I've lost
For that which can never be.
I cloak the horror of what I am
and pray you never see.

He sat in his favorite chair before the fire, gazing, unseeing, into the flames. She permeated his house, his thoughts, his dreams. Never before had a woman affected him like this, taking hold of his every waking moment, tormenting him with her nearness. He spent his nights hovering near her while she slept, watching her, listening to her breathe, to the beat of her heart, the sound of the blood flowing through her veins. She smelled always of flowers. Even when the hunger lay dormant within him, he was drawn beyond his power to resist being with her, to touch the smoothness of her cheek, to run his fingers over her lips and imagine his mouth there.

She was so beautiful, this child-woman who wandered through his house by day and sustained him through the night. He knew her thoughts, heard the tears she sometimes shed in the night. It pleased him to satisfy her every want, to dress her in fine clothes, to provide the best food and wine that money could buy. He took pride in her ability to learn, and ordered books and music he thought would please her.

It was the least he could do, he thought, for she gave him life, and no matter how he tried, he could never repay her for that.

He knew the moment she fell asleep. He heard the change in her breathing, felt a change in the house itself, as if the life went out of it while she slumbered.

He would not go to her tonight. He would take to the streets and ease his craving there. Yet even as the thought crossed his mind, he knew it for the lie it was. Already, he was rising, her innocence calling him, beckoning him, the single light in the darkness of his existence.

Soundlessly, he climbed the stairs and opened the door to her room. She locked her door each night, but no lock made could keep him out.

And then he was standing beside her bed, gazing down at her. It was a warm night, and she had thrown off the covers. Her nightgown had ridden up, exposing a long length of softly rounded thigh.

His body stirred to life, hunger and desire riding him with whip and spurs as he sat down on the bed beside her.

He was bending over her when he realized that she was awake and staring at him.

Certain she was dreaming, Rhianna closed her eyes and opened them again. The tall dark figure was still there, hovering over her, like smoke.

"Lord Rayven?" She couldn't see his face in the darkness, yet she knew somehow that it was he.

"Go to sleep, Rhianna," he murmured. "You're very tired. Your eyelids are heavy, so heavy you can no longer keep them open."

"No . . ."

"Sleep, sweet Rhianna. Sleep is what you need."

His voice, deep and melodic, winding around her like a soft cocoon.

Her eyelids fluttered down, and she was following a narrow path through the darkness. She tried to turn back, but her feet refused to obey. Her heart was racing; she could hear the blood pounding in her ears as she drew ever closer, wondering who awaited her in the shadows tonight, the man who took her in his arms and held her as if she were a precious gift, or the one who preyed upon her flesh. Would she awake feeling loved and protected, or sobbing with fright? Or would this be the night she wouldn't awaken at all? . . .

She came awake to the sound of her own cries. Disoriented, she looked around, her pulse gradually slowing as she realized the nightmare was over and she was safe in her room.

She glanced at the door. The key was still in the lock. It had all been a dream, and yet this one had been so real, so vivid, she would have sworn Lord Rayven had entered her room last night, that she had awakened to find him sitting on the bed beside her, his dark eyes glowing with an unholy light as he bent over her.

Rhianna shook her head to clear the images from her mind. Just a dream. That's all it had been, just a dream. She brushed a lock of hair from her neck, her fingers pausing as they encountered what felt like an insect bite.

She spent the day in her room and tried to study her lessons, but she couldn't concentrate. She tried to take a nap, but sleep eluded her. She had no appetite for lunch.

Bevins looked in on her several times, his brow lined with concern. Once, she asked him to look at the marks on her neck. A shadow passed over his eyes as he examined the tiny wounds. *It's nothing, miss,* he had assured her. *A bite of some kind, I would say. Perfectly harmless.*

At dusk, she shook aside her lethargy, bathed, and dressed for supper.

Bevins had just served the first course when Rhianna felt a sudden tingle. Glancing over her shoulder, she saw Lord Rayven standing in the doorway, dressed, as before, in impeccable black.

"My lord." She started to rise, startled by his unexpected appearance, unnerved by the fact that he was a man of title and property, while she was nothing more than his servant, no matter that she had yet to serve him in any way.

He motioned for her to remain seated as he took the chair across from her. "Do you mind if I join you?"

"Of course not. It's your house, after all."

She toyed with her napkin as he settled back in his chair. A moment later, Bevins entered the room bearing a crystal decanter and a wineglass, which he set in front of Rayven.

"Thank you, Bevins," Rayven said. "That will be all."

"As you wish, my lord. Good evening, miss."

When they were alone again, Rayven studied the girl's face, noting the faint smudges beneath her eyes. "You are well?"

"Yes, my lord."

"And are you happy here?"

Her gaze slid away from his. "I am not unhappy, my lord." She gestured at the platters of meat and fowl in the center of the table. "Will you not eat something, my lord? Bevins is a very fine cook." She felt her cheeks flush. "I don't suppose I need tell you that."

A faint smile hovered over his lips. "Thank you, no. How are your lessons coming along?"

"Nicely, I think. Bevins says I have a talent for music, but it's reading I love."

"Indeed?"

"Oh, yes! Tales of brave knights and fair ladies, far-off lands, dragons and sorcerers."

Rayven's hands clenched in his lap as he watched her face, so alive, so expressive. So young. Heat flowed through him as she went on, her voice filled with the excitement of discovery. Had he ever been that young, that eager to learn?

Rhianna bit down on her lip, suddenly conscious of Rayven's gaze on her face. His eyes, as black as midnight mist, seemed to be searching her very soul.

"I'm . . . I'm sorry," she stammered. "I didn't mean to run on like that. It must seem silly to you."

"Not at all. Perhaps . . ." He took a deep breath. "Perhaps you would read aloud to me this evening."

"Oh. I . . . I'm still learning. I'm afraid you would soon be bored."

"It would please me very much, Rhianna."

"Very well then, if you're sure."

"Quite sure."

"Would you care for a glass of wine, my lord?"

At his nod, she lifted the decanter and filled his glass, noting, for the first time, that the wine was dark and red. Like blood.

His fingertips brushed hers as he took the glass from her hand. She was startled by the little frissons of heat that leapt from his skin to hers, by the jumbled images that filled her mind, images of a man writhing in pain, bleeding, screaming.

As quickly as it had appeared, the vision was gone, leaving her to wonder if she had seen anything at all.

Rayven leaned back in his chair, his gaze fixed upon her face. Had she felt it, too, the mystical flame that had sparked between them? He had glimpsed a well-spring of hope within her, a yearning for a home and family of her own, longing for the home she had left behind. What, if anything, had she sensed in him?

Rhianna took a deep breath, unsettled by the tension between them. "Would you mind if I shared your wine?"

"I doubt you would find it to your liking."

She glanced at the dark liquid in the decanter, then reached for her own glass, which was filled with water.

"Finish your supper, Rhianna," he said. "You need to keep up your strength."

"Why? I never do anything more strenuous than play the piano."

"Because you're hungry."

Obediently, she picked up her fork and began to eat. She *was* hungry, after all.

Later, he sat in a chair before the fire, sipping from his wineglass, while she read to him. Time and again, she glanced in his direction, expecting him to be bored or asleep, but always she found him watching her, his fathomless black eyes burning with a strange fire, a warmth hotter and more penetrating than the heat radiating from the crackling flames in the hearth.

"Tell me about yourself," he said, surprising them both.

"There's little to tell, my lord. I have four sisters, all younger than I." Her voice turned bitter. "My father sold me. Surely that tells you all you need to know."

"It tells me he needed money."

"He could have sold his horse."

A wry smile curled Rayven's lip. "And would you have pulled the plow in the horse's stead?"

She lifted her chin defiantly. "I have done so in the past."

Her admission touched a chord within him. Proud, she was, in spite of her poverty.

"You'll never have to do so again."

"Why did you buy me?"

Rayven shrugged, unable to admit the truth. "Why do you think?"

"I don't know." Her gaze slid away from his. "I thought that . . . I mean . . ."

"Go on. What did you think?"

"Nothing."

"Tell me." She heard the sliver of steel beneath his softly spoken command.

"I thought you bought me so I wouldn't have to disrobe in front of the others."

"You're very perceptive, sweet Rhianna."

"But why? You never . . ." Fire climbed into her cheeks, and she bent her head to the book.

"I never come to your bed?"

She didn't look up, but she nodded.

"And that bothers you?"

"Oh, no," she said quickly. It didn't bother her, not really, although it stung her pride to think he found her so ugly as to be completely undesirable.

"Rhianna, look at me."

Slowly, she met his gaze.

"You are a beautiful young woman," he said quietly. "But you are young. Far too young for me." His hands clenched in his lap. "Be glad I do not come to your bed." A shiver ran through her as his gaze held hers. "You would not like what would happen if I did."

She stared into his eyes, caught in their darkness, in blackness that was icy cold yet hotter than flame. It was like looking into eternity, she thought, into an endless black void filled with such yearning that she wanted to weep.

Muttering an oath, Rayven stood up. "Go to bed, Rhianna," he said curtly.

Frightened by the seething turmoil in his voice, she scrambled to her feet and hurried from the room. Panic lent wings to her feet, and she fairly flew up the stairs to her bedchamber. Inside, she turned the key in the lock, then collapsed on the bed, feeling as though she had just escaped, though from what, she couldn't say.

Chapter Four

I shadow my gaze in your presence
and pray you may ne'er be part,
Of the hunger that claws at my vitals
of the evil that blackens my heart.

Rayven stared after her, his hands curled into tight fists. It had been a mistake, joining her at supper. Never before had he spent time with the women he brought here. He used them as long as it was safe, then he paid them handsomely and sent them away. Far away, with a warning never to return. He had never watched any of the others so avidly while they slept, or burned with such longing for the touch of their flesh.

But Rhianna . . . She drew him in ways he didn't understand. She was no different from the others. All had been young. All had been beautiful. Though none had been quite so young, or quite so beautiful, as Rhianna. All had been born in poverty and ignorance. But none had expressed such an eagerness to learn.

He should send her away now, before it was too late.

But he knew he would not.

Releasing a deep breath, he reached for the wineglass on the table. He stared at the deep red liquid for a long moment, suddenly sickened by the blood and wine concoction that had sustained him for four hundred years. With an oath, he hurled the goblet into the fireplace and stalked out of the room.

Rhianna sat back on her heels, an immense feeling of satisfaction warming her as she surveyed her handiwork. It had taken hours and hours of hard work, but the castle gardens bloomed with color. Months ago, there had been nothing out here but barren ground and a few scraggly weeds. Now, there were flowers of all kinds and colors, lacy ferns and shrubs.

At home, she had spent long hours laboring in the vegetable patch, hoeing, weeding, nurturing the tender plants that fed the family. There had been no time or space to waste on flowers.

Rising, she pressed a hand to her back. But this . . . She closed her eyes, basking in the sun's warmth, in the heady fragrance that rose all around her. This had been a labor of love. She had planted vegetables, too, but only the ones she liked.

Removing the wide-brimmed hat that shaded her face, she walked along the narrow dirt path that wove in and out of the flower beds. In addition to flowers, she had planted fruit trees, thinking they would add not only beauty for the eye and shade from the sun, but a bountiful harvest.

When she reached the end of the garden, she stared at the maze that rose up near the castle's outer wall. The hedges that formed the maze were the only thing in the garden that had not needed care. She had wandered to the edge of the maze several times, but she had never found the courage to go inside. There was something ominous about the place, though she couldn't say what. Perhaps it was her fear, however irrational, of being lost in it.

With a sigh, she sank down on one of the marble benches that were scattered through the garden. It had been three months since the night Lord Rayven had joined her in the dining room. Why had he sought her out that night? Why hadn't he sought her company again?

She had been at the castle for almost six months now. Anything she desired was hers for the asking. She had all the clothes she would ever need. She had become an avid reader and she had discovered she had a talent for playing the pianoforte, and for painting. In truth, she had everything she had ever wanted—everything except someone to share it with.

When she was bored, Bevins drove her to the marketplace in the next town for a day of shopping and then, like a silent shadow, he followed her wherever she went. It would have been fun, buying whatever caught her eye, taking lunch in one of the inns, if it hadn't been for the boldly curious stares people sent in her direction. Save for the shopkeepers, no one spoke to her, though all who saw her nodded politely. It amazed her that gossip from her small village had spread to the next town, that everyone she met seemed to know she was living in Castle Rayven. Sometimes she heard Rayven's name mentioned, always in hushed whispers, always followed by the sign to ward off evil. It gave her a sad, lonely feeling.

Once, she had asked Bevins if she might invite her mother and sisters to the castle. He had replied, "No, miss, you may not," in such a way that she had never asked again.

Occasionally, she wondered if he might permit her to go visit her family, but she never found the nerve to ask.

Sometimes, she felt like a princess in a fairy tale, imprisoned in a magic castle but cut off from the rest of the world.

And always, lurking in the back of her mind like a dark shadow, was Rayven. She never saw him, never heard his voice, save in her dreams. She wondered what he did all day, if he was even in the castle. For all she knew, he could have left months ago. Rayven. He was like a riddle with no answer, a puzzle that could not be solved. Why had he brought her here?

It was a thought that stayed foremost in her mind the rest of the day, and followed her to bed that night.

He stood in one of the rooms in the east tower, staring out the window, his gaze drawn to the yard below. Bathed in the dancing silver shadows of the moon, the white roses glowed like ethereal blooms planted in some mystical garden. He felt a sudden longing to wander through the grounds during the light of day, to see the myriad colors of the flowers that Rhianna had nurtured, to touch the petals her hands had touched. In the darkness, the bright rainbow colors looked muted, devoid of life.

Turning away from the window, he donned his cloak and drew on his gloves. Perhaps a midnight ride would soothe him; if it did not, he would go to Cotyer's and squander the remaining hours of darkness at one of the gaming tables and lose himself, for a few hours at least, in a semblance of normalcy.

Leaving the room, he locked the door behind him, then made his way swiftly along the dark hallway and down the stairs.

His steps slowed as he approached the stables. Abruptly, he turned away and made his way to the side yard. The fragrance of hundreds of flowers, of freshly turned earth, and grass and trees, rose up around him as he walked slowly down the narrow pathways, pausing now and then to caress the velvety softness of a rose. Rhianna had done this, had turned ugliness into beauty. He wondered if, offered the chance, she would be able to work the same miracle in his life.

A ripple in the air, the scent of warm skin, alerted him to her presence. He whirled around, his gaze piercing the darkness.

"Come out," he said. "I know you are there."

She stepped from behind a hedge, her cheeks flushed, her hands worrying the folds of her robe. Moonlight washed her hair in silver, turned her skin to alabaster.

"What are you doing out here at this time of night?" he demanded.

"I . . ."

"Speak up, girl. You needn't be afraid."

"I saw you from my window, and I wondered what *you* were doing out here at this time of night."

"I was thinking of you," he admitted.

His words sent a thrill of excitement racing down her spine. "Were you, my lord?"

He nodded, his gaze sweeping over her. She wore a voluminous robe of apricot-colored velvet. A froth of white lace framed her face. Her feet were bare and oddly provocative. "Why aren't you asleep, sweet Rhianna?"

"Because, my lord," she replied candidly, "I was thinking of you."

"Indeed?" Surprised by her candor, delighted to know he had been in her thoughts, he took a step closer. "What were you thinking?"

"I was wondering what I had done to displease you."

"You please me very well, Rhianna." Far too well for my peace of mind, he mused, and shoved his hands deep into the pockets of his trousers to keep from reaching for her, from taking that for which he hungered.

"I've not seen you in months, my lord." She should have been glad of that, she thought, for he was most mysterious, and, sometimes, a little frightening. And yet the few short hours she had spent in his presence had been intoxicating.

"You should be glad you've not had cause to see me," he replied brusquely.

"Should I?"

He gazed deep into her eyes, probing her thoughts, feeling her loneliness, her confusion.

She was a young girl on the brink of womanhood, yearning for something she did not fully understand. Like a finely crafted violin, she awaited the touch of the master's hand to bring forth the music locked within her.

Drawn into the depths of her eyes, he moved slowly toward her. Needing to touch her, steeling himself to be rejected, he pulled off his gloves and tossed them aside. A gasp—or was it a sigh?—escaped her lips as his hand stroked her cheek.

"My lord?" He heard her uncertainty in the trembling of her voice.

"I will not hurt you," Rayven said, praying he spoke the truth. "I want only to touch you. Your skin is so soft, sweet Rhianna. So soft . . ." Bending his head, he brushed her lips with his. "Sweet," he murmured, "as I knew you would be."

She stared up at him, caught in the web of his gaze, in the shivers of pleasure that undulated through her. There was fire in his touch, magic in his kiss, that it could make her feel so changed.

With a low groan, he took a step back, the twin talons of hunger and desire clawing their way to life.

Taking her hand, he started walking toward the maze.

A sense of dread filled Rhianna's heart as they reached the entrance. With a wordless cry, she tugged on his hand.

"What's wrong?" he asked.

"The maze." She shook her head. "It frightens me."

"There's nothing to fear."

She looked up at him, her eyes luminous in the moonlight. Her hand was small and warm in his.

He could see the pulse racing in her throat.

"Come, Rhianna," he whispered, his voice low and seductive. "Don't be afraid."

As though mesmerized, she fell into step beside him. Her gaze darted nervously from right to left as they went deeper into the maze. Soon, tall hedges rose on every side, cocooning her in a silent world of greenery.

She lost track of time until it seemed as though she had been walking through the maze for hours. Rayven was a tall, dark figure beside her. The moon cast silver highlights in his hair. His black cloak floated from his shoulders like thick black fog. She had never seen a cloak like his. It seemed alive somehow, moving when he moved, surrounding him in protective folds. His profile was sharp, all hard planes and angles, yet curiously beautiful. She wondered if this was what death looked like, dark and seductive.

It took her a moment to realize he had stopped walking. Glancing around, she saw what had once been a rose garden, though all that remained now were a few dead plants. In the center of the small garden was a bronze statue of a snarling wolf, and beside it, the figure of a raven carved in black marble.

A shiver of unease tiptoed down her spine. An odd choice of ornamentation for a garden, she thought.

Conscious of Rayven's gaze, she turned to face him. "I . . . I'm sure it must have been very lovely, once."

He raised one dark brow, his lips curved in wry amusement. "Do you think so?"

"I don't know. But it could be."

He turned away from her and stared at the statues, felt the darkness rise up within him, heard the wildness calling to him, bidding him to shed the thin veneer of humanity and run wild and naked through the night.

"My lord?"

Her voice, the underlying fear, drew him from the edge of darkness. Feeling as though he, too, were made of cold marble, he turned to face her once again.

"Could you work a miracle here, sweet Rhianna?" he asked softly. "Could you change this ugliness into beauty?"

Rhianna looked into his eyes, wondering if he was talking about the garden, or himself.

He placed a finger beneath her chin and tilted her face up. "Could you, sweet Rhianna?"

"I'll try, my lord."

"Would you kiss me, girl?"

"If you wish."

"No, Rhianna, not as I wish. I want you to take me in your arms and kiss me of your own free will."

He was lonely, she thought, as lonely as she.

Time slowed, and she became acutely aware of her surroundings. She felt the cool dampness of the grass beneath her feet as she stepped toward him, until their bodies were almost touching. His cloak was soft beneath her fingers as she placed her hands on his shoulders. Her nostrils filled with his scent, a wild musky scent that made her think of damp grass and rain.

And then she rose on her tiptoes and kissed him. His lips were cool and firm. When she started to draw away, his arm curled around her waist, holding her close against him. She felt the tremors that shook his body, sensed that he was keeping a tight rein on his emotions, sensed the underlying strength that dwelt in him.

Her eyelids fluttered down as his tongue traced her lower lip, then plunged into her mouth. Heat and fire exploded within her, radiating outward, until she felt as though she were melting in his arms. Distorted, disjointed images flickered in her mind—a wolf crouching over its prey, an enormous black bird drinking blood from a crystal goblet, a thick gray fog moving through the darkened streets of the village.

She heard Rayven swear under his breath as he let her go.

Like a slate wiped clean, the images disappeared, and she blinked up at him, feeling dazed and suddenly bereft.

"Rhianna? Rhianna!"

"Aye, my lord?"

"Are you all right?"

"I . . . I don't know. I thought I saw . . ."

"What?"

She shook her head. "I don't remember."

Cursing softy, he pulled her into his arms, his chin resting lightly on her head. "I beg you to forgive me, sweet Rhianna," he whispered hoarsely.

"Forgive you, my lord? But why? What have you done?"

"I hope you never find out," he replied, his voice suddenly harsh.

He held her for a long while, letting his power move over her, calming her. She closed her eyes, soothed, like a child, by the steady beat of its mother's heart beneath her cheek.

He knew the moment sleep claimed her. Murmuring her name, he gathered her into his arms. With her eyes closed and the moonlight shimmering on her face, she looked like a princess in a fairy tale.

A wave of tenderness swept through him as he carried her out of the maze and into the silent darkness of the castle.

In her room, he put her to bed, still fully clothed, and drew the covers over her. She was innocence personified, he thought, and for the first time in years, he hated who he was, what he was, because it denied him all hope of a normal life, of love. He would never have a wife, never know the quiet joy of holding a child he had fathered.

Tenderness turned to regret, regret turned to anger, and anger burned into a hot fierce rage. He had resigned himself to his lonely life shortly after he'd been made. Knowing such things would be forever denied him, he had put all thought of a home and family out of his mind, his heart.

He had thought himself content, happy even, until Rhianna. Seeing her, holding her, had awakened feelings and desires that had lain dormant within him for centuries.

With a low-throated growl, he bent over her, hating her for the power she had over him, for the weakness he felt when he looked at her. His hand brushed a lock of hair from her neck.

Her scent filled his nostrils, stirring his hunger, kindling his desire. If this was all of her he could have, then so be it, he thought, and let loose the beast that dwelt within him.

Chapter Five

I look into her eyes
and find forgiveness there
and for a moment—
one brief, sweet shining moment,
I see an end to my despair.

It had been a mistake to touch her, to kiss her. Having once tasted of Rhianna's sweetness, he could think of nothing else. He sought her out at supper, sipping from his wineglass while he watched her eat, listening with rapt attention while she told him how she had spent her day. She had a bright mind, a keen intellect, and a delightful sense of humor. Bevins had told him she was a quick study, that she was making remarkable progress.

Rayven saw the results for himself each night when she read to him, as she was doing now.

He sat in his favorite chair, staring into the flames of a fire that did little to warm the coldness within him, listening to her read. The sound of her voice washed over him like silken sunshine, softer than eiderdown, hotter than the flickering flames that danced in the hearth. Through heavy-lidded eyes, he watched her, wondering how it was possible for her to grow more beautiful with each passing day. Her cheeks bloomed with color, her eyes sparkled, her skin glowed with youth and life. The firelight cast golden shadows on her profile. Mesmerized like a love-struck youth, he basked in her nearness, in the breathy sound of her voice.

Several minutes passed before he realized that she had stopped reading, that she was staring back at him.

"Is something wrong, sweet Rhianna?"

"No, my lord."

"Why have you stopped reading?"

A faint smile played over her lips. "I stopped some time ago."

He frowned. "Will you tell me why?"

"Because the story is over, my lord."

He looked at her for a long moment, feeling quite the fool, and then he laughed.

Rhianna stared at him. She had rarely seen him smile, never heard him laugh. It was a wondrous sound, deep and rich. And contagious. She felt a wave of answering laughter rise up within her, mingling with his, until the walls echoed with the sound.

And then, without knowing quite how, he was kneeling before her, and the laughter died in her throat.

"Rhianna." He took her hands in his and kissed each one. "Do you know how long it's been since I laughed like that?"

"No, my lord."

"A very long time," he replied, his gaze burning into hers. "Longer than you can imagine."

"Then I'm glad I made you laugh."

"What can I give you in return?"

"My lord?"

"A new dress to match the color of your eyes? A chain of fine gold?"

"I want nothing, my lord. You have already given me too much. And I . . ." She looked away. "I have given you nothing in return."

Guilt, sharper than the thorns on the roses she loved, pricked his conscience. She had given him far more than she imagined. More than he had any right to take.

"Name your prize, sweet Rhianna. You have but to name it, and it's yours."

"Anything I want? Truly?"

"Truly."

"I should very much like to have a mirror in my room."

He sat back on his heels, his dark eyes suddenly shadowed and cold. "A mirror?"

She nodded, her expression eager. "You've given me so many fine things. I want to see how I look."

"Very well," he said, his voice tight. "You shall have one."

"Did I say something wrong?" she asked, her eyes filled with confusion.

He shook his head, then rose slowly to his feet. "Go to bed, girl."

She stood up. As always, his size surprised her. He moved with such stealth, spoke with such quiet, she often forgot how very big he was. Tall and broad shouldered, he towered over her. "Will you not tell me what I've done to displease you so?"

He turned away from her to stare into the fire. "Go to bed." His voice was brittle, like frozen glass.

"Very well, my lord."

He listened to the sound of her footsteps, muffled by the thick carpet, as she crossed the floor.

"Good night, my lord."

He could feel her watching him, waiting for a reply, heard her sigh as she opened the door and left the room.

Rayven stared into the flames. He could sit in this room and pretend he was a man like any other. He could pretend she was his, that she was there because she wished it. He could surround himself with riches, but he could not hide from the truth any more than he could walk in the sunlight, or see his reflection in a mirror. Such simple things, forever denied him.

The mirror that Bevins delivered to Rhianna's room the following afternoon was quite the most exquisite thing she had ever seen, a full-length looking glass set in a frame of burnished oak. And in the top corner, etched in spidery script, were her initials.

"Oh, it's beautiful," she murmured. She ran her hands over the wood, traced the letters of her initials.

"Lord Rayven will be pleased that you approve."

"Oh, I do! Is he home? I must thank him."

"He is unavailable, miss."

"He's never here during the day," Rhianna said, pouting. "Where does he go?"

"I'm sure I don't know, miss."

"You don't?"

"No, miss." The hesitation in his voice told her he was lying. "Will you be coming down for dinner, miss?"

"No, I don't think so." She turned away from the mirror. "I think I'll take a nap."

"Very good, miss." With a slight bow, Bevins left the room.

Rhianna went to the window and stared down into the gardens. She'd been here for months, and only now had she realized she had never seen Rayven during the day. Why had Bevins lied to her? Was Rayven here? Upstairs, perhaps?

Curious, she crossed to the door, opened it, and peeked out. There was no sign of Bevins. Tiptoeing from her chamber, she made her way down the corridor toward the east tower.

Her footsteps echoed loudly in her ears as she climbed the narrow winding stairway. Ninety-nine steps. She was breathless when she reached the top.

Pausing to catch her breath, she glanced down the long corridor. There was no light up here save for what little filtered through the shuttered windows set in the thick stone walls.

On tiptoe, she made her way down the hallway. She stopped at the first door, her hand trembling as she reached for the latch. The door opened without a sound.

Peering inside, she saw that the room was filled

with furniture—brocade sofas, chairs covered in faded embroidery and horsehair, curved settees covered in damask. There were tables in all sizes and shapes, chairs made of rich dark oak and mahogany, delicate stools and marble-topped commodes. All were covered with a layer of dust, as if they had not been used for decades.

Closing the door, she crossed the hallway to the opposite room. It, too, was crowded with the furniture of another era.

The next room was filled with works of art: statues, paintings, bronze figures, vases made of crystal and porcelain, china figurines, a huge sculpture of a raven hewn in black wood. These, too, were covered with dust and cobwebs.

Ahead was the tower room itself. She knew, without knowing how she knew, that this was Rayven's personal lair. Moving cautiously, she approached the door. She pressed her ear to the smooth wood, and when she heard no sound from inside, she put her hand on the latch.

Heart pounding, she opened the door and stepped inside. There was no light at all in this room. Heavy black velvet draperies covered the windows. Crossing the floor, she drew back the curtains, then turned and looked around. The room was empty.

Puzzled, she let the draperies fall back into place. Why had Rayven forbidden her to come here? What possible reason could he have for not wanting her to see rooms filled with old furniture, or this empty tower?

From out of nowhere came the chilling sensation that she was not alone. Unreasoning panic rose up within her, driving her out of the room.

She ran down the hall, down the stairs, a silent sob rising in her throat as images of darkness and death swirled through her mind.

She ran blindly through the castle until she reached her chamber. Inside, she locked the door, flung the windows wide. Sitting on the bed, she clutched a pillow to her chest and stared at the sunlight pouring through the window, hoping it would dispel the darkness that seemed to enfold her like thick black smoke, permeating her very soul. And in the center of that darkness, she sensed a loneliness so deep it broke her heart.

Rayven sat across the table from Rhianna, idly swirling the liquid in his goblet, watching the crystal catch the candlelight. "We're going to the opera next week. I want you to go out and buy something suitable to wear."

"My lord, surely I have no need of more gowns."

"Do it to please me. Something blue, to match your eyes, I think."

"Very well, my lord, if it will please you."

"So, what did you do today?"

Rhianna swallowed hard, her gaze sliding away from his. "Today, my lord?"

"Yes, today."

"I . . . Bevins brought me a new piece of music."

"Will you play it for me?"

"If you wish, though I've not yet mastered it."

"You are a most biddable creature, sweet Rhianna."

"My lord?" She looked at him askance, not knowing if he was praising her or complaining.

Rayven considered her over the rim of his glass. He had never kept a woman who was so agreeable, one who asked for nothing, who seemed to take genuine pleasure in his company. It stroked his male vanity to think she cared for him, even a little. The others had done his bidding, but he had been ever aware of the fear in their eyes, the lust for what his wealth could buy. He had given them whatever they asked for, had smothered them in gifts—jewels, furs, costly raiment—deeming it a small price to pay for what he took.

He tilted his head to one side, regarding her through half-lowered lids. He had sensed her presence in the tower, had smelled the lingering fragrance of her perfume, her very essence, when he woke that evening. He had never kept a woman who dared defy him. For that act of courage, he would buy her a sapphire necklace to match her new gown.

"What else did you do today?" he asked silkily.

Fear rose up in her throat. *He knows,* she thought frantically. *He knows what I've done, and now he'll punish me.*

"You've been here some time now," he remarked in that same deceptively mild voice.

"Yes."

"I trust you've gone exploring."

"You said I might have the run of the castle, my lord," she replied, a definite quaver in her voice.

"So I did. Save for the east tower."

Rhianna nodded, unable to speak past the fear coagulating in her throat.

"You remember my warning?"

She nodded, then crossed her arms lest he see her trembling.

"See that you do not disregard my wishes again."

"Yes, my lord."

He smiled at her over the rim of his goblet as he drained the glass. Rising, he offered her his hand. "Come," he said. "I wish you to play for me."

"Thank you, my lord."

His brow lifted in a gesture she had come to recognize as mild amusement. "For what, my sweet Rhianna?"

"For not being angry with me. For being so kind."

"Kind?" He laughed softly, the rich full sound filling her with sensual pleasure. "Of a truth, no one has ever called me that before."

"Indeed, my lord?"

"Indeed, my sweet."

"Then I shall do so often, if it would please you."

"You please me," he replied. And so saying, he lowered his head and covered her mouth with his, kissing her with an intensity that drained the strength from her limbs even as it seemed to draw all the air from her lungs.

She stared up at him, feeling strangely light-headed, when he drew his lips from hers.

Rayven smiled down at her, his dark eyes burning. "Never doubt that you please me very well."

Long after Rayven had left her, she could feel the heat of his lips, the urgent hardness of his body against hers. Though she had never known a man, she was not totally ignorant in the ways of men and women, but she had never dreamed that such pleasure was part of it. The women in the village whispered of putting up with a man's base nature, of enduring the hardship of the marriage bed. They had never mentioned the wonder of it, the fluttery feeling in one's stomach.

Earlier, he had listened to her play, dismissing her mistakes with a wave of his hand. It had been an easy piece; normally, she would have played it without hesitation. But she couldn't forget his touch, couldn't keep her hands from trembling with the memory of being in his arms, of touching him. Even now, it seemed as if the imprint of his long lean body had been burned into hers.

It seemed an effort to move, yet at the same time she seemed to be floating over the floor, up the stairs.

In her room, she removed her shoes and stockings, dropped her gown over the back of a chair, and slipped into bed.

She dreamed of him that night, dreamed that he was there, in her room, sitting beside her on the bed, his dark cloak floating over her like a shroud as he bent his head toward her. In the uncertain light of her room, his eyes seemed to glow like smoldering coals. She felt his hands grip her shoulders, felt his lips at her throat, felt the familiar lassitude steal over her as his teeth grazed the tender skin of her neck. Sensual pleasure mingled with pain. She moaned softly as his hands tightened on her arms. And then his voice, whispering in her ear.

"Only a dream, sweet Rhianna," he murmured, his voice hypnotizing her with its power. "Only a dream . . ."

Her eyelids fluttered down, but not before she saw him rise from her bed like a dark mist. She blinked once, and he was gone, as if he'd never been there.

But, of course, it was only a dream.

Chapter Six

Her touch has rendered me helpless,
her trust weakens the chains of the past.
Dare I believe in the love she offers?
Have I found an end to this darkness at last?

Rhianna's eyes widened as she stepped into the opera house. Except for the occasions when Bevins had taken her shopping in the neighboring town, it was the first time she had been out of the sheltered valley where she had been born, the first time she had been to the city. She couldn't help staring at the women, as beautiful as butterflies in their flamboyantly colored gowns of silk and satin.

She lifted her chin defiantly, trying to pretend she was one of them, that she belonged there. Her gown was just as fashionable, just as costly. The sapphires at her throat were fit for a queen. But, try as she might, she couldn't help feeling like a serving girl playing dress up in her mistress's clothes.

Once her initial awe wore off, she realized people were staring at Rayven. She heard snatches of conversation as Rayven escorted her up the stairs to his private box.

"It's Rayven . . ."

"Haven't seen him here in years . . ."

". . . a new mistress . . ."

". . . so young . . ."

"She's lovely . . ."

". . . odd . . . he never changes . . ."

She was certain her cheeks were red with embarrassment by the time they reached their box. Sitting there, she hid her face behind her fan.

"Pay them no mind, sweet Rhianna," Rayven said. Taking the seat beside her, he settled back in his chair, a bored look on his face.

"They're talking about us."

"Let them. Did I tell you how beautiful you look in that gown?" And indeed, she did. The deep blue velvet complemented the creamy smoothness of her skin and made her eyes seem darker.

Rhianna nodded, wishing she could just disappear. Never before had she been the object of so much discussion, so much speculation. She hadn't had to hear the words to know they thought she was Rayven's mistress.

She risked a glance at the box across from theirs, shrank back as she recognized the tall, blond man. He had been at Cotyer's the night her father auctioned her to the highest bidder.

He had seen her, too. Smiling, he inclined his head in her direction and then blew her a kiss.

She heard Rayven mutter something under his breath and then, to her relief, the curtain parted and the opera began.

Rhianna had never seen or heard anything like it—the costumes, the actors, the music, the dancing. Even though she couldn't understand the language, she had no trouble following the story of a rich young man in love with a peasant girl.

At intermission, Lord Montroy appeared at their box. He sketched a bow in Rayven's direction, then bowed over Rhianna's hand.

"Good evening, my dear," he said, and she heard the hint of a smile in his voice. "How well you look."

"Thank you."

Montroy dropped into one of the chairs, his long legs stretched negligently before him. "Can't remember the last time I saw Rayven at the opera," he remarked. "You must be a good influence on him."

"I . . ." She shook her head. "It was Lord Rayven's idea, not mine." A smile lit her face. "But it is wonderful, isn't it?"

"You're enjoying it, then?"

"Oh, yes, it's a wonderful play. I've never seen anything like it."

Rayven sat back in his chair, his arms crossed over his chest, as Montroy conversed with Rhianna. His detachment rapidly turned to anger as Montroy began flirting with Rhianna, complimenting her hairstyle, comparing the blue of her eyes to the sapphire necklace she wore. He watched Rhianna's cheeks turn scarlet as she murmured a polite thank you. His hands clenched into tight fists, the mild anger he'd felt quickly turning to fury as she laughed softly at something Montroy said.

"Enough." The word, softly spoken, cut across Montroy's flowery compliments like a knife through butter.

With lazy grace, Montroy stood up, murmuring his farewells as he bent over Rhianna's hand, then turned to Rayven. "Will we see you at Cotyer's later, my lord?"

"No."

Montroy looked at Rayven with what could only be called a smirk. "A foolish question, indeed," he said. "Good night, my lord."

"Montroy."

Rhianna fanned herself, not daring to meet Rayven's gaze. She had not missed the hint of anger in his voice, though the reason for it eluded her.

She was grateful when the performance resumed.

Rayven had seen the opera many times, and it was Rhianna's face he watched during the last act. As he had suspected, she wept when the heroine killed herself rather than face life without the hero, though why a woman would want a weak-willed man like the hero was quite beyond him.

When the curtain came down, he offered her his handkerchief. "Dry your eyes, sweet Rhianna. It was only make-believe, after all."

"But it was so sad. They loved each other so much."

"Rubbish! If he'd loved her, he would have disobeyed his father and married her instead of shackling himself to a woman he didn't love."

"Yes," Rhianna murmured, "I suppose he would have."

Gaining his feet, Rayven draped her cloak over her shoulders. "Ready?"

With a nod, Rhianna stood up and placed her hand in his. She held her head high as they left the box and made their way outside.

It was a beautiful moonlit night. A bright yellow moon hung low in the sky. She stood beside Rayven, conscious of the people nearby, aware of their curious stares, their whispered words as they speculated on her relationship with Castle Rayven's dark lord.

She was relieved when Bevins arrived with the carriage.

As Rayven helped her inside, she was aware of his hand at her arm. His touch was firm, cool. She settled her skirts around her as he entered the other door and took the seat beside her. There was something vastly intimate about being alone with a man in a closed carriage. Rayven's hard-muscled thigh brushed against hers as he shifted in the seat. The scent of his cologne tinged the air.

He rapped on the roof, and the carriage lurched forward. They drove in silence for several minutes. Rhianna glanced out the window, admiring the moonlit countryside.

"Montroy finds you quite attractive, my sweet."

Rhianna turned her head to look at him, surprised by his blunt remark. "My lord?"

"Don't play coy with me, girl. I saw the way he looked at you. The way you looked at him."

"I don't know what you mean."

"Don't you?"

Rhianna met his gaze, confused by the carefully

banked anger in his eyes, by the hard edge of jealousy in his voice.

"If you have any plans for meeting him on the sly, put them out of your mind."

"My lord, you misjudge me!" Rhianna exclaimed, shocked that he would even think such a thing. "I have no interest in the man."

"No?"

"No."

"Forgive me, sweet Rhianna," he murmured, astonished by his reaction to the thought of her with another man. Never before had be been possessive of the women he brought home, but then, none had been as lovely, or as innocent, as Rhianna McLeod.

"Please don't be angry with me, my lord."

Rayven blew out a long breath, then reached for her hands, kissing first one and then the other. "I could never be angry with you. Nor Montroy, either, I suppose. One can hardly blame the man for being attracted to you."

He kissed the back of her right hand again; and then, ever so slowly, he removed the glove from her right hand, bent his head and licked her palm. Rhianna gasped as a rush of potent heat shot up her arm.

Heart pounding, she met his gaze, felt the fire burning in his eyes engulf her. "My lord . . ."

Slowly, inexorably, he drew her into his arms until his face blotted everything else from her sight. Slanting his mouth over hers, he kissed her, his teeth grazing her lips, his tongue exploring the soft inner flesh of her mouth, until she was breathless, almost dizzy from the tumult of emotions swirling through her. Her skin felt tingly, every nerve ending vitally alive.

Hardly aware of what she was doing, she leaned into him, a soft moan rising in her throat as her breasts were crushed against his chest.

"Rhianna, ah, Rhianna." He groaned softly. "Do you know what you're doing to me?" His hands slid up and down her back, erratic as the beating of her heart.

He drew her more fully against him, his lips raining kisses on her eyes, the tip of her nose, the curve of her cheek. His tongue laved her neck, she felt his teeth nibble at her earlobe, then graze the tender flesh beneath her ear.

A low groan rumbled deep in his throat and then, abruptly, he pushed her away.

Dazed, she blinked at him, then leaned toward him, wanting him to kiss her again, to continue the strange magic his touch wrought upon her senses.

"Don't." The tone of his voice had the effect of a slap.

With a muffled cry, she scooted into the corner, her heart pounding wildly—not with desire, but trepidation. What had she done? Why was he looking at her like that, his eyes burning yet cold?

The rest of the journey passed in silence. Rhianna kept her gaze downcast, her hands tightly folded in her lap.

When they reached home, Rayven practically flew out of the carriage. She stared after him, wanting to call him back, but he was swallowed up by the darkness so fast it was almost as if he had vanished completely.

Bevins handed her from the carriage, then preceded her into the castle, lighting the lamps in the downstairs rooms.

"Would you care for a cup of tea, miss?" he asked, "or some cocoa, perhaps?"

"Cocoa, please. I'll take it in the parlor."

"As you wish, miss."

Removing her cloak and remaining glove, Rhianna went into the parlor and sat down on the sofa, trying to comprehend what had happened in the carriage. She was new to desire, but certainly she had not been mistaken in thinking Rayven wanted her. Heaven knew she had wanted him, would have surrendered her virtue there, in the carriage, had he not thrust her away. Had she done something to displease him, and if so, what?

"Would you care for a fire, miss?" Bevins asked. He handed her a cup of hot chocolate.

"Yes, please. It's quite chilly in here."

Bevins nodded, then turned away to see to the fire.

"Has Lord Rayven come in yet?" she asked.

"No, miss. I shouldn't wait up for him if I were you."

"Do you know where he's gone?"

Bevins hesitated. "No, miss. Will that be all?"

"Yes, Bevins. Thank you."

"Good night, then."

"Good night."

Staring into the flames, Rhianna sipped the cocoa, feeling it relax her. Funny how life turned out, she mused. She had been afraid to come to this place, afraid to leave home, afraid of Rayven, yet all her fears had proven groundless. There was nothing to fear in the castle. She had food to eat and beautiful clothes to wear. She had learned to read and write, to appreciate poetry, to play the pianoforte, to paint. Even her fear of Rayven had been unjustified. Until the last few weeks, she had hardly seen him at all. Sometimes, it seemed as though he were afraid of her.

Putting the cup aside, she tucked her feet beneath her. Why had Rayven brought her here? If he didn't want her for his mistress or a housemaid, what did he want her for? So far, she had done nothing to earn the money he had paid for her.

Rayven. Why wasn't he married? He was rich. He was handsome. Even the scar on his cheek couldn't detract from his roguish good looks. Just being near him made her come alive, made her blood run hot and her stomach quiver with longing. Surely bedding him would not be a hardship in spite of what her mother had said about such things. . . .

Heat that had nothing to do with the warmth of the flames suffused her cheeks at her wayward thoughts. With a sigh, she closed her eyes, summoning his image to mind, the high wide forehead, the finely shaped nose, his beautiful dark eyes that could burn her with a look, his full lips . . .

She felt her body tingle in every place where he had touched her. If only he hadn't pushed her away . . .

Rayven stood at the foot of the sofa, watching her sleep. Her hair had come loose from its pins and fell across the arm of the sofa like a river of gold silk. She sighed in her sleep, her sweet pink lips curving into a smile that was both sweet and seductive. Of what, or of whom, was she dreaming?

Unable to resist, he knelt beside her, staring at the slow steady beat of the pulse at the base of her throat. He closed his eyes and took a deep breath, breathing in the scent of her. She smelled of soap and perfume and powder, of the roast beef and Yorkshire pudding she had eaten for dinner, of cocoa. He placed his fingertip over the pulse in her throat, felt the blood thrumming through her veins, felt his mouth water as he remembered the warm, sweet, coppery taste.

Even before he opened his eyes, he knew she was awake and watching him. He heard the change in her breathing, the escalation of her heartbeat.

"My lord," she murmured. "I'm sorry if I did something to offend you."

"Offend me?"

"In the carriage."

"You did nothing amiss, sweet Rhianna."

"Then why . . ."

"It is not my wish to hurt you, Rhianna."

"You weren't hurting me." Heat climbed up her neck and into her cheeks. "Quite the opposite, my lord."

"Ah, child," Rayven murmured, stroking her cheek. "If you only knew."

"Knew what?"

"Nothing. I would not frighten you with my past, or bore you with my present."

"I don't understand."

"There is no need for you to understand. All you need know is that you please me very well."

"Then won't you kiss me again?" She saw the refusal in his eyes and pressed her fingertips over his lips. "Just one kiss, my lord."

Taking her hand from his mouth, he kissed her palm. When he looked at her again, there was a glint of amusement in his dark eyes. "Would it please you so much?"

"Oh, yes."

"One kiss, and then you must go to bed."

She nodded, her eyelids fluttering down as his lips met hers. There was such sweetness in his kiss, such longing. Unwilling for him to leave her, she wrapped her arms around his neck and deepened the kiss, hoping he would know how much she wanted him.

His arms tightened around her, and he lifted her off the sofa, cradling her in his lap, his mouth ravishing hers in a most delightful way.

She was drowning in pleasure, melting with desire, and then, into her mind came a vision of darkness, and yet it wasn't darkness as she knew it, but a total absence of light, and interwoven with the darkness was an awareness of pain and anguish so vivid it felt like her pain, her anguish.

She squirmed in his embrace, felt his arms tighten around her. She tried to open her eyes, but the darkness increased, and she felt herself being engulfed in that horrible blackness . . .

"Rhianna?"

"No. No, no . . . please."

"Rhianna, open your eyes. There's nothing to fear."

She blinked at him, feeling as though she had just emerged from a waking nightmare. "What happened?"

"Nothing."

"But . . ."

"It was only a dream, my sweet, nothing more."

"But I was awake!"

"No. You fell asleep in my arms." He looked down at her, his smile strained, his eyes dark and compelling. "To bed with you, I think," he said, and stood up, carrying her with him as though she weighed nothing at all.

"I can walk, my lord."

"No need."

Effortlessly, he carried her up the long flight of stairs to her room. "Rest well, sweet Rhianna."

"Good night, my lord."

He bowed his head, then left the room, his long black cloak swirling around his ankles like smoke.

Chapter Seven

Sunk in the depths of a black and bitter despair, Rayven stood before the hearth, staring into the flames. He could not keep her here any longer, could not put her life at risk. It was enough that he stole the very essence of her life. He would not take her heart and soul, as well.

And yet, how could he let her go? He had walked often in her dreams, losing himself in her sweetness, her purity. In the power of her dreams, he could walk in the sun again, feel its warmth on his face. He could see the world bathed in light instead of darkness. Walking beside her, he could pretend he was human again, a man again.

She was dreaming now, and in her dreams she walked along the banks of a sparkling blue river, pausing to pick a bouquet of bright yellow daisies, to wade in the sun-dappled water, and he walked beside her, feeling the sunlight like a benediction on his face.

He drew his mind from hers. It was dangerous, letting his thoughts meld with hers. It was getting harder and harder to restrain himself, to keep his hunger under control, to keep his diabolical thirst separate from his desire. He could not, would not, defile her.

With a sigh, he turned away from the fire.

Tonight would be the last time.

He was there, beside her bed, the same dark shape that had come to her so often in the past. A black velvet cloak lined with midnight-blue silk billowed around him, like the wings of a raven. She could not see his face, yet she recognized his touch.

She felt his lips move over her brow, her cheeks, her temple, felt the heat of his tongue, trailing fire, as it slid down her neck. She turned her head to the side, her hands grasping his arms, her eyelids closing in ecstasy as his teeth grazed her tender flesh.

She heard his low growl, like that of a wolf, felt the painful, pleasurable bite of his teeth, followed by the touch of his tongue stroking her neck. And then came the words, oddly familiar, soft-spoken hypnotic words that carried her down, down, into the darkness of a dreamless sleep. . . .

Rhianna woke with a cry, bolting upright in bed. Her gaze darted around the room.

It was dawn, and she was alone.

And yet, the dream had seemed so real. She lifted a trembling hand to her neck, terrified of what she would find. Her breath rushed from her lungs in a sigh of relief when her fingers encountered nothing but smooth skin.

Weak with relief, she fell back on the pillow. There were no teeth marks on her neck.

It had only been a dream, after all.

She woke to the sound of a knock on her door. Her first thought was that it was Rayven, and then she heard Bevins's voice requesting entrance.

"Yes," she called, "come in."

"Good morning, miss," Bevins said in his carefully modulated voice.

"Good morning. Is something wrong?"

"Wrong? No, miss. I've come to inform you that Lord Rayven has made arrangements for you to go to Paris."

"Paris? But why?"

"You are to be tutored there. It seems Lord Rayven feels I have taught you all I can. He wishes for you to be instructed in more than merely reading and writing. He wishes for you to be taught etiquette and acquire other feminine arts."

Rhianna could only stare at him. To her knowledge, no woman in their town had even received a formal education, though a few fortunate ones could read and write their names.

For a moment, she let herself be caught up in the possibilities, and then she shook her head. "I don't want to leave here."

"I'm sorry, miss. The arrangements have been made."

"How soon?"

"Sunday a week, miss. Lord Rayven has instructed me to take you to town to purchase whatever you think you might need. An account has been opened in your name in the bank near the school."

"He is most generous," she said, blinking back her tears.

"I have always found him so."

"Thank you, Bevins."

"Breakfast will be ready when you are."

Rhianna shook her head. "I find I have no appetite this morning."

"I understand, miss."

She was going away to school. It was something she had never even dared dream of. Yet the thought of leaving this place, of leaving Rayven, filled her with inexplicable sadness.

The days passed all too quickly, and soon it was her last night at the castle. After the evening they had spent at the opera, she had expected Rayven to seek her out, but he never did.

That night, at supper, she asked Bevins if Rayven was at home.

"I believe so, miss."

"Would you take me to him?"

"I'm afraid that's impossible."

"Why?"

"Because it is."

"But I'm leaving in the morning. I just want to tell him good-bye and . . . and thank him for his kindness."

"I know, miss. I am sorry."

He meant it. She could see it in his eyes, hear it in his voice.

Leaving the table, she went outside. She would miss this place, she thought as she wandered through the gardens. She had been happy here. Far happier than she had ever expected. She wondered how her mother was, if her sisters ever thought of her. No doubt they missed her help in the house and fields, but did they ever miss *her*? She had not missed them as much as she'd thought she would. In truth, she had hardly thought of her family at all these past months. To think of them living in poverty while she dwelt in luxury was far too painful. The few times she had let herself think of home, she had been filled with an overpowering sense of guilt, though why that should be so, she didn't know. She had not left her family by choice. And yet, being sold to Rayven had turned out far better than she had ever hoped. She had long ago forgiven her father for selling her. Rayven had been kind to her, generous, undemanding.

Hardly aware of what she was doing, she followed the path that led to the labyrinth. It didn't frighten her anymore. Drawing her shawl around her shoulders, she walked on until she reached the heart of the labyrinth.

Rayven looked up, startled to find Rhianna gazing down at him.

He slanted her a wry grin. "No mortal has ever crept up on me like that before," he remarked.

"No mortal?" she asked, confused by his odd choice of words.

"Thank you for this," he said, ignoring her question. He gestured at the roses and shrubs that grew in artless profusion around the statues so that the wolf and the raven seemed to rise up out of a crimson sea. "It's beautiful."

Rhianna nodded. She had spent the past week here, wanting to leave something of herself behind, something for him to remember. She had planted dozens of bloodred rosebushes interspersed with delicate lacy ferns. The result was striking and somehow masculine. She thought it suited Rayven perfectly.

"I'm leaving tomorrow," she said quietly.

"I know." Oh, yes, he thought, he knew. Even now the thought of her going was tearing him apart inside.

"Why are you sending me away?"

"It's for the best."

"Best for who?"

"For you. For me."

"I don't want to go."

He stood up, towering over her, his dark eyes glowing. He was tall and lean, his shoulders broad, his arms well-muscled. She noticed that the scar on his cheek was shaped like a V. Funny, she had never noticed that before.

Following an inexplicable urge, she traced the fine white line with her fingertip, felt a catch in her heart as his hand covered hers.

"Rhianna."

"Please, Rayven, please don't send me away."

"Ah, Rhianna, I would keep you with me forever if I could."

"And I would stay. Only ask me to stay, and I will."

He shook his head. "No."

His hand tightened on hers as tears welled in her eyes and trickled down her cheeks. In the moonlight, her tears sparkled like flawless diamonds, but they were far more precious to him than jewels. They denoted caring and affection, willingly given, and for that he would always love her. And because he loved her, he would let her go.

"Someday you will thank me for this, sweet Rhianna."

"No," she said, sobbing.

She twisted away from him, her blue eyes awash with tears. "I'll never forgive you. Never!" she cried, and then she was running away from him, taking the sunlight from his life, leaving him in the vast empty darkness of the night, alone, as he had always been alone.

He contemplated leaving the castle, certain he could not stay there now, could not walk the rooms she had walked, breathe the air she had breathed, and know he would never see her again.

He would have to leave soon at any rate. He had overheard the men in Cotyer's talking about him, wondering why they never saw him during the day, why he never joined them for dinner, why his appearance never changed, why he didn't seem to age.

And yet, even knowing he should go, he knew he would not. The castle was filled with her essence, and as painful as it would be to be reminded of her, it was better than forgetting.

He laughed softly, bitterly. As if he could ever forget.

Part Two
Four Years Later

Chapter Eight

Millbrae Valley, 1847

Blinking back her tears, Rhianna stood at her father's graveside. She had left the convent school as soon as she received word that her father was dying, but she had arrived too late to bid him a last good-bye.

Standing there, she remembered how kind and jolly he had always been when she was a little girl, before times got hard and the laughter forever left his eyes. Once, she had thought him calloused and unfeeling. And even though she had understood his reasons, she had hated him for selling her to Rayven, but she had forgiven him for that long ago. She wished she had told him so. She murmured the words under her breath, hoping he could hear them.

She glanced at her sisters, who stood on the opposite side of the grave. They had grown from pretty little girls into lovely young women since she had last seen them. Aileen, the eldest, was engaged to be married in the spring. Rayven had given her a generous dowry that would enable her and her future husband to buy a small piece of land and build a home of their own.

She had been surprised to see how well they all looked. Their clothes were new and fashionable. The cottage, once little more than a hovel, was in good repair. Two large rooms had been added. A small stable had been built behind the cottage. It housed three milk cows, a goat, a sheep, and two fine horses.

When she'd questioned her mother about the changes in their circumstances, Ada had explained that Lord Rayven had refurbished the cottage and built the barn. Each year he sent a generous allowance.

"It was so good of you to think of our needs, Rhianna," her mother had said, "especially when your father sent you away."

"I had nothing to do with it," Rhianna had replied, though of course, in a way, she had.

"But why else would he do such a thing?" her mother had asked. "We are nothing to him."

He had done it because of her, Rhianna thought, and knew she could never repay him for his kindness to her family, for the education he had provided her.

The graveside service was brief. When the last prayer had been said, her mother dropped a handful of earth on the simple wooden coffin, and then each daughter, starting with the youngest, did the same. Rhianna knew it was a sound she would never forget.

Putting her arm around her mother's shoulders, she led her away from the grave.

Back at the cottage, Rhianna brewed a pot of tea, then sat at the table across from her mother.

Rhianna picked up her cup, holding it in both hands, hoping the warmth would ease the coldness that she'd felt inside ever since she left the convent.

"How is Lord Rayven?" she asked after a while.

"How should I know? I heard he left the castle shortly after he sent you to Paris."

"He's not here?"

The coldness that had invaded her body now crept into her heart. He was gone. For four years, she had dreamed of seeing him again. Such a short time they had spent together, yet he had been in her thoughts every hour of every day, in her every dream at night.

"An odd man, that one," her mother mused. "I only saw him once." Ada shivered. "Such cold eyes. Never have I seen such cold eyes."

"Cold?" Rhianna shook her head. He had not seemed cold to her. Lonely. Isolated. But not cold. She had seen the warmth in those eyes. The heat of desire. The flame of passion.

"Did he say where he was going? When he would be back?"

"Not that I recall." Ada sipped her tea. "Did he . . . Forgive me, Rhianna. I said I wouldn't ask, but I must know. Did he defile you, child?"

"No, Mother. He was kind to me."

"Kind?"

Rhianna nodded. "I had the best of everything

while I was with him. He sent me to the best school in Paris, made sure that I had new clothes every year. I was the only girl who had a room of her own. He sent me an allowance each month so I would have spending money of my own. In truth, he has been most generous to me. And to you, it seems."

"Aye. It's glad I am that you're back, child. Have you come home to stay?"

Rhianna thought of what it would be like to live in the village again. She would miss Paris, miss her companions at school. But this was Rayven's home. Surely one day he would return. And she would be here when he did.

"Yes," she decided, "I'm here to stay." And knew that she would have stayed in any case. Her mother had never been strong; now she looked frail.

Ada smiled. Setting her cup on the table, she stood up. "I'm tired. I think I'll go lie down for a while."

"Rest well, Mother."

"Welcome home, daughter." Giving Rhianna an affectionate squeeze on the shoulder, she left the room.

Her sisters came in then. Aileen, the eldest, was now 17. Lanna was 15, Brenna almost 14, and Bridgitte had just turned 12. Subdued by the funeral, they sat at the table, reminiscing about their father, remembering the good times and ignoring the bad.

"He never forgave himself for what he did to you," Aileen remarked. "Even though the money Lord Rayven paid him put food on our table." She paused, her fingers toying with the sash of her dress. "Was it awful, living with Lord Rayven?"

"No." Rhianna glanced around the cottage. How different it looked. And yet, even though it was now clean and well-equipped, it still looked like a hovel when compared to the castle's opulent furnishings.

She spent a quiet evening with her mother and sisters, reminiscing about old times, listening to their plans for the future.

Later, when everyone else had gone to bed, Rhianna saddled one of the horses and rode to Castle Rayven.

The castle was as she remembered it, a stark and lonely sentinel looming over the town. The mist, ever constant, shrouded Devil Tree Mountain, so that only the tallest spires were visible from a distance.

He wasn't there. She knew that, yet she needed to see the castle again, to walk through the gardens, to say good-bye. . . .

Dismounting at the side gate, she tethered the horse to a tree, opened the gate, and stepped into the garden. Gone were the beautiful flowers she had planted, the shrubs, the roses. The trees, once flourishing, were dry skeletons.

Heavy hearted, she wandered up and down the narrow twisting paths. All her hard work gone for naught.

Only the maze remained, standing stark and green against the gray stone walls.

With a sigh, she made her way back to the side gate and took up her horse's reins. It was time to go. Everything she had planted, everything she had once hoped for, was gone, like a bad dream.

* * *

She was here. Cloaked in the shadows of never-ending night, he watched her walk along the moonlit paths. She had changed in the last four years. Youthful curves had matured. She moved with womanly grace and self-assurance, and he watched her with a sense of pride, knowing that he was, in part, responsible for what she had become, though her inner beauty had always been there.

Rhianna. Her name rose in his mind, chasing away centuries of darkness. *Rhianna . . . Why have you returned? Come to torment me anew? To remind me of what can never be? Rhianna . . . beloved . . . how I have yearned for you . . . dreamed of you . . . Rhianna . . .*

"My lord?" She turned around, expecting to see him standing behind her, his dark cloak swirling around him like smoke, but there was no one there.

Confused, she peered into the shadows. She had heard his voice so clearly, she could not have imagined it.

Dropping the horse's reins, she hurried along the narrow brick path that led to the front of the castle and pounded on the door.

She waited. And listened. And knocked again.

After what seemed an interminable length of time, the door creaked open. "Good evening, miss," Bevins said.

"Bevins! What are you doing here?" He looked much the same, she thought, though his hair seemed grayer than before, thinner with the passage of time.

He lifted one brow. "Why, I live here, miss."

"But I thought Lord Rayven had gone."

Bevins cocked his head to one side, and she had the strangest impression that he was listening to a voice only he could hear.

"Bevins? He is gone, isn't he?"

"Yes, miss. He left soon after you departed for Paris."

"You didn't go with him?"

"No, miss. My place is here."

"Is he . . . Will he be coming back, do you think?"

"I cannot say, miss. Might I ask why you left Paris?"

"My father died. I came home for the funeral."

"I am sorry, Miss Rhianna. Please accept my condolences."

"Thank you, Bevins." With a sigh, she turned to go, and then she paused. "Are you quite certain he's not here?"

"Why do you ask?"

"No reason. I mean, that is, I thought I heard him call my name."

Bevins blinked at her, astonishment evident in his eyes. "You heard his voice?"

Rhianna nodded. "At least I thought I did. He . . . he sounded so sad. I suppose I must have imagined it."

"Yes, miss."

"Well, I'd better be going. If you hear from Lord Rayven, please give him my best, and my thanks for being so kind to my family."

"I will, miss. And may I say that Paris must have agreed with you, for you have blossomed into a lovely young woman. I know Lord Rayven would be pleased."

"Thank you, Bevins. Good night."

"Good night, miss."

Shoulders sagging, Rhianna walked down the steps to collect the horse. It was sheer nonsense, of course, thinking she had heard his voice. It was only that she had missed him so much these past four years. Missed him, and dreamed of him.

Standing at the side gate, she looked up at the windows of the east tower. "Rayven," she whispered, "I know you're here."

Hidden in the shadows of a lonely tower room, a man clad in the darkness of the night heard her plea, and wept bloodred tears.

She went back the next night and the next, wandering through the gardens for an hour, hoping he would come to her, hoping she would feel his presence and know he was there.

But he did not seek her out.

Sometimes, as now, she sat on one of the stone benches, lost in thought as she gazed up at the east tower, wondering where he was, what he was doing, wondering at the overpowering urge that brought her to this place night after night, the certainty that he was nearby. Strange, she had no desire to come here during the day. Was it because she had never seen Rayven when the sun was up? What a puzzle he was, a man as dark and mysterious as the night itself.

Rising, she walked toward the maze, her heartbeat increasing as she drew nearer.

"There's nothing in there to be afraid of." She spoke the words aloud, hoping to bolster her flagging courage. "There's nothing there in the darkness that isn't there in the light." Yet, even as the words left her lips, she wondered if that was true.

Straightening her shoulders, she took a deep breath and stepped into the maze. Greenery rose all around her, enfolding her, embracing her. Feeling as if she were being guided by an unseen hand, she went steadily onward, anticipation quickening her footsteps, until she reached the heart of the labyrinth.

She came to an abrupt halt as she glanced around. She had expected the roses within the maze to be dead, like the ones in the gardens, but the bushes here were full and green. Her gaze lingered on the statues, the bronze wolf and the black raven captured forever in metal and marble.

Shivering, she wrapped her arms around her waist. There was something ominous about the statues tonight. She had the eerie feeling that the wolf and the raven were watching her, waiting for a chance to pounce.

She was turning away when she saw a flash of movement from the corner of her eye. She glanced over her shoulder, her mind telling her that she was imagining things again.

But it wasn't her imagination this time.

Rayven materialized out of the shadows near the statue of the wolf, the moonlight shining in his thick black hair, his cloak enfolding him like a living thing.

"My lord," she murmured, suddenly breathless.

"Good evening, Rhianna." His tongue lingered over her name, drawing it out, making her shiver, as though he had caressed her.

"You're here." She glanced at the statue of the wolf. It looked different somehow. "Bevins said you weren't here."

"Why are *you* here, sweet Rhianna?"

"My father . . ."

He shook his head. "I know why you have come home. Why are you *here*?"

"I missed you, my lord. Being here, on the castle grounds, made you seem less far away."

"You missed me?"

Rhianna nodded. "You find that so hard to believe?"

He laughed, but there was no humor in the sound. "I find it impossible to believe."

" 'Tis true, nonetheless. I am sorry if it displeases you."

"It does not displease me, sweet Rhianna," he replied quietly. "How long will you be here?"

"At the castle?"

"In Millbrae."

"Oh. I've come home to stay."

"No. You must not."

Rhianna looked up at him, surprised by the vehemence in his voice. "It seems my presence displeases you as much as my honesty, my lord."

"Nothing about you displeases me, sweet Rhianna. It is only your well-being I am thinking of."

"My lord?"

"Your future, Rhianna. I would see you wed to a man worthy of you, not some farmer who will make you old before your time, who will plant a babe in your womb every year, and see you to an early grave."

"You wish me to marry?"

"Is it not your wish, also?"

"Yes, of course, but . . ."

His gaze held hers. "But?"

"I don't want to marry for wealth, my lord, but for love."

"Love." The word was a whisper, a wish unfulfilled, a dream unborn.

"Have you never been in love, my lord?"

Slowly, he shook his head, his dark eyes filled with such pain, such stark loneliness, that she wanted to weep. Was it only her imagination, or did his cloak seem to wrap more closely around him, as if to comfort him?

"And you?" he asked. "Have you, in your few short years of life, found love?"

"Aye, my lord, though I fear he does not return my affection."

"Then he is a fool!"

A faint smile curved Rhianna's lips. "On that, at least, we are agreed."

Rayven fought back his anger. The urge to destroy the cur who failed to return her love rose up within him, and with it an all-consuming jealousy. "Who is this man?"

"Can you not guess?" Rhianna replied, her voice hardly more than a whisper.

Rayven closed his eyes, pain ripping through him. If he survived another four hundred years, he would never forget this moment, the love shining bright and clear in her eyes, the wonder of it.

A long shuddering sigh escaped him, and then he opened his eyes.

"Go away from here, Rhianna," he said, his voice brusque, his eyes as cold as black ice. "Leave my house and never come back."

She recoiled as if he had slapped her, the hurt in her eyes scorching his soul.

"Be gone," he said. "Pray I never see you again."

"As you wish, my lord," Rhianna said, and turning on her heel, she fled his presence without a backward glance.

Behind her, a black wolf lifted its melancholy cry to the night.

Chapter Nine

She cried for hours after she returned home, and all the while she berated herself for her foolishness. He had never led her to believe he was anything more than mildly fond of her. She had amused him with her naïveté, nothing more. She had laid her heart bare, and he had scorned it, and her.

She would not humiliate herself in such a fashion again. And she would marry for love, or she would not marry at all.

Clinging to that thought, she fell asleep.

The maze rose up in the night, a twisting wall of greenery that separated her from the rest of the world. Drawn into its heart, she collapsed near the statue of the bronze wolf. She drew a deep breath, and her nostrils filled with the scent of roses. Only then did she notice that they were no longer red.

Dozens of blooms grew on the trees, but they were all black.

Curious, she picked one, gasping as a thorn pricked her finger. A drop of bright red blood oozed from the wound, and suddenly Rayven was there, towering over her, his dark eyes ablaze with an unholy light as he took her hand in his and slowly licked the blood from her finger . . .

"No!" The sound of her own horrified cry roused her from sleep and she sat up, glancing wildly around the room. "Only a dream," she whispered as she snuggled under the covers again. "Only a dream."

The familiar words hovered in the back of her mind.

"Only a dream . . ."

She closed her eyes, but sleep eluded her. With a restless sigh, she sat up and gazed out the window, her mind filling with images of Rayven as she had seen him last, his fathomless black eyes filled with torment. He was lonely, so lonely. Why? He was a handsome man. A wealthy man. Why did he not marry and raise a family? Why did he live in that cold, lonely castle? Why had he sent her away?

She had learned much in the four years she had been away. She had, on rare occasions, flirted with young men. In Paris, she had learned the power of a coy glance, a shy smile, a come-hither look. She knew when a man wanted her. And Rayven wanted her. He had wanted her from the beginning. Why, then, had he turned her away? Why had he bought her in the first place? She had assumed he had wanted her to warm his bed. She wondered now if he had bought her simply for companionship. But surely a man like Rayven had no need to purchase feminine companionship.

She thought of all the strange rumors she had heard about him, about his peculiar habits. Since returning home, she had overheard other things, stories told in hushed whispers that hinted at evil, at bargains made with the devil. Was it possible that the people of the town believed such outrageous tales? Her friends and neighbors were a humble, superstitious people, frightened of what they didn't understand, of what couldn't be easily explained.

Snuggling under the covers once more, she closed her eyes. As much as she had loved Paris, she was not going back.

This was her home. This was where she belonged, and she would not let anyone, not even the master of Castle Rayven, chase her away.

The next day was market day. With her mother's list in hand, Rhianna took the carriage Rayven had bought for her family and went into town. It was good to see familiar country faces again. Because of Rayven's generosity, she was able to purchase fresh bread, prime cuts of meat, and a bottle of fine red wine.

She was sitting in the window of a tearoom, wondering if Rayven would haunt her thoughts forever, when she saw Dallon Montroy. He saw her at the same time. Tipping his hat, he crossed the road, a broad smile on his face. He was as handsome as she recalled. Several women turned to stare at him, their gazes frankly admiring. He wore a coat of dark green broadcloth trimmed in black velvet, buff-colored breeches, and black boots. His linen was impeccable; a diamond stick-pin sparkled in his cravat.

"Good afternoon, Miss McLeod." He bowed over her hand. "May I join you?"

"Please do."

"It's been a long time," Dallon said. His gaze moved over her, warm with affection and approval. "Your stay in Paris seems to have agreed with you."

"Thank you, my lord," Rhianna replied, acutely aware of the admiration in his eyes.

"I was sorry to hear about your father," Montroy said. "Is there anything I can do for you or your family?"

"No, thank you. Lord Rayven has been most generous."

"Indeed." Montroy sat back in his chair. "Are you returning to France soon?"

Rhianna shook her head. "No. As much as I loved Paris, I've decided to stay here. It's home, after all." *And Rayven is here.*

A slow smile spread over Montroy's face. "That's good news indeed," he said. "There's a new play at the theater. I'd like very much to take you."

"Would you?"

Montroy chuckled softly. "If you'd like to go. And if you think you could tolerate my company for the evening."

"I should like that very much indeed," Rhianna replied. In truth, it would be no hardship to spend time with Montroy. With his dark blond hair and blue eyes, he was quite the most blatantly handsome man she had ever met, and she had met many during the last four years.

"Good. I shall pick you up Saturday at six."

"I'll be ready."

"Very well." Rising to his feet, he took her hand in his. "I hate to leave you, but I have a business appointment." He kissed her hand. "Till Saturday next, Miss McLeod."

"Till Saturday."

Montroy arrived at six o'clock sharp. Rhianna grinned openly as she introduced him to her sisters. One and all, they stared at him, hardly able to speak coherently as he bowed over their hands. Even her mother seemed awestruck.

"I'm sorry about my family," Rhianna remarked later, in the carriage. "They've never met anyone quite like you. My youngest sister asked me if you were a prince."

"And what did you tell her?"

"Why, I said you were, of course."

Dallon laughed softly as he took her hand in his and gave it a squeeze. "Hardly that."

For a time, they rode in silence. Montroy studied the girl beside him. She was even more beautiful than he remembered. Four years at school had refined her, given her an aura of self-confidence that she had lacked before. It occurred to him that it was past time for him to marry and father an heir.

He thought of little else during the play. None of the ladies he knew could hold a candle to the young woman sitting beside him. True, she came from a poor family, but he was a wealthy man and the fact that she had no dowry mattered not at all. There was only one drawback that he could see, and that was the fact that everyone in the valley knew Rhianna's father had sold her to Rayven, that she had lived in his house. Dallon didn't care a whit what the people of Millbrae Valley thought, but it would likely cause a stir should his family ever find out.

But he would jump that fence when he came to it.

After the play, he took her out for a late supper. She continued to charm him with her openness, her candor. Flirting came naturally to her; it wasn't something she had learned at school, or studied in front of her looking glass.

By the time his carriage drew up outside her home, his decision had been made.

"Thank you for a lovely evening," Rhianna said.

"It was my pleasure," Dallon replied gallantly. He kissed her hand and then, unable to help himself, he drew her into his arms and kissed her.

Rhianna closed her eyes as his lips touched hers. It was a pleasant kiss, gentle, tender. Unbidden came the thought that, while Montroy's kiss was pleasurable, it had no fire. Comparing Montroy's kiss to Rayven's was like comparing the warmth of a firefly to the warmth of the sun.

His arm tightened around her briefly before he let her go. "Will I see you tomorrow night?"

"If you wish."

"Seven?"

Rhianna nodded.

"Good night, Miss McLeod."

"Good night, my lord."

He came for her promptly at seven the following evening, and every night for a week thereafter. They went to a ball at Lord Tewksbury's, to supper in the city, to another play, to the opera.

As much as she enjoyed Montroy's company, she couldn't help feeling that she didn't belong in the crowd he associated with. They dined with barons and counts. Once, she found herself dancing with an earl. On the outside, she knew she looked as though she belonged. The gowns Rayven had bought her were every bit as costly and fashionable as those of the other women. Thanks to the training she had received at the convent, she knew how to behave at the dinner table, which fork to use with which course, but on the inside, she was still a country girl, unsure of herself, in awe of the highborn men and women who were Montroy's contemporaries.

She said as much one night, at supper.

"Nonsense," Montroy exclaimed. "There's no shame in being born poor."

"But . . ."

"I'll hear no more of it," Dallon said firmly. He took her hand in his. "You're more beautiful than any of them, Rhianna. You have no need to feel inferior simply because your father was a farmer and not an earl. Don't forget, Gaskell wasn't always an earl. Not all of us are born to our titles."

Rhianna smiled at him, reassured, at least for the moment. "Will I see you tomorrow night?" she asked.

Dallon shook his head. "I'm afraid not. I've agreed to meet Tewksbury and Rayven at Cotyer's."

The mere mention of his name caused a sharp pain in her heart.

"Is something wrong?" Montroy asked. "You look pale of a sudden."

"I feel a headache coming on," Rhianna said apologetically. "Would you mind if we went home?"

"Of course not." He summoned the waiter, took care of the bill, and wrapped her cloak around her shoulders.

Minutes later, she was comfortably settled in his coach, a blanket over her lap. She closed her eyes to discourage any conversation and all the while, in the back of her mind, she heard Montroy's voice telling her he was meeting Rayven tomorrow night. She wished she had the nerve to follow Montroy to Cotyer's so that she might see Rayven again, if only from a distance.

She bid Montroy good night and went into the house. Standing at the window, she watched his coach pull away. Overcome by a terrible sadness, she removed her cloak and went into the bedroom she shared with Lanna. Montroy cared for her. He might even ask for her hand in marriage, but she knew she would never love him as she loved Rayven.

Why had he sent her away? After living at the convent in Paris, she understood what it was like to be lonely, to be different from those around you. She knew, from the rumors she had heard, from things Rayven himself had said, that he felt estranged from society, though she didn't understand why. Was there some incident in his past that made him feel inferior?

She told herself it didn't matter, that she didn't care. He had sent her away, first to Paris, and then away from the castle, sent her away and told her, nay, warned her, never to return.

So be it, she thought, blinking back tears she

refused to shed. If he didn't want her, she knew someone who did.

At the invitation of Lady Tewksbury, Montroy escorted Rhianna to a masquerade ball at Tewksbury Hall the next week.

Dallon dressed as Robin Hood, complete with bow and feathered cap. It seemed only natural that Rhianna should go as Maid Marian.

They arrived at eight, had supper at nine. It was after ten when Dallon led her into the ballroom. A huge crystal chandelier cast soft candlelight over the dancers. The orchestra was partially hidden behind a wall of lacy ferns.

She danced with Dallon, and with Tewksbury, and then with Dallon again. He flirted with her shamelessly, declaring her to be the most beautiful woman in the room. His hand caressed her bare shoulders, his lips brushed her cheeks, her eyelids.

Light-headed from too much wine, feeling lonely because Rayven had rejected her, she allowed Dallon to kiss her. She even kissed him back, telling herself it didn't matter. Rayven didn't want her. He had even told her to marry someone else. Why not marry Montroy? He was young and handsome and rich, and he adored her. He would never send her away.

At the end of the waltz, Montroy left her for a moment to fetch her a glass of champagne.

Feeling suddenly warm, Rhianna left the crush inside the ballroom and went out on the balcony that overlooked a rather exotic topiary. A breeze ruffled her skirts and cooled her flushed cheeks.

Away off in the distance, she could see the tall

spires of Castle Rayven. In spite of her resolution to put him from her mind, she wondered what Rayven was doing, if he ever spared a thought for her.

A sudden chill caressed her nape, and with it the sense that she was no longer alone.

She whirled around, gasping when she saw a tall man standing in the doorway. He was dressed all in black save for the stark white death's-head mask that covered his face. A wide-brimmed black hat adorned with a curling black feather was pulled low over his brow. A cloak of fine black velvet billowed around him.

He held out his hand. "May I have this dance, my lady?"

His voice caressed her, calling up images of roses and moonlit nights. She never thought to refuse him, but willingly placed her hand in his.

He held her close, his body brushing intimately against hers at every turn. Trapped in the web of his gaze, she let him waltz her around the balcony. The music faded into the distance. The crush of people inside the ballroom ceased to exist. There were only the two of them, dancing beneath a sky sprinkled with stars, and the awareness that crackled between them, as sharp as a sliver of glass.

She gazed into his eyes, fathomless black eyes that stared back at her, eyes that burned with hell's own fires.

Suddenly breathless, she murmured his name.

His arm tightened around her waist, drawing her closer. Her body burned at his nearness; her heart was pounding furiously.

Was it he?

It had to be.

Slowly, he lowered his head toward hers, until the dark eyes blazing from behind the mask burned everything else from her sight, until she saw nothing, was aware of nothing, but the man who held her. She lifted her face for his kiss, felt the touch of his cool lips scorch a bright path to the very heart and soul of her.

When he drew his mouth from hers, she stared up at him, a curious lethargy stealing through her limbs. If not for the strength of the arms around her, she thought she might have melted at his feet, like butter left too long in the sun.

She wasn't aware that the music had ended until she saw Montroy standing in the doorway.

Her partner bowed over her hand and then, his cloak swirling about him like smoke, he walked away from her to disappear in the darkness at the far end of the balcony.

"Who was that?" Rhianna asked, though she was certain, within her heart, it had been Rayven.

Montroy glanced after the man in the black hat and cloak. "I don't know."

"I thought . . ."

"Thought what?"

"I thought it was Rayven."

"Rayven? Here?" Montroy chuckled softly as he handed her a glass of champagne. "He loathes masquerades. Loathes parties of any kind. I've never known him to attend one."

"Have you seen him at Cotyer's recently?"

Dallon nodded. "Blast the man. He's impossible to beat, you know. Sometimes I think he knows what cards I've been dealt before I do."

"Indeed?" She stood on tiptoe, trying to see over the heads of the crowd.

"Come," Montroy said. He placed her glass on the balcony railing, then took her hand in his. "I believe this is my dance."

She dreamed of Rayven that night, dreamed that he came into her room, that he was standing beside her bed, his long black cloak enfolding him like loving arms, a hideous mask hiding his face. Not the white mask he had worn to the ball, but a mask with glowing red eyes and sharp white fangs dripping blood.

She woke with a cry on her lips. Or was she still dreaming? She blinked into the darkness. Was he there, in the corner, or was that merely a shadow cast by the moonlight?

Heart pounding, mouth dry, she stared into the darkness of her room. "My lord?"

"Go to sleep, sweet Rhianna."

"Let me see your face."

"You would not like what you see. Sleep now. Sleep, sleep, go to sleep . . ."

She struggled to stay awake, but could not resist the hypnotic sound of his voice. Her limbs grew heavy; her eyelids refused to stay open.

"Please come to me," she begged, though it was an effort to think, to speak. "I know you're there."

"This is only a dream, Rhianna. Only a dream . . ."

How could it be a dream, she wondered, if he was telling her to go to sleep?

And then she was asleep, or was she merely dreaming she was asleep? Confused, she tried to call his name, to climb out of the lethargy that was dragging her down, down, into nothingness. . . .

She woke determined to see him again.

In spite of her resolution, it took her a week to get up the nerve to travel the narrow winding road that led up Devil Tree Mountain to Castle Rayven.

She dressed carefully for her journey. The gown she chose was of royal blue velvet. The bodice had a square neck, the sleeves were long and fitted, the skirt was bell-shaped, the hem trimmed with black fur. She wore her hair down, caught away from her face by two jeweled combs.

Donning a voluminous dark brown cloak, she took a last look in the mirror before leaving her room.

Not wanting her mother or sisters to see her, she tiptoed out the back door, saddled one of the horses, and rode out of the yard.

It was a bit frightening, riding through the night toward Castle Rayven. The trees cast ominous shadows on the road. She felt her heart drop into her stomach as an owl swooped past her head.

Dark clouds gathered overhead, shutting out the moon and the stars. A cold wind rushed down from the mountain, keening sadly as it swept across the land.

She was shivering by the time she reached the castle. Dismounting, she tethered the horse, then climbed the steps and knocked on the door.

Several minutes later, the door opened with a creak.

"Miss McLeod," Bevins exclaimed. "What are you doing here?"

"I came to visit Lord Rayven."

Bevins looked momentarily taken aback. "No one has ever come to visit before," he remarked in astonishment. "Is Lord Rayven expecting you?"

"No. Is he here?"

Bevins hesitated a moment, then nodded.

"Can I see him?"

Bevins frowned. "Truly, miss, I don't know what to do."

"Is something wrong?"

Bevins took a step forward. "He's been in quite a bad mood, miss," he said, his voice lowered conspiratorially. "I'm not sure that seeing him just now is a good idea."

"Bevins!"

Rhianna jumped back, her eyes widening as Rayven stepped into the hallway.

Very slowly, Bevins turned around to face his master. "Sir?"

"You may go, Bevins," Rayven said, his voice like ice.

"Yes, my lord. Good night, Miss Rhianna."

"Bevins, you have my leave to go."

"Yes, my lord," Bevins said. He sent Rhianna a glance that might have been meant to be reassuring, then hurried down the hallway.

Like statues, Rhianna and Rayven stood staring at each other until the sound of Bevins's footsteps disappeared.

"What are you doing here?" Rayven asked, his voice carefully controlled. His eyes, those depthless black eyes, held hers captive.

"I . . . that is . . . I . . ." She couldn't speak, couldn't think coherently, with him staring at her like that.

She licked lips gone suddenly dry. He looked so angry, so ominous standing there. He wore black, always black, she thought. Had she made a mistake in coming here? Had she been mistaken at the ball? Perhaps it hadn't been Rayven at the masquerade after all.

He walked down the hallway, rapidly closing the distance between them, until they were only an arm's length apart. "I told you never to return here."

Rhianna nodded. She slipped her hands into the pockets of her cloak and balled them into tight fists to still their trembling. "So you did, my lord."

"Then why are you here?"

She lifted her chin, refusing to let him intimidate her. "If you never wanted to see me again, why did you come to the masquerade? Why did you dance with me?" She took a deep breath. "Why did you kiss me?"

He stiffened. She saw his hands clench at his sides, and knew it was not to still their trembling, but to restrain his anger.

"I know it was you," Rhianna said, "so you needn't try to deny it."

"Leave my house," Rayven said, biting off each word. "Leave now, while you can."

Rhianna looked deep into his eyes. Past the anger lurking there, beneath the harsh timbre of his voice, she sensed the loneliness that plagued him.

"I've missed you, my lord," she said quietly. "I had hoped you missed me."

A muscle twitched in Rayven's jaw. It was the only visible sign of the tension that was spiraling through him. He drew a deep breath, and the scent that was hers assailed his nostrils—the soap she bathed with, the mutton and cheese she'd had for supper, the scent of her hair and skin, the fragrance of her perfume. He could smell the nervousness that made her heart beat fast, smell the blood that flowed in her veins.

A sharp blast of wind buffeted Rhianna's cloak, its chill breath making her shiver. A moment later, there was a blinding flash of lightning, followed by a tremendous clap of thunder, and then it began to rain.

Rayven swore under his breath. Even the elements seemed to be conspiring against him. He took a step back so she could cross the threshold.

"Come in," he said, though there was no warmth in his voice, no welcome in his eyes.

"My horse . . ."

"Bevins will see to it," Rayven said brusquely. "Come in."

Afraid he might change his mind, Rhianna quickly did as bidden. She unfastened her cloak, felt Rayven's hands at her shoulders as he took it from her and hung it on a wooden clothes peg, then shut the door.

Wordlessly, he walked past her.

She hesitated only a moment, then followed him down the long narrow hallway that led to the library. How many hours had she sat in this room, reading to him? she wondered. How often had she watched him, wishing he would take her in his arms, that he would kiss her as she had longed to be kissed? Had he known how she felt? Was that why he had sent her away?

She paused in the doorway as a horrible thought crossed her mind. Perhaps he was in love with someone else. Perhaps he hadn't wanted to be bothered with her silly infatuation. Only it wasn't some childish infatuation she felt for him.

He sat down in his favorite chair, his back to her. "Come in, Rhianna," he invited softly.

Feeling suddenly shy, she crossed the floor and took a seat in the chair across from his. It seemed strange to sit there, as if she were his equal. Most nights, she had sat on the floor with her back to the hearth.

She glanced around the room, finding it exactly as it had been the last time she had seen it four years ago. An ancient-looking sword hung over the massive fireplace. A long oak table covered with a black lace cloth stood beneath a pair of tall, stained-glass windows. A narrow shelf made of dark oak held several pewter figurines in the shapes of snarling wolves and ravens in flight. There was no other furniture in the room save for the two high-backed chairs.

"You should not have come here." His voice was low and soft.

"I'm sorry if my presence upsets you."

One corner of his mouth turned down in a wintry smile. "You have no idea what your presence does to me."

"I am most happy to see you again, my lord," Rhianna said candidly. "I had hoped you would feel the same."

"Rhianna, I have longed for you these past four years in ways you cannot begin to imagine."

She shook her head. "Then why are you so angry with me?"

"I am not angry."

He looked angry, she thought. His hands were curled over the arms of the chair, his knuckles white with the strain. His posture was stiff, unyielding. She could almost see the tension radiating from him.

"What is it, then?" she asked.

"I fear you are not safe here."

"Not safe?"

He stared past her, listening to the rain drumming on the roof. It was going to storm all night, he mused bleakly. There was no way he could send her home, not now.

His gaze skimmed her face and figure. She was so beautiful. Her skin was the color of honey; her hair fell down her back in a mass of sun-gold waves. She watched him through guileless blue eyes, her affection for him evident in every glance.

She could not stay here. The years without her had not lessened his desire. He wanted her, burned for her, ached for her in ways unknown to mortal man.

Hunger roared through him. Hunger for her touch, for the very essence of her life.

He felt it rise up within him, demanding to be fed, felt the thirst clawing at his insides. Her nearness, the remembered sweetness of her, magnified his longing, his need for this one woman above all others.

His fingernails dug into the arms of the chair, gouging the wood. His breathing became shallow and erratic. "Rhianna."

"My lord?" She leaned forward, her eyes narrowed as she studied his face. "Are you well, my lord? Can I get you a glass of wine?"

"Go to your room."

"But . . ."

"Go!"

She didn't argue, didn't waste time saying good night. Bolting from her chair, she fairly flew out of the room and up the stairs to the chamber that had once been hers.

Inside, she locked the door, then stood with her back against the portal, her breath coming in labored gasps.

She had fled from him once before. The memory came surging back, as bright and clear as if it had happened only yesterday instead of years ago. She remembered feeling as though she had escaped a terrible fate that night.

She felt much the same way now.

When her breathing returned to normal, she noticed that the room was just as she had left it. Crossing the floor to the armoire, she opened the elaborately carved double doors. Inside were the dresses she had not taken with her when she left for Paris. She had regretted leaving so many behind, but Rayven had given her more clothes than any one woman could wear in a lifetime.

Closing the doors, she went to the dresser and opened the drawer that had held her nightgowns. Selecting one, she undressed, drew on the gown.

She was about to climb into bed when she noticed that the full-length mirror Rayven had given her had been covered with a dark cloth.

Curious, she thought, as she removed the cloth. She gazed at her reflection. She had been but fifteen the last time she looked in this mirror. She had grown a little taller, her figure was more rounded, more womanly, but other than that, she looked much the same. She wished suddenly that she was beautiful, that she had curly red hair like her friend at the convent, Leanna, that her eyes were emerald green instead of ordinary blue, that her breasts were larger, her waist smaller. No wonder Rayven had sent her away. Why would he choose her when he could have his pick of beautiful women?

Turning away from the mirror, she drew back the covers and slipped into bed. If the rumors were true, he'd had many, many women, yet he had married none of them. She couldn't help wondering why. Surely a man of his wealth and breeding desired an heir.

A baby, she thought dreamily, a son with Rayven's black hair and eyes. Closing her eyes, she imagined herself as Rayven's wife, the mother of his children.

As he had so many times in the past, he stood beside her bed, watching her sleep. The softness of her skin tempted his touch, and he curled his hands into tight fists to keep from stroking her cheek. How beautiful she was! And how he adored her. The years without her had been the worst torture he had ever endured. He had thought of her daily, hourly, the memory of her face, her laughter, tormenting him far worse than any pain the heat of the sun might hold. The remembered sweetness of her lips, the nectar of her essence, had forever spoiled him for the taste of anyone else.

Ah, how he had burned for her, the yearning within him more excruciatingly painful than the dark hunger that plagued him. Rhianna.

He had watched Montroy dancing with her at Tewksbury's masquerade, and he'd wanted to kill the man, to rip the heart from his chest. Never in all his four hundred-and-thirty-one years had he experienced such blinding jealousy, such hatred, such an intense urge to destroy. He had known it would be a mistake to attend the masquerade, just as he had known, from the minute Montroy had mentioned the ball over drinks at Cotyer's, that he would go. Just to see her. But seeing her had not been enough. He had wanted, needed, to hold her in his arms.

His fingernails cut into his palms as he fought the urge to gather her into his arms, to kiss the soft curve of her cheek, to run his tongue along her neck . . .

A red mist rose up before his eyes. Hunger cramped his stomach and ran like molten lava through his veins. He felt his fangs lengthen, felt the urge to feed rise up within him, a ravening beast straining to be released.

"No." The word whispered past his lips. He would not. Could not.

Fear drove him toward the door.

"My lord?"

He stopped, his hands clenched at his sides.

"My lord? Is that you?"

"Go to sleep, Rhianna," he said. Slowly, he glanced over his shoulder, unleashing the full force of his gaze upon her. "Go to sleep, my sweet, and dream your young girl's dreams while you still can."

She gazed into the dark depths of his eyes and felt a familiar lassitude steal through her. Her eyelids felt unbearably heavy. With a soft sigh, she closed her eyes.

Just before sleep claimed her, she thought she heard the hauntingly lonely cry of a wolf.

Chapter Ten

As usual, Rayven was nowhere to be found in the morning.

Bevins smiled cheerfully as he moved around the dining room, serving her favorite breakfast, pouring her a cup of cocoa. "I trust you slept well, miss?"

"Yes, thank you." Rhianna glanced out the window. Gray clouds hung low in the sky, broken by an occasional flash of lightning. She had always loved storms—the thunder, the lightning, the soothing sound of the rain pounding on the roof, pattering against the windowpanes. "Will Lord Rayven be coming down for breakfast?"

Bevins shook his head. "My lord has offered you the shelter of his house," he said, following her gaze, "until the storm passes."

"Did he?" Odd, she mused, when he had seemed so anxious for her to be gone.

"He would not have you catch a chill, miss. There's a cozy fire in the library, should you wish to read, and also in the conservatory, should you wish to play."

"Thank you, Bevins." She sipped the hot chocolate he had placed before her, relishing the smooth rich taste. "I thought you told me Lord Rayven wasn't here."

"Did I?"

"You know you did. Why did you lie to me?"

A guilty flush climbed into the old man's cheeks.

"The last time I came here, you said he had left the castle shortly after he sent me to Paris."

Bevins shifted uncomfortably. "I only told you what I was instructed to say, miss," he replied quietly. "It would have been better for all concerned if you had believed me."

"Better? What do you mean?"

Bevins glanced at the door; then, heaving a sigh, he sat down at the table across from her. Rhianna stared at him in surprise. Never before had he sat at table with her, or crossed the fine line between servant and friend.

"Miss Rhianna, I know you think yourself in love with Lord Rayven," he said, speaking quickly, as though he feared being caught speaking to her so candidly. " 'Tis true my lord has a certain appeal that most women find hard to resist."

"I didn't realize my feelings were so transparent," Rhianna muttered dryly.

Bevins leaned across the table, his voice somber. "You must believe me when I tell you it isn't safe for you to stay here."

Rhianna frowned. Rayven had said practically

the same thing the night before. "I don't understand."

"Lord Rayven is a man compelled by dark appetites, miss. Appetites he cannot always control. You would be wise to leave this place and never come back."

"Dark appetites?" Rhianna shook her head. "Whatever are you talking about?"

Bevins glanced at the door again, his expression wary. "I cannot explain, miss, except to say that Lord Rayven is not like other men. He is driven by forces you cannot comprehend. It is why he lives in solitude."

"I don't believe you. If he's such a monster, why has he never harmed me? Why did he send me to school and provide for my family?"

Bevins took a deep breath. "I've said too much already, miss." Rising, he placed a fatherly hand on her shoulder. "Go home, Miss Rhianna. As soon as the storm passes, go home."

Smothered in darkness, Rayven felt his anger bubble to the surface. How dare Bevins interfere in his personal life! What right did the man have to warn Rhianna away from him?

Muttering an oath, he took a deep breath, the anger washing out of him between one breath and the next. Bevins had said nothing that he, Rayven, had not said himself. If Rhianna were wise, she would leave his house and never return.

He had no illusions about what he was. He reeked of evil, of death. He had done things, horrible things, atrocious things, committed acts that had damned his soul forever. No matter that he had not chosen this life for himself. Once the deed had been done, he could have ended it. He could have walked into the sunlight and destroyed the creature he had become.

He gazed into the darkness that shrouded him, a distant memory rising up in his mind . . .

"I don't want it!"

He screamed the words as he struggled against her, but his puny mortal strength was as nothing compared to hers.

"But you will take it," she said, her black eyes wise with knowledge beyond his understanding. "You are a warrior, Rayven of Millbrae. You will not submit. You will not surrender. You will fight with every ounce of strength you possess to survive." She laughed softly, confidently. "You would drink me dry if I let you."

"No! Never!"

"But you will." The certainty in her voice, the red glow in her eyes, had filled him with terror.

Effortlessly, she had held him close while she raked one bloodred nail across his cheek. "I have marked you," she said, "so that you will always remember me."

And then she pressed him back on the couch, holding him effortlessly in spite of his violent struggle to escape. He cried out as he felt the sharp bite of her teeth at his throat. Revulsion rose within him as he realized she was drinking his blood.

He wanted desperately to fight her, but he had no strength left. There was a buzzing in his ears, his heart was beating frantically, a hazy red mist rose up in front of his eyes.

"No, don't . . ." Weakness engulfed him, his heartbeat slowed and grew heavy, and he felt the blackness of oblivion descending. And with it a

nameless fear, worse than the fear of death.

"Please . . ." He formed the word but no sound emerged from his lips.

"You want to live?" Her breath was hot against his ear. "Then drink."

He was too weak to move, to obey. He tried to see her face, but saw nothing at all.

"Drink!"

He didn't want to submit, but the will to live rose strong within him. He was, after all, a warrior, born to fight, to conquer.

He opened his mouth, and she pressed her wrist to his lips.

"Drink."

His mouth closed over her flesh. A rush of liquid flowed over his tongue, warm and slightly salty. It slid down his throat like liquid fire, and suddenly he was clinging to her arm, drawing the blood into his mouth, revulsion and delight warring within him. His heartbeat thundered in his ears, growing ever stronger, beating in rhythm with hers. Power surged within him, igniting a craving for more.

"Enough!" She wrenched her arm from his grasp. "Enough, I say!"

He stared up at her, dazed, his gaze lingering on the redness around her mouth, the blood oozing from the gash in her wrist. A gash that was closing, healing, even as he watched.

Horror descended slowly. Lifting his hand, he wiped his mouth, then stared at the scarlet wetness on his fingertips. Her blood. He had been drinking her blood.

Slowly, seductively, she licked the redness from her lips. "You are mine now," she said, "always and forever mine."

"No." He shook his head, numb with the horror of what he had done, what he would become.

"You died tonight," she told him, her voice calm and detached, as if the words were of no significance. "When you wake tomorrow night, you will be as I am."

He had not wanted to believe. Had refused to believe. Even when the violent tremors wracked his body, even when, with the sun's rising, darkness the likes of which he had never experienced enveloped him. Even when he woke the next night and saw the world through new eyes, he had not wanted to believe.

But it was true.

He had become a vampyre, damned to spend his life in darkness, to be forever at the mercy of the Dark Gift, forced to live in the shadows, to exist on the blood of others, or perish . . .

Vampyre . . . the word echoed and re-echoed through the corridors of his mind as the familiar darkness encompassed him once more.

She was still in the house when he awoke. He felt her presence with his first conscious breath. Why hadn't she left?

Rising, Rayven bathed and donned fresh clothing. Leaving the tower, he hurried downstairs, only dimly aware that it was still raining.

Rhianna was sitting in the library, her feet curled underneath her. For a moment, he stood in the doorway, watching her. She wore a gown of pale green velvet tied with a dark green sash. Her slippers were of the same dark green. Her hair fell over her shoulders, shimmering like fine gold silk in the firelight. A slender gold chain circled her throat. The rain falling against the windows made a pleasant counterpoint to the crackling flames.

As though suddenly aware of his presence, she looked up, her cheeks turning rosy when she saw him watching her.

"Good evening, my lord." She put the book she had been reading aside, pleased that her hand didn't tremble, that her voice was calm.

"Good evening, sweet Rhianna."

He entered the room on silent feet and sat down in the chair opposite hers. His cloak settled lovingly around him, enfolding him like the wings of a great black bird.

"I meant to leave," Rhianna said, his nearness making her suddenly nervous, "but Bevins said I should wait out the storm."

Rayven nodded. His whole being seemed to be reaching for her, yearning for her. Hungering for her. Did he really want her to go? Why not let her stay? She could live comfortably here. His wealth could buy her whatever she desired. He would make sure she lacked for nothing . . .

He clenched his jaw. He could never give her the things every young woman wanted. He could provide for her and protect her, but he could never give her children. He could stay by her side, but he could never share her whole life. He could care for her when age and disease took their toll, but he would not grow old with her. And in the end, he would stand by her grave, looking exactly as he did now.

"You can send me away if you want," Rhianna said, unnerved by his silence, by the fierce glitter in the depths of his hell-black eyes. "You can send me away, or you can leave, but I'll always be here when you come back."

"You're not afraid of me, are you?" he asked, his voice touched with wonder.

"Afraid? Of you?" She shook her head. Sometimes he made her feel apprehensive, but she had never been truly afraid. She knew, in the deepest part of her being, that he would never intentionally harm her.

"You should be." He spoke the words calmly, as if commenting on the inclement weather.

"Do you want me to be afraid?"

"It would be better if you were."

"Better for whom? You speak in riddles, my lord."

"Pray you never understand them."

He turned the full force of his gaze upon her, and in spite of her brave words to the contrary, she felt a sudden chill of unease. Clasping her hands in her lap, she took a deep breath. "Shall I leave?"

"You are welcome to stay," he said, one hand idly stroking the rich velvet of his cloak, "until the storm ends." He would offer her a bribe, he thought, offer to grant her anything she desired, anything that would take her away from this place. From his presence.

He regarded her through narrowed eyes. "I am going to grant you a boon, Rhianna. One wish. Ask for whatsoever your heart desires above all else, and it shall be yours."

"You can do such a thing?"

A faint smile tugged at the corner of his lips. "You would be surprised at what I can do."

Rhianna frowned, certain she was imagining

things, yet she would have sworn his cloak wrapped itself more tightly around his broad shoulders, that it soothed him in some way.

"Anything?" she asked.

"Only name your heart's desire."

"And you will grant it to me? You promise?"

Rayven nodded. "What will it be?" he asked curiously. "Riches? A fine house staffed with servants? A return to Paris? A large dowry for yourself and your sisters? Only name it, and it's yours."

"I wish to stay here with you," she replied quietly, "for as long as it pleases me to do so. I wish to live in your house and spend time with you each night."

Rayven stared at her. Of all the things he had imagined she might ask for, the most obvious had never occurred to him. "Ask for something else."

"No. You gave me your word." Her gaze met his. "Is it your intention to break it?"

"No." His voice was choked, hoarse, as though it were an effort to speak. "One year. I will give you one year."

Her smile was radiant. Triumphant. "Thank you. Would you ask Bevins to pick up my things in the morning? Oh! I must write a note to my mother and let her know I shall be staying here. Would you ask him to come for it before he goes?"

Rayven nodded curtly. Then, feeling like a spider caught in its own web, he stood up, his expression bleak, his eyes as cold as the rain pummeling the windowpanes.

"I pray you do not regret your choice," he said, and swept out of the room, his cloak swirling around his ankles as though blown by an angry wind.

Chapter Eleven

Bevins climbed the stairs to the east tower, aware of the unrest that troubled his master. He had been in Rayven's employ for over fifty years. He had been but a youth of fourteen when the vampyre saved his life. In exchange, Bevins had sworn to dedicate the rest of his life to serving Rayven.

Crossing the floor, he stood in the doorway of the inner chamber in the east tower, his expression carefully neutral as he watched Rayven remove his cloak and toss it over the back of a chair.

Bevins eyed the cloak warily. It was a most unusual garment, often seeming as though it possessed a life of its own.

"What am I to do?" Rayven asked, his voice rising with anger. "She cannot stay here! I cannot bear it."

Bevins remained silent, knowing no answer

was expected. Never had he seen his master in such an agitated state.

Rayven raked his hands through his hair, a string of vicious oaths escaping his lips as he paced the floor, his long legs carrying him from one end of the room to the other in less than a half-dozen strides.

He paused abruptly, turned, and went to the window of the outer room. He could feel the tension building within him as he stared into the garden below. How many nights had he stood here, gazing out over the castle walls, wishing she was here, wishing for one more night, one more hour in her presence? But a year?

He groaned softly. He had sent her away because he was losing control of his desire, of the fierce hunger that drove him relentlessly, urging him to take what he needed, to bring her across the vast gulf that separated them so that she might ease the loneliness of his endless existence. He had always been arrogant and selfish, but he had never been cruel, and so he had sent her away to protect her from his own desire.

And now she was here again, in the castle again, in his life again, and it was as if she had never gone away. Her scent was everywhere—on his skin, his clothes, in the very air he breathed.

"Is there anything else you wish this evening?" Bevins asked.

"What?" Rayven whirled around. He had all but forgotten the other man was in the room. "No. Go to bed. Wait. Tomorrow morning you will go to Rhianna's and collect her belongings. She also wishes you to deliver a note to her mother."

Bevins nodded. "I shall see to it." He took a deep

breath. "Will you be coming down tomorrow night?"

"I promised her, didn't I?" Rayven snapped, his voice like death.

"Yes, my lord. And will you also be joining her at supper?"

"Yes." Rayven clenched his hands into tight fists, his expression bleak. "Don't forget the wine."

Bevins nodded curtly, then left the stark tower room, closing the door behind him. He heard the sound of the bolt being shot home.

It was going to be a long year, he thought. For all of them.

She was waiting for him at the supper table the following night. Dressed in a rich plum-colored gown, with a matching ribbon in her hair, she fair took his breath away.

"Good evening, my lord," Rhianna said, smiling up at him. He was clad in black from head to heel. He looked dark and dangerous, a midnight rogue who made her heartbeat quicken and her insides quiver with desire. "I'm so glad you decided to join me."

He took the seat across from her. "I said I would, did I not?"

"Yes, but I thought you might have changed your mind."

His eyes narrowed. "My word, when given, is as good as that of any other man."

"Yet you feel as though I tricked you somehow."

"I thought you would likely ask for something that would be of benefit to you or your family."

He picked up the crystal decanter and poured himself a glass of wine.

"Yes, my family. You have been most kind to them, my lord. I thank you for that, and for the generous dowry you have given my sister."

He made a vague gesture of dismissal with his hand. "Why do you insist on staying here when you know I want you gone?"

Rhianna watched him drain his glass, wondering why he downed it so quickly. Wasn't wine to be savored?

"Because, my lord, in this one instance, my pleasure means more to me than yours."

She pushed her plate away and stood up, offering him her hand. "Shall we go into the library? Bevins has laid a fire, and I have a new book I wish to read."

Rising, Rayven took her hand in his, felt the quick jolt of awareness that passed from her hand to his.

She stared up at him through wide blue eyes. "My lord," she murmured, and he knew she had felt it, too.

Unable to help himself, he drew her into his arms. He gazed into her eyes for a timeless moment, and then he kissed her. It was a brutal kiss, violent, angry, filled with a fierce longing that could never be fulfilled. His hands tightened on her shoulders as he deepened the kiss, bruising her lips.

"You should leave this house, sweet Rhianna," he growled. "Leave now, while I am still able to let you go."

Dazed by the intensity of his kiss, she could only shake her head.

He kissed her again, his tongue plundering the softness of her mouth. His hands moved over her, hot and restless, molding her body to his, letting her feel the rigid evidence of his desire.

Her head fell back over his arm, exposing the slender curve of her neck. His gaze fastened on the pulse throbbing wildly in the base of her throat. He could hear the rapid beat of her heart, smell the blood heating in her veins. And then he felt the prick of his fangs against his tongue.

Abruptly, he thrust her away, his hands curling into tight fists at his sides.

"Rhianna, I beg you, ask another boon of me. Anything," he whispered, his voice laced with desperation. "I'll give you anything else. This castle, if you wish it, my fortune, anything."

"I want only to stay here, with you, my lord," she replied softly. "I know when the year is up, you will send me away, but I want to spend this time with you."

"I only hope it will not prove to be your undoing," he muttered under his breath, and turning away from her, he left the room.

He hunted that night, hunted for prey as he had not hunted in years, knowing that tonight, a few sips of Rhianna's precious blood would not be enough to still the awful hunger that her mere presence stirred within him.

A year, he mused as he bent over his helpless victim. Compared to the centuries behind him, to the eternity that stretched before him, twelve months was less than a moment in time, yet he feared it was a year that would see his end, or hers.

Rhianna began her seduction the following night, determined to have him in her bed before the year was out. He had made it clear that he did not love her, that he would never marry her, but she was determined that he would be the first man to bed her.

She had dreamed of him for four long years, dreamed and yearned, and now she meant to have him. She had heard whispers of how easy it was to seduce a man. Not all the girls in the convent school had been as innocent as she, and those who had traded their virtue for knowledge had been most eager to share what they had learned. Men were easily led by a pretty face, they had told her, and by the promise of an easy conquest.

To her regret, Rayven seemed to be the exception to the rule. No matter how brazenly she flirted with him, no matter how boldly she teased and tempted, he refused to succumb to her enticements. She knew he wanted her. She could see the hunger in his eyes, hear it in his voice, feel it in the way his arms trembled when he occasionally weakened and drew her close. But always, at the last, he thrust her away and left the room.

He had done it every night for so long.

Tonight had been no exception.

She stood beside the fire, staring after him, wondering if she lacked some vital feminine attraction.

With a sigh, she dropped down into Rayven's favorite chair. He had left his cloak draped across the back, and she drew it into her lap, idly stroking the fine velvet. How alive it seemed as she spread it over her legs. Of its own accord, it seemed to press against her, warming her. Soothing her.

Suddenly weary, she closed her eyes, felt herself swept away into a world of darkness.

Her hands clutched the smooth velvet as disjointed scenes filled her mind—she saw Rayven walking along a dark dusty path, his cloak floating behind him like ink splashed against the darkness of the night; she saw a dark gray mist surround a drunken man, heard the man's faint cry of terror, and over all hung a mist of darkness and the scent of blood; she saw a sleek black wolf standing over the carcass of a deer, heard a long, lonely howl echo in her ears . . .

She woke with a start, her brow damp with perspiration, her heart pounding wildly in her breast.

Tossing the cloak to the floor, she scrambled to her feet and ran out of the room.

Dallon Montroy came calling late the following afternoon. Bevins showed him to the front parlor, his face a mask of disapproval as Rhianna made the man welcome.

"Bevins, will you please bring us some tea," Rhianna requested, "and a few scones, perhaps?"

"As you wish," Bevins replied. He fixed her with another disproving stare, then left the room.

"And now, my lord," Rhianna exclaimed softly, "what brings you to Castle Rayven?"

"You, of course," Montroy said. "Why else would anyone make such an arduous journey."

"Not arduous, surely?" Rhianna teased.

"I would have climbed a mountain twice as high to see you smile again," Dallon replied gallantly.

"Indeed?" Rhianna mused. "And would you have crossed crocodile-infested waters, as well?"

"To be sure." His smile faded as he took her

hands in his. "Why have you come back here, Rhianna?" he asked, his tone and expression grave. "Did Rayven force you? Threaten you in some manner?"

"Of course not. I'm here because I choose to be here."

"I don't understand."

"It's quite simple, really. Lord Rayven said he would grant me anything I asked for, and I asked to live here. He's letting me stay for a year."

Montroy stared at her as if she were speaking in a language he couldn't quite understand. "You asked to stay here? With him? But why?"

"I'm afraid I can't explain it."

Montroy raked a hand through his hair, thinking that, if he lived to be a hundred, he would never understand the workings of the female mind. "Well, I wish you'd try!"

Rhianna shook her head. "I can't." She studied him a moment, then frowned. "Why are you so distressed? I thought you were his friend."

"Rayven has no friends."

"Why ever not?"

"Because he wishes for none. He is a solitary man."

"You play cards together at Cotyer's."

Montroy nodded. "True enough, but he keeps us all at arm's length, and allows no familiarity. He's never accepted any invitations extended to him, nor offered any in return."

"I find that passing strange."

"As do I, I assure you."

Montroy released her hands as Bevins entered the room bearing a silver tea tray.

Back stiff, Bevins placed the tray on a low table,

fixed Rhianna with a warning glance, and left the room.

Taking a seat, Rhianna poured tea for Montroy, then herself.

After a moment, Montroy sat in the chair across from hers. "I'm afraid it will be most difficult, courting you here."

Rhianna added milk and sugar to both cups, then handed one to Montroy. "You intend to court me, my lord?"

"I thought you had guessed that by now."

"But . . . I mean . . ." Rhianna shook her head. "Surely you intend to marry a lady of quality."

"I do, indeed." He smiled at her, the dimple in his cheek deepening. He had every intention of marrying Rhianna, and he would tell her so, when the time was right. "May I call upon you again?"

"Dallon, you must know that there can be nothing between us but friendship. I love Rayven."

Montroy nodded, convinced that he could win her heart if given the chance.

Rhianna hesitated, wondering if Rayven would object, and then she put such concern aside. He was never about during the day. Why should he care what she did? He had made it quite clear he had no interest in her, that he intended to send her away when the year was done.

"Rhianna?"

She regarded Montroy a moment more, and then nodded. "I shall be delighted to have you call on me."

Montroy smiled, obviously pleased. "There is a new play at the theater. Would you care to attend?"

"Yes, I think so." She smiled thoughtfully. Nothing else had worked. Perhaps jealousy would produce the results she sought.

"Rhianna, it matters not to me, but . . ." Montroy put his cup on the table and raked a hand through his hair. "Aren't you concerned about what the people in the village will say about your living here, with him?"

"I never gave it any thought," Rhianna said. And, indeed, she hadn't. Thinking about it now, she realized it didn't matter what anyone thought. She was determined to stay here, with Rayven, and she was willing to sacrifice her reputation to do so.

"Are you sure this is what you really want?" Montroy asked quietly.

"I'm sure."

"Then I'll say no more about it."

They passed the next hour in quiet conversation, and then Montroy took his leave.

Rhianna had just sat down to supper when Rayven entered the dining room. He stood towering over her, a fierce scowl on his face.

"What was Montroy doing here?" Rayven demanded brusquely. He had caught the man's scent even before he left the east tower.

"He came calling, my lord," Rhianna said, trying to keep her voice from shaking. "I did not think you would mind, since he is your friend."

Rayven's eyes narrowed. "Did he tell you that?"

"Tell me what?"

"That we were friends."

She started to lie. She wanted to lie, but found she could not, not when Rayven's dark eyes were fixed hard upon her face.

"What did he say?" Rayven asked, his voice low and silky smooth.

"He said . . . he said you would not accept friendship."

Rayven glanced over his shoulder as Bevins entered the room. "You will not allow Montroy, or any other man, into my house again. Is that clear?"

"Yes, sir," Bevins said.

With a curt nod, Rayven turned his attention back to Rhianna. "Is that clear to you, as well?"

"Yes, my lord, but . . ."

"But what?"

"But why? Why do you shut yourself up in this castle? Why not let Lord Montroy visit you here? I think he would be your friend, if you would but let him."

"I have no need to explain my reasons to you, Rhianna. Suffice it to say that no one is welcome here."

"Including me?"

"Most especially you."

"You are most rude, my lord."

He smiled then. It was most unexpected, and most welcome.

"I apologize for my behavior, sweet Rhianna, but I fear you must learn to tolerate my moods if you insist upon staying here."

"Indeed, I shall, my lord," Rhianna retorted. "For neither your foul temper nor your bad manners shall drive me away."

Rayven sat down in the chair across from her and reached for the glass of wine that Bevins had poured for him. He lifted the crystal goblet, studying the contents a moment before he took a drink.

A look of pleasure crossed his face as he set the goblet on the table. "Finish your supper, sweet Rhianna, and then I should like to visit the maze."

"As you wish, my lord."

"Indeed, my sweet. Exactly as I wish."

It was most disconcerting, dining under his watchful eye. Her hands trembled, she knocked over her water glass, spilled a bit of gravy in her lap. And all the while, she could feel his unblinking gaze upon her, as black as the night sky.

When she finished eating, he donned his cloak, then draped a warm shawl around her shoulders.

The gardens lay quiet under a hunter's moon. He took her hand and they walked toward the maze. Rhianna tried to think of something amusing to say, some bit of small talk to ease the taut silence that stretched between them, but nothing came to mind.

"Perhaps, in the spring, you will work your magic in the gardens again," Rayven remarked after a while.

"If you wish, though I would have your promise that you will not let everything die again when I'm gone."

"You have it."

"I think I shall plant daisies near the summer house this time," Rhianna said, thinking out loud. "And more roses, of course."

"Red ones," Rayven said.

"And yellow ones, too."

"No, just red. And white." Red for the blood that sustained him; white for the purity of the woman beside him.

"Then I shall have yellow daisies."

He smiled in defeat.

"Why didn't you look after the roses in the garden as you looked after the roses within the maze?" Rhianna asked as they strolled along the winding pathway.

"I warned Bevins of dire consequences should the roses in the maze be allowed to die."

"Why such concern for the one and not the other?"

Rayven stopped. Turning her to face him, he took both her hands in his. "You planted the roses in the garden for your own pleasure," he explained, his thumbs making lazy circles over the backs of her hands. "But you planted the roses in the maze for me."

The look in his eyes made her heart beat fast. His touch sent shivers up her arms. The sound of his voice moved over her and through her. His voice. She had never heard another like it, deep and rich, filled with arrogance and command.

"Why do you live so alone?" she asked. "Why do you let no one get close?"

"I am a solitary creature by nature," he replied.

"You have an odd way of speaking of yourself," she said, "as if you were different from everyone else."

"Do you think I am not?"

And in that moment, she knew that he *was* different. Different from her, different from anyone else she had ever known, though she could not say why. And then she remembered an odd remark he had once made.

"Do you recall the night before I left for Paris?" she asked as they continued walking.

"I remember." It had been the worst night of his life.

"You said something that night, something I thought most peculiar."

"Indeed?"

"Yes. You said no mortal had ever crept up on you before."

He hesitated a moment before answering, and it seemed as if he withdrew into himself a little. "Did I?"

Rhianna nodded. "Don't you think that's odd?"

"Explain yourself," Rayven said, though he knew exactly what she meant.

"You used the word *mortal* as if it applied to me, but not to you."

"Did I?"

"You know you did!"

To distract her, he drew her into his arms. "You are the most beautiful woman I've ever known," he said, his voice husky. "Your eyes are as blue as a midsummer sky. Your skin is like alabaster kissed by the sun. And your hair . . ." He ran his fingers through the hair at her nape. "Your hair is as soft as the finest silk."

With a sigh, she melted against him, her face turned up to his, inviting his kiss.

His lips brushed hers. "Are you in love with Montroy?"

Rhianna blinked at him. "What?"

"Are you in love with Montroy?" he demanded. His hands tightened on her shoulders, his eyes burning with a fierce anger.

"No, my lord."

"I don't want you to see him again."

"I thought you wanted me to marry and have children." She tilted her head back to better see his face. "Isn't that what you said?"

"Not Montroy." He bit off each word, refusing to admit that he was jealous of the man, of any man. "Not Montroy," he said again, and hated the man because he could give Rhianna all the things she deserved.

"Very well, my lord, I'll not see him again so long as I am in residence here."

He wanted to shake her, to make her promise she would never see the man again, not now, not ever.

"There's just one thing," Rhianna said. "I gave him leave to call on me."

"Bevins will send him away."

She couldn't help it. She smiled, pleased at the notion that he was jealous of her affection for Montroy. Surely it was a good sign.

Clasping her hand in his, Rayven turned and headed back toward the castle.

"I thought we were going to sit in the maze awhile," Rhianna said, quickening her steps to keep up with him.

"Not tonight," Rayven said, his voice almost a growl. Not tonight, he thought, when his black heart burned with jealousy, when the rage running through him kindled his hunger until he was almost mad with the need to hunt.

At the castle door, he drew her into his arms, his cloak enfolding them both in a cocoon of lush velvet and warm silk. She was trembling when his mouth covered hers.

"You are mine, sweet Rhianna," he murmured. His eyes burned into hers, his breath fanned her cheek like a flame. "For this year, you belong to me and no one else."

Chapter Twelve

He didn't join her at supper the following night. Rhianna picked at her food, hardly tasting the succulent roast beef Bevins had prepared.

She glanced up at the sound of footsteps, felt the hope in her heart grow cold when Bevins entered the room.

"Is the meal not to your liking, Miss Rhianna?" Bevins asked solicitously. "I can prepare something else, if you wish."

"No, thank you." She pushed her plate away. "I find I have little appetite this evening."

Bevins nodded, a wealth of understanding in his eyes.

"Would you bring me a glass of wine?" she asked. "Perhaps the vintage Lord Rayven prefers?"

A look of horror crossed Bevins's face, and then he shook his head. "It's a very strong vintage, miss," he said. "Might I recommend something more . . . subtle?"

"Never mind." Rising, she dropped her napkin on the table. "I don't suppose you know where he is?"

"In the gardens, I believe."

"Thank you, Bevins." She smiled at him. "If he asks, I won't tell him that you told me."

"He'll know," Bevins said, a note of resignation in his tone. "Best take a wrap. The night is cool."

Her feet felt suddenly light as she grabbed her shawl and left the house.

The maze, she thought. He would be in the maze.

Her footsteps slowed as she neared the entrance to the labyrinth.

Did she dare? Why not? Everything else had failed.

Feeling somewhat reassured by the darkness, she began to undress and then, wrapped only in her shawl, she ran toward the heart of the maze.

Rayven drew in a deep breath. He had known she would seek him out, had sensed her presence long before she stepped into view.

But he had not been prepared for the sight that greeted his eyes. Silver moonlight danced in her hair like fairy dust, caressed her face, her long slender legs. A lacy white shawl that revealed far more than it hid, covered her from her shoulders to her knees.

He stood up, his breath trapped in his throat.

She took a step toward him, then stopped, all bravado gone now that she was in the lion's den.

Hunger and desire rose up within him, hotter

than the flames of an endless, fiery hell.

She was Venus rising from the sea, Eve before she tasted the apple.

"Rhianna." Her name whispered past his lips, soft as a sigh. The last desperate prayer of a dying man.

His cloak wrapped more tightly around him.

"Good evening, my lord," she said, and let go of the shawl.

It slid to the ground, pooling around her feet like star dust, and he was tempted to do the same, to drop to his knees and worship her beauty, to beg her forgiveness. Surely such a goddess could absolve him of his sins.

"Leave me, Rhianna." It was not a demand, but an urgent plea for salvation.

Slowly, she walked toward him, and it seemed as if the moonlight followed her.

"Rhianna . . ."

"I love you," she said softly.

"Don't." He tried to draw his gaze from her face, from the sheer beauty and perfection of her slender figure. Her breasts were high and firm, her belly flat, her waist so narrow he was sure he could span it with his hands.

She was the first completely naked woman he had seen in over four hundred years, the first woman who had professed to love him since he became Vampyre. The first who had begged for his touch.

He waged a silent inner battle, the last vestiges of honor and humanity at war with the monster he had become.

"My lord?" Her voice was soft and sweetly entreating as she reached a tentative hand toward him. "Rayven?"

The sound of his name on her lips was like music to his ears.

"Rhianna, please." He forced the words past a throat gone dry. "Please don't do this to me. I'm afraid . . ."

Slowly, she lowered her arm. "You? Afraid?" Disbelief flickered in her eyes.

Rayven closed his eyes, an image of the first and only woman he had ever taken to his bed since he'd been made Vampyre rising in his mind. She had been nothing more than a harlot, a woman whose favors he had purchased to ease the hunger of the flesh. She had been young, but wise beyond her years. He had felt nothing for her, had thought he could satisfy his lust without arousing his hunger.

He had been wrong, and his error in judgment, in control, had cost the woman her life. That had been almost four hundred years ago, he mused. Fearful of the consequences, he had not sought a woman's affection since.

He had learned to control the desires of the flesh, to keep his lust under tight rein, until Rhianna. Knowing he dared not possess her had made it easier to hold his passion in check. He had never, in his wildest dreams, expected her to want him.

Certainly he had never expected to find her standing naked before him on a moonlit night, silently begging for his touch.

"I can't." He took a step backward, and his cloak wrapped itself more tightly around him, as if to shield him from harm. "I can't."

He wanted to turn away, to leave her before it was too late, but the yearning in her eyes held him spellbound. No woman had ever looked at him with such longing, such tender regard.

Rhianna stared at him, her longing turning to confusion. "Is there . . . ?" She felt a rush of embarrassment flood her cheeks. "Are you . . . ?" The fire in her cheeks burned hotter. "I mean . . ." She took a deep breath and said it all in a rush. "Are you unable to perform, my lord?"

The thought amused him even as it pricked his vanity. Was that what she thought, that he was some impotent fop? If only he were, he thought wryly. How much easier it would be for them both.

A breeze stirred the land, ruffling the leaves on the rosebushes. Rhianna shivered, not from the cold, but from the knowledge that she had offered herself to him, heart and soul, and he didn't want her.

She felt suddenly cold inside and out, naked to the very depths of her soul. She had not felt this vulnerable, this exposed, since that awful night in Cotyer's Tavern when she stood next to her father in front of a crowd of leering men.

Certain she would never be able to face Rayven again, she bent down to retrieve her shawl.

And felt his hands on her shoulders; strong, capable hands drawing her up, pulling her close.

"Rhianna, if I could have one wish, it would be to make love to you here and now. But I dare not." He saw the question in her eyes, the doubts. "It has nothing to do with you. Believe me when I say I want you as I've wanted no other woman."

Tears glistened in her eyes, clinging to her

lashes like morning dew. Tears of shame and humiliation. "I don't believe you."

"Rhianna, please . . ."

She shook her head. "I was wrong to come here, wrong to think I could make you care." She stepped away from him, feeling suddenly bereft as his fingers slid from her shoulders. "I'll leave here tomorrow, and you need never see me again."

It was what he wanted, what he knew was best for her, yet her words pierced the deepest regions of his worthless soul. And in that instant, he knew that he could not face a future without her. Four hundred years of solitude were enough.

"Rhianna! Don't go." The words were dragged from the depths of his heart.

"My lord?" A tiny flame of hope ignited in Rhianna's breast, warming her inside and out.

"Stay with me, Rhianna. Give me the year I promised you."

"It will be my pleasure, my lord."

In a single fluid movement, he bent over, picked up her shawl, and draped it around her shoulders. "You are the most beautiful, desirable woman I have ever known." His hands tightened on her shoulders. "We will have our year, sweet Rhianna. A year to get acquainted."

He was standing behind her. Slowly, he lowered his head, his lips grazing the side of her neck. "Go back to the house," he said, his breath fanning the hair at her nape. "I'll see you at dinner tomorrow night." *After I've fed the beast within.*

"As you wish, my lord."

He watched her walk away and feared, in that instant, that he would never be able to let her go.

* * *

She had been afraid she wouldn't be able to face him again, but she felt surprisingly calm when he joined her at the dinner table the following evening.

She had dressed with care in a dress of soft blue wool. The color matched her eyes. The dress, while modest in cut and design, still managed to outline her every curve. She wore her hair in loose waves down her back because he liked it that way.

"Good evening, sweet Rhianna."

"Good evening, my lord."

He sat down across from her and picked up the glass of wine that Bevins had poured for him as soon as he entered the room.

Rayven took a sip, nodded his approval to Bevins, then sat back in his chair.

"So," he said, regarding her over the rim of his goblet, "what did you do today?"

Rhianna met his gaze, unable to shake off the feeling that he knew exactly how she had spent the day.

"I learned a new piece of music this morning," she said, "and this afternoon, I began to prepare the soil for the new rosebushes."

He nodded, one brow arching upward as he waited for her to continue.

"I took a nap this afternoon, and then I read for a while." She met his gaze squarely. "What did *you* do today, my lord?"

"How I spend my days is none of your business, my sweet."

"Forgive me, my lord," she said, her voice icy. "I did not mean to pry."

"Didn't you?"

"I've never seen you during the day. I simply wondered what it was that kept you away from the castle from dawn till dark."

"I hope you never find out."

His reply should have made her angry, but it was spoken so softly, and with such bitterness, that she found herself feeling sorry for him, wishing she could do something to erase the sudden sadness in his eyes.

"Tell me about Montroy," Rayven said.

"There's nothing to tell. He came by this afternoon, and Bevins sent him away."

"No doubt I shall hear all about it next time I visit Cotyer's," Rayven muttered.

"I'm sure Lord Montroy thought it quite rude, being sent away as if he were a stranger."

"To be sure," Rayven agreed.

"But you don't care."

"Not a whit."

"I don't understand you."

Setting his glass aside, he leaned across the table to brush his knuckles gently over her cheek.

"You never will, Rhianna," he said quietly. "There are things I cannot tell you, things you must never know." He smiled, but it was a sad smile. "Things you would not want to know even if I could tell you."

But she wanted to know. She wanted desperately to know where he went during the day, what secrets lay behind the sadness that shadowed his eyes, why he lived in self-imposed isolation in a huge drafty castle on top of a fog-shrouded mountain.

"Can you tell me why you never dine with me?"

Slowly, he shook his head.

"Are you ill? Is that why you live here alone, why I never see you during the day?"

"Ill?" He smiled that melancholy smile again. "I suppose you could call it that." He picked up his wineglass and took a drink. "Finish your supper, my sweet, and then I should like you to read to me. Something sad and tragically romantic, I think."

A short time later, they retired to his study. Rhianna sat on the floor, her skirts spread around her, her back to the hearth. They came here rarely. The room was paneled in dark wood and held little furniture save for a large desk and a few chairs. She wondered why he had chosen to come here tonight.

Rayven sat in the chair beside the hearth, his cloak loosely wrapped around him. Bevins had refilled his wineglass, and he stared into the ruby-red depths while she read. He knew Rhianna didn't care for this room, but tonight its very darkness appealed to him.

Occasionally, Rhianna slid a glance in his direction, wondering at his somber mood. He seemed more withdrawn than usual tonight, his thoughts turned inward, wandering paths he would not share. She wondered if he had been wounded by some great tragedy in his life. Had he been the victim of some terrible malady, or had some woman hurt him so badly that he had turned his back on life and vowed never to love again?

After an hour, she closed the book and stood up. "I'm going to ask Bevins to make me a cup of hot chocolate," she said. "Would you like some?"

Rayven looked up at her, a corner of his mouth

turned down in wry amusement. "What do you think?"

"I just thought I'd ask." She put the book aside and gestured at his empty glass. "Would you like more wine?"

With a nod, he handed her the crystal goblet.

Bevins was sitting in the kitchen, polishing a silver tea pot. He stood up as she entered the room. "Something I can do for you, miss?"

"Yes. I'd like some hot cocoa, please." She handed him the empty glass. "And Lord Rayven would like some more wine."

A hint of something—disapproval, perhaps—flickered in the depths of Bevins's eyes as he took the goblet from her hand. "I'll see to it immediately."

"I'll wait," Rhianna said. Sitting down in the chair Bevins had vacated, she picked up the cloth he'd been using and began to polish the teapot.

"Miss Rhianna . . ."

"What?"

"I don't think . . . that is, you shouldn't . . ."

Rhianna frowned. "Shouldn't what?"

He jerked his chin toward the silver. "You needn't do that."

"I want to. How long have you worked for Lord Rayven?"

"More years than I care to remember."

"Do you know why he's so sad?"

"Sad, miss?"

Rhianna nodded. "I've never seen such sadness in a man's eyes before. Sometimes it makes me want to cry."

Bevins blinked at her, his expression at first surprised and then disbelieving, as if she'd just expressed sympathy for a wild animal. And then he turned away to fill a pan with milk. "You're very perceptive for one so young," he remarked as he lit the fire and placed the pan over it.

"You know why he's so sad, don't you?"

Bevins shook his head. "I'm afraid I couldn't say."

"Couldn't, or wouldn't?"

"I don't know, miss, truly I don't."

"Has he ever been in love? Been married?"

"Not to my knowledge."

Rhianna set the teapot aside. Propping her elbows on the table, she rested her chin on her folded hands. "I wish I could make him happy."

"You do, miss. I'm sure of it."

"Do you really think so?" He had begged her to stay, but he hadn't seemed happy about it.

Bevins glanced at the kitchen door, his expression wary, as if he feared being overheard. "He needs you, miss. He needs you, and he doesn't like it."

"Did he tell you that?"

Bevins shook his head and then, to discourage any further conversation, he turned away and busied himself at the stove.

Rhianna watched in amazement as he removed the pan of milk from the stove and set it aside, then took another pan from the cupboard, poured some wine into it, and placed it over the fire.

"What are you doing?" she asked.

"Lord Rayven likes his wine to be quite warm."

Bevins prepared her cocoa, then poured the wine into the crystal goblet and set both containers on a tray. "Anything else, miss? A biscuit, perhaps?"

"No, this is fine." She reached for the tray.

"I'll bring them to you, miss."

"That won't be necessary," Rhianna said, smiling, and lifted the cup and the goblet from the tray. "Thank you, Bevins. Good night."

"But, Miss Rhianna . . ."

"What is it?"

"Nothing." He glanced quickly at the goblet in her hand, then looked away. "Good night, miss."

Rhianna left the kitchen, her steps slow as she returned to the study. Warm wine? She stopped in the hallway, glanced around to make sure she was alone, and took a sip from Rayven's goblet. Warm or cold, she knew she had never tasted anything like it. It was thicker than any wine she knew of and had a strange flavor that made her stomach churn.

She licked her lips clean so Rayven wouldn't know she had tasted his drink. A special vintage, indeed, she thought, grimacing. Well, he could have it.

He was standing in front of the hearth, gazing into the flames, when she returned to the study. He stood with his back to her, one arm braced against the mantle. His cloak fell in soft folds down his back, and she noticed again how the thick black velvet seemed to cling to him.

He didn't turn around as she stepped into the room. He seemed to be deep in thought, and she wondered if he even knew she was there.

But of course he did. He was attuned to her every breath, her every movement. Without looking, he knew exactly where she was in the room. He could feel her gaze on his back, knew when she placed his wineglass on the table beside his chair, knew she was exactly five steps behind him, slightly to his left. Knew she had been talking about him to Bevins.

"Did you learn anything?" he asked, his voice deceptively mild.

"My lord?"

"From Bevins. Did he tell you anything you didn't know?"

"I don't know what you're talking about."

"Don't you?" He turned to face her, his cloak swirling around his ankles.

"I . . . I just asked him if he knew why you're so sad," Rhianna replied, and then she frowned at him. "How do you know I asked about you? Were you spying on me? Eavesdropping?"

He shook his head. He had no need to spy on her. His preternatural hearing had allowed him to hear every word that had passed between her and his servant.

"Why *are* you so sad?" Rhianna asked.

His eyes narrowed to ominous slits as he met her gaze.

"Bevins said you needed me," she went on, determined not to let him frighten her into silence. "Do you?"

I need you, he thought. *Need you in ways you cannot imagine. Ways that would sicken you if you knew.*

He watched her eyes widen with alarm as he closed the distance between them. Taking the cup from her hand, he placed it on the table, then took her in his arms.

"This is what I need," he said, and crushing her body to his, he kissed her, his tongue boldly plundering her mouth.

Almost immediately, he drew back. Staring down at her, he took a deep breath. No, he hadn't been mistaken. She tasted of wine. And blood.

"What have you done?" he demanded, his voice no less intimidating for its softness.

"Done?" She stared up at him, her heart pounding.

Rayven took a deep breath and then bent his head to hers again, savoring the taste of his wine on her tongue. He closed his eyes as he deepened the kiss. She felt sorry for him, did she, thought he'd experienced some horrible tragedy in his life.

His arms imprisoned her as he kissed her again, and yet again. He'd teach her to feel sorry for him.

Rhianna moaned softly as his mouth punished hers. She tried to turn her head, but his hands came up to imprison her face. A red haze swam before her eyes and then, within the crimson mist, she saw a man running from a dark shadow. She heard his cry of terror as the darkness engulfed him, saw a pair of eyes that burned with hell's own fury . . .

The man's fear took hold of her. She felt death hovering over her, stealing her breath, her life, and she began to struggle wildly in Rayven's embrace. She had to get away, away from those hideous red eyes.

"My lord! Rayven! You're hurting me!"

Slowly, her words penetrated the thick red haze that had settled over him. Muttering an oath, he released her.

Rhianna stumbled back, her heart pounding frantically as she stared up at him. His cloak rippled, as though it had a life of its own, and she knew, *knew,* that Rayven's cloak had been the dark shadow she had seen in her mind.

"What happened?" she gasped. "Who was that man? What have you done?"

He looked down at her, his dark eyes glittering like shards of black glass. "Now you know what I need," he said.

She stared at him, her thoughts churning as she sought to decipher his meaning. She tried to draw her gaze from his, but could only stand there, weak and helpless as a mouse in the jaws of a lion.

Caught in the web of his hypnotic eyes, unable to think or speak, she could only stare up at him, silent, vulnerable.

Abruptly, he pivoted on his heel, his cloak swirling like black smoke around his ankles, and then he was gone.

Rhianna sank to her knees, her arms wrapped around her body to still its trembling.

She didn't understand what had just happened, but she knew, for the first time, what it was to be truly afraid.

Chapter Thirteen

He didn't join her at supper the next night. Rhianna couldn't help feeling relieved. She wasn't ready to face him again, not until she understood what had happened between them, until she could make sense of the strange vision she had seen while Rayven was kissing her.

After spending a few minutes toying with her food, she pushed her plate aside and left the dining room, wandering through the downstairs until she came to the library.

With a sigh, she ran her gaze over the books lining the walls, but none appealed to her. And then, as if it were inevitable, she found herself in his study. She had never gone there without him before, and she couldn't help feeling she was trespassing as she wandered around the room.

And then she saw it, a small book sitting on his desk. Curious, she picked it up and thumbed through the pages. Most were blank, but a few had writing on them.

Mesmerized by the words, she sat down, hardly aware that Bevins entered the room a short time later and laid a fire in the hearth.

The book was written in a bold hand and she knew, without knowing how she knew, that Rayven had written the words, dark words, troubling words. . . .

During the night,
I am the creature before you,
pale and tall and straight
dark eyes firing toward you
gliding, lifting, steering, directing
I am the silent and the powerful
a moonlit field of smooth, untouched snow

But he
Yes, him, the other me
Oh, he would tremble in your grasp
his lily hand would crumble to your touch
he would twist to press your lips to his
he would stroke your silken cheek
and slide his corroded lips along your
dovelike neck.
Not I, you understand, the other me
he who squints
and hesitates
and weakens
in the daylight.

Her heart was pounding erratically as she turned the page to the next poem.

I can feel it coming
through the tears in the darkness
quickly approaching as I conceal
myself
quaking underneath
the shadows in the light.

Shivers ripple my moist skin
The urgent itching on the
surface tormenting me
keeping me locked in.
I run my tongue over
my lips
And I am found, as always.

Then it begins
My resistance bleeds away
and I am filled with
the emptiness of my being.
Awareness is replete.

The trial is ended

Sated by the shattering
my knowing
why
and left alive
for the next visit

The darkness has taken a piece of my soul.

She closed the book and stared into the flames dancing merrily in the hearth as she tried to understand what she had read.

Lord Rayven is a man compelled by dark appe-

tites, miss. She heard Bevins's voice in the back of her mind. *He is driven by forces you cannot comprehend. You would be wise to leave this place and never come back.*

Last night, she had decided Bevins was right. She had tried to leave the castle early that morning, only to find that all the doors were locked. She had gone looking for Bevins, but, for once, he was nowhere to be found.

Now, sitting in front of the fire, her whole body tensed as a chill skittered down her spine.

He was here.

She had heard no sound to betray his presence, no footsteps as he entered the room, but suddenly he was there before her, a tall figure clad all in black. He stood before the hearth, the fire crackling behind him. *Like a demon rising from the bowels of hell.*

He lifted one black brow in amusement. "A demon, Rhianna?" She heard the rueful smile in his voice. "You are more right than you know."

She tried to think of something clever to say, but nothing came to mind. Like a bird trapped by a hungry cat, she could only stare at him, waiting for him to strike her down even as she wondered how he had known what she was thinking.

He glanced at the book in her hands, wondering how much she had read, if she understood the connection between his dark words and the blackness in his soul.

"You're afraid of me now, aren't you?" he asked, knowing her fear had nothing to do with what she had read and everything to do with what had passed between them the night before.

She couldn't speak past the lump in her throat.

"Aren't you?" His voice was sharp, demanding an answer.

"Yes, my lord." She crossed her arms over her chest. "I should like very much to go home now."

"Would you?"

She nodded vigorously. "Yes, please. Please . . ." Tears filled her eyes and spilled down her cheeks. "Please let me go home."

The sight of her tears smothered his anger. Murmuring her name, he reached for her, drawing her out of the chair and into his arms. The book fell, unnoticed, to the floor.

"I will not hurt you, Rhianna," he said quietly. "Please believe me."

"No. I just want to go home. Please, my lord, please let me go home."

"Rhianna . . . sweet Rhianna." Gently, he caressed her cheek.

She flinched at his touch, as though fearing he would strike her. Once, he had wanted her to be afraid of him, to be wary for her own sake. Now, the knowledge that she was afraid of him burned into his soul, as painful as the touch of the sun on his preternatural flesh.

"Rhianna, I warned you once to go while you could. Now I fear it is too late." He shook his head with regret. "I find I cannot let you go."

She gazed up at him, his face blurred by her tears. Even so, she could see the loneliness that haunted his eyes, the sadness that she had once yearned to wipe away.

Slowly, he lowered his head, and she felt the touch of his lips on hers, cool, gentle. His arms held her lightly, with warm affection. Would he let her go if she stepped away?

Heart pounding, she drew away and took a step backward. And he let her go, his arms falling to his sides, his eyes dark with an inner torment she could not fathom.

"You once begged me to let you stay," he said, his voice moving over her like a dark wind. "Now I am begging you."

She felt the tears dry on her cheeks. "I've changed my mind."

"Too late, Rhianna. Shall I go down on my knees and plead with you, my sweet?"

"No!" She could not bear to think of him kneeling at her feet, his arrogance humbled, his pride broken.

"Won't you take pity on me, my sweet Rhianna? A year is not so long, after all."

"And if I stay, will you let me go when the year is up?"

"You have no choice, Rhianna. You will stay."

"Then why are you asking me? I don't understand."

"I want you to stay with me of your own free will. I want your company to see me through the long lonely nights. I want to see your smile, hear your voice, your laughter." He smiled ruefully, as if he had discovered a truth about himself, one he did not like. "I need you."

He needs you, miss. He needs you, and he doesn't like it. She heard the echo of Bevins's voice in her mind again.

"Will you stay with me, Rhianna?"

She wanted to say no. She wanted to go home. But she found she could not refuse him. "Yes."

"Because you want to?"

She nodded again, surprised by the discovery that she did, indeed, want to stay.

Stepping into the inner chamber of the east tower, Bevins laid out a change of clothing for Rayven, then gathered up his master's dirty laundry and linen.

"Thank you, Bevins. That will be all."

Bevins turned to go, then hesitated in the doorway. Taking a deep breath, he turned around. "I've never known you to be deliberately cruel before."

"I've never known you to care before."

"She's a fine lass. I'd not see her destroyed."

"Is that what you think I'm going to do?"

"Isn't it?"

"Have I destroyed any of the others?"

"She's not like the others, and you know it. You'll not be able to hide what you are from her forever, my lord. She cares for you too much to be deceived for long."

"Yes, she does." Rayven turned away from the accusation in the other man's eyes. Even after he had pleaded with her to stay, he hadn't expected her to agree. Last night, she had been terrified of him, of the dark images that had flooded her mind when they kissed, a vision conjured up by his touch, and by the wine she had sipped from his glass. He could end all her fears, bind her to him so that she would want only him. He had only to initiate her, and she would do anything he asked, stay with him for as long as she lived, be miserable when they were apart.

"Let me take her home, my lord."

"No."

"It's wrong to keep her here."

Slowly, Rayven turned around, his gaze locking on that of his servant.

Fear took hold of Tom Bevins, the same cold, paralyzing fear that had engulfed him the first time he had looked into the vampyre's eyes some fifty years before. How clearly he remembered that night. He had been knifed in a street fight and left for dead behind one of the gambling hells, his life slipping away drop by crimson drop when a dark cloud overshadowed him. He had felt a sharp stabbing pain in his neck, and then a voice, low, seductive, had offered to save him.

Desperate to live, Tom had watched, uncomprehending, as the stranger hovering over him had made a slit in his own wrist, then pressed his bleeding flesh to Tom's lips. A few drops of the stranger's thick dark blood had miraculously revived him. In exchange for his life, Tom had sworn to serve Rayven as long as he drew breath. It had been, for the most part, a good life. He had never wanted for food or shelter or been denied anything else he had desired. But Rayven owned him, body and soul. It was a fact he forgot on occasion.

But there was no forgetting now.

"Do not interfere," Rayven warned.

And in the back of his mind, Bevins heard the unspoken threat: *I gave you your life. I can take it back again.*

"Will that be all, my lord?" Bevins asked. At his master's curt nod, he started toward the door.

"Bevins."

"Yes, my lord?"

"I will not harm her."

Bevins nodded. It was a promise, and an apology, all in one.

"I don't understand you," Ada said. She didn't look up from the dough she was kneading. "I cannot believe you decided to stay with that dreadful man?"

"He asked me to stay," Rhianna replied, bending the truth only a little. "He's been kind to me, to us. How could I refuse?"

She glanced past her mother to where Bevins was standing in the doorway, his arms crossed over his chest. He had insisted on accompanying her. To protect her, he had said, but she knew better. He was there to make sure she returned to the castle by nightfall.

Ada stared at the lump of dough in the bowl. "I just thought that when you returned from Paris, you would stay here, with us, with your family."

"I'll come to see you often," Rhianna promised. "It's only for a year, after all." Only a year, she thought, and already a month was gone.

"Will he let you come to your sister's wedding?"

"Of course," Rhianna replied brightly, though inwardly, she wasn't sure.

Ada looked up and met her daughter's gaze, wondering what Rhianna was holding back.

"I've got to go," Rhianna said. Rising, she rounded the table and bent over to give her mother a hug. "Tell the girls I'm sorry I missed them. I'll see you at the wedding."

Ada placed her hand over her daughter's, marveling at how soft and smooth Rhianna's hands were. Once, they had been rough and calloused, the nails broken and uneven from hard work.

Now, Rhianna had hands like those of a fine lady. Perhaps she was wrong to worry so.

"Good-bye, Mama." Rhianna gave her mother one last hug, then left the cottage.

Outside, Bevins handed her into the carriage. Taking his place on the seat, he took up the reins and clucked to the horse.

"Your mother is quite lovely," Bevins remarked.

Rhianna slid a glance in his direction, surprised by his observation, and more surprised that he had voiced it aloud. "Do you think so?"

Bevins nodded as he turned the horse onto the road. "You look much like her."

"Thank you." Rhianna folded her hands in her lap and sat back, enjoying the beauty of the countryside as they passed by. "Have you ever been married?"

"No, miss."

"How long have you been with Lord Rayven?"

Bevins hesitated. "A very long time."

"Surely he wouldn't object if you had a family of your own."

"I'm afraid it's not possible."

Not possible, she mused. What an odd way to phrase it. "Why do I never see him during the day?"

"I couldn't say, miss."

"But you know, don't you?"

"Would you like to stop in the village for anything?" Bevins asked, blatantly changing the subject.

"Yes," Rhianna answered. "I'd like to stop at the confectioner's."

They traveled in silence until they reached the village. Rhianna bought a small bag of peppermint candy for herself, and another, larger bag, to take to her mother and sisters on her next visit. As she stepped out of the store, she saw a little girl of perhaps seven sitting near the door. The child's hair was dirty and stringy, her dress faded and tattered along the hem.

"Are you lost, child?" Rhianna asked.

The girl looked up at her through wide brown eyes, then, shyly, held up a fistful of primroses. "Buy a flower, my lady?"

"Of course," Rhianna said, and then realized she had no money. "Bevins?"

"Come along, miss."

"I want to give her something."

Bevins shook his head. "Lord Rayven won't like it."

"Then don't tell him." Rhianna smiled down at the girl. "I'll take them all."

A muscle clenched in Bevins's jaw as he reached into his coat pocket and withdrew a handful of coins. He wouldn't have to tell Rayven anything. The vampyre would know.

The child's face lit up as she handed Rhianna the bouquet, then took the coins from Bevins.

"Thank you, lady," she exclaimed, clutching the money to her chest. "Oh, thank you!"

Rhianna grinned as she watched the little girl run down the street. "Shall we go?"

They had almost reached the carriage when she heard Montroy calling her name. Turning, she saw him striding toward her.

"Let's go, miss," Bevins urged.

"In a minute." She smiled up at Montroy as he took her hands in his. "Hello, Dallon."

"Rhianna." He lifted one of her hands and kissed it. "How pretty you look."

"So do you."

Montroy grinned, pleased by her reply, and by her welcoming smile. "Come along," he said. "I'll buy you a cup of tea."

"All right."

Bevins cleared his throat. "Miss Rhianna, we need to go."

"Later," she said, placing her hand on Montroy's arm.

"I would remind you of your promise, miss," Bevins said sternly.

"What promise is that?" Montroy asked. He glanced from Rhianna's face to Bevins's and back again.

"Nothing." She lifted her hand from his arm and took a step back. "I promised to be home by . . . by . . ." Her voice trailed off. She had no idea what time it was.

"By three, miss," Bevins interjected smoothly. "We're late already."

"Yes, we are. I'm sorry, my lord, but I really must go."

"Surely you have time for a cup of tea," Montroy urged.

"I can't, really. I'm sorry."

"Very well, I shan't try to keep you." Montroy bowed over her hand, certain that Rayven had extracted her promise not to see him again. "If you should ever tire of him, if he ever harms you in any way, come to me."

"Thank you, my lord. You're most kind."

"Be careful, Rhianna," Montroy said earnestly. "Rayven is . . . Just be careful."

"I will. I really must go."

He helped her into the carriage, stood watching as Bevins clucked to the horse. What hold did Rayven have over her, he wondered. Somehow, he would find out.

"Lord Rayven is very rich, isn't he?" Rhianna remarked. She had sat in silence for some time, watching the countryside pass by. The fields were green and gold. Sheep grazed on the hillsides.

Bevins nodded. Rich did not begin to describe his master's wealth.

"He should do more with his money," Rhianna mused. "He could ease the suffering of so many."

Bevins smiled in spite of himself as he imagined Lord Rayven walking among the town's peasants, his black cloak billowing around him as he scattered gold coins like confetti.

"Don't you think so?" Rhianna asked.

"It isn't my place to tell Lord Rayven what to do, Miss Rhianna." Bevins turned to face her. "Nor yours."

With a little humph of pique, Rhianna sat back, her arms folded over her breasts. Somehow, she would find a way to convince Rayven to ease the poverty in the village.

Later that night, Rhianna sat at the table, staring, unseeing, into the bowl of mutton stew growing cold in front of her. All thoughts of helping the poor in the village had fled her mind as she contemplated seeing Rayven again. How strange life was! When she wanted to stay, he wanted her to go. When she wanted to go, he urged her to stay.

Had she imagined it all, she wondered, the disconcerting vision of that man being pursued by darkness, the sense of evil? Her fear had been real enough, but it seemed foolish now. Rayven would not harm her.

Now you know what I need. What had he meant by those cryptic words?

And then he was there, filling the room with his presence. Clad in a loose-fitting white shirt, snug black breeches, and soft leather boots, he crossed the room on silent feet to take the chair opposite hers.

"Good evening, sweet Rhianna."

She inclined her head in his direction. "My lord."

"No appetite this evening?" he asked, gesturing at the untouched bowl of stew in front of her.

Rhianna sighed. "I'm not very hungry."

A shadow of concern passed over his face and then was gone. "Are you well?"

"Well enough. Might I ask you something?"

"You may ask me anything."

"But you won't answer."

"What do you want, Rhianna?"

"A favor."

He lifted one black brow. "Another boon?"

"I want to help the people in the village. Many of them have had a bad year."

"And you intend to help? How?"

"There's a deserted storehouse near the end of town. I'd like to turn it into a shelter to house the poor."

"Indeed?"

Rhianna nodded, warming to the subject. "It wouldn't have to be anything elaborate. Just some beds, really."

"You don't want me to feed them, too?"

"Of course. I thought we could ask John Dunsmore if he'd send food over at night. And milk for the wee ones."

"And you want me to fund this endeavor?"

"Yes."

He smiled faintly, amused by the idea of feeding those who had, on occasion, nourished his own hunger.

"Let Bevins take care of it," he said. "I don't want you directly involved."

"Why not?"

"I want you here."

"But there's nothing for me to do all day."

"I thought you were going to replant the gardens."

She had forgotten that for the moment, but she couldn't spend all her time among the flowers, and said so.

"I want you here," he repeated firmly. "You take care of the gardens, Rhianna, and I'll have Bevins procure the warehouse and stock it with beds and whatever else you think necessary."

"You're most kind, my lord."

"You're to tell no one about this," Rayven said. "I'll have your promise."

"You have it."

"Are you going to finish your supper?"

Rhianna shook her head. "No."

"Come then," he said, rising. "I wish to go for a walk."

Bevins was waiting for them at the door. He handed Rayven his cloak, then draped a light cotton shawl around Rhianna's shoulders.

She frowned as she stepped outside. How had

Bevins known they were going outside?

The night was cool, but not cold. A bright yellow moon hung low in the sky. Millions of stars twinkled above, sparkling like tiny diamonds against a bed of indigo velvet.

Side by side, they walked down one of the narrow paths. She knew somehow that they would end up at the maze, and she wondered what there was about that one place that drew Rayven to it.

"How is your mother?" Rayven asked after a lengthy silence.

"She's fine. She wants me to come home. I'm afraid she doesn't understand why I've decided to stay here."

He said nothing.

"My sister's getting married soon. Will you come to the wedding?"

"I've not been invited."

"I'm inviting you."

"When is the happy occasion to take place?"

"This Sunday evening, after Mass."

"I doubt I should be welcome."

"I should very much like you to be my escort." She smiled up at him. "I'm sure Bevins would like a night off."

"I'll think about it."

"All right."

They were in the maze now. As always, the place filled her with apprehension, though she could not say why. There was nothing to fear.

When they reached the heart of the labyrinth, Rayven sat down on one of the wrought-iron benches and indicated she should sit beside him.

Suddenly nervous, Rhianna sat down beside him, smoothing her skirts in place.

Rayven sat back, his arms crossed over his chest. "You saw Montroy today."

Rhianna licked lips suddenly dry. "Yes, my lord."

"Tell me what happened."

"Why don't you tell me? You seem to know everything I say and do." She regarded him through narrowed eyes. "I'd like to know how you manage that."

"I can read your mind, my sweet."

"That's impossible."

"Is it?"

"Isn't it?" She stared at him, wondering if he was telling the truth.

"You promised not to meet him while you lived here, with me."

"We didn't 'meet.' I saw him on the street and he said hello."

"And invited you to tea."

"Bevins told you, didn't he?"

Rayven shook his head. "I can smell Montroy on you," he said quietly. "Montroy smells of expensive tobacco and horse and a rather strong cologne."

Rhianna felt her heart skip a beat as Rayven studied her, his nostrils flaring as he took a deep breath.

"You carry the scent of the tea and toast you had for breakfast, the lavender soap you bathed with," he said, his voice moving over her like a caress. "You had mutton and potatoes for lunch. Your hands smell of primroses and peppermint. There's a faint scent of powder and perfume. And overall," he went on, his voice low and intimate, "the unique fragrance that is yours, and yours alone."

Rhianna could only stare at him, stunned by his words. How could he know such things?

He didn't tell her that he could hear the sound of the blood flowing in her veins, or that, if he opened his mind, he could hear the voices of the people in the village—their laughter, their tears, the harsh breathing of those who were ill, the prayers of the hopeful, the desperate, the dying.

He could hear their thoughts, sense their presence. He knew their fears.

And yet he was ever on the outside of life, looking in.

He closed his eyes, and his senses filled with the woman at his side. She reminded him of sunshine and roses on a warm summer day. Her hair, her skin, carried myriad scents that called to him, arousing the beast in him as well as the man.

Rhianna. With a low groan, he reached for her, wishing he could bridge the vast gulf between them, wishing that, for one day, he could be a part of her life. He whispered her name as he dragged her into his arms and crushed her close. His kiss was tinged with desperation. Rhianna, Rhianna.

She struggled against him, frightened by the rush of need that leaped from his lips to hers. A sense of hopelessness, of desolation, washed over her.

Abruptly, he let her go. Rising, he turned his back to her and drew his cloak more closely around him. The heavy velvet molded itself to him. "I didn't mean to frighten you."

"I begged you to make love to me not long ago,"

she reminded him. "I offered myself to you freely. You needn't take me by force."

"Forgive me, Rhianna. Sometimes I forget who I am. What I am."

"What are you?"

"Your worst dream come true."

"You're talking in riddles again."

"Shall I tell you the answers?" he wondered aloud. "Shall I tell you truths you will not believe and watch your eyes fill with revulsion? Shall I lower the mask I wear and watch you run screaming from my presence?"

He turned around to face her. His eyes gleamed, even in the darkness. His cloak shifted and rippled, as though trying to pull him away.

"I need you, Rhianna."

In a single, fluid movement, he knelt in front of her and took her hand in his. His skin was firm, cool, belying the fire that blazed in his eyes.

"I need you," he said again, more fervently this time. "Be patient with me, Rhianna." His dark gaze held hers, silent, imploring. "I swear by all that I hold dear that I will not hurt you."

"You worry me, my lord," she murmured. "Can you not explain what it is that troubles you so?"

"I wish I could." The burden of the secret he had carried for over four hundred years weighed heavily upon him. What a relief it would be to tell her everything. As a man, he had once shed his sins by confessing them to a priest; he wondered now if he could ease the sadness, the loneliness, of centuries by confiding in Rhianna. Would she be able to understand? Would she be able to forgive him for the lives he had taken when first he'd been made, when the hunger had been excruciating, when he'd been afraid and confused?

"Look at me," he said. "What do you see?"

She gazed into his eyes, felt an ache in her heart, an ache that spread to her soul and brought tears to her eyes. "Darkness. Sadness. Loneliness."

His gaze burned into hers. "What else do you see?"

"Don't ask me," she begged. "I cannot bear it."

"Rhianna . . ."

"I see death wrapped in darkness. And blood. So much blood. On your hands . . ."

She lowered her head to stare at their joined hands, then slowly met his gaze again. "Who are you? What are you?"

"Swear to me on the life of your mother that you will not leave me if I tell you."

"I have already promised to stay a year."

He shook his head, his fingers tightening around hers. "Swear it."

"I swear on the life of my mother that I will not leave you."

"Then look deep into my eyes, Rhianna, and see the truth for yourself."

His eyes were deep and black and filled with the mysteries of the universe. They drew her in, until she saw nothing else, and then, rising up out of a black mist, she saw Rayven. He looked as he did now, save there was no scar on his cheek. His eyes, though black, seemed more alive; his face and arms were browned by the sun.

And then she saw a woman. She felt Rayven's hand squeeze hers and knew, in a distant part of her mind, that she was seeing his past. But how was that possible?

"Her name is Lysandra." She heard Rayven's voice, speaking softly in her mind.

He had seen her first at court. He had been a knight in those days, a warrior renowned for his pride, his bravery in battle. He was the boldest, the bravest, and proud of it. He had never been defeated in battle, nor unseated in tournament.

Lysandra had been married to an earl—Rayven could no longer recall the man's name. He had seen Lysandra and been smitten at first glance. Clad in a gown of unrelieved white silk, her black hair arranged in curls atop her head, she had been the most beautiful woman he had ever seen.

He had been unprepared for the heat that passed between them when her gaze met his. Her eyes were deep and black, like pools of liquid ebony. Her skin was pale, almost translucent, ever cool to the touch.

Like a besotted fool, he had attended every gathering in hopes of seeing her again. He remembered the night he had first spoken with her, danced with her. Kissed her. Her lips had been as smooth and cool as iced satin.

He had been charmed by her beauty, fascinated by the mystery that lurked in the depths of her eyes. He had never thought himself in love with her, but his lust had run hot, fueled by her come-hither smiles. Her kisses, stolen in dark corners and moonlit gardens, had left him feeling drugged and desperate for more.

She had teased and tempted him for months, playing a game he'd never had a chance of winning. Too late, he had learned it wasn't an affair she wanted, but his life.

"And so I was made Vampyre . . ."

His voice was still low. She heard it in her mind, but refused to accept what he was telling her. There was no such thing. It was not possible.

"She left me the night she made me," Rayven went on, his voice devoid of emotion. "When I woke the next night, I was ravenous."

"Stop!" Rhianna clapped her hands over her ears. "I don't want to hear any more."

He went on as though she hadn't spoken. His words rang clearly in her mind. Unable to shut them out, she clasped her hands in her lap.

"I had no one to tell me what was happening to me, no one to teach me how to be a vampyre. I shall never forgive her for that," he said, his voice laced with anger. "I did not realize the awesome powers I possessed. I was driven by a hunger that was excruciating.

"In the beginning, I thought it would drive me mad. All I knew was that blood eased the pain, and that the sunlight that I had once loved now meant death. Even then, I didn't want to believe. And then, one night, I looked in a mirror . . ."

He had never forgotten the slow horror that had spread through him when he stared into that glass, expecting to see his image reflected back at him, and saw only the room behind him.

"I ran away from my home, from all who knew me. I had hoped that I would be able to live some semblance of a normal life in another place, that I would be able to marry and have children. I know now how foolish those hopes were, but in the beginning I didn't realize that I had lost all hope of living as a man. In time, I learned that I was not a man at all."

Restless now, he stood up, his gaze fixed on something only he could see.

"I was in Italy when I met another vampyre. Salvatore was one of the ancient ones. He taught me what it meant to be a Vampyre, told me that I could be a monster, striking terror in the hearts of mortals, or I could hide myself away and live off the blood of beasts, or I could dwell somewhere in the middle, neither man nor monster.

"And that is what I have done. I never stay longer than fifteen or twenty years in any one place. I have already stayed here too long. Soon I shall go to one of my other dwellings and stay there until people began to talk about my strange way of living, until they begin to notice that I do not age, and then I shall move again."

"You're telling me the truth, aren't you? You're not making this up just to scare me?"

Rayven nodded.

"What about Bevins? Does he know what you are?"

"Of course. We are more than master and servant. My blood runs in his veins." There had been times when taking blood from Bevins had meant the difference between life and death. Yet he had never taken enough to bequeath the Dark Gift to his servant. In over four hundred years, he had never made another Vampyre.

"You fed on him?" He didn't miss the quick look of revulsion in her eyes.

He nodded curtly, wondering if she would ask the question he dreaded.

"When you bought me from my father, were you going to feed on me, too?"

So, he thought, there it was. He took a deep

breath and then, very slowly, he nodded.

"But you didn't?" She lifted her hands to her neck, her fingers exploring. There were no marks. Relief whooshed from her lungs in a deep sigh.

And then she frowned. There had been marks once, soon after she came to the castle the first time. She had asked Bevins to look at them for her, and he had assured her there was nothing to worry about.

"I rarely drank from your neck," Rayven said quietly, "and when I did, I had only to run my tongue over the wounds to heal them." But he had forgotten that one night.

"You drank my blood?" She stared at him, wondering why the idea didn't repulse her. She should be fainting or screaming hysterically. She should be horrified. Instead, she felt remarkably calm, as if she were listening to a story that had nothing to do with her.

"No more than a thimbleful at a time." He took a step back. His cloak wrapped around him, enfolding him. "Had I given you my blood in return, we would be bonded."

"What does that mean, bonded?"

"It means you would be able to read my thoughts as I can read yours."

"That's what you've done to Bevins, isn't it? He's your slave?"

"No. We share only a bond." A bond born of blood and a vow.

That didn't seem so bad, Rhianna mused. She wished she could read his thoughts now. Perhaps then she would be better able to understand him.

"There's another bond," Rayven said. "A deeper bond, one more binding."

"Oh?"

She wasn't sure she wanted to hear it.

"It's a bond that cannot be broken except by death. Mine, or yours. You don't know how I've longed to make you mine, Rhianna, to bind you to me. And yet I could not, for to do so would be to take away your freedom, and I found I could not do that to you."

"Why have you told me all this?"

Rayven took a deep breath. "I needed to tell someone. After four hundred years, I wanted someone to understand." Slowly, he shook his head. "I know now that is impossible."

"You've been alive for over four hundred years?"

He shook his head, a rueful grin on his lips. "I was alive for twenty-seven years. I have been Vampyre for four hundred and three."

"But that would mean you were born in . . ."

"Fourteen hundred and twelve, my sweet."

"It's not possible."

He said nothing, simply watched her through fathomless black eyes.

"And you drink human blood to survive?"

"Rarely, and only a little at a time."

"How can you?" she asked, repelled.

How to explain it to her, to make her understand that it wasn't awful? He shook his head and then sighed, knowing she deserved an answer, abhorrent as it might be.

"I don't know how to describe it to you, Rhianna. There's nothing in your experience I can compare it to. When I drink, it's like becoming a part of that person. I can feel the beat of their heart; I know their thoughts, their fears. You cannot imagine what it's like—the power, the hunger. Before I learned to control it, when I thought I had to take a life to survive . . ." He shook his head again. "I can't explain it."

"If you no longer drink human blood, what do you drink? What is it that Bevins brings you in the evening?"

"It's wine mixed with blood. From sheep, usually, although any kind of blood will do." But he needed human blood, as well, though he didn't tell her that. It was why he had bought Rhianna in the first place. There was a freshness, a strength, in the pure, sweet blood of a virgin that could be found nowhere else.

"You drink the blood of sheep?"

"I keep a small flock on the north side of the castle beyond the gate."

"Oh?" She was staring at him, her expression dazed.

"I've sickened you, haven't I?"

"A little," she admitted. But, mostly, she felt sorry for him. Four hundred years of living alone, never able to trust another living soul. Four hundred years since he had seen the sun, felt its warmth on his face. Four hundred years since he had tasted food, drunk a glass of cool, clear water. Four hundred years without a friend to confide in, a woman to love.

She envisioned him bending over her, his teeth piercing her flesh, drinking her blood. Tried to imagine herself living as he lived, forever cursed to dwell in darkness, to forego the simple pleasures of life.

Wanting to comfort him somehow, she gazed deep into his eyes and there, in the inky black depths, she caught an image of Rayven as he had been four hundred years ago. The pain and fear and rage he had experienced when he first became Vampyre, the centuries of loneliness that had followed, and overall the never-ending scent of blood and death. He was a vampyre. Child of Darkness. Undead . . .

Darkness engulfed her, deeper than hell, darker than black. With a strangled sob, she felt herself slipping into a swirling vortex that had no beginning and no end.

Chapter Fourteen

Rayven caught her before she toppled from the bench. Lifting her easily in his arms, he looked down at her, his gaze instinctively drawn to the pulse beating in her throat. Perhaps he should not have told her. If he wished, he could wipe it all from her mind, make her forget everything he had said.

And yet, it had felt good, cleansing somehow, to tell her the truth. He had wanted her to know, had wanted no lies between them in the time they had left. And when their year together was up, he would leave this place, and it wouldn't matter if she told anyone or not. No one would believe her. In spite of all the stories and rumors that circulated among the villagers, none of them truly believed him to be a monster.

Rhianna had never believed it, either, but she knew the truth now.

Tomorrow he would find out if she was strong enough to accept it, to live with it. And with him.

And if she wasn't . . .

He shook the thought away as if it were no more than a troublesome insect. There would be time enough to worry about that tomorrow. Tonight, he would hold her while she slept and pretend, for a little while, that she knew what he was, and loved him in spite of it.

Effortlessly, he carried her back to the castle, up the winding staircase to her chamber. Gently, he lowered her onto the bed, took off her shoes and gown. Removing his boots and cloak, he sat down on the bed, his back to the headboard. Aching with need, he drew her into his arms and covered them both with his cloak.

He sat there through the night, watching her sleep, listening to the soft, even sound of her breathing. Tenderness engulfed him as she snuggled against him, her arms wrapping around his waist.

Do you know? he wondered. *Do you know it's me?*

He lifted a hand, his knuckles lightly stroking the downy curve of her cheek, marveling at the smoothness of her skin, so warm compared to the coolness of his own. With his forefinger, he traced the line of her mouth—soft and sweet. Her lips parted slightly, and she made a low, sleepy sound in her throat.

"Rhianna." Desire surged through him, painful in its intensity. "Open to me, my sweet," he whispered.

"Rayven . . ." Her eyelids fluttered open. She had been dreaming of him, and now he was there, gazing down at her through black eyes that blazed with a deep inner fire.

"Kiss me." He lowered his head toward hers. "Kiss me . . ."

She tilted her head back, uttered a soft moan as his lips claimed hers in a searing kiss that drove all rational thought from her mind even as it made her toes curl with pleasure.

He shifted his position so that they were lying face-to-face, their bodies pressed together from shoulder to thigh. Desire unfurled within her at the touch of his hard lean body molded so intimately against her own.

His tongue traced her lips. He heard the rapid beat of her heart, felt his hunger roar to life, felt his fangs ache with the need to drink and drink and drink, to fill himself with her sweetness, her very essence.

Rhianna groaned softly. Instinctively, she pressed herself against him, wanting to be closer. Her hands slid under his shirt, caressing the smooth line of his back. She felt as if she were on fire. His skin was cool beneath her fingertips, yet she knew he was as aroused as she. His breathing was harsh and erratic, his hands restless as they slid up and down her sides, his fingers brushing against the curve of her breast.

She felt his teeth graze her throat, and she lifted her hair away from her neck, wanting to feel his tongue against her skin.

His hand cupped her buttocks, drawing her close against him, letting her feel the visible evidence of his desire. The fact that her kisses, her nearness, had the power to arouse him excited her. Never before had she felt passion like this, known such longing, such need.

She whispered his name, wanting him to touch her everywhere at once. She tugged at his clothing, wanting to feel his bare skin against her own.

"Rhianna." His voice sounded heavy, drugged. "We've got to stop."

"No." She clung to him, her fingers kneading his back and shoulders, her hips moving against him, urging him to ease the ache spreading through her. "Kiss me," she whispered. "Touch me."

"Rhianna . . ." The image of the last girl he had taken to bed rose within him. They had to wait, wait until the hunger was sated and under control.

But she didn't want to wait. Her agile fingers tossed his cloak and shirt aside until nothing separated them but the thin material of her chemise. He could feel the warm sweet heat of her breasts against his chest.

A low growl rose in his throat as her hand boldly caressed his thigh.

"Rayven, please . . ." She moved restlessly on the bed, driven by an urgency she didn't understand, couldn't resist.

He felt her need as if it was his own. His body was on fire for her. He felt the sharpness of his fangs against his tongue, felt the hunger rise up within him as he stripped her of her undergarments and tossed his trousers aside.

She was beautiful, her body smooth and unblemished, a temptress with slender legs and softly rounded hips, a siren with breasts that had been fashioned for his hands and his alone.

Trembling with need, he lowered himself over

her, his weight braced on his elbows as he buried his face in the hollow of her shoulder. "Rhianna, are you sure?"

He felt her nod as she wrapped her arms around him and held him close.

Hunger and desire pounded through him, and with them the knowledge that the waiting of four hundred years was about to come to an end. And then, like a warning blast of hot air, he felt the sun creeping over the edge of the horizon.

With a low cry, he reared back, his gaze moving to the window. Through a narrow gap in the heavy curtains, he could see the faint light of the sun, feel the coming warmth of a new day.

"What is it?" Rhianna asked. "What's wrong?"

"I must go."

"Go?" She looked up at him, her eyes filled with confusion. "Where? Why?"

"It's dawn." With fluid grace, he vacated the bed. Grabbing his cloak, he draped it over his shoulders. "Till tonight, sweet Rhianna," he said, his voice hoarse with unfulfilled desire.

"Rayven, wait . . ."

But he was already gone.

That afternoon, she sat in front of her dressing table, absently brushing out her hair. He was a vampyre. She told herself she should be grateful that the dawn had sent him from her bed before he'd claimed her innocence.

Vampyre. Last night, drugged by his kisses, at the mercy of the passion that had flowed through her like warm honey, she had been incapable of rational thought. She had known nothing but need, hot urgent need that had left her blind and deaf to everything else.

Now, in the cold light of day, she wondered how she could have forgotten it for even a moment.

Vampyre . . . images of emaciated monsters with yellow fangs dripping blood rose in her mind.

Vampyre . . . hideous, unnatural creatures who stalked the night in search of prey, drinking the blood of innocents.

Vampyre . . . ghouls who slept in coffins by day because they could not abide the pure light of the sun.

Vampyre . . . how could it be true? If he was truly a vampyre, why wasn't she repulsed by him? Why was she still alive? Would she become what he was?

Rising to her feet, she went to the windows and threw the curtains open wide. The sun felt warm on her face.

She had never seen Rayven during the day. Never seen him eat.

She pressed her forehead against the cool glass. Was he sleeping in his coffin even now?

The thought made her shudder.

The east tower. That was where he slept. That was why he had forbidden her to go there. She frowned. She had found nothing when she went there, only an empty room.

She was across the room, her hand on the latch, before she realized what she was doing. She paused in the hallway, listening, wondering what Bevins was doing.

Lifting her skirts, she ran down the corridor to the staircase that led up to the east tower.

Her heart was beating loudly in her ears when she reached the tower room. Taking a deep breath, she opened the door and stepped inside. As before, there was nothing to see—no furniture, no pictures, only a single window covered by thick, black velvet draperies.

She opened the curtains, then stood in the center of the room, slowly turning around. At first she saw nothing, and then she discerned a faint break in the pattern of the stone wall across from the window.

Heart pounding, palms damp, mouth dry, she pressed her hand to the wall, gradually moving her hand over the surface.

She gasped as she felt the wall move, and then a portion of the wall slid open, revealing another room beyond.

Poised to flee, she stood in the doorway and peered inside. There were no windows in this chamber. Sunshine from the room behind her spilled through the open doorway. Though the light was faint, she could make out the shape of a large cherry wood armoire on the wall across from her. A wolf's head was carved into one door, a raven on the other.

A large fireplace took up the far corner of the room.

She took another step forward and glanced to the right. A huge tapestry covered the wall. Woven in shades of forest green and brown, it depicted several scenes. In one, a raven was perched on a tree branch. Below, a black wolf with bloodred eyes sat on its haunches, howling at the moon. Another scene portrayed several men armed with spears in pursuit of a wolf. A third scene illustrated a wolf standing on its hind legs, its teeth bared in a vicious snarl.

Drawing her gaze from the tapestry, she turned her head to the left, felt her heart jump into her throat. A huge bed covered with a black canopy was situated on a raised dais. And lying on the bed, his arms folded across his chest, was Rayven. She could only stare as images imprinted themselves on her mind. The sheets and pillow slip were black. A comforter, also black, was folded across the foot of the bed. His cloak covered him, enfolding him like loving arms.

His face, framed by his black hair, looked very pale. He did not seem to be breathing.

Alarm skittered through her. Had he died during the day? The urge to go to him, to make sure he was still alive, rose strong within her, and with it, snatches of folklore she'd heard about ways to destroy a vampyre.

Cut off its head. Stuff its mouth with garlic. Drive a stake through its heart and into the ground beneath so that it couldn't rise again.

Last night, he had told her what he was, and she had thought she believed him. But hearing his words had not prepared her for this.

The villagers had been right all along, she mused. There was a vampyre in their midst, and she knew where he slept.

"Oh, Rayven," she whispered. "Oh, Rayven, what am I to do?"

"Rhi . . . anna."

His voice, though barely audible, sounded in her ears like thunder.

He was awake. Awake and watching her

through heavy-lidded eyes as dark and deep as pools of liquid ebony.

She stood in the doorway, mesmerized by his gaze, unable to move.

"Have you come to destroy me?" There was a note of bitter resignation in his voice, but it was the forgiveness in his eyes that tugged at her heart.

"No." She shook her head, pity welling up within her. "No."

"Come to me." His voice was soft, so soft, filled with longing.

She couldn't. Wouldn't. But her feet were moving of their own accord, carrying her across the floor, up the two stairs of the dais, until she stood beside the bed.

"Rhianna . . . please don't . . ." His voice was low, as if speaking were an effort. His eyelids fluttered down, then opened again. "Don't hate me."

"I don't." She lifted one hand, wanting to touch him, yet afraid. "Are you in pain?" she asked. "Can I get you anything?"

The ghost of a smile played over his lips. "The sun . . . daylight . . . I cannot abide it."

"It's true," she murmured in wonder. "Everything you told me. All true."

He nodded once, briefly. "Lie with me."

She glanced at the bed. It wasn't a coffin, after all, just a large bed carved of wood.

Vampyre . . . Would he wrap her in his evil embrace and drain her dry?

It was a foolish thought, and she shook it away. If he had wanted to kill her, he'd had plenty of opportunity before now.

With a sigh, she sat down on the mattress, then

stretched out beside him, her head pillowed on his shoulder.

He smiled at her, his arm drawing her close to his side. There was a soft whoosh as the panel slid shut, and then his eyelids fluttered down and he was asleep once more.

And she was in the monster's lair.

She gave a little start as she felt his cloak slide out from beneath her, felt the smooth silk lining slither up over her bare arms, until it covered them both.

Hidden panels that shut of their own volition and a black velvet cloak that seemed almost alive. It was beyond her comprehension, beyond the realms of reality.

Suddenly weary, she closed her eyes. And slept.

He was aware of her there beside him all through the day. Her hair brushed his cheek like a skein of golden silk. Her arm rested across his chest, the warmth of her flesh penetrating the cold that enveloped him in his deathlike sleep. The clean fresh scent of her skin wrapped around him, the slow steady beat of her heart was as comforting as a lullaby. Her thigh pressed intimately against his, bequeathing erotic dreams to one who never dreamed.

He woke as the setting sun turned the sky to flame, and her face was the first thing he saw. Emotions rose within him, hot and swift and unfamiliar. For over four hundred years, he had awakened to the darkness of a lonely room, and now an angel lay sleeping beside him, her hair spread like sunshine across the pillow, her lashes like dark fans against her cheek.

And he knew in that moment that he had never loved her more.

She stirred in his arms, her eyelids fluttering open, an uncertain smile on her lips.

"You look surprised," he murmured. "Did you think I would drink you dry while you slept?"

She shook her head, but even in the dark, he could see the telltale flush that climbed into her cheeks.

"Rhianna, you have no idea what it means to me, to wake up and find you here beside me."

"I'm glad it pleases you, my lord."

"It does," he said. "Very much."

"Is there . . . is there a candle in here?" She glanced around, unnerved by the unrelieved darkness. There were no windows in the room, no hint of light. "It's so dark."

She felt him turn away from her; a moment later, there was a soft whoosh as a fire sprang to life in the hearth. Soft golden light filled the room, creating dancing shadows on the walls and ceiling.

Rhianna stared at the flames as if they had risen from Satan's own pit. "How . . . how did you do that?"

"A bit of vampyre magic," he replied. Bevins insisted on keeping a supply of wood in the fireplace, though Rayven had often told him it was unnecessary. For once, he was glad the man hadn't listened to him.

"Oh." She stared into the fireplace for a moment, then frowned. "I had expected . . . That is . . . Aren't . . . aren't vampyres supposed to sleep in coffins?"

"Some do."

"But you don't?"

"I find them narrow and confining." He could survive the day outside a coffin, but a thick layer of his native soil was spread beneath the mattress.

A muscle worked in his jaw as he sat up. The cloak fell away, pooling in his lap. "Have you any other questions about my . . . affliction?"

Rhianna sat up, her shoulder brushing against his. "Are there truly ways to . . . to kill a vampyre?"

"Plotting my destruction, are you?"

"Of course not."

"A hawthorne stake through the heart is said to be effective. I believe a stake made of ash or blackthorn will also suffice. Fire will certainly destroy me. Another sure method of destroying a vampyre is to cut off his head."

She swallowed the bile rising in her throat, sickened by the images his words conjured in her mind. "And what of holy water?"

"Holy water has a rather unpleasant effect, though I doubt it would be fatal unless I fell into a pool of it."

Rhianna frowned, searching her mind for other snippets of vampyre lore she had heard through the years. "And garlic?"

Rayven grinned. "The smell is most unpleasant, but will not deter me."

"And crosses?"

"A silver one would burn me should I touch it."

"And those made of wood?"

"They will not save you."

The words chilled her, but there was no menace in his voice, only mild amusement.

Rhianna frowned thoughtfully. "Why are you telling me how to destroy you?"

"Because someday you may need to know."

She didn't want to dwell on what that might mean. Casting about for some other topic of conversation, her gaze settled on his cloak. It spread over the bed like a shimmering pool of ebony. She stared at it warily for a moment, remembering how it had covered her the night before.

She poked at it tentatively, as if afraid it might attack her. As always, the rich velvet was warm to the touch, seeming to pulse with a life of its own.

"It won't bite you," Rayven remarked, one brow arched in wry amusement.

"Are you sure? It is the strangest garment I have ever seen. This afternoon . . ." She broke off with a shrug. "Never mind."

"What?" he urged. "Tell me."

"I know it's impossible!" Rhianna exclaimed. "But I'd swear it moved. Oh, I know I must have been imagining it, but it seemed to cover me of its own volition."

She shook her head, her eyes wide with awe and disbelief. "And the panel in the wall, it closed all by itself."

She looked at him, waiting for him to explain that which was unexplainable. "How is it possible? Am I going mad?"

Rayven caressed her cheek with the back of his hand. "You're quite sane, my sweet. I caused the panel in the wall to close, just as I caused it to open when I sensed you were on the other side."

"You did? But, how?"

"Like this," he said, and a moment later, the

portal slid open and then closed again, leaving no trace of its existence.

Rhianna blinked up at him, astonishment evident in her eyes. "Would you mind leaving it open?"

"As you wish," he said agreeably, and the narrow door opened once again. "Is that better?"

"Yes, thank you." She glanced at him, at the door, and back at him again. "Did you manipulate the cloak, as well?"

"No."

"No?" She cast a wary glance at the puddle of black velvet in his lap.

With a sigh, Rayven stroked the smooth velvet. "I don't know how to explain my cloak. Indeed, I don't know if it can be explained. I fashioned it myself, though I cannot recall how it was done, nor where the material came from. The night after I was made Vampyre, my hands created it with a knowledge of their own. My blood, the very essence of my life, is woven into the fabric. And because the blood of my mother is in me, a part of her dwells within the cloak."

"And it's that part of her that soothes you, isn't it?" She smiled, as if she had just solved a mystery. "I've seen the way the cloak enfolds you when you're unhappy, or weary, as if to comfort you."

He nodded, surprised by her perception, and by her ready acceptance of what was, for the most part, completely incomprehensible.

"You have a beautiful soul, Rhianna McLeod," he said quietly. "Do you think me cruel to keep you here against your will? To make you live with a monster when you deserve so much more?"

A man like Montroy, he thought, sick with jealousy. That was what she deserved. *A husband who could give her children, who could offer her a home filled with sunlight and laughter.*

"Is that how you see yourself, my lord? As a monster?"

"Don't you?"

"No."

"What do you see, sweet Rhianna?"

"I'm not sure. But you're far too kind to be a monster."

"Kind?" He made a low sound of derision in his throat. "No one has ever accused me of that before."

"You have been kind to me, kind to my family. And now you've shown kindness to the town as well."

"That was your idea, not mine."

"You could have said no."

"Not to you." He cupped her cheek in his palm, the heat of her skin warming him. "Rhianna, I wish . . ." He drew his hand from her face and stood up, turning away so that his back was to her.

"What do you wish?"

"Nothing. Wishes are for fools."

Rising, she went to stand behind him. He was so tall, so strong, and yet so vulnerable. Fearing she would be rebuffed, she slid her arms around his waist and pressed her cheek to his back. "Won't you tell me what you wish?"

He folded his arms over her hands and bowed his head. "I wish I could be mortal for you, Rhianna, that I could love you, that I could make love to you, as a mortal man. I wish I could stand beside you on a warm summer morning and watch the sunrise, that I could share your days as well as your nights. I would cherish you with each breath, shower you with the riches of the world. I wish I could father your children and watch them grow, that I could work beside you, and grow old at your side."

He took a deep breath, willing away the images his words had created in his mind. "I can do none of those things." He turned around to face her. "If I weren't a monster, my sweet, I would release you from your promise. I would send you away from here and bid you well. But I have ever been a selfish knave and find that I cannot let you go. Not now. Not after the joy of having you rest beside me." His dark eyes burned into hers. "Perhaps not ever."

She looked up at him, her expression serene. "Have I asked to be released from my promise?"

"You should."

"Why? You just said you would not let me go."

He traced the curve of her cheek with his forefinger. "True enough," he agreed, "and yet, I doubt I could deny you anything. Even your freedom, should you ask it of me."

"I promised you a year, my lord, and unless you send me away, I intend to honor that promise."

"Rhianna . . ." He had no words to express his feelings, no words to tell her how precious she was to him at that moment as she looked up at him, her eyes filled with acceptance, and trust. "What a rare creature you are," he murmured.

"You look extremely pale, my lord," she mused. "Shall I call Bevins?"

"No." He turned away from her again lest she see the hunger burning in his eyes. "Why don't you go freshen up for supper? I shall join you later."

"Will you not kiss me before I go?"

"Not now." His voice was harsh.

"Very well, my lord."

The hurt in her voice was like a slap. "Rhianna, wait." He took a deep breath; then, when he was certain the hunger was under control, he took her in his arms and kissed her. "I'll see you as soon as I can."

She noticed the change in him when he entered the library two hours later. His face seemed less pale, his eyes less bright, his attitude more relaxed.

He hesitated in the doorway, aware of her scrutiny. "Shall I leave?"

"No." Why had she never noticed there were times when he looked pale, and times when his color was more—she swallowed—normal? She tried to analyze her feelings now that she knew what he was, what he did to survive. She expected to feel revulsion; instead, she felt only compassion.

He crossed the room and took a seat across from her. She wore a dress of pale pink trimmed with white lace. Her hair fell over her shoulders and down her back like a waterfall of spun gold. And her eyes . . . He gazed into her deep blue eyes and saw the daylight sky he had not seen in over four hundred years.

He longed to touch her, but made no move toward her for fear of frightening her. She would need time to adjust, to accept.

"How do you bear it?" she asked after a lengthy

silence. "How can you drink . . . I don't understand how you can do it, drink the . . . the blood of animals."

They had discussed this before, but he understood her need to try to understand. "It is necessary for my survival," he replied patiently.

"Do you need to . . . to drink it every night?"

"No."

"How long can you go without it?"

"Comfortably for a week or so. Any longer than that becomes . . . stressful."

"You fed well tonight, didn't you? Your skin looks almost . . ."

"Human?"

She nodded, thinking what a strange conversation this was. She knew what he was, knew it was true, and yet a distant part of her mind still refused to accept it.

"You told me that you usually drink the blood of animals. Were you lying to me?"

"No." He hesitated, wondering how much to tell her, how much more she could accept. "I can survive on the blood of animals, as you could survive on locusts and ants, if necessary. But would you want to? It isn't natural for you to eat such things, any more than it is natural for me to drink the blood of animals. I need human blood."

I need your blood. He did not say the words, but she heard them in her mind, and in her heart.

Rhianna stared at him. "All those other girls," she said slowly. "The ones who were here before me. You didn't defile them, the way the townspeople think, did you? You drank from them."

Rayven nodded, his expression impassive. He saw the revulsion in her eyes, felt as though a vast gulf were opening between them, an abyss he would never be able to cross.

"And that was why you bought me, wasn't it? To . . . to feed on."

"The blood of beasts will satisfy the hunger," he said, his voice carefully neutral, "but it gives me no pleasure, nor will it sustain me indefinitely. From time to time, I need human blood. Sometimes I crave it. To go without it for long periods of time weakens me." He took a deep breath and let it out in a long, weary sigh. "You cannot imagine the pain that comes with abstinence."

He glanced at the pulse throbbing in her throat. The blood of beasts was vile, but Rhianna's blood was like the finest wine, the sweetest nectar.

"What happened to the other girls who stayed here before me?"

"I sent them away."

Rhianna swallowed hard. "Alive?"

"What do you think?"

"I don't want to believe that you killed them. If you tell me you didn't, I'll accept your word."

"I did them no harm. But I have killed in the past, Rhianna. And will do so again, if necessary. Don't try to imagine that I'm noble. Or kind. I am a vampyre, and we are, by our very nature, killers. We trust no one, especially others of our kind, and guard our territory jealousy."

She heard his emphasis on the word "we," but couldn't deal with the idea that there might be others like him living nearby. Not now, not when she was trying so hard to understand what made him as he was.

"Are you still trying to scare me away, my lord?" she asked, forcing a smile.

Rayven shook his head. "I just want you to be aware of what you're dealing with."

He stood up. "Think about what I've said, Rhianna. If you're still here tomorrow night, I'll know you've decided to stay until the year is up. If you leave, I will provide for you and your family as long as you live."

She wanted to tell him that she still loved him, that nothing he could say or do would change her mind, but she couldn't form the words.

"Good night, sweet Rhianna." His voice moved over her like a cold winter wind, and then he was gone as if he had never been there at all.

Chapter Fifteen

She didn't leave. She spent a sleepless night, remembering everything he had said, everything that had passed between them since that fateful night at Cotyer's, and when dawn came, she knew she couldn't leave him.

She had expected him to be glad, to spend his every waking moment in her company. Instead, she had the feeling he was avoiding her. Though he joined her each night at supper, he seemed withdrawn. She had thought, after what he'd told her, after the day she had spent sleeping beside him, that he would take her to his bed. Instead, he held her at arm's length, his gaze warning her to keep her distance. It was most confusing.

Tonight, he was late. She picked at her food, wondering if she had dreamed the whole thing. In the cold light of day, all he had told her seemed like a fable—reading minds and magical cloaks, living on the blood of sheep mixed with wine, being forced to live forever in the darkness. It was inconceivable.

She sensed his presence even before he entered the dining room. Looking up, her gaze met his, and she knew that it was all true. He was a vampyre. Alive and yet dead. It explained so much: the despair she sometimes saw in his eyes, why she had never seen him during the light of day, why she never saw him eat, why his skin was ever cool to the touch.

She felt a burst of hysterical laughter bubble in her throat. She had been afraid he had bought her to shame her, to defile her, when all he had wanted was to drink her blood.

"Hungry, my lord?" she asked bitterly. Leaning back in her chair, she slowly and deliberately bared her throat to his gaze as all her dreams of a future with Rayven dissolved in a crimson sea of impossibility. He would not marry her. She would never bear his children.

"Rhianna, don't." He turned away from the revulsion in her eyes, from the sight of her bared throat, the pulse beating wildly. The scent of her despair, her blood, flooded his senses.

"I'm sorry. Forgive me," she murmured, and burst into tears. She would leave this place in a few months. Someday she would marry. She would have children and grandchildren, but Rayven would still be here, locked in chains of eternal darkness, forever alone and lonely.

"Rhianna!" Muttering an oath, he knelt in front of her and took her hands in his. "Rhianna, don't cry. Please don't cry. I cannot abide your tears. You needn't stay here any longer. I'll send you home tomorrow. Tonight, if you wish. Only please don't cry."

"I'm not crying for me," she said.

He stared up at her, stunned by the realization that she was weeping for him.

"Is there nothing that can be done for you?" she asked, sniffing back her tears.

"Done for me?" he asked, frowning.

"Can you never be mortal again?"

Slowly, he shook his head. "No."

"I'll stay with you," she promised. "I'll stay as long as you want me."

"Ah, Rhianna, you have no idea how that tempts me." Never to be alone again. To have someone to share his life. He would show her the world, shower her with diamonds and emeralds, grant her anything she desired. She would never want for anything. She could sleep days at his side. Her face would send him to sleep and welcome him when he awoke . . .

Slowly, he shook his head. He could not condemn her to the kind of life he led, expect her to shun the daylight, to spend her life with a man who was not a man at all, simply to ease his loneliness. He might be a monster, but even he could not be that cruel.

His loneliness, the complete and utter sadness in the depths of his eyes, caught at her heart and made her soul weep. "Don't send me away," she begged softly. Leaning forward, she pressed a kiss to his brow.

He slipped his arms around her waist, his face pressed against her breasts. Her warmth engulfed him, dispelling the cold that was his constant companion as sunlight chased away the chill of night.

"I won't." He drew in a shaky breath. "God forgive me, I won't."

A sense of peace, of coming home, filled her soul as she stroked his hair.

"My sister is to wed on the morrow," she reminded him. "Say you'll come with me to the wedding."

"If you wish." He no longer seemed to have any will of his own, he thought with wry amusement. She spoke, and he yearned only to obey.

"I do." He looked up to see her smiling down at him. "You are most agreeable, my lord."

"It seems I can deny you nothing."

"Nothing, my lord Rayven?"

"What would you have now, Rhianna? A chest filled with sapphires to rival the color of your eyes? Gold to match the color of your hair?"

"What I want is of infinitely more worth, my lord."

"I cannot imagine what it might be."

"Can't you?"

She was flirting with him, he mused. And quite brazenly, too. "Tell me, my sweet, and it's yours."

"A kiss," Rhianna said, drawing out the word until it was a caress. "One kiss."

"Only one?"

"Or two."

"Or twenty?" Rayven murmured, covering her mouth with his.

Rhianna made a low sound of assent deep in her throat as she wrapped her arms around his neck. This was what she wanted, she thought as his touch drugged her senses. To be here, in his arms, for the rest of her life.

Time ceased to have meaning as his tongue stroked her lower lip, as his hands slid up her rib cage, his thumbs lightly stroking her breasts.

"Rayven . . . please . . ."

He drew back to look at her. His breathing was ragged, his eyes alight with a fierce inner glow.

"Don't turn me away again," she pleaded softly.

"Rhianna, I want you more than you can imagine . . ."

"But?"

"I'm afraid I'll hurt you, that . . ."

"What?"

"Rhianna, I can't always separate my desire from the hunger that plagues me. I'm afraid that, in the heat of passion, the lust for blood will overcome my self-control."

"Does it always happen that way?"

"I don't know. I've only taken one woman to my bed since I was made Vampyre."

"Only one? In four hundred years?"

"The lust for blood has ever been more powerful than the lust of the flesh." Until Rhianna, he thought. Until she came and threaded hope into the lonely tapestry of his life.

"What happened to that girl?"

"She died in my arms."

Rhianna sat back in the chair, unable to suppress the shudder of fear that skittered down her spine.

"Rhianna, I could not live with the guilt if anything I did should cause you harm."

"Have you . . . taken nourishment this evening?"

"Yes." Knowing he would see her, remembering what it had been like to hold her while he slept, he had fed, and fed well.

"Are you hungry now?"

He shook his head, the certainty of what was coming next exciting him even as it filled him with a sense of dread.

He needed her, needed her as surely as she needed him. Knowing that gave her the courage to shake off her fear. Rising to her feet, she took his hand and drew him up beside her. "I've waited for you long enough, my lord."

The words were spoken so softly, he doubted a mere mortal could have heard them.

Rayven shook his head. "I cannot, Rhianna. Please do not ask this of me."

"I'm not afraid."

His fingers curled over her shoulders. "But I am."

"Did you love that other girl?"

"No."

"Do you love me?"

He nodded, unable to deny it.

Her smile was as bright as the sunlight he would never see again, as warm as a mother's love.

"You're sure this is what you want, Rhianna?"

For answer, she took his hand in hers and turned toward the door.

Helpless to resist, he followed her up the winding staircase to her room.

Inside, her courage seemed to desert her, and she stared up at him, her eyes wide and uncertain.

"We don't have to do this," Rayven said.

"No, I want to. I just don't know what's expected of me."

"We could start with a kiss," Rayven suggested, hoping it would put them both at ease.

He drew her into his arms, felt the nervous tremors that shook her from head to foot.

"Rhianna." He murmured her name as he claimed her lips.

She was sweeter than honey, warmer than a summer day. It was like standing next to a ray of sunshine, he thought. Holding her in his arms chased away the chill that seemed ever to hold him in its grasp, and he drew her closer, absorbing the heat of her, the softness. Her breasts were crushed against his chest; he could feel the rapid beat of her heart, sense the passion blossoming within her.

She responded to his kiss ardently, pressing herself against him, her arms sliding around his neck. She moaned softly as his lips slid over her throat, along her shoulder.

"Rhianna, Rhianna, do you know how often I have dreamed of this moment?"

She made a wordless sound of assent, drawing back a little so she could see his face. The heat in his eyes threatened to scorch her very soul, and she thought how wonderful it was that an innocent such as she could arouse such a man.

He released her long enough to remove his cloak. She watched as he tossed it over a chair, felt her breath catch in her throat as she caught sight of herself in the mirror.

For a moment, it was as if the world came to a stop and she saw everything in frozen moments of time: her reflection, her hair slightly mussed, her cheeks rosy, her lips slightly swollen from his kisses. She saw his cloak, spread like a river of velvet blackness over the chair. She saw the bed behind her. But Rayven, who stood beside her, cast no reflection in the glass.

Startled, she glanced at him, assuring herself that he was there. She looked in the mirror again, felt the blood drain from her face.

"What is it?" Rayven looked at her askance and then, slowly, he followed her gaze. Her image stared back at him from the mirror, her blue eyes wide, her face ashen. "Rhianna?"

"I . . . You . . ." She drew in a deep breath, let it out in a long, shaky sigh. "The mirror . . . You don't . . . Why can't I see you?"

He went suddenly still. "I'm not sure," he replied stiffly. "There are many theories, the foremost being that vampyres cast no reflection because they are composed of unnatural flesh."

Vampyre . . . She knew that was what he was, but she had refused to dwell on it, had tried to pretend that it didn't matter, that it was some sort of rare disease rather than a state of being. She knew now why there had been no mirrors in the castle, knew the heavy draperies over the windows weren't there simply to shut out the light.

Taking a step back, she gazed up at him. In an unconscious gesture of self-protection, she crossed her arms over her breasts.

Rayven did not miss the significance of her action. Drawing himself up to his full height, he moved to the far side of the room. "I told you what I am," he said, his voice cold and slightly defensive.

"I know, but I guess I never really realized what

it meant. It doesn't matter. Truly, it doesn't. It just startled me for a moment."

"Startled?" He lifted one black brow in bitter amusement.

"You look ready to faint."

"Do I?" She smiled wanly. "Can you blame me?"

"No. This isn't going to work, Rhianna. I'll have Bevins take you home in the morning."

"No!" She hurried across the floor and placed her hands on his shoulders. "It doesn't matter." She gestured at the mirror. "I just didn't know about this. You never said . . ." She crossed her arms over her breasts again, suddenly remembering that he had imparted this knowledge to her when he told her about Lysandra and how he had become a vampyre. "I'm sorry, I forgot."

She thought of all the other things he had told her about vampyres. It had all sounded so unreal, so improbable. She knew now that, in spite of his ability to open and close doors and start fires with the power of his thoughts, in spite of his need for blood, deep down, she hadn't really believed he was a vampyre. "Is there anything else I should know? I mean, I've heard stories about vampyres, of course, but . . ."

She bit down on her lower lip to stop her inane babbling. Even after all she had seen, after all he had said, she didn't want to believe it was true. Tears stung her eyes as she looked up at him, hoping he would tell her it had all been some horrid mistake.

"Ah, Rhianna, you are so young, and I feel so very old."

"Tell me."

"I believe I've told you everything you need to

know." His gaze moved to the slender column of her neck, to the pulse that throbbed so invitingly. The scent of her blood teased his nostrils.

Overcome with tenderness, he took her hands in his and kissed each one, his lips cool against her flesh. "I think I'd better go."

"But . . . I thought that . . ."

"Another time, Rhianna."

He was both relieved and disappointed when she didn't argue.

"Will I see you tomorrow night, my lord?"

"If you wish."

"Will you accompany me to my sister's wedding?"

"Do you think that would be wise?"

"I don't know. Perhaps it would be good for you to spend more time with people and less time locked away in this castle."

He looked skeptical. "What time is the wedding?"

"Seven, my lord, at Millbrae Chapel." Rhianna bit down on her lower lip. "Can you . . . I mean, you won't . . . ?"

He laughed softly. "I assure you, the church will not collapse if I enter, my sweet. Nor will I disintegrate into a smoldering pile of ash." Bending, he pressed his lips to the top of her head. "Until tomorrow night."

Chapter Sixteen

Rayven waited at the bottom of the staircase, speechless, as he watched Rhianna descend the steps, a vision in a swirl of pale pink satin and ivory lace, an angel with a cloud of golden hair and eyes the color of a mid-summer sky. The gown revealed the slender curve of her neck and a modest expanse of honey-hued skin. Pink slippers peeked from the ruffled hem of her gown.

"How pretty you are, my sweet," Rayven said. Taking her hand in his, he pressed it to his lips.

A wave of color washed into Rhianna's cheeks as she saw the admiration in his eyes.

"You look very handsome yourself, my lord," she replied, feeling suddenly shy.

Clad in tight-fitting black breeches, soft black leather boots, a white shirt, and a black broadcloth coat trimmed in black satin, he looked every inch a gentleman of quality and wealth.

The word "vampyre" whispered down the corridor of her mind. Resolutely, she pushed it away. She would not think of that now.

"Do you still think this is a good idea?" he asked as he placed a white woolen shawl around her shoulders, then reached for his cloak.

"You needn't accompany me if you'd rather not," she said.

His knuckles brushed her cheek. "I was only thinking of you, of your reputation."

"I don't care what others think, my lord," she replied, "so long as I am with you."

A bit of warmth, like the touch of sunlight, settled around his heart. "As you wish," he said, and offered her his arm.

The church, made of wood and hewn stone, was set against the hills. The light from dozens of white candles filled the room, bathing the painted faces of the wooden saints in a soft amber light.

The pews were filled with friends and family, and Rhianna smiled at her mother and sisters as she took her place among them. For a moment, she held her breath, waiting. Waiting for what? she mused. For the church to collapse? For the priest to come forward, cross in hand, and cast Rayven out of the church?

"Relax, my sweet." Rayven whispered. He took her hand in his and patted it reassuringly. "My presence will not cause the chapel to go up in flames. The priest will not renounce me as a spawn of Satan."

Rhianna felt her cheeks grow hot as he put her fears into words.

In spite of his mocking words, Rayven was not

as at ease as he would have had her think. Time and again his gaze was drawn to the large wooden crucifix mounted on the wall behind the altar. He had not been inside a church in almost four hundred years. The last time he had entered a church had been soon after he had been made Vampyre. He had taken shelter inside a small chapel to escape the light of the sun. Huddled within one of the tiny confessionals, he had begged forgiveness for the blood he had spilled, for the lives he had taken.

Now, sitting beside Rhianna, he was acutely conscious of the whispers erupting behind him as the townspeople voiced their surprise at seeing him there. He rarely left the castle, except on those occasions when he went to Cotyer's.

"He never seems to change . . ."

"What do you suppose he does up in that castle?"

". . . nerve, to bring him here . . ."

". . . not natural, the way he lives . . ."

The whispers and speculation came to an abrupt halt as the village priest and the groom took their places at the altar. Moments later, Rhianna's sister walked down the aisle.

She was a pretty girl, Rayven mused, radiant on this, her day of days. She wore a modest ivory gown and veil and carried a bouquet of primroses and delicate ferns.

The groom, Creighton York, was tall and rather thin, with dark brown hair and brown eyes.

Rayven slid a glance at Rhianna as the priest began to speak. He didn't have to probe her mind to know what she was thinking, to know she was imagining herself standing at the altar, repeating the vows that would bind her to the man she loved. A single tear slid down her cheek as her sister's new husband lifted her veil and kissed his bride.

A sharp pain pierced Rayven's heart. Some day, Rhianna would stand at a similar altar and say the words that would forever bind her to another man. He could not abide the thought. The anguish of knowing she belonged to another would be his undoing.

On that day, when he knew she was forever lost to him, he would go out to meet the sun.

There was a party after the ceremony. Creighton York was the only son of a middle-class family. His father, Langston, was the village silversmith. The reception was held in the town hall.

Rayven stayed in the background, relieved that there were no mirrors in the large wooden building. He stood in a corner, comfortable in the shadows as he watched Rhianna move about the room, mingling with the guests, laughing with her sisters, pausing to speak to her mother, helping Mistress York at the table.

She was a vision, his Rhianna, a faerie queen in a swirl of pink skirts. There were other women present—some younger, some who possessed more generous curves—but there were none more fair of face, none as vibrant and alive as she. In a room filled with living beings, her scent, her blood, stood out like a beacon shining across a midnight sea, tantalizing his senses.

Rhianna looked up, her gaze drawn to his like a bee to pollen. Rayven stared back at her, his eyes dark and compelling. Before she realized what she was doing, she was moving toward him, unaware of the people who spoke to her as she passed by.

She blinked up at him. "My lord?"

"May I have this dance, sweet Rhianna?"

"Dance?" Only then did she notice that the musicians were playing, that others were dancing.

She stepped toward him, a sigh of contentment whispering past her lips as he took her in his arms and whirled her around the floor. She had never danced with a man who was so light on his feet, whose very touch made her whole being tingle with yearning and forbidden desires. She looked into his eyes, fathomless black eyes that held her spellbound, until she was aware of nothing and no one save the dark lord of Castle Rayven.

Vampyre.

The arm around her waist tensed as the word crossed her mind. *He knows,* she thought, *knows what I'm thinking.* He had told her once that he could read her mind, and she had refused to believe him, but she believed it now.

Leaning back a little, she gazed into the depths of his eyes. *Kiss me, my lord, kiss me now.*

And, ever so slowly, he lowered his head and brushed his lips across hers.

She gloried in his kiss even as she contemplated what it would mean to live with a man who could divine her every thought. A man who was not a man at all.

When the dance ended, he escorted her across the hall and handed her a glass of wine, then sat beside her while she ate a piece of wedding cake. Later, there were toasts to the bride and groom, and then Aileen and Creighton took their leave. Shortly after that, Rhianna went to bid her mother and sisters good night.

"Come home with us," Ada urged. She slanted a glance in Rayven's direction, shuddered as his hell-black eyes locked on hers. "Please, daughter, come home where you belong."

"I can't, Mama. I've promised to stay with Lord Rayven for a year."

Ada shook her head. "I don't understand you, daughter. What hold does he have on you?"

"I love him," Rhianna said quietly. "That's the hold he has on me. He has granted me a year to be with him, only a year, and I will not leave him one day sooner."

Ada shook her head again. "I fear he has bewitched you."

Rhianna bit back a smile. "I assure you, Mama, he is neither witch nor sorcerer."

"I'll wager he is not a mere man, either," Ada snapped. "He's evil, Rhianna. Why can you not see that?"

"He's not evil, Mama. He's been kind to me, to our family. Have you forgotten that Aileen would have had no dowry if not for Lord Rayven's generosity? Have you forgotten that he provided the means to enlarge our cottage, that he's the one who made it possible for us to keep our land after Papa died, that he's put clothes on our backs, food on our table?"

"I've not forgotten," Ada replied in a hushed tone. "But I fear his generosity is not born of kindness, Rhianna. I fear it is only a matter of time until we learn his true purpose."

Rhianna shook her head. She started to tell her

mother about the shelter in the village, then closed her mouth, remembering she had promised Rayven she would tell no one.

"I've got to go, Mama," she said. She gave her mother a quick hug, kissed her sisters good-bye. "I'll see you all soon."

She was unusually silent in the carriage as they rode back to the castle. Rayven regarded her through narrowed eyes, wondering what was bothering her. Was it her mother's disapproval? A touch of melancholy because her sister seemed happily wed? Or was she trying to find a way to tell him she had changed her mind about spending a year in the company of a vampyre?

"Rhianna?"

She turned toward him, her face in shadow. "Yes, my lord?"

"What troubles you?"

"My mother. She thinks you're evil, that there's some nefarious reason why you're being so kind to me and my family."

"And what do you think?"

"I think I shall die if you don't kiss me."

"Ah, Rhianna . . ."

"Are we never to make love, my lord?"

"Would you marry me, Rhianna?"

"Marry you," she gasped.

"Is the thought so repugnant?"

"No, but . . ."

"Only for what is left of our year, Rhianna. For what remains of the time you promised me, I should like you to be my wife."

"And then?"

"And then I shall free you from your vows."

His proposal left her speechless. Marry him?

"I shall make it worth your while, my sweet." He took her hands in his, delighting in the warmth of her skin. "I want you, Rhianna, more than I have ever wanted anything. More than I yearn to see the sun again."

"You need not marry me, my lord," she said softly. "I should think I've made it quite clear that I want you, as well."

"Ah, Rhianna, to my surprise, I find that there lingers within me a scrap of conscience. I would not take your maidenhead, nor steal your innocence, without benefit of marriage." He kissed her palm, his tongue stroking the sensitive flesh, sending shivers of delight racing through her. "Say yes, sweet Rhianna."

She could not see his face in the darkness, but she could feel his eyes on her—deep black eyes that glowed with a fierce inner fire.

Vampyre.

"I will not hurt you, Rhianna McLeod."

"I know." She looked at her hands, enfolded in his. Strong hands, yet he had ever been gentle with her.

Lord Rayven is a man driven by dark appetites. Bevins's words, spoken earnestly, warning her to be careful.

He's evil, Rhianna. Why can't you see that? She heard her mother's voice echo in the back of her mind.

She searched Rayven's eyes and knew he was aware of her thoughts, her doubts.

"Rhianna . . ."

"I will marry you, my lord, whenever you say."

"Tomorrow night."

"So soon? I had hoped . . ."

"What had you hoped, my sweet?"

"To be married in a church, in a gown of white silk, and a veil, with my mother and sisters beside me."

"You shall have it."

"By tomorrow night, my lord? I think not."

"Arrange for the wedding you have always dreamed of, Rhianna," he said. "All I ask is that you don't make me wait too long, and that you agree to have the ceremony performed in the chapel here, in the castle."

"There's a chapel here?"

Rayven nodded. "How much time do you need?"

"Two weeks should be time enough, my lord."

Bevins was astonished at the news. Rhianna's mother was horrified, her sisters speechless.

Montroy was stunned.

Sitting across from Rayven at Cotyer's several nights later, Dallon shook his head in disbelief. "She agreed to marry you?"

Rayven nodded. He could sense the jealousy radiating from the other man, the anger, see it in the way Montroy's fist clenched around the mug in his hand. "I never thought . . . I never thought you would get married."

"Nor I," Rayven replied. He glanced around the hall, nodded at Tewksbury and Jackson, who were involved in a never-ending card game.

"I suppose you'll keep her locked up in that blasted castle," Dallon said, his voice tight. "Damn it, Rayven, you can't make a prisoner of her!"

Rayven didn't move, didn't change his expression, yet Montroy knew he had gone too far.

Dallon cleared his throat. "I just meant that she deserves better than that."

"She will not be a prisoner," Rayven said. "She will be my wife. As such, she will be free to come and go as she pleases."

Dallon nodded again. He didn't miss the warning in Rayven's eyes, or the fine edge in his voice, and he knew it would be wise to change the subject.

"She wants to be married in church with her family beside her," Rayven remarked. He took a deep breath, and his nostrils filled with the odor of strong whiskey and cigar smoke and overall, the warm thick scent of blood.

Montroy sat back in his chair. He took a deep breath, striving to compose himself. "You can hardly blame her for that."

"She has asked her two oldest sisters to stand up with her."

Rayven cleared his throat and glanced around the room. In four centuries, he had never asked a favor of another man.

With a sigh, he looked at Montroy again. "I have no friends to speak of," he said tonelessly. "But I would consider it an honor if you would stand up with me."

Dallon blinked at him, obviously at a loss for words, and then he nodded.

"I should be most pleased, my lord," Montroy replied soberly, though he wondered how he could bear to be present while Rhianna pledged her heart to another. "When is the marriage to take place?"

"In ten days."

Ten days, Montroy thought, and wondered if

there was anything he could say to change Rhianna's mind before it was too late.

During the next week, Castle Rayven enjoyed more company that it had known in over four hundred years. Rhianna's mother and sisters came often to help with sewing Rhianna's wedding gown and to plan the wedding dinner.

It should have been a happy occasion, Rhianna mused. There should have been smiles and laughter as they sat in the solarium working on her gown, but anyone looking at her mother's face would have thought they were preparing for a wake. Ada muttered repeatedly that no good would come from this marriage, that there was something amiss within the castle, that Lord Rayven was not the nobleman he seemed. Rhianna did her best to ignore her mother's dire warnings, though sometimes, when she was alone, she wondered what good could come of marrying a vampyre.

Her sisters thought it romantic that she was marrying the mysterious dark lord of the castle. They oohed and aahed as she showed them around, marveling at the tapestries that hung on ancient walls, at the huge fireplaces in the main hall, at the heavy swords crossed over the hearth. They ran through the gardens; they were enchanted by the maze.

Bevins, on the other hand, was enchanted with Rhianna's mother. He made any number of excuses to enter the solarium when Ada was there, pausing in the doorway whenever he passed by, stopping to inquire if they wished refreshments. Ada pretended to be unaware of Bevins's interest, but Rhianna noticed the way her mother's eyes sparkled when Bevins was near, the way her cheeks flushed when their hands accidentally touched.

Bridgitte was the first to mention it aloud. They were in the solarium, turning the hem on Rhianna's wedding dress, when Bevins entered the room with a tray of tea and biscuits. He served them each in turn, smiled at Ada, and left the room.

"I think he likes you, Mama," Bridgitte remarked. "He always gives you the biggest biscuit, and his eyes smile when he looks at you."

"I don't know what you're talking about," Ada retorted.

"It's true." Brenna grinned at her younger sister. "Maybe we'll have a new father soon."

"Hush, Brenna," Ada admonished.

"He's nice looking, mama," Lanna added. "And his eyes do smile when he looks at you."

"Nonsense!"

"It isn't nonsense, Mama," Rhianna said. "He told me he thought you were a fine-looking woman."

"When?" Ada asked, her cheeks flaming. "When did he tell you such a thing?"

"The first time he brought me home."

Flustered and flattered, Ada bent her head over her sewing so her daughters couldn't see her flushed cheeks. It had been years since a man had looked at her in such a way. More years than she cared to remember. She might have found Bevins's interest flattering if it had been anyone else, but she wanted nothing to do with anyone in Rayven's employ. It was hard enough to stand by and watch her daughter make what Ada thought was the biggest mistake of her life. She jabbed the needle through the material, silently berating her husband. But for Vincent, Rhianna and Rayven would never have met.

At dusk, Rhianna's mother and sisters took their leave. Rhianna had invited them to stay for dinner each night, but Ada had always refused. She had made any number of excuses, but Rhianna knew the truth, knew that her mother was afraid to be in the castle after dark. There were too many stories of strange goings on at Castle Rayven, too many rumors of ghosts and ghouls prowling the grounds. Each night before she left, Ada made the sign of the cross on Rhianna's brow and admonished her to say her prayers and keep her rosary close at hand.

Tonight was no different. Rhianna stood at the door, the touch of her mother's calloused thumb lingering on her brow as she watched her mother's carriage drive away.

With a sigh, Rhianna closed the door and made her way into the dining room. She sat down at her usual place, smiling at Bevins as he set a plate before her.

Moments later, Rayven entered the room. He kissed her on the forehead, then took his customary seat across from her. A moment later, Bevins placed a decanter and goblet in front of him.

Rhianna glanced at the decanter, at the dark red liquid that shimmered within the crystal. She looked away as Bevins filled the goblet and handed it to Rayven.

Sheep's blood and wine. How had he existed on such a thing for over four hundred years?

She stared at her plate, at the mutton and potatoes and freshly baked bread, and tried to imagine what it would be like if she could never eat solid food again, if she were forced to drink the blood of people or animals to survive.

She thought of all the things she loved—bread and cheese and chocolate. Sunshine, and grass wet with dew. Swimming in the lake on a hot summer day. Working in the gardens with the sun on her back and the scent of freshly dug earth filling her nostrils. Watching children at play . . . things forever lost to the man sitting across from her.

This was how it would be when they were married, she thought. They would never share a meal, or walk hand in hand in the gardens in the morning when the dew sparkled on the ground. She would never know the wonder of motherhood. She would change her life to conform to his. The moon would become her sun, the night her day.

She was suddenly aware of the silence in the room. She could feel his gaze burning into her. Taking a deep breath, she forced herself to meet his eyes.

Pain. Stark, unrelenting pain. And beneath it all, the loneliness of four hundred years. How did he bear it?

He said nothing, only stared at her, and she knew that he had divined her every thought, that he had felt her revulsion, her pity. She could feel the rage that bubbled beneath the surface, his anger, his bitterness.

She felt her heart skip a beat as he lurched to his feet. For a moment, he stared down at her, and then, his cloak whipping around his ankles, he left the room. A moment later, she heard the slam of a door and knew he had left the castle to prowl the gardens, knew that, sooner or later, he would go to the maze. He would sit in the shadow of the wolf and the raven and stare into the darkness that was a part of him. How did anyone survive centuries of darkness?

She sat there a moment and then, slowly, rose to her feet to follow him.

"I wouldn't, miss."

"Bevins, I didn't see you."

"Let him be, Miss Rhianna."

"I can't. He's hurting . . ."

Bevins nodded. "Aye, miss, but he's used to it long since."

She stared at Bevins as if seeing him for the first time. "All this time, you've known what he is and never told me." And then a new thought occurred to her. "Are you one, too?"

Even as she asked the question, she knew it was impossible. "Does he . . ." She tried to find a way to phrase it delicately, and found none.

"He has drunk from me in the past, miss, when there was no one and nothing else available."

"Your loyalty runs very deep."

"He saved my life, miss. Could I do less?"

Rhianna glanced at the window. She could see nothing but darkness beyond. Rayven was out there, alone and lonely, and it was her fault. She had driven him away, into the night.

"I must go to him." She was heading for the door as she spoke. "Is he in the maze?"

"No, miss."

"No?" She stopped and turned around. "Has he left the grounds?"

"No, miss."

"Bevins!"

"I'm sorry, Miss Rhianna."

"Then I'll find him on my own," she exclaimed, and stormed out of the castle.

Outside, she stood shivering in the darkness. And then, suddenly, she knew where he was.

It took her twenty minutes to find her way to the gate in the north wall. She was shivering from the cold by then, but she had come too far to go back for a wrap. A chill mist dampened her hair.

The gate opened on well-oiled hinges, and she closed it carefully behind her. The damp grass muffled her footsteps and soaked her shoes. And then she saw them, a small flock of sheep huddled against a rock. They didn't spare her a glance as she approached. She peered into the darkness, trying to see what held their attention.

At first she saw nothing, and then she saw a bit of white against the dew-damp grass, and above the body of the sheep she saw a pair of eyes. Dark eyes that glittered with an unearthly red glow.

And then a dark shape rose up from behind the carcass.

The wolf had black hair. Blood dripped from its fangs. A low growl rumbled deep in its throat, sending a frisson of terror running down her spine.

Go away! Rayven's voice echoed in her mind. *Go!*

Slowly, she took a step backward, and then another, and another until, driven by a nameless horror, she turned and ran for the safety of the castle.

Bevins was waiting for her at the door. He asked no questions, simply wrapped a warm woolen blanket around her shoulders and led her up to her room. As if she were a child, he helped her out of her clothes and into her nightgown. He brought her a cup of hot tea and sat beside her while she drank it. When the cup was empty, he took it from her hands, then tucked her into bed.

Rising, he extinguished all the candles save one, and then, sitting down in the chair beside the bed, Bevins took her hand in his and settled back to wait out the night.

Chapter Seventeen

Rayven stood at the window in the east tower, staring at the sky. He could sense the dawn approaching, feel the deathlike sleep waiting to overtake him, feel the encroaching darkness that would soon envelop him like a shroud.

He ran his hands over his cloak, felt the material curl more tightly around him, enfolding him like a cocoon spun of silk and velvet.

Rhianna had seen him in wolf form in the field, his hackles raised, his fangs bared and bloody. The image of her horror, her revulsion, had branded itself in his mind so that he saw it every time he closed his eyes.

Well, he mused, turning away from the window, that was that. She would not want to marry him now. No doubt she would leave the castle as soon as she woke, and he would not stop her.

Knowing he would never see her again, he left

the tower and made his way to her chamber.

Bevins rose to his feet as his master stepped into the room.

"How is she?" Rayven asked.

"Sleeping peacefully, my lord."

Rayven nodded. "When she asks to leave here today, I want you to help her pack her things, then take her home, back where she belongs."

"My lord?"

"I was a fool to think there could be anything between us."

"She loves you, my lord, I'm sure of it."

Rayven shook his head. "She has a tender heart. I fear it is only pity she feels for me, and I cannot live with that. I would not have her marry me because she feels sorry for me, because she's afraid of hurting me." He shook his head again. "It's time to move on. I'm leaving here next week."

"Leaving?"

"I've been here too long already. Start packing your things, and mine, too."

"As you wish, my lord, but . . ."

Rayven's head jerked up, his gaze darting toward the window. " 'Tis dawn," he said, his voice tight. "We will discuss it later."

Bevins sighed as he watched his master leave the room. It was a pity that one so horribly cursed should be denied the one thing he yearned for, the one thing that might bring him happiness. And yet, there had been no happiness for his master or himself. Nor, he mused ruefully, were they likely to find any.

"I didn't mean to hurt him."

Bevins whirled around. "I thought you were asleep, miss."

"I felt his presence and I woke up. Why did he . . . The wolf, it was him, wasn't it? He told me he could change into a wolf, but I didn't really believe it."

"Aye, miss, 'tis true enough."

Rhianna sat up and tucked the covers under her arms. "Why did he do it? Kill that sheep, I mean?"

"It's his way when what he is becomes too painful to endure. There was a time when he took his anger out on mortals, but he's not killed anyone since I've been with him."

"I didn't mean to hurt him," Rhianna said again. "I'd forgotten he could read my mind."

"It's natural for you to be repulsed by what he is."

"I suppose so."

"Will you be leaving this morning?"

"I don't know." She stared out the window. The curtains were open, and she could see the beginning of a new day. The sky was pale blue, splashed with vivid hues of gold and pink and crimson.

He hadn't seen the sun in over four hundred years. . . .

"Bevins, I want you to go into town for me. I need some new brushes."

He woke as he always did, coming instantly awake, his senses reaching out to explore the castle. Bevins was in the kitchen preparing dinner. A stew of some kind, heavily flavored with onions and thyme.

Was she gone? Sitting up, he probed for her presence. Her life force beckoned him like a candle shining in the darkness. For a moment, he closed his eyes, his relief at knowing she was still there almost painful in its intensity. Perversely, he wondered why she hadn't left when she'd had the chance.

Rising, he dressed quickly, then hurried down the winding staircase, his passing no more than a blur of movement on the darkened stairway.

When he reached the bottom landing, he paused and took a deep breath.

She was in the dining room.

He took hold of his cloak, rubbing the soft velvet between his thumb and forefinger, wondering how he could face her after last night. She had not yet seen him at his worst, when the blood lust was on him, when his eyes were sunken and burning with need. She had not seen him then, when he looked more monster than man, when his skin was stretched paper thin and the hunger clawed at his vitals, demanding to be fed.

But what she had seen last night was bad enough. With his emotions raw with hurt and longing, he had taken on the wolf form and killed one of the sheep. He had ripped out the animal's throat, hoping to alleviate his frustration in a burst of violence and bloodshed. Until last night, no one, save Bevins, had ever seen him like that.

He took a deep breath, chiding himself for his cowardice. He had to face her sometime.

She looked up as he entered the room. Her smile was forced, and her eyes reflected a myriad of emotions: fear, pity, compassion, anxiety.

"Good evening, my lord," Bevins said, breaking the heavy silence.

Rayven nodded curtly, and Bevins left the room. He returned a few moments later bearing a heavy silver decanter and a crystal goblet.

Rhianna's gaze was drawn to the thick red liquid as Bevins filled the goblet and placed it in front of his master.

Rayven met Rhianna's gaze as he lifted the glass. Slowly, deliberately, he took a long swallow, savoring the thick, slightly salty taste of the warm liquid.

Try as she might, Rhianna could not suppress a shudder of revulsion as he drained the goblet, then placed the glass on the table.

Wordlessly, Bevins lifted the decanter and refilled the goblet.

Rayven lifted his glass, his gaze capturing Rhianna's as he stared at her over the finely cut crystal. "Why are you still here?" he demanded brusquely.

"Because I wish to be here, my lord," she replied, her voice barely audible. "Because you need me."

"I don't need you, or your pity," he said, his voice razor sharp. "I don't need anyone."

"Don't you?"

He lifted the goblet and consumed the contents in one long swallow. "Get out," he said brusquely. "Out of my sight. Out of my house!"

Rhianna stared at him a moment, stunned by the harshness in his voice, by the barely suppressed rage blazing in the ebony depths of his eyes. She didn't stop to wonder if his anger was directed at her or himself. Frightened and confused, she lurched to her feet and ran out of the room.

The sound of her footsteps flying up the stone stairs echoed like thunder in his ears.

"What have I done?" he whispered brokenly. "What have I done?"

"My lord, the wedding is to take place tomorrow night."

Rayven stared into his empty goblet. A few bright drops of liquid clung to the crystal, reminding him of crimson tears. "I cannot marry her," he said heavily. "I cannot let her marry me."

"Her family is coming this evening."

"See that she leaves with them."

"As you wish, my lord."

Slowly, Rayven rose to his feet and walked to the window. Pushing the heavy drapes aside, he peered into the darkness beyond. Never had the night seemed so dark, so empty.

"I cannot go on without her." In response to the grief in his voice, his cloak wrapped more tightly around him, but, for once, the garment's gentle caress failed to soothe him. "Bevins, what am I to do?"

"Survive, my lord, as always."

Slowly, Rayven shook his head. "I cannot." The memory of the one day she had slept at his side rose up to torment him. He remembered how he had awakened, how her face, beautiful in repose, had been the first thing he had seen. He could not abide the thought of never knowing such happiness again.

He whirled around. His cloak swirled around him, then pressed against him once more.

"I cannot," he whispered hoarsely, and fled the room.

Blending into the shadows, he sought shelter in the darkness of the night, and knew he would never find refuge in the shadows again.

Traveling with preternatural speed, he left Millbrae Valley far behind, his destination the city. He prowled the darkness for hours. Wandering through the fog-shrouded streets of London, he tortured himself by watching the couples strolling by. He listened to their laughter, stopped outside a cozy home to watch a mother nurse her babe, watched a father comfort a sobbing child.

Moving on, he saw a young couple embrace in the moonlight. The scent of their blood, their rising passion, teased his senses.

He moved down a quiet residential street, pausing in front of house after house to listen to the conversations of the inhabitants. He listened to children laughing, a husband arguing with his wife about the cost of a new bonnet, heard a mother crooning a lullaby to her newborn daughter.

Mundane sounds.

Ordinary sounds.

Human sounds.

And over all and through all, he saw Rhianna's face, heard the soft music of her voice.

Never before had he yearned for mortality as he did that night. Never had his existence seemed so empty.

He stalked the streets of the East End, his nostrils filling with the scent of humankind—the cloying perfume of a harlot, the stink of unwashed bodies near the wharf, the fragrance of powder and soap and fine tobacco as he returned to the wealthy part of the city.

He stalked Park Lane, hating the wealthy inhabitants who ate and slept in their fancy houses, those members of the ton who spent their days fox hunting and shopping on Bond Street. Despising himself for it, he envied the rich young men who rose early in the morning to go riding in Hyde Park, who went on to spend the afternoon at their clubs, who spent their nights at the opera in the company of other equally rich and spoiled young men and women.

And always the blood called to him, thick and rich and hot with life. But he refused to hunt, refused to give in to the need roaring through him. He welcomed the pain, using it to remind him of what he was, to remind him that he had long ago lost any right to love a mortal woman.

And then he smelled the dawn.

He swore under his breath, cursing his foolishness, the anger that had kept him away from home too long.

The sun chased him through the streets, its heat taunting him, filling with him terror as he contemplated what would happen if he didn't reach shelter before the light found him.

For a moment, he considered surrendering to the dawn. If he couldn't have Rhianna, what point was there in living? But then a bright ray of warm golden light scorched his left cheek, singed the skin of his left hand. The pain, the acrid stench of his own burning flesh, spurred him on.

He felt the searing heat of the sun on his back as he burst through the castle door and slammed it behind him, then raced up the stairs to the east tower.

He was breathing heavily by the time he reached his sanctuary. The left side of his face and the back of his left hand felt as though they were on fire.

Grimacing with pain, he closed the door behind him. And then he saw it—the sun rising over a mountain lake. Bright ribbons of color were splashed against a dawn sky—brilliant shades of orange and ocher and scarlet. The lake, its surface as smooth as a mirror, reflected the colors back to the sky. Flowers blossomed near the edge of the water. Red and yellow, pink and lavender, and pure clean white. A blue bird perched on the limb of a willow tree, its dark eyes so bright they seemed alive.

He stared at the painting, the agony of his seared flesh forgotten. She had given him a sunrise, one he could enjoy without fear.

Rhianna . . . He lifted his hand to his cheek, surprised when his fingertips encountered wetness. He stared at the single red tear on his finger. Rhianna . . .

"My lord?"

Had he conjured her presence with his tears? He covered the left side of his face with his right hand, hid his left hand in the deep folds of his cloak. "Did I not tell you to go?"

"I cannot leave you, my lord," she replied quietly. "I promised to stay with you a year, and you . . ." She moved toward him. "You have promised to marry me."

He whirled around, his hand still covering his face. "Are you mad? Why did you not leave?"

"What has happened to your face?"

"Nothing." He turned his back to her. "Go away, Rhianna."

"I will not leave you."

"Go. Now." His left hand clenched beneath the folds of his cloak. He closed his eyes and took a deep breath. The pain of his wounds increased his hunger. He needed blood to heal, and the blood of sheep would not suffice. *Rhianna*. "Go!"

He flinched at the touch of her hand on his back. He could feel the darkness gathering around him. Soon, he would succumb to the dreamless sleep of the undead.

"You're in pain!" she exclaimed. She pressed her hand against his back. "I can feel it." She took hold of his shoulder, trying to turn him toward her. It was like trying to move a mountain. "What has happened to you?"

"Nothing. Go away, Rhianna. The dawn . . . I must rest."

Determined to find out what was wrong, she moved around to stand in front of him. His eyes burned into hers, but he didn't resist as she drew his hand away from his face.

"Rayven!" One side of his face had been horribly burned. The skin was red and raw and oozing. "What happened?"

He loosed a long sigh that seemed to carry all the sorrow of the world. "I was careless."

"Careless?" She curled her fingers into her palm to keep from touching him.

"I was late getting home. The sun . . ." His words trailed off and he shrugged.

"The sun did this to you?"

He nodded once, wearily.

"What can I do?"

"Leave it alone, Rhianna. It will heal by itself."

"It will?" She looked at him dubiously.

He nodded again. Reaching up, he unfastened his cloak and tossed it on the mattress. "Go away,

Rhianna." He lurched toward the bed, his strength ebbing as the sun rose higher in the sky. He fell back on the mattress and closed his eyes. "Tell Bevins I need him."

"If you tell me what you need, I'll get it for you."

He groaned as if he was in pain, then shook his head. "Get Bevins."

"You need blood, don't you, to help you heal?" She didn't know what made her ask that, but she knew it was true.

"Rhianna . . . please. Get Tom."

It was the first time she had heard him use the other man's first name. Somehow, it made his need seem all the more urgent. He needed blood, and suddenly she needed to give it to him, to be the one who eased his suffering.

Going to the bed, she sat down on the edge of the mattress. Gently, she smoothed a lock of hair away from his brow, then stroked his uninjured cheek.

Rayven's eyelids fluttered open. For a moment, she thought he would send her away and then, with a sigh, he turned on his side and reached for her hand. His movements were sluggish, his eyes heavy-lidded, as he kissed her palm. His lips were cool and dry, sending shivers up her spine as his tongue teased the tender skin of her wrist. He looked up at her, his dark eyes alight with an inner fire, and then he drew her into his arms, arms that held her immobile, arms that were as hard and inescapable as steel bars.

She felt a sudden apprehension as his lips skimmed the length of her neck, shivered uncontrollably as his mouth closed over the tender flesh. There was a sudden, sharp pain, but before she could protest, the hurt was swallowed up in a wave of pleasure that was oddly sensual.

He was drinking her blood. She should have been sickened, shocked, disgusted. Instead, she felt a rush of satisfaction. He was in need, and she was answering that need in the most intimate way possible.

A strange languor settled over her. His mouth was warm, strangely erotic, and she pressed herself against him, wanting to be closer. His tongue stroked her skin, once, twice. She moaned softly as he drew he away.

"Rhianna? Rhianna!" He shook her slightly. "Answer me!"

"Don't stop," she murmured.

Fear for her life dispelled the lethargy that dragged him down toward darkness. With an effort, he sat up, one arm holding Rhianna against him. He stared in horror at the twin marks that marred the perfection of her throat. What had he done?

Bevins! His mind screamed the name.

Moments later, Bevins appeared in the doorway.

"Bring her something to drink. Hurry!"

Bevins left as quickly as he had arrived. Minutes later, he returned carrying a cup of hot tea heavily laced with brandy.

"Rhianna, drink this." Rayven held the delicate china cup to her lips, his brow furrowed as he watched her swallow the contents.

Rhianna gasped as she took a sip of the tea. She had never tasted spirits before, and the brandy burned a bright path down her throat to her stomach.

"All of it," Rayven urged.

Heat suffused her as she obediently drank the rest of it.

Rayven smiled as the color returned to Rhianna's cheeks. "Are you all right?" he asked anxiously.

She hiccupped, then grinned up at him. "What happened?"

"I fear I may have taken more than I should have."

Bevins glared at Rayven, his mild brown eyes glinting with anger as he realized why Rhianna had looked so pale when he first entered the room, why she appeared disoriented and weak.

"You didn't!" Bevins exclaimed. "Tell me you did not use this child to quench your fiendish thirst!"

Rayven looked away, unable to face the censure in his servant's face. For the first time in over four hundred years, he was embarrassed by what he had done.

"Why didn't you call me?" Bevins asked, his voice thick with accusation. He glanced at Rhianna's flushed cheeks. "It's one thing to take a little from time to time. That, I can understand. But this, to use her like one of your blasted sheep . . ."

Rayven's head snapped up, his dark eyes filled with warning. "You will be silent," he said curtly, "or I will silence you forever."

Bevins quickly swallowed the retort that rose to his lips.

"It was my idea," Rhianna said, unnerved by the tension that vibrated like a living entity between the two men. "He told me to call you, but I didn't."

"Look how pale she is." Bevins took a step forward, worry evident in his furrowed brow. "You've taken too much."

Rayven shook his head. He hadn't taken enough to put her in danger. It was just that it was the first time he had taken more than a thimbleful.

Muttering an oath, he fell back on the bed, unable to fight the darkness any longer. "Take care of her . . ." he murmured, and then the blackness claimed him.

Chapter Eighteen

She was asleep at his side when dusk released him from his prison of darkness. Her hair was spread across his pillow, a splash of gold against the black silken case. Her arm rested on his chest, her head was pillowed on his shoulder. One slender leg was nestled between his.

The heat of her smooth sweet flesh against his own, the flowery fragrance of her hair, the scent of her blood, had him awake and aching between one breath and the next.

What was he to do with her? She refused to be intimidated by him, refused to leave when he gave her the chance. Last night, when she should have run screaming from his presence, she had offered him the very essence of her life. No other woman had ever come to him willingly, nor looked on him with love. No other woman had ever looked past the monster to the lonely man who yearned to be free of the darkness that housed him.

Rhianna . . . She had looked into his heart and soul and given him a gift that he could not buy at any price—she had given him the sun he had not dared look upon for four centuries.

Turning his head, Rayven studied the painting. Even in the darkness, he could see it clearly; the warm hues of the sunrise, the azure blue of the lake, the bright bold colors of the flowers, the bird sitting slightly askew on the branch of a tree. So long since he had seen flowers in the clear light of day, a bird, a lake sparkling in the sun. He had seen paintings created by masterful artists, but none more beautiful than this.

Rhianna . . .

He brushed a featherlike kiss across her cheek. She had given him a glimpse of the sun again. If he had any honor at all, he would give her her freedom in return. He would leave her now, while she slept. Leave and never see her again.

But he wouldn't. Couldn't. In four hundred years, she was his one chance for happiness. Tonight she would be his bride. He would coddle her and love her for what was left of their year, and then he would send her back to her own world, where she belonged. His heart, which he had thought as hard as the stone walls of his castle, seemed to crumble at the thought.

With a sleepy sigh, she stirred in his arms, opened her eyes, and smiled up at him. Such beautiful eyes she had, he mused, as blue as a summer sky at midday.

"Good evening, my lord," she murmured. Her sleep-roughened voice caressed him like velvet.

"Good evening, Rhianna."

"Might we have some light?"

With a soft grunt of acquiescence, he fixed his gaze on the bedside candle, which instantly blazed to life. "Is that better?"

"Yes, thank you."

"I never thanked you for the painting."

"Do you like it?"

"Very much." His fingertips stroked the soft curve of her cheek. "Why did you not leave when I told you to go?"

"Because you need me, my lord, no matter how you may wish to deny it."

"And why are you here, beside me?"

"You once said you liked having me here beside you when you woke," she replied candidly. "Should I go?"

"No." His arm tightened around her. "My death-like sleep does not frighten you?"

"A little."

"You are a most amazing child."

"I'm not a child, my lord." Though she supposed, to one of his vast age, she seemed very young indeed. "Your face." She lifted a hand to his cheek, her eyes wide with wonder. His skin, though still red, didn't look nearly as bad as it had the night before. " 'Tis much better."

Rayven glanced at his hand. The awful rawness was gone, though the skin had not completely regenerated. Other injuries healed overnight while he slept, but burns always took longer to heal.

"No doubt I'll frighten your mother even more when she sees my face."

"The wedding!" Rhianna bolted upright. "What time is it?"

"Near six."

"Six. And we're to be wed at seven! Why didn't you wake me sooner!" she exclaimed, and then blushed furiously.

Rayven laughed softly as color flooded her cheeks. "You have not changed your mind, then?"

"No, but I've got to go." She stood up and ran a hand through her hair. "I'll never be ready in time. I've got to bathe, dress, arrange my hair . . ." She bent to brush a kiss over his lips. "I've got to go."

"Take your time, sweet Rhianna. There's never yet been a wedding that wouldn't wait for the bride."

The chapel was located on the far side of the castle. Built of white stone, it shimmered beneath the light of a full moon. An intricately carved wooden cross stood to one side of the arched double doors. Lacy willows whispered secrets to the night, while shadows played hide and seek with the moon.

He stood in the darkness, his gaze fixed on the chapel. He had been inside only once in all the years that the castle had been his.

He whirled around as a familiar scent reached his nostrils. "Madam." He bowed at the waist.

"Is there nothing I can say to persuade you to call off this wedding?"

Rayven shook his head. "Nothing. She will be mine."

"What are you?"

He glanced away, then met her gaze once more. "I love your daughter, Mistress McLeod. I swear I will do her no harm."

"I don't believe you."

He shrugged. "I find your concern well-placed but rather late."

"What do you mean?"

"Have you forgotten her own father sold her to me?"

Hot color surged into Ada McLeod's cheeks. "Of course I've not forgotten!"

"I could keep her with me for the rest of her life," Rayven said quietly. "Do not begrudge me a single year." He lifted his head, his senses testing the breeze. "She's here," he said, and whirling away from Rhianna's mother, he disappeared into the darkness.

He entered the chapel through a side door and took his place at the altar. The light from a dozen tall wax candles filled the edifice with a soft golden glow.

Dallon Montroy stood beside him, his expression solemn. Montroy, who preferred coats in brilliant hues of green and gold, looked almost subdued in a dark blue coat, striped cravat, and buff-colored breeches.

Tom Bevins, looking solemn and quite handsome in a dark brown suit and cravat, sat alone in the front pew on the left. Rhianna's mother sat on the right. Brenna and Bridgitte, clad in gowns of lavender and blue, sat on either side of their mother.

Rayven did not miss the furtive glances that Bevins sent in Ada's direction, or the faint flush that rose in Ada McLeod's cheeks when she caught Bevins looking her way.

The priest took his place at the altar. Moments later, Aileen walked down the aisle, followed by

Lanna. They wore matching pink gowns trimmed with dark velvet ribbons.

And then he saw Rhianna. Aileen's husband, Creighton, walked her down the aisle, but Rayven had eyes only for Rhianna.

She wore a gown of white silk and brocade. The bodice was square cut, the sleeves long and fitted. A gossamer veil covered her face. She looked like an angel, he thought, the very essence of purity and light.

He was aware of Ada McLeod's tears, of the jealousy that radiated from Montroy like waves of heat off hot desert sand. He sensed Bevins's good wishes, the misgivings of the priest.

The small chapel seemed to resonate with the sound of their combined heartbeats, their thoughts clamored inside his head, a chorus of unwanted voices.

Why are you doing this, daughter? Where did I fail?

I love you, Rhianna. I pray you will be happy.

Does she know what she's doing? Is it too late to warn her?

I'll miss you, Rhianna. Please come and see us often.

He felt Ada McLeod's motherly concern, Montroy's broken heart, the priest's anxiety, Bridgitte's sense of loss, Brenna's curiosity as she wondered what had happened to the left side of his face, Aileen's hope that her oldest sister would be happy, Lanna's certainty that all the wealth in the world would not be enough to make her live in Castle Rayven with its dark lord.

He took a deep breath, and his nostrils filled with the scent of the blood flowing in their veins.

But he had fed well this night, and the hunger slept within him.

And then Rhianna was there, at his side, and he blocked everything from his mind but the beauty of the young woman who was about to become his bride. He could hear the excited drumming of her heart as she looked up at him. Her skin was soft and warm, her eyes shining with love as she placed her hand in his.

Together, they turned to face the priest.

The ceremony was brief. He listened to the words that bound them together and thought he had never heard more beautiful words spoken in all his life.

And then it was over, and she was his. He could not stay the trembling of his hands as he lifted the veil from her face. Never, in four hundred years, had he imagined a moment like this. Time lost all meaning as he gazed down at her, imprinting her image deep in his mind and heart so he could recall the quiet beauty of her face and form when she was gone.

"You may kiss the bride," the priest repeated in a loud whisper.

Rayven nodded. And then, with a near-forgotten sense of reverence, he drew Rhianna into his arms and kissed her. *I love you, sweet Rhianna. I swear to love you and care for you so long as you are mine.*

Rhianna looked up at him when he ended the kiss. Had she imagined his voice in her mind?

"I love you, sweet Rhianna," he said quietly. "I swear to love you and care for you so long as you are mine."

He repeated the words with quiet intensity, the

same words she had heard in her mind. Before she could ponder what it meant, her mother and sisters surrounded her.

"Congratulations, my lord," Dallon said, offering Rayven his hand. "I hope you and your bride will be happy together."

"Thank you, Montroy," Rayven replied sincerely. "I know how hard this has been for you."

"Indeed." Montroy glanced over at Rhianna. Never had she looked more beautiful, more innocent. More desirable. "Would you mind if I kissed the bride?"

"It's tradition, I believe."

With a nod, Dallon made his way toward Rhianna. "I wish you every happiness," he said, taking her hands in his.

"Thank you, Dallon."

His gaze held hers. "You are happy then? This is what you want—not what he wants?"

"Believe me, Dallon, it's what I want. I've never been happier."

"Then I'm glad, for your sake." Bending, he kissed her cheek, then whispered, "If you ever need anything, you have only to send word, and I'll be here."

"Thank you, Dallon."

With a nod, he turned away and left the chapel.

Bevins had prepared a late supper for the guests. If anyone thought it odd that the groom didn't eat, no one said anything.

When the meal was over, Aileen insisted on giving Creighton a tour of the castle and urged Rhianna and her mother and sisters to go along, even though they'd already seen it.

With a helpless shrug, Rhianna went with the others.

Alone in the dining room, Rayven sat back in his chair, one hand curled around a crystal goblet. He drained the glass in a single long swallow, refilled it, and drank again.

She was his bride. Soon, he would make her his wife in the most intimate sense of the word. The mere idea frightened him as nothing else had.

He filled the glass a third time, determined to drown the hunger in a river of blood in hopes that his bride would be safe in his arms. "Have I done the right thing, Tom?"

Bevins paused in the doorway. Even after fifty years, it sometimes surprised him that his master could read his thoughts, could sense his presence even before he entered the room.

"My lord?"

"I'm . . ." he took a deep breath as he contemplated the crimson droplets that shimmered in the bottom of the goblet, ". . . afraid."

"She loves you, my lord. She trusts you."

Rayven nodded. "But can I trust myself?"

Bevins crossed the floor. Kneeling before his master, he rolled up his shirtsleeve and extended his arm. "Take what you need, my lord."

Rayven lifted the empty goblet. "This should be sufficient."

"On this night, the blood of sheep may not be strong enough to keep the hunger at bay."

Rayven nodded, silently admitting the truth in his servant's words. And then, humbled by the understanding in Bevins's eyes, ashamed of the need that controlled him, his fingers closed around the other man's wrist.

* * *

"Have they gone?" Rayven stood up as Rhianna entered the study.

"Yes. Why did you not come out and say goodbye?"

He snorted softly, remembering the way Rhianna's mother had looked at him, as if he were a bug that needed squashing. "I doubt I was missed."

"Rayven, what a thing to say!"

"Your mother bears me no love, my sweet, and your sisters look upon me as though I were a cross between an ogre and a warlock. I thought to spare them all my odious presence."

She wanted to argue, but knew it was useless. Her mother had spent the last ten days trying to talk her out of marrying the Lord of Castle Rayven; her sisters had admitted he was quite handsome, but they, too, feared she was making a grave mistake.

"You look wondrous fair, my sweet Rhianna. White suits you, but then, what else would an angel wear?"

"And black suits you," she replied.

She smiled as her gaze moved over him. His black broadcloth coat emphasized the spread of his shoulders; the velvet lapels added a touch of elegance. He wore a black cravat, black trousers, and black boots. The white of his fine linen shirt provided a stark contrast.

"Truly, I have never known so handsome a man in all my life."

He chuckled softly as he swung her into his arms and carried her up the winding staircase to the east tower. "And have you known many men in your short life?"

"No, nor do I desire to do so. You are man enough for me, my lord."

"I am not a man at all," he said quietly, and emphasized that fact by opening the tower door with the power of his mind.

Rhianna placed her hand over his mouth as he carried her into his bedroom, then set her on her feet. "We will not dwell upon that tonight, my lord husband."

She removed her hand from his mouth and replaced it with her lips, kissing him deeply, passionately. She had no need to be cautious now. He was her husband, and she could touch him to her heart's content. To prove it, she pressed herself against him, the silk of her gown whispering against his clothing.

Rayven groaned low in his throat as her tongue skimmed his lower lip, gasped with surprise when she bit him.

"Careful, love," he warned. "You will not like what my blood will do to you."

She leaned back a little so she could see his face. "What will it do?"

"Enough of it will make you as I am, a creature damned for eternity, doomed to live forever in darkness. You do not want that, my sweet."

He did not mention that to make her as he was he would first have to drink from her, take her to the point of death, or that she would then have to drink his accursed blood to return from the abyss of eternity.

"Surely a little would not harm me," she remarked, repulsed yet intrigued by the thought of tasting his immortal blood.

"No." A tremor of excitement tightened his loins as he imagined her teeth at his neck.

"Will you help me out of my gown, my lord?" she asked, her eyes shining with mischief.

"It will be my pleasure."

"I hope so, my lord," she retorted, and turned her back to him so he could unfasten the tiny cloth-covered buttons that began at the neck of her gown and ended just past her waist.

He was surprised to find his fingers trembling as he began the task. He lowered his head, kissing her nape, the shallow vee between her shoulders, as he removed her gown and undergarments until she stood before him wearing only her wedding slippers and stockings.

Dropping to his knees, he removed her slippers, then slid his hands over the curve of her calf. He paused to massage the hollow behind her knee, then his hand moved up the length of her thigh, lingering there a moment before he slowly drew the stocking from her left leg. Then his hands moved to her right leg and began all over again.

Rhianna shivered with pleasure as his hands caressed her calf, her thigh. His hands, though cool, caused her insides to flame with desire.

When he stood up, she began to undress him, her hands eager, curious, as they rid him of his coat, his vest, his cravat and shirt.

She grinned as his breathing increased in tempo with every item of clothing she tossed aside. He was trembling visibly by the time he stood naked before her.

Head tilted to one side, she regarded the man

who was now her husband. He was tall and lean, broad-shouldered and slim-hipped. His skin was the color of pale cream, unblemished, save for the half-healed burns on his left cheek and hand. His legs were long and straight, his stomach ridged with muscle. Her breath caught in her throat, and she felt her cheeks flame, as her gaze skimmed over that part of him that made him a man. For some reason, she hadn't expected him to be so well-endowed.

Rayven basked in the warmth of Rhianna's gaze upon his naked flesh. The touch of her eyes was like fire, chasing away the cold, the darkness. It had been over four hundred years since a woman had looked at him with longing instead of terror. . . .

He glanced at the bed, and into his mind came the image of the last woman he had taken to his bed. Even now, after more than four hundred years, he could see her clearly, her brown eyes open and filled with horror. Her body, drained of blood, had been almost as white as the sheet upon which she lay. The drops of bright red blood that had fallen from his lips had added a garish note of color to the macabre scene.

His desire shriveled at the memory.

"What is it?" Rhianna asked. "What's wrong?"

He looked down at her, his eyes filled with torment and a deep-seated fear. "Rhianna . . . I cannot . . ."

She knew immediately what he was afraid of. Slipping her arms around his neck, she drew his head down and kissed him.

"It will be all right, my lord husband," she murmured. "I'm not afraid."

"Rhianna . . ."

She kissed him again, her hands gliding over broad shoulders, sliding over his chest, each touch a little bolder, until he was on fire for her, until his fear was smothered by the love he felt for this woman who had taken him into her heart, into the very sanctuary of her soul.

He carried her to the bed and placed her reverently upon it. For a timeless moment, he stared down at her, imprinting her image on his mind against the time when she would be gone, and then, gently, he lowered himself over her and sheathed himself within her welcome embrace. She was warm wine and honey in his arms, intoxicating and sweet, and he knew if he lived a thousand years, he would never forget this night.

Rhianna cried his name as all thought, all reason, was swept aside in a whirlpool of sensation. She felt loved, cherished, protected, but it was more than that and she knew—knew—that what she shared with Rayven was far beyond what she would have experienced in the arms of a mortal man.

Love and longing and flesh merged together. She sensed he was holding back, knew he was afraid of hurting her. Closing her eyes, she felt her soul blend with his, and as her passion bloomed, she let her heart speak to his, assuring him of her love, promising that he would never be alone again.

For a moment, she was overwhelmed by feelings she knew were his—fear of causing her pain, the loneliness of four centuries, the constant yearning for that which was forbidden, and then, swept up in an ocean of need, she plunged over the abyss into ecstacy, his name a cry on her lips as she convulsed beneath him.

And then she felt Rayven's body convulse, heard him whisper her name as he buried his face in the hollow of her neck.

Seconds later, she felt the quick sharp bite of his teeth at her throat, felt a wave of heat surge through her that blended with the shudders of pleasure rippling through every fiber of her being. Never had she felt such exquisite rapture. Warmth spread through her. She was drifting, floating in a hazy world of sensation, drowning in a sea of crimson silk . . .

"Rhianna? Rhianna?"

His voice drew her back to reality. She shook her head, wanting to sink deeper into the scarlet cocoon.

"Are you all right?" Rayven asked anxiously. "Did I hurt you? Rhianna? Rhianna, speak to me!"

Slowly, her eyelids fluttered open and she smiled up at him, her blue eyes glowing with pleasure. "I've never been more all right in my whole life, my lord husband."

Weak with relief, he stared at the two tiny puncture wounds in her neck. The hunger had not overpowered him. He had not savaged her throat, or drained her to the point of death. He had taken only a little, a single swallow, no more, and it had been enough. One swallow of her sweet essence had appeased his hellish thirst as completely as loving her had fulfilled his desire.

Relief washed through him. Perhaps there was hope for them after all. Gently, tenderly, he ran his tongue over the tiny wounds in her neck. They would be gone by morning.

Rolling onto his side, he carried Rhianna with him, holding her close. The musky scent of their lovemaking filled the room.

Rhianna sighed with contentment as she made lazy circles on his back. "Tell me what it was like in the beginning," she said, "when you were first made Vampyre."

"I've already told you how I was made."

She shifted in his arms, her bare breasts brushing against his chest. "I want to know more. I want to know everything."

Absently, his hand stroked her hair. "In the beginning, the hunger ruled me. I was terrified of the hunger, of the pain that engulfed me when I abstained. I killed and killed again."

He looked past Rhianna, remembering the beginning as if it had been yesterday, regretting the lives he had taken that he might have spared.

"Once I had been a knight, a man of honor. Now I was nothing but a monster ruled by fear. Each life I took added a burden of guilt to my soul, or what was left of it. I hated what I had become, hated the killing, hated the hunger that was my master. I longed for death, but I was afraid." He laughed softly, bitterly. "I, who had once been a knight without equal, lacked the courage to give myself to the sun and end the hell in which I was living.

"It wasn't until years later, when I met Salvatore, that I learned I didn't have to kill to live, that I could take a mortal's blood without taking his life. Lysandra had never told me that, never taken the time to explain that it wasn't necessary to kill to appease the hunger. But then, she enjoyed the hunt, the smell of fear. The kill."

He felt the old anger rise within him as he spoke her name. She could have told him so much, made his transition from mortal to immortal so much easier to bear.

"I'm glad she made you a vampyre," Rhianna murmured, snuggling closer against him.

"Are you?" he asked, surprise evident in his voice.

"Indeed." Rhianna gazed into his eyes and saw herself reflected in the inky depths. "If she had never made you what you are, you would have died long ago, and I would never have known you."

"I love you, Rhianna," he whispered, his voice raw with emotion. "You will never know how much you mean to me."

"You could show me, my lord husband," she said with a beguiling smile.

His arms tightened around her, as though he feared she might disappear from his sight.

"I shall do my best," he murmured, brushing his lips across hers. "So long as I am able."

Chapter Nineteen

Rhianna woke shortly after four the following afternoon, her lips turning up in a smile as she remembered the night before. Making love to Rayven had been everything, and more, than she had hoped.

Rayven. Her husband. After lighting the candle on the bedside table, she rolled over and felt the smile fade from her lips when she saw him lying beside her.

Hardly breathing, he lay as still as death beneath the blankets. The skin on his left cheek, once ravaged by the faint light of the rising sun, was nearly healed.

She stared at him a long while, a part of her joy diminishing with the full realization of what it meant to be married to a vampyre. They would never get up early in the morning and watch the sunrise together; never linger over a quiet breakfast; never share the joy of watching their children grow. He would never be able to accompany her when she went shopping in the village, or stroll down a fashionable street in the middle of the afternoon.

From this day on, she would have to spend the daylight hours alone, or adjust her days to his.

Leaning forward, she pressed her lips to his cheek. His skin, always cool, seemed more so now.

Drawing away, she glanced at her surroundings. There were no windows in this room, no lights of any kind save for the single candle guttering on her bedside table.

Feeling suddenly trapped, Rhianna slid out of bed and made her way to where she thought the door should be. She ran her hands over the smooth stone, her movements becoming jerky with desperation when she couldn't find the way out. It had to be there! But where? She felt a surge of panic as she realized that she couldn't get out, that even though the chamber held a bed and a table, it was no more than a crypt.

She glanced at Rayven, lying still as death upon black silk sheets.

Vampyre. Undead.

She knew he would never hurt her, knew there was nothing to fear. She reminded herself of how much she loved him, of the ecstasy she had found in his arms the night before, but to no avail. A wild unreasoning panic grasped her firmly in its clutches, and at that moment, she had no thought save to escape.

"Help me!" She pounded her hands on the cold stone wall. "Help me! Bevins, please, let me out!"

The underlying hysteria in her voice, the rapid thudding of her heart, penetrated Rayven's deathlike sleep. Rhianna! She was afraid, in danger . . .

"Rhianna . . ."

She whirled around at the sound of his voice, too frightened to wonder how he could be awake when the sun was up. "I can't get out!"

With an effort, he focused on the faint light of the candle, fighting through layers of darkness toward consciousness. Summoning what energy he could, he focused his mind on the doorway, heard her sigh of relief as the portal slid open, and then she was gone.

For a timeless moment, he stared at the open door and at the empty room beyond. And then the darkness enveloped him once more.

Later, sitting in her room after a hot bath, Rhianna realized how foolish she had been to flee from his presence. The room where he passed the day was only a room, after all.

Feeling sheepish, she slipped into a sleeping gown of pale blue silk, drew on a matching robe, and climbed the stairway to the east tower. She would spend what was left of the day beside him so she would be there when he woke.

She was smiling with anticipation when she entered the outer room, thinking how pleased and surprised he would be to find her there, but the portal that led to the inner chamber was closed.

Crossing the floor, she found the distinguishing mark in the stone and placed her hand on it, but nothing happened. She pushed against it, then knocked softly, hoping he would hear her, and then she called his name.

"Rayven?" She pressed her ear to the stone, but could hear nothing but the sound of her own heartbeat.

Frowning, she called again, and then again. Discouraged, she went to the window and watched as the sun sank from sight in a blaze of crimson. The color reminded her of blood and death, of red wine in a crystal glass. She had married a vampyre. The thought, which should have given her pause, filled her with joy. She was his, truly his, and soon he would rise to be with her again. Anticipation fluttered deep within her heart.

She whirled around when she heard the portal slide open. Rayven appeared in the doorway. He was dressed all in black from his shirt to his boots, and his cloak fell in graceful folds to the floor.

Rhianna smiled when she saw him, her heart skipping a beat as her gaze moved over him. How handsome he was, and how much she loved him!

"Good evening, my lord." She started toward him, then stopped, her smile frozen in place by the icy expression in his eyes.

His gaze swept over her as if she were a stranger. "What are you doing here?"

"I wanted to be with you when you awoke."

He lifted one black brow in a look of clear disbelief. "I find that difficult to believe, madam, considering your eagerness to flee my presence earlier."

Rhianna lifted her chin, determined to make him understand. "It wasn't you I was running from."

"Indeed? Need I remind you there was no one else in the room?"

"It was the room I was running from, my lord, not you."

He regarded her a moment, then glanced over his shoulder into the room behind him.

"What was it that frightened you?" he asked, his voice heavily laced with sarcasm. "The bed? The armoire?" His gaze was hard and cold as it met hers again. "The table, perhaps?"

"It was the room," she repeated. "I felt trapped because I couldn't get out. I couldn't find the door, and there are no windows, and . . . I . . . It was foolish, I know, but I couldn't help it."

He crossed his arms over his chest, his eyes like shards of black glass as he stared at her. When he spoke, his voice flowed over her like a wave of dark, bitter water. "Are you sure it wasn't the corpse on the bed that frightened you, madam?"

She regarded him a moment, dismayed by his anger, and then she realized it wasn't anger he was feeling, but a keen sense of disappointment, and hurt. "Rayven, don't! Please, don't."

"I cannot change what I am, madam, not even for you."

"I'm not asking you to change."

"Look at me, Rhianna. This is what I am."

She wanted to look away, to run from the room, away from the pain she had caused him. Instead, she held her ground and met his gaze.

And he let her see him as he saw himself, a man who lived but did not grow old, who was, and was not. Four hundred years a vampyre, and the hunger was still his master. He had learned to control it, but never to subdue it. He unleashed it now, let it rise up within him until he knew his eyes burned with need. He drew back his lips so that she could see the sharp white fangs he had kept carefully hidden from her view.

It was a sight that had terrified others. It terrified Rhianna, as well. Every instinct she possessed urged her to flee, to run from his presence and his house and never return.

Instead, she clenched her fists at her sides and held her ground, determined to prove that she wasn't afraid of him, to convince him once and for all that she loved him, that it didn't matter what he was so long as he loved her in return.

A strangled sound that might have been a growl or a sob rumbled deep in his throat. He took a determined step toward her, wondering if she would bolt from the room. He saw her eyes widen as he closed the distance between them, sensed her uneasiness. He could hear the frightened pounding of her heart, see the rapid pulse throbbing in the hollow of her throat, but she stood firm. Everything she was feeling mirrored in the clear blue depths of her eyes.

Taking a deep breath, Rayven leashed the ravening beast within him. He had let her see him as he was. Would she leave him now? A part of him, that part that feared for her safety, prayed she would go, even as the more selfish part of his nature hoped she would stay. *You could make her stay.* He dismissed the thought before it was fully formed. He would not keep her against her will.

"Rhianna, will you come to me?"

"Always, my lord," she replied tremulously.

Hardly daring to believe, he held out his arms, and waited.

With more bravery than he thought she possessed, she took the steps that put her within his grasp.

She looked up at him, love and trust shining in her eyes as he drew her into his arms and then, with a sigh that seemed to come from the very depths of her soul, she rested her cheek against his chest and closed her eyes.

"Could we not leave your chamber door open, my lord?" she asked after a time.

Tenderly, he stroked her hair. "If you wish, my sweet. I shall have Bevins install a bolt on both sides of the tower door, and you shall have the only keys. You must promise to lock the door from the outside if you leave the inner chamber during the day."

"As you wish, my lord."

He held her close for endless moments, basking in her nearness, chiding himself for his earlier fit of temper. It had taken years for him to adjust to being Vampyre; he was a fool to think Rhianna could adjust to what he was in a matter of days. And yet they had so little time . . .

He grinned as he heard the faint rumble of her stomach. "Come," he said, taking her hand, "let us go down and see what Bevins had prepared for your supper."

"I *am* hungry," she admitted. "Have you eaten nothing in all these years?"

"Nothing."

"Have you tried?"

He nodded curtly. He had tried, but only once. That had been enough. Soon after he'd been made, before he had fully accepted what he was, he had gone into a tavern and ordered a meal. He had forced it down even though the smell of cooked meat had sickened him. And then he had gone outside and been violently ill. He had not endeavored to eat solid food again.

Rhianna sighed and shrugged. "It doesn't matter."

"Would you prefer to dine alone?"

"No," she said quickly. "Please don't think that. It's just that Bevins is such a good cook, I wish you could enjoy what he prepares."

When they reached the dining room, Rayven held her chair for her, then took his usual place across from her.

A few minutes later, Bevins entered the room bearing a large silver tray that held a covered plate, a decanter, a crystal goblet, a silver teapot, and a delicate china cup. He placed the decanter and goblet in front of Rayven, then served Rhianna's dinner.

"Thank you, Bevins," Rhianna said, smiling at him. "It smells wonderful."

"Thank you, madam."

"Bevins, I want you to install a heavy lock on the tower door, both inside and out, and give the keys to Rhianna."

"Yes, my lord. I'll see to it tomorrow, first thing."

Rayven had expected his bride to make changes in his life, and she did. In the weeks that followed, she transformed the interior of the castle from a dark, dreary place into a home.

The fireplace in his chamber, which had been used but rarely, blazed cheerfully every evening, adding warmth and light to a room that had ever been cold and dark.

She stripped the black canopy and linens from the bed. The new canopy cover was made of dark blue velvet with gold tassels. The new sheets were white linen, the comforter the same dark blue velvet as the canopy.

She brought in a delicate oil lamp made of amber glass and brass so she could read in bed.

She bought a small cherry wood table and two overstuffed chairs covered in a cheery blue print so they could sit in front of the fireplace in the evening.

Gradually, her clothes took up residence beside his in the armoire, her shoes rested beside his, he found gaily colored ribbons and silk stockings mixed in with his gloves and cravats.

His bedchamber, once as cold and barren as the grave, soon became a room vibrant with the life of its mistress.

Sitting before the hearth late one night, waiting for Rhianna to join him, he realized anew how alone, how separate, he had lived from the rest of humanity.

And he wondered how he would ever let her go.

She had voiced a desire to visit London, where she had never been, to stay in one of the plush hotels, to take in a play, to dine in one of the city's fanciest restaurants. And Rayven, finding himself more deeply in love with her with each passing day, never thought to deny her.

Deciding they would make a holiday of it, they packed a small trunk and left the castle two nights later.

She was thrilled by the idea of spending time in London. Rayven had told her she could spend her days shopping, so long as she took Bevins with her, and he had told her she could buy whatever she pleased for herself, for her family.

He really was the most generous of men, she thought as she watched the countryside pass by in a blur of moon-dappled trees and rolling hills. The shelter in the village now housed five women, two infants, a crippled old man, and a homeless ten-year-old boy, providing them with a place to live, clean beds to sleep in, food to eat. Because Rayven had declared that he did not believe in handouts, Rhianna had found ways for those who lived in the shelter to help each other. The women took turns doing the washing and the ironing, the old man looked after the babies when their mothers were busy, and the boy gathered firewood. It was an arrangement that suited everyone.

Pushing thoughts of the shelter aside, she glanced over her shoulder at her husband. He was watching her, a half-smile playing over his lips.

"Why are you looking at me like that?" she asked.

"Like what, my sweet?"

"Like I was a mouse, and you a hungry cat."

"Perhaps because I am hungry, and you look very tasty."

A shiver of anticipation ran down her spine, followed by a little chill of apprehension. "Did you not eat before we left home?"

"A glass of wine."

"It did not satisfy you, my lord?"

Slowly, he shook his head. She could feel his gaze on the pulse throbbing in her throat, felt her heart begin to beat faster as she imagined him bending over her, his teeth grazing her tender flesh.

"Rhianna . . ." His voice was low and raw, and underlying it like a dark shadow, she heard the faintest hint of pain.

"My lord?" She hid her hands in the folds of her skirt to hide their trembling.

His dark gaze met hers. She saw the unspoken question in the depths of his eyes, knew he would not take what she did not offer freely. They had made love often in the two weeks since their marriage, but he had not drunk from her again. Remembering that he had once told her he must occasionally take human blood to survive, she wondered if he had taken nourishment elsewhere. The thought of Rayven turning to another woman to satisfy his need for blood filled her with an odd sort of jealousy. She was his wife, after all. If he needed sustenance, she would give it to him.

She tilted her head to one side, granting him easy access to her throat.

Wordlessly, his fingers closed over her shoulders as he drew her into his embrace. She sighed with delight as his lips teased the sensitive skin along her neck. She closed her eyes as she felt the sharp prick of his fangs, gave herself over to the sensual pleasure that flowed through her at his touch.

Too soon, he drew away, his dark eyes filled with concern. "Rhianna?"

She gazed up at him through eyes hazy with desire. "Surely you can't have taken enough so soon."

"Quite enough." He caressed her cheek, loving her for her willingness to give him that which he needed, despising himself for being at the mercy of what he was, for having to take the very essence of her life to survive. "Rhianna . . ." He wanted to tell her how very precious she was to him, how much her generosity meant to him, but there weren't words enough to convey what he was feeling.

She snuggled against him. "I love you, Rayven," she murmured, and then, with a sigh, she fell asleep in his arms.

He watched her sleep, one hand idly stroking her hair. Never before had he realized the awesome responsibility that came with love.

Rhianna glanced around, unable to believe the splendor of her surroundings. Rayven had taken two adjoining suites in London's finest hotel.

She walked around, admiring the paintings, the plush carpets, the luxurious draperies, while Bevins unpacked their belongings. Rayven sat in a chair, watching her, his mouth turned up in wry amusement.

"You're pleased?" he asked.

"Oh, yes. It's lovely. What shall we do first?"

"Whatever you wish, my sweet."

"Could we go for a walk?

"If you wish." Rising, he settled his cloak on his shoulders, then helped her into her coat. It was new, made of deep rich burgundy velvet trimmed in black fur.

Rhianna glanced in the mirror, smiling at her image. She looked like one of the ton, she mused. No one, seeing her now, would ever guess that she had been born in a small, remote village, or that she was the daughter of a poor farmer who had sold his oldest daughter to provide for the rest of his family.

She was suddenly eager to go shopping, to buy gifts for her mother and sisters. New dresses and hats and perhaps a trinket or two. The only thing that marred her excitement was the fact that Rayven would not be able to go with her.

Standing behind Rhianna, Rayven felt his heart swell with emotions he had not experienced in centuries—love, jealousy, tenderness, an almost overpowering urge to protect her. His hands clenched at his sides with the knowledge that what she most needed protecting from was himself.

"Ready?" She whirled around, her cheeks flushed, her eyes glowing.

With a nod, he offered her his arm and they left the hotel.

They spent the next two hours wandering the streets of the city. Most of the shops in Knightsbridge had closed for the night, so she was surprised when, every time Rayven knocked on a shop door, they were permitted to enter.

"I sent Bevins round earlier to make arrangements," Rayven explained.

She felt like royalty as she moved through some of London's most exclusive shops. She had only to look at something, to wonder what it cost, if her mother would like it, what her sister would think, and it was hers. A brown-and-gold-striped dress for her mother, a hat for Aileen, a lacy parasol for Lanna, a bride doll for Brenna, a darling stuffed animal for Bridgitte.

"But you've bought nothing for yourself," Rayven remarked.

"I have everything I need."

"Then I shall pick something for you," he said, and guiding her into a jewelry shop, he purchased a small gold heart-shaped locket on a fine gold chain.

"It's beautiful," Rhianna exclaimed softly. She turned her back to him while he fastened the chain.

His lips brushed her nape. "It's to remind you that my heart is yours," he murmured. His breath fanned her skin, making her shiver with anticipation of the time when they would be alone again.

Rhianna's fingers brushed the locket. "I should like to have our portrait done to put inside," she remarked as they left the shop.

Rayven was about to refuse outright, but then he saw the eagerness in her eyes. "One day, perhaps."

Bevins was waiting for them when they returned to the hotel.

"My bride has made numerous purchases," Rayven remarked. He helped Rhianna out of her coat and tossed it over a chair, then shrugged off his cloak and laid it across the foot of the bed. "They should be arriving on the morrow."

"Yes, my lord. I'll take care of everything. Will there be anything else?"

"No. You may retire for the night.

"Yes, my lord." With a slight bow in Rhianna's direction, Bevins took his leave.

Rayven moved up behind Rhianna and began to unfasten her gown. She shivered with pleasure as his fingers brushed against her skin.

"You are so beautiful," he murmured, dropping

kisses on her shoulders. Her gown slid to the floor. "So warm. So alive . . ." He caressed her out of her undergarments until she stood naked before him. "I cannot believe you are here, that you are mine."

She turned to face him, her arms twining around his neck as she pressed herself against him. "Believe it, my lord Rayven," she whispered huskily, and covered his mouth with hers.

Rayven's arms circled her waist, drawing her closer, reveling in the warmth of her body, the flowery scent that clung to her skin, the softness of her hair. She pulsed with warmth and life, intoxicating him with her nearness. Her heartbeat increased as he deepened the kiss. The scent of her desire filled his nostrils; he could smell the blood flowing in her veins, hot and sweet.

Her hands trembled with eagerness as she divested him of his clothing until there was nothing between them but desire.

"Rhianna . . ." Just her name, but she heard the words he couldn't say, heard the love in his voice, the need, the fear. Always the fear, she thought, saddened that their love was tainted by it.

With a smile of reassurance, she took him by the hand and led him to the bed. Drawing back the covers, she sat down on the mattress and drew him down beside her.

"Love me, my lord." She caressed his cheek. "I think I shall die if you don't kiss me."

She regretted her choice of words as soon as they left her lips. Though unspoken, she heard Rayven's reply echo in her mind: *And you might die if I do.*

She pressed herself against him, loving the

touch of his bare skin against her own. He fell back on the mattress, carrying her with him, his arms locking around her waist in a desperate embrace, his mouth closing over hers, his tongue teasing hers.

Desire unfurled within her, like a flower opening to the sun. Threading her fingers through his hair, she kissed him with all the love and passion in her heart. Her hands skimmed his body, boldly exploring, learning anew what made him smile, what made him groan with delight.

She gazed into the depths of his eyes, felt the heat of his desire sear a path to the very core of her being. With a low groan, he rolled over, carrying her with him until she lay beneath him.

Eyes blazing with a clear black flame, he buried himself deep within her. The world seemed to tilt as their bodies merged. His hands caressed her, igniting fires of pleasure where they touched. He whispered her name, his voice rough.

She cried out as she was swept into a maelstrom of sensations—the cool sheets beneath her, the heat of Rayven's kisses, the smoothness of his skin, the fire in his touch, the husky sound of his voice as he whispered to her in a language she did not understand. And always she had the feeling that he was holding back, that he was afraid to let go for fear of hurting her.

She called his name as the waves of ecstacy crested in an explosion of heat and color, closed her eyes as rivers of pleasure rippled through her.

She felt Rayven's teeth at her throat, felt him convulse one last time. Joy rose up within her as shudders of delight wracked his body. He sighed deeply, and she felt the tension drain out of him.

"Did I hurt you?" he asked gruffly.

"No, my lord." She forced him to look at her. "I love you, Rayven. Please don't let your fear of what might happen ruin what we have."

"Rhianna, you don't understand . . ." How could he tell her how it was, how closely the lust for blood was tied up with his desire, that he would never be free of the fear that plagued him, that he would ever be afraid that the hunger would overpower his self-control, that one night his control would shatter and he would drink and drink until he had destroyed her.

"I love you with all my heart and soul," she said again, more forcefully this time. "Please believe that."

He rose up on his elbows and stared down at her. Was it possible that his love for her was stronger than the hunger, that his love for Rhianna would protect her from the blood lust? Maybe she was right, he mused. One small sip of her precious blood quieted the hunger stirred by his desire.

"I'm not afraid of what you are, my lord. I believe in the power of our love, but you have to believe, too."

Her words soothed his troubled soul as nothing else could. Rolling onto his side, he cradled her in his arms and held her tight.

"I pray you are right, beloved," he murmured.

"I know I am. I love you."

"And I love you." He pulled his cloak over the two of them, then drew her into his arms once more.

It had been centuries since he had dared to

pray, but now he closed his eyes and beseeched the God of his youth to protect the woman who rested so trustingly in his arms, even if it meant protecting her from himself.

Chapter Twenty

They had been in London for almost two weeks the night Rayven rented a carriage and they went for a drive through Hyde Park, down Rotten Row. It had once been known as the *route du roi,* Rayven informed her. The king's path. The park had once been owned by Westminster Abbey, he added, but Henry VIII had closed it off, stocked it with deer, and kept it as a royal chase. Charles I had opened it to the people in 1635.

Rhianna nodded as she gazed at the vast green expanse. Rayven had been alive during the reign of Henry VIII. He had been alive when Charles I opened Hyde Park.

"Rhianna. Rhianna?"

"Hmmm?"

"Would you like to go to supper?"

"What?"

Rayven cocked his head to one side. "You seem

far away, my sweet. Is something wrong?"

"No, no, nothing's wrong."

Unable to resist, Rayven let his mind touch hers. He drew in a sharp breath as he followed the path of her thoughts, wondering if she would ever fully accept him for what he was.

"Does what I am bother you so much?" he asked quietly.

"Bother me?" She shook her head. "No, my lord. It's just so hard to comprehend. It's astonishing to realize just how long you've lived, how much you've seen."

Rayven nodded. Kings and queens had come and gone, yet he remained.

"What did you ask me before?"

"I wondered if you were hungry."

"Yes, a little."

He took her to dinner at The King's Arms. It was an elegant restaurant, the finest she had ever seen. The tables were covered with fine white linen cloths and matching napkins. Sparkling crystal glassware and gleaming silver added to the opulence of the setting. Dark red velvet drapes hung at the windows; the chairs were covered in the same rich fabric.

As she glanced around the room at the equally elegant men and women who occupied the surrounding tables, Rhianna wondered what her mother would think if she could see her now.

Sitting there, waiting to be served, she was aware of Rayven's dark-eyed gaze moving over her. Feeling self-conscious, she ran her hand over her hair, then fingered the gold locket at her throat. "Is something wrong?"

"No." He shook his head, thinking how lovely

she was. The mauve gown she wore complemented the color of her hair and skin. The room was filled with fashionably dressed women, yet she put them all to shame.

"You're staring at me."

The corner of his mouth crooked up in a smile as he leaned across the table. "I fear I cannot help it. You are the most ravishing woman in the room."

A faint flush crept into her cheeks. "Thank you."

He lifted her hand, his lips brushing her fingertips, and wondered how he had survived four centuries without her. She smiled, and he no longer missed the sun. She laughed, and he forgot the loneliness that had been his constant companion. She touched him, and stilled the hunger that had tormented him for so long he could scarce remember a time when it did not. Rhianna.

He had never been more conscious of time passing than he was now. Each day brought him closer to losing her, closer to the time when he would go back to his empty life, his empty bed.

And yet, even as each day made their future separation more painful, he knew he had to let her go. It would be cruel to subject her to a life with him. Already, she was changing her ways to his. She stayed up until dawn so that she could be with him until the deathlike sleep claimed him. Once an early riser, she slept later each day, losing precious hours of daylight. He did not want to subject her to a life spent in darkness. He did not want to rob her of the beauty of the daylight world. She loved the sunshine, the flowers. There was no sun in the darkness of his world; the brilliantly hued blossoms she loved faded to gray in the light of the moon.

Rhianna ordered dinner; he ordered a glass of red wine.

She had just finished dinner when Rayven heard a familiar voice. Looking up, he saw Dallon Montroy making his way toward their table.

"Rayven," the viscount said, inclining his head.

"Montroy."

"Rhianna." Dallon took the hand she offered and brushed his lips across her knuckles.

"How are you, Dallon?" she asked, smiling up at him. As always, he was dressed to the nines, from his smartly cut redingote with its black velvet collar to his gray-and-black-striped trousers.

"Quite well, thank you. No need to ask how you are," Dallon said, his gaze moving over her appreciatively. "It seems married life agrees with you. And you," he said, glancing at Rayven. "Mind if I join you?"

"Of course not," Rhianna said.

Montroy sat down in the booth beside Rayven. "What brings the two of you to London?"

"Shopping," Rhianna said with a grin. "I fear Lord Rayven will be a pauper by the time we return home."

"No fear of that," Dallon said, chuckling softly. "I daresay he could afford to buy out half the shops in the city. Isn't that right, my lord?"

Rayven grunted softly. "Perhaps."

"What brings you to London?" Rhianna asked.

"Business," Montroy replied with a grimace. "Fortunately, it will be concluded quickly. I'm planning to go to the theater later. If you're not busy, you're welcome to join me in my box."

Rhianna looked inquiringly at Rayven.

"Whatever you wish, my sweet," he replied coolly.

"I think not," Rhianna said, "but thank you for the invitation."

Dallon nodded, all too aware of Rayven's jealousy. He was about to take his leave when the strains of a waltz filled the room. Feeling suddenly reckless, and a little curious to see if he could prick Rayven's eternally cool demeanor, he said, "With your permission, Rayven, I should like to dance with Rhianna."

A muscle ticked in Rayven's jaw as he fought to keep hold of his temper. "Perhaps you should ask her."

Rhianna looked at her husband. Tension hummed between the two men like a wire drawn taut. "My lord?"

"It's up to you, my sweet," Rayven said.

"I should like very much to dance, if you don't mind."

With a curt nod, Rayven gave his consent. He did not want her dancing with anyone else, especially Montroy, but he couldn't dance with her himself, not here, where the small dance floor was lined with gilt-edged mirrors from floor to ceiling.

Montroy rose smoothly to his feet and offered Rhianna his arm. With a half-smile at Rayven, she stood up and placed her hand on Dallon's arm.

Hands clenched into tight fists, Rayven watched them wend their way toward the dance floor. Jealousy made a hard, ugly knot in his belly as he watched Montroy twirl Rhianna around the floor. Rhianna's skirts swirled around her ankles; the lamplight streaked her hair with gold. How well they looked together, two mortals in the prime of life, their skin glowing with good health, young hearts beating fast as they whirled around the room. He didn't miss the admiration in the viscount's eyes, or the way the man smiled at Rhianna.

He's in love with her, Rayven thought. The knowledge filled him with the urge to kill, to rip out Montroy's heart and grind it into the dust.

He took a deep breath, his hands clenching and unclenching, as he watched them walk back to the table. Rhianna's cheeks were rosy, her eyes shining, as she took her seat across from him.

Schooling his features into an impassive mask, Rayven lifted his wineglass and drained it in a single swallow.

"Thank you, Dallon," Rhianna said.

She smiled at Montroy, and Rayven was consumed with the urge to strike out at the other man, to grab Rhianna by the arm and shout to the world that she belonged to him.

"I should be going," Dallon said. He kissed Rhianna's hand, then sketched a bow in Rayven's direction. "Good evening, my lord."

"Montroy."

Dallon felt himself go suddenly cold, as if ice had formed on his spine, as his gaze met Rayven's. For a moment, he couldn't move, couldn't breathe, could scarcely think.

Then Rayven looked away, and the world was set to rights again.

Dallon shook his head, wondering if he had imagined the coldness, the unspoken warning he had read in Rayven's devil-black eyes.

"Good night," he said again. Turning on his

heel, he stifled the urge to bolt from the room.

"Did you enjoy your dance?" Rayven asked.

"Yes, very much," Rhianna replied, "though I would rather have danced with you."

"Another time," he said. "Are you ready to go?"

Rhianna nodded, perplexed by his clipped tone, his curt manner. Surely he could not be angry with her because she had danced one dance with Dallon.

Bevins was waiting outside with the carriage. He took one look at Rayven's face and quickly opened the carriage door. He felt a rush of compassion for Rhianna as he handed her into the coach, nodded at Rayven, then closed the door behind them.

They rode in silence back to the hotel. Rhianna stared out the window of the carriage, wondering what she had done to make her husband so angry with her.

"He's in love with you."

"What? Who?"

"Montroy."

"That's absurd. He doesn't know anything about me."

"Love isn't based on knowledge," Rayven replied quietly. "If it was, you would not be sitting here with me."

Rhianna turned to face him. Even in the dim light, he could read her expression clearly. Her eyes were filled with confusion and compassion. How foolish she was, to think she knew him because he had told her a little of his life, because they had made love. He had done things of which he was ashamed, things for which his soul would be forever damned.

His gaze moved over her, his heart aching at the vast gulf that yawned between them. She had no concept of evil. If she did, she would have run screaming from his presence before she ever let him touch her that first time. She was the epitome of innocence, of goodness.

Filled with self-revulsion, he curled his hands into tight fists. He should never have defiled her with his touch, never should have interfered in her life.

Rhianna reached for his hand and squeezed it. "I'm sorry, my lord husband."

Rayven frowned. "For what?"

"For whatever I've done to upset you so."

"You've done nothing amiss, Rhianna."

"What's wrong then? Won't you tell me?"

He gazed deep into her eyes, felt the love he saw reflected in their clear blue depths soothe his anger, his doubts. She was his. For one year. And already more than three months had gone by. Never before had time passed so quickly.

"Tell me," he urged softly. "Tell me that you love me."

She moved closer to him, her arms wrapping around his waist as she gazed up at him. "I love you," she said fervently. "Never doubt it, my lord. I love you more than I ever thought possible."

With a wordless cry, he crushed her to his chest, his mouth closing over hers in a fierce passionate kiss that left her lips bruised. His tongue plundered the depths of her mouth, his hands stroked her hair, caressed her thighs, lingered over the sweetly rounded curve of her breast.

"Mine," he whispered hoarsely. "Tell me that you're mine."

"You know I am," she replied, hardly able to speak for the rapid beating of her heart. "Rayven, please, tell me what's troubling you."

"Not now." He bent her backward on the seat, his hands delving under her skirts, lifting her petticoats, parting her drawers.

"My lord . . . Rayven . . ." She gasped as his fingertips slid over the sensitive flesh along her inner thigh. "The hotel . . . We'll be there soon."

"Don't make me wait, Rhianna. I need you. Now." He drew back, his dark eyes seeking hers, waiting for her to refuse him.

In answer, she drew his head toward hers and kissed him. She didn't know what demons were driving him; she only knew she could not refuse him.

He fumbled with his trousers, and then he was on top of her, his weight resting on his elbows as he plunged deep within her. His breath fanned her face, his tongue swept into her mouth, branding her as his.

It was quick and fierce. She cried out once and then clutched his shoulders as pleasure washed over her. His hands and lips were like lightning, burning hot wherever they touched, until the storm he had unleased within her culminated in a crash of thunder that left her breathless.

He rode the storm with her, his lips worshiping her, his voice filled with adoration as he whispered his love. She felt the sharp prick of his teeth at her neck, the sudden sensual sweetness that exploded within her as he shuddered convulsively, then lay still, his breathing harsh and uneven against the curve of her throat.

Feeling replete, her heart swelling with tenderness, she stroked his hair. It was soft and silky. She felt him tremble as her hands caressed his nape, heard him mutter something unintelligible under his breath as he sat up.

He fastened his trousers, then rearranged her undergarments, quickly and efficiently, as if he did such a thing every day.

"I'm sorry," he said gruffly. "Forgive me."

"There's nothing to forgive."

"I took you like a rutting stag."

Sitting up, she smoothed her skirts. "I'm sorry you did not find it pleasurable, my lord husband."

He stared at her. "And you did?"

Rhianna nodded. She glanced out the window, surprised to find they were on a country road. "Where are we?"

"Outside the city."

"But . . ." She felt a rush of color wash into her cheeks. "How did Bevins know . . ."

"I spoke to his mind, my sweet, and told him we wished to take the long way home."

"Oh." Her cheeks burned hotter with the knowledge that Bevins knew what they had done.

A smile played over Rayven's lips as he rapped on the roof of the carriage. Moments later, the coach swung around, heading back to London.

Rayven put his arm around Rhianna's shoulders, and she snuggled against him, warm and trusting as a child. Moments later, she was asleep.

When they reached the hotel, he carried her to their suite. She murmured something unintelligible but didn't waken as he undressed her and put her to bed.

For a moment, he stood watching her sleep, noting the thickness of her lashes, the soft sensuality of her mouth, the golden halo of her hair.

He undressed, intending to join her in bed; then, reluctant to retire when it was so close to dawn, he went to the window and stared into the night. Once, the darkness had been his only companion. He had welcomed it, knowing it hid his ugliness from the world. And then Rhianna had come into his life, chasing away the darkness, the loneliness, making him wish for a way of life that was forever lost to him, stolen from him centuries ago.

Closing his eyes, he pressed his forehead against the cool glass and imagined what it would be like if he were a mortal man again. In his mind's eye, he saw himself walking hand-in-hand in the sunlight with Rhianna, saw her nursing a fair-haired infant, saw himself surrounded by children.

A fierce ache tore at his heart as he turned away from the window and slammed his hand against a table. The wood shattered beneath the force of the blow. A splinter an inch thick pierced his palm.

"Rayven!" Rhianna sat up in bed, the covers clutched to her breast as she peered into the darkness. "Rayven!"

"I'm here," he replied. "Go back to sleep."

"What was that noise?"

"Nothing."

She lit the lamp, then slid out of bed and hurried to his side. She frowned at the taut line of his jaw, then gasped when she saw the sliver of wood embedded in his flesh.

"What happened?" She stared up at him, waiting for an explanation.

He shook his head, not wanting to explain, not certain he could explain.

"Here, let me help you," she said, reaching for his hand.

"No!" Muttering an oath, he jerked the splinter from his flesh. Dark red blood flowed freely from the wound to pool in his palm.

Cursed blood. Unholy blood.

Not knowing what possessed him to do such a thing, he cupped his hand and drank the blood from his palm, feeling a perverse pleasure at the look of horror that spread across her face.

Rhianna took a step back, her gaze searching his. He was trying to shock her, to frighten her. Why?

Turning away, she went to the commode and soaked a cloth in water, then carried it back to him. Wordlessly, she took his injured hand in hers and pressed the cold cloth to his palm, holding it in place between her hands.

"Won't you tell me what happened?" she asked quietly.

He felt his gaze drawn to hers, felt the anger drain out of him, vanquished by the love shining in her eyes.

"I was wishing," he said gruffly, "wishing for things that can never be." He lifted his other hand to her cheek, his knuckles running back and forth over her soft flesh. "Wishing that I could spend my days at your side, that I could give you . . ." He took a deep breath. "Wishing I could give you a son."

"Oh, Rayven," she murmured, "It's what I wish for, too."

Slowly, he shook his head. "It will never happen, Rhianna. I cannot father a child."

"Why not?" she asked, perplexed. "You're able to . . ." A faint flush tinged her cheeks. "You know."

"You still don't understand, do you, my sweet?" He shook his head. "The dead cannot create life."

She looked up at him, saddened by the bitter sorrow in the depths of his eyes. Certain no words could comfort him, she led him back to bed, drew him into her arms, and held him close until the dawn took him away.

She didn't go out at all that day. Shopping held no appeal, nor did the thought of mingling with other people. She had always taken her life for granted, assumed she would marry and have children, watch her children grow up and have children of their own. She would watch the seasons change, count the passing years, until her life ended.

What was it like for Rayven, to remain forever the same while all around him the world changed, people changed? What would he do when Bevins was gone? Who would look after him? Who would guard his lair while he slept his deathlike sleep? He had said he would soon have to leave the valley, that he had already stayed too long. What was it like for him, to watch others grow old and die, to know he dared not stay too long in any one place lest people notice he never changed, that the passing years had no claim on him?

She knew without doubt that the people in the valley would destroy Rayven if they knew what he was. Vampyre. Undead. He was supposed to be a monster, yet he had treated her with naught but kindness. At her urging, he had provided a shelter for the poor and the homeless, insisting she tell no one what he had done. He could have preyed upon the villagers without mercy, taking what he needed to survive, yet he existed on the blood of sheep mixed with wine, taking human blood only when necessary, and then only in small amounts.

She should have been afraid of him, appalled at what he was, yet she felt only pity and compassion, and an overwhelming feeling of love that defied logic or reason. She loved him and she wanted to spend the rest of her life with him.

She spent the day in their room, watching him sleep, thinking how beautiful he was until, needing to touch him, she stretched out beside him on the bed, her head pillowed on his shoulder.

Rayven woke at dusk to find Rhianna asleep in his arms. It still surprised him to wake and find her there, especially after what had happened the night before. For centuries, there had been no one beside him when he aroused from his deathlike sleep. No one in his bed. No one of importance in his life save Bevins. And then he had purchased a dirty-faced girl from her father, and his whole world had changed. He had brought other girls to the castle. None stood out in his mind. They had become a faceless blur in his memory. They had stirred nothing within him—not affection, and certainly not love. They had made no changes in his life, held no interest for him other than the sustenance they had unknowingly provided.

Rhianna. She had not been the first girl he had brought to his castle, but he knew she would be the last.

Chapter Twenty-one

Rhianna walked slowly down the street, lost in thought.

In the past three weeks, Bevins had taken her on several sightseeing tours. They had gone to Madame Tussaud's Wax Museum. Rhianna had been surprised to learn that the museum had been founded in 1776. She had been fascinated by the lifelike wax figures of the famous and the infamous, repulsed by the Chamber of Horrors that depicted gruesome scenes from the Battle of Trafalgar.

Bevins had taken her to see St. Paul's Cathedral, which was over a hundred years old. The dome had been breathtaking, the nave a thing of exquisite beauty.

She had stared in wonder at Westminster Abbey. It was there, in that magnificent edifice, that all the kings and queens of England had been crowned.

They had gone to see the Tower of London, where two of Henry VIII's wives had been executed, as well as Sir Thomas More and William Penn. Rhianna had shivered as she imagined being imprisoned in the Tower of London to await her execution. She had imagined the fear of kneeling on the gallows, of waiting for the ax to fall.

They had walked through the Traitor's Gate, seen the Bloody Tower and the Wakefield Tower.

They had toured Trafalgar Square, watched the changing of the guard at Buckingham Palace, and all the while she had wished it was Rayven walking beside her, showing her the sights.

London was an amazing city, so different from the quiet village where she had spent most of her life. So filled with activity and noise—the incessant sound of wheels and horses' hooves making their way over the pavement, the bell of the muffin man, the cries of street peddlars who sold everything from eggs to knives, dolls, rat poison and books. Street urchins were everywhere, carrying packages, holding horses for finely clad gentlemen, fetching cabs, or doing cartwheels in the street in hopes of earning a ha'penny.

Now she paused to peer into one of the shop windows. It seemed strange to be out on her own, without Bevins hovering in the background. He had gone off on an errand of some kind, and she had grabbed at the chance to go out alone. No doubt Bevins would be angry with her when she got back to the hotel, but she hadn't gone far and wouldn't be gone long.

She tilted her head to one side, admiring one of the bonnets displayed in the window of the millinery shop. It was a darling little thing, a confection of natural straw, colorful flowers, and lavender ribbons. She didn't need another hat; she had bought several in the last few weeks. But she wanted this one, and there was no reason why she shouldn't have it. Rayven had given her carte blanche to buy whatever she wished.

She was about to enter the shop when she saw Dallon Montroy striding down the street toward her. Women on both sides of the street paused to look at him as he passed by, and she couldn't blame them. Old or young, they turned to watch him as he walked toward her. He cut quite a dashing figure in his hunter-green coat, mustard waistcoat, and buff-colored breeches. The sun gilded his hair, making him look very much like the prince Bridgitte had once thought him to be.

"Rhianna!" he exclaimed, catching both her hands in his. "How nice to see you. And how very pretty you look." He smiled at her, his eyes twinkling. "That's a most fetching gown."

She flushed with pleasure as his gaze moved over her in a boldly admiring glance. "Thank you, Dallon. It's good to see you, too."

He nodded toward the shop window. "See something you like?"

Rhianna nodded. "That one," she said, pointing. "The straw one with the ribbons and flowers. It's darling."

"Then you should have it." He smiled at her as he offered her his arm.

"I really don't need another bonnet," she said, but she didn't argue as he led her into the shop.

Dallon plucked the bonnet from the window, then stood to one side, his arms crossed over his chest, while she tried it on.

The shopkeeper, a rather buxom woman with curly gray hair, beamed at the prospect of a sale as Rhianna admired herself in the mirror.

"It's perfect, madam. Imported from France." The shopkeeper slid a glance at Dallon, and Rhianna knew the woman thought he was her husband. "It suits the lady well, don't you think so, my lord?"

"Indeed," Dallon said. "We'll take it."

Rhianna met his gaze in the mirror, and shook her head. "No, Dallon."

"I want to," he said, and ignoring her protests, he paid for the hat, insisting she wear it.

Feeling lighthearted, Rhianna tied the ribbons under her chin.

"Come," Dallon said, taking her by the arm, "let's go have tea so everyone can see how pretty you look in your new chapeau."

Rhianna shook her head. "I'd like to, really, but I can't."

"Of course you can."

"I need to get back." She glanced at the setting sun. Rayven would be waking soon. He would expect her to be there. "Rayven will be . . ."

"Rayven will be what?"

"Waiting for me."

"Let him wait, Rhianna. A little jealousy is good for a man."

"Is it?" she asked dubiously.

"One cup of tea," he urged. "What can it hurt?"

"I can't, Dallon. Please, I must go."

"What's he done to you, Rhianna?" Montroy

asked, his voice sharp with concern. "You're his wife, not his slave. You're entitled to a life of your own, friends of your own."

"You don't understand . . ."

"I had hoped to be more than your friend, Rhianna," Dallon said quietly. "But that's not possible now."

"Dallon, you mustn't say these things to me. It isn't proper."

"I know, and I'm sorry. But I can't help the way I feel." He took her hand in his, his thumb sliding back and forth across her knuckles. "Please don't deny me the pleasure of a few minutes of your company."

She knew she should refuse, knew Rayven would be angry if he found out, but she couldn't ignore the gentle pleading in Montroy's eyes, or rebuff his offer of friendship.

"Very well," she said. "But I must be back at the hotel before dark."

"You will be. I promise," Dallon said.

They spent a pleasant hour talking about trivial things. She told Dallon about her tour of the city; he told her about the new carriage he had purchased, together with a pair of high-stepping matched grays to pull it.

Feeling relaxed and at ease in his presence, Rhianna forgot about the time until she realized the sun had set.

"I'll be late!" she exclaimed.

"I'll walk you back to the hotel."

"No! Good-bye, Dallon. Thank you for the hat, and the tea." Jumping to her feet, she grabbed her reticule and ran out of the café.

Her heart was pounding, her brow sheened

with perspiration, when she reached the hotel. Forcing herself to take a deep calming breath, she opened the door to their bedroom and stepped inside.

Rayven was standing at the window, looking out. He turned around as she closed the door. His dark gaze swept over her from head to heel.

"I'm sorry I'm late," Rhianna said. Tossing her handbag on a chair, she smoothed her skirts, removed her gloves. "Where's Bevins? I should like to order supper."

"I've ordered for you."

"Oh?" She clasped her hands to still their trembling. "Thank you."

"Where have you been?"

"Shopping. I . . . I got a new hat. Do you like it?"

He nodded, his dark stare fixed upon her face.

"I think I'll freshen up."

"You cannot wash away your lies, Rhianna."

She swallowed hard, her fingers worrying the folds of her skirt. "Lies, my lord?"

"You've been with Montroy again."

There was no point in denying it. "Yes. We took tea together."

"Where?"

He was watching her intently, his dark eyes unblinking. His very stillness intimidated her.

"In a little tearoom just down the street. Across from the millinery shop."

His eyes narrowed ominously as he crossed the room, and then he was standing in front of her, so close she could feel the heat of his breath upon her face. "Did he buy you the hat?"

She swallowed against the fear congealing in her throat. "Wh . . . why do you ask?"

"His scent is on the bonnet, on your hands. Did he buy it for you, Rhianna?"

"He saw me admiring it in the window and bought it for me. I didn't want him to, but he insisted."

A muscle clenched in his jaw. She had spent time with Montroy. Alone.

"Nothing happened," Rhianna said. She laid a placating hand on his arm. "We had tea, that's all. I'm sorry I wasn't here when you woke. Please forgive me."

He turned away from her, not wanting her to see the jealousy that was eating at his soul. "There's nothing to forgive. You're not a prisoner here, Rhianna. It's unfair of me to expect you to lock yourself in this room until nightfall."

"Oh, Rayven." She closed the distance between them. Slipping her arms around his waist, she laid her cheek against his back, wishing she could ease the hurt she had caused.

"I'm sorry," he said stiffly.

"You've nothing to be sorry for."

"I want to kill him," he said gruffly. "I'm jealous of every hour, every minute, you spend with anyone else."

"There's nothing for you to be jealous of. Dallon is just a friend, nothing more. That's all he'll ever be."

"I know." Rayven took a deep breath and released it in a long, slow sigh. "I've never been in love before," he said, as if confessing a guilty secret. "I look at Montroy and see what I might have been had I not lusted after Lysandra. What's the good of living four hundred years if one has to live alone?"

One of his hands covered hers, his thumb tracing aimless patterns across the back of her hand. "When I was young, I had dreams of glory. I was the finest knight of the realm. I had a name men respected and feared. I had lands and riches, my pick of desirable women. I could have had a good life, a wife, children. But I threw it all away to chase a woman who looked like an angel and turned out to be the spawn of the devil."

"I'm sorry, Rayven, so sorry." She kissed the faint hollow between his shoulder blades. "But I said it before, and I'll say it again. I'm glad you're a vampyre. If you'd never met Lysandra, you would have died hundreds of years ago, and I would never have met you."

She walked around to stand in front of him. "I love you, my lord husband," she said fervently. "I'm glad you bought me from my father. You've given me a wonderful education, provided for my mother and sisters far better than my father was able. I love you," she said again. "No one but you."

With a sigh, he drew her into his arms and held her close. "You have no idea how much you mean to me, Rhianna," he murmured, "and I fear there aren't words enough to tell you. Forgive me for my jealousy. I have no excuse except that I've never loved anyone before."

She stood on tiptoe, wanting to kiss him, to reassure him, only to draw back as there was a knock at the door.

"Your supper is here," Rayven said.

"I'll get it." She pressed a quick kiss to his cheek, then went to open the door.

A young man dressed in hotel livery handed her

a covered tray. "Will there be anything else, madam?"

"No, thank you." Closing the door, she carried the tray to the table. "Will you sit with me while I eat?"

With a nod, Rayven crossed the floor and sat down opposite her.

"You never told me where Bevins is."

"He asked for the night off."

"Oh?" She lifted the tray, and the aroma of roast mutton and potatoes filled the room.

"Rhianna."

She looked up, her smile fading. "What?"

He looked at her a long moment, then slowly shook his head. "You make me ashamed of what I am."

"Ashamed? Why?"

He shook his head. How could he explain it to her when he didn't understand it himself? He had thought himself long since resigned to what he was. He forced himself to drink the blood of sheep when it gave him no pleasure, denying what he craved, denying what he was. He shut himself up in Castle Rayven, or in one of his other holdings, keeping out of the way of mortals, protecting them even as he shut himself up in a prison of his own making. He had been proud of himself for learning to control the fierce hunger that drove him, pleased that he no longer had to kill to feed, that he had found a measure of peace within himself.

And then he had bought Rhianna and realized anew how vast was the gulf between himself and the rest of the world. Her goodness and light emphasized the darkness that dwelled within him.

And he was ashamed of the lives he had taken, the blood he had spilled, the evil that slept restlessly within him, under control but never completely vanquished. He still could not believe that she loved him, knew he was unworthy of her affection.

Just this one year. Please, just let me have this one year, and then I'll let her go.

"Rayven, talk to me."

"There's nothing to talk about."

"You're brooding again, worrying about me, about us, aren't you?"

"I think you begin to know me too well."

"Has there been no happiness in your life these past four centuries?"

He sat back, his expression thoughtful, and then he nodded. "Of course."

"Tell me about those times."

With a sigh, he began to tell her of his past.

In the beginning, after he had learned to control the hunger, when he had come to terms with what he was, he had traveled the world. The jungles of Africa, the wonders of Egypt. He had toured France and Spain and Greece, spent a year in South America wandering through the ruins of an ancient culture. During that long-ago time, he had learned to read and gained an appreciation for the written word.

He had learned to appreciate fine art, had developed a love for music, for the theater. He had courted many beautiful women, though he had allowed none to get close to him. And when he tired of being a vagabond, he had come back here, to the land of his birth, to the place where, one fateful night, his life had been changed forever.

He had been Vampyre for a hundred years when he'd bought the castle at the top of Devil Tree Mountain and withdrawn from the rest of the world. And every twenty or thirty years thereafter, when people began to wonder about him, he had taken his leave. But he always returned to this place.

Rhianna sat back, sighing. "You've seen so much," she murmured. "Done so much." She shook her head. "I should think you would be glad for the opportunities you've had."

He grunted softly. "Indeed." How like her, he thought, to be able to see the good and ignore the rest. Perhaps he had survived too long. Perhaps it was time to end it before the bitterness growing inside him devoured him.

Jaw clenched, he stood up and reached for his cloak.

"Where are you going?"

"Out." He gestured at her plate. "You've had your dinner, and now I must go hunt my own. Something thick and hot."

"You're doing it again," Rhianna said accusingly. "Trying to shock me, to make me think you're some kind of monster. Why? Why do you keep doing that?"

"It's what I am." He ran a hand through his hair, guilt and regret and self-reproach rising up within him. She brought out the best in him, he thought ruefully, and the worst, as well. He wanted to be worthy of her love and yet, for some perverse reason he didn't understand, he found himself trying to provoke her hatred.

"Very well, my lord," she said angrily. Pushing the tray away, she got to her feet, rounded the table, and stood in front of him. "You think yourself a monster." She titled her head to the side and drew her collar away from her neck, exposing the curve of her throat. "Prove it."

He looked at her as if she had gone mad. "What are you doing?"

"I want you to prove to me what a monster you are. Go on, rip out my throat. Drink your fill."

He stared down at her, his nostrils filling with the scent of her anger. He could hear the blood thrumming in her veins, hot and heavy, hear the rapid beat of her heart.

His gaze locked on the pulse beating in the hollow of her throat. He licked his lips, remembering the sweet taste of her blood on his tongue.

"I'm waiting." She stared back at him, her blue eyes daring him to take what she was offering.

He felt his fangs lengthen, felt their sharpness against his tongue. His breathing grew harsh, his hands clenched into fists as he felt the hunger rise up within him, urging him to wrap her in his embrace, to drink and drink and drink.

It's what you are, the hunger urged. *Why fight it any longer?*

His hands reached for her. As if they belonged to someone else, he watched his fingers curl over her shoulders. She was so fragile, he could easily break her in two. Slowly, he drew her closer, closer, until her face filled his vision. Her eyes were wide, deep blue pools filled with love and compassion and acceptance.

He took a deep breath and inhaled the scent of fear. It struck him with the force of a mortal blow, overpowering the hunger within him.

"Rhianna." With a harsh sob, he sat down.

Drawing her into his lap, he crushed her against him. "You foolish girl."

"You only proved I was right, my lord," she said, her hand caressing his cheek. "You're not a monster at all."

She glanced over his shoulder as the door swung open and Bevins entered the room.

"Ah," he said, clearing his throat. "Forgive me. I didn't mean to disturb you.

"It's all right," Rayven said. He set Rhianna on her feet and stood up. "I was just going out."

"Will you be needing anything else this evening?"

"No, Bevins. Good night."

"Good night, my lord. Lady Rhianna." With a bow, he went into the small room that adjoined their suite and closed the door.

"You've said you don't like the blood of sheep," Rhianna remarked. "Why don't you take what you need from me instead?"

Rayven shook his head. "No." His voice was harsh, not with anger, but gratitude.

"And if I were to insist?"

"No, Rhianna. I would not use you so." There might be a time when he would need her blood to survive, a time when he might need more than the very small amount he allowed himself when they made love, but he would not drink from her as he drank from others, would not use her to satisfy his hunger, tempting as it might be.

She placed her hands flat against his chest. "Would you let me eat locusts and ants if it was unnecessary, my lord?"

"It's not quite the same thing, my sweet," he said ruefully.

"Please don't refuse me, Rayven. It's something I want to do for you. Something I need to do."

At a loss for words, he shook his head.

"Rayven . . ."

"No, Rhianna. I'm grateful for your offer, more grateful than you'll ever know, but I cannot accept."

She studied his face, wondering why he was being so stubborn. "Very well, my lord," she said. "But the offer stands."

He nodded. "I shan't be gone long," he said, and gathering his cloak, he left the room.

She was asleep when he returned. It had taken him longer than usual to find someone suitable for his purposes; after he had quenched his hunger, he had walked through Hyde Park, comfortable in the darkness.

Now, he stood at the foot of the bed, watching her for a long while, marveling anew at her generosity of spirit. No other woman in all the world would make such an offer, he mused, and he loved her the more for it. In desperate times, he had taken blood from Bevins, but that was in payment of an old debt. Rhianna had offered out of love.

With a sigh, he went to stand in front of the fireplace, his arm braced against the mantle as he stared into the cold hearth. A fire sprang to life at the blink of his eye and he stared, unseeing, into the flames.

Who would have thought that one young woman could make such vast changes in his life in such a short time?

How would he ever let her go?

Chapter Twenty-two

They stayed in London another two weeks, and then returned to Millbrae.

Rhianna felt a growing sense of anticipation as the carriage climbed the long, fog-shrouded hill to the castle. Once, the fortress had loomed cold and forbidding; now it was home.

Rayven helped her from the carriage, his gaze sweeping over the grounds. He had taken residence in a great many lands in the last four centuries; of them all, Devil Tree Mountain and its stark castle had always been his favorite abode, and yet he had never thought of Castle Rayven as home until now. Until Rhianna.

Swinging Rhianna into his arms, he opened the front door and carried her into the hall. "Welcome home, Lady Rhianna."

Rhianna laughed softly as he carried her down the corridor into the study.

The weeks they had spent in London had been wonderful. It had, she thought, been the best time of her entire life. She had slept at Rayven's side during the day, toured the theaters and concert halls with him in the evening.

Twice she had talked him into taking her blood, not just a sip, but enough to soothe his hunger. He had not wanted to, had argued against it, but, in the end, she had convinced him it was something she needed to do, wanted to do. And because he hated to deny her anything in his power, he had relented. The experience had left her feeling weak as a newborn babe, but she had found a deep satisfaction in nourishing him with her life's essence.

Setting her on her feet, Rayven dropped a kiss on her forehead; then, with a glance, he lit the lamps and started a fire in the hearth.

He could hear Bevins moving through the house, carrying their trunk and then Rhianna's valise into the tower room, making another trip to the carriage to unload the things she had purchased for her family.

Rhianna stood in front of the fireplace, shivering against the chill in the room, until Rayven put his arms around her, drawing her into the deep silken folds of his cloak.

With a sigh of contentment, she rested her head against his chest and closed her eyes. This was where she wanted to be, where she belonged.

"Tired?" he asked.

"Not really." She wrapped her arms around him, wanting to be closer, wishing she could climb inside his heart and soul and discover the secrets he refused to share.

"Hungry?" He stroked her hair lightly, all his senses vibrantly attuned to her nearness.

"No." She drew back a little so she could see his face. "Are you?"

He smiled down at her, his eyes filled with such love that it made her heart skip a beat.

"No." He had taken her blood twice in the last two weeks. He dared not take more so soon, nor was there any need.

At first, he had refused to drink from her. It was one thing to savor her sweetness in the throes of passion, another to take enough of her precious blood to still the hunger that burned within him. In the end, because he found it impossible to deny her anything within his power, he had done as she asked. Savoring the sweetness of her blood had made him realize anew just how much he had loathed the blood of sheep.

It was difficult now to remember that he had bought her for the sole purpose of satisfying his hunger. Miraculously, a few sips of her precious blood pacified his hunger far more effectively than had the blood of countless other women, women whose names and faces he could no longer recall.

"Will you be needing anything else tonight?" Bevins asked.

Rayven shook his head.

"Would you mind if I . . ." Bevins cleared his throat. "Would you mind if I took the carriage this evening?"

"Of course not," Rayven said, then frowned. "Where are you going?"

"I . . ." Bevins cleared his throat. "I thought I'd go look in on Mistress McLeod."

Rhianna glanced over her shoulder. "You're going to see my mother?"

"If you've no objection, milady?"

"No, of course not," Rhianna said.

"I, uh . . ." Bevins ran a finger around the inside of his collar. "I just thought perhaps she might like to know you're well."

"Of course," Rhianna said. "Give her my love. And tell her I'll be by to see her soon."

"I'll do that," Bevins said. "Good night, my lord. Lady Rhianna." With a slight bow, he left the room.

"Well," Rhianna said, "what do you make of that?"

Rayven shook his head. For the first time, it occurred to him that he had thoughtlessly condemned Bevins to endure the same lonely life he himself had lived.

"It was never my intention to rob Tom of a normal life," he remarked. "And yet that is what I've done. I spent so much time worrying about protecting my own existence, I never gave any thought to how lonely he must have been all these years."

"You had good reason to worry, my lord," Rhianna said.

Rayven shook his head. "It was wrong of me. Why did I not realize it sooner?"

Ada McLeod blinked in surprise when she saw Tom Bevins standing at her door. Her first thought was that something had happened to Rhianna.

"What is it?" she asked anxiously. "What's that monster done to my daughter?"

"Miss Rhianna is quite well, madam."

"Thank the Lord." She peered over Bevins's shoulder. "Did she come with you?"

"No, Mistress McLeod. I, uh, I just wanted to come by and assure you that she is well, and . . ." He tugged at his collar, then cleared his throat. "Quite well."

"Would you care to come in and sit a spell, Mr. Bevins?" Ada asked, alarmed by the sudden flush in his cheeks.

"Yes, thank you, madam."

"Come along, then."

Bevins followed her into the kitchen, sat down at the table at her invitation.

"Would you care for a cup of tea, Mr. Bevins?"

"Yes, thank you."

Lifting a pot from the fire, Ada filled two cups. She placed one in front of Bevins, then sat down across from him. She didn't feel comfortable having the man in her house, but she was eager to hear news of her daughter. "Sugar?" she asked. "Milk?"

"No, thank you, madam."

"Now, then, sir, what brings you here at this late hour?"

"I was wondering if I might have permission to, uh . . ."

"To what?"

"I should very much like to call on you, Mistress McLeod."

"Call on me?" Ada stared at him in disbelief. She was forty years old and the mother of five children. Long past the age when men came courting.

"Yes, madam."

Ada folded her hands in her lap, her cheeks growing hot with embarrassment. "I don't know what to say."

"Say yes, Mistress McLeod."

Ada shook her head. "I can't allow you to come calling, Mr. Bevins."

"I see." He shook his head. "No, I don't see. I thought, that is . . . Why not?"

Ada lifted her chin and met his gaze squarely. "I have no liking for the man who employs you. I don't trust him. He's evil. He has bewitched my daughter."

Bevins shook his head. "Mistress McLeod, I assure you that the rumors you've heard about my master are false."

"I think not. There's something peculiar about him." She shook her head. "I know not what it is, but I know he's not like other men."

Bevins let out a sigh of resignation.

"You admit it, then?"

"My lord's ways may seem strange to you, Mistress McLeod, but he is a good man."

"I've heard nothing of his goodness."

"The stories told in the village are lies," Bevins said, wondering how to steer the subject away from his master.

"They can't all be lies," Ada argued. "And even if they are, it's been my experience that most lies are based on an element of truth. There's something odd about him, I'm thinking, something that doesn't ring true. I've lived in the valley all my life, and never once have I seen that man in the village in the light of day, nor has anyone else that I know of. 'Tis an evil man who shuns the light, who has no friends." She stared into her tea cup, sadness dragging at her features. "I fear for my daughter's well-being."

Bevins fidgeted in his chair. "Mistress McLeod, my Lord Rayven may not live like other men, but he loves your daughter, and while she lives with him, no harm will befall her. I can promise you that."

"You're very loyal."

"He saved my life many years ago."

"Indeed?"

"Yes, madam." Bevins stood up. "I'm sorry to have troubled you, Mistress McLeod."

"Good evening to you, sir."

Bevins started toward the door, then turned back, knowing if he didn't speak now, he would never have the courage to do so again.

"Mistress McLeod, I came here tonight because . . ." He took a deep breath and finished in a rush, "Because I'm lonely, and I thought maybe, if you were lonely, too, you wouldn't mind my company. I know you don't approve of my master, but can you not look past that and judge me on my own merits?"

Ada blinked up at him, somewhat taken aback by his impassioned declaration. "I don't know what to say."

"I should be getting back," Bevins said, his courage deserting him as quickly as it had come. "My lady said to tell you she will be coming to visit you very soon."

"Thank you," Ada said. Rising, she followed Bevins out of the kitchen to the front door of the cottage. "Give Rhianna my love."

"Yes, I will."

"Mr. Bevins?"

"Yes, madam?"

"I should be honored to have you call on me."

Bevins bowed from the waist. "It will be my pleasure, madam."

Ada stared after him, her eyes narrowed thoughtfully. Tom Bevins knew a great deal about Castle Rayven and its dark lord. If she was careful and clever, she might yet learn the secrets that lay hidden within the mist-shrouded walls of the castle.

"He's home," Rayven said.

Rhianna glanced up from the embroidery in her lap, her eyes filled with curiosity. "I didn't hear anything."

Rayven smiled; a moment later, Bevins entered the study.

"Yes, my lord?"

"I believe Rhianna wishes to talk to you."

"Yes, milady?

Rhianna looked at her husband. He was watching her, his dark eyes alight with mischief.

"I was just wondering if all is well at home."

Bevins nodded. "Quite well, milady."

"Won't you sit down, Tom?" Rhianna asked, gesturing at the chair across from Rayven.

"No, thank you, milady."

"Did you have a nice visit with my mother?"

"Yes, milady. She said . . ." Tom cleared his throat. "She said I might call on her again."

Rhianna met Rayven's amused glance.

"That is, if you have no objection, milady."

"No, of course not." Rhianna smiled at Bevins. "I think you and my mother suit rather well."

"Thank you, milady. Will either of you be needing anything further this evening?"

"No," Rayven said, answering for them both. "You may retire."

"Thank you, my lord." Bevins bowed, then left the room.

"Is he always so formal?" Rhianna asked.

Rayven nodded. "Why do you ask?"

"The two of you have been together so long, it just seems strange, that's all. I'd think you'd be friends by now."

"I made it clear from the beginning that I would not welcome his friendship."

"Oh? why?"

"I've let no one close to me since I became Vampyre," he replied quietly. "No one, but you."

Rising from her chair, Rhianna went to sit in his lap. "I wish I could make you forget the past," she whispered, caressing his cheek. "I wish I could make you happy."

"You make me happy, beloved," he replied. "Never doubt that for a moment."

"How can I help it, when you always look so sad?"

He smiled faintly. "Do I?"

Rhianna nodded. "You try to hide it from me, but I can see it in your eyes, even now. What is it that troubles you so, my lord husband?"

With a sigh, he wrapped his arms around her and drew her close, his face pressing against the warmth of her breasts. What hurt more? he wondered. The thought that he would soon have to release her from her vows? The certainty that she would one day marry another? Or the knowledge that she would grow old and die while he stayed forever as he was?

"My lord?"

He took a deep breath, his nostrils filling with the warm sweet scent of her perfume, her hair, her skin, the blood that was the very essence of her being. Hunger and need stirred to life within him.

"Rhianna?" Her name whispered past his lips, soft as a sigh.

She pressed a kiss to the top of his head. "Yes, my lord?"

His hands slid down her back as he cursed the darkness within him, the hunger that made him weak. He wondered how she could love him when he asked so much of her and gave so little in return.

Rhianna drew back a little so she could see his face. "Rayven?"

"I need you."

Smiling, she tilted her head to the side, then swept her hair over her shoulder, baring her throat. "Then take what you need, my lord."

He rose from the chair in one smooth, effortless motion, carrying her with him as if she weighed less than nothing at all.

"I need more than that, my sweet Rhianna," he replied, his voice rough with emotion.

He brushed his lips over hers, then carried her swiftly up the dark winding staircase, his cloak billowing out behind him like the devil's breath.

It was obvious early on that Bevins had fallen in love with Rhianna's mother. His step was lighter, and he smiled frequently for no apparent reason. And every Friday evening he asked Rayven if he might borrow the carriage on Saturday night.

"Mayhap we'll have another wedding soon," Rayven mused as they lingered at the dinner table one night.

"Maybe," Rhianna replied dubiously. Bevins had been seeing her mother once a week for over three months now.

"You don't think so?"

Rhianna made a vague gesture with her hand. "I think . . . That is, it doesn't seem as though . . ." She shook her head, not certain how to say what she was thinking.

"Go on."

"I think she's using him."

Rayven frowned. "Using Bevins? To what end?"

"Never mind."

"Tell me, Rhianna."

There was no way to ignore that tone of voice, or the look in his eye.

"Well, we both know she's never liked you. Or trusted you. She's heard all the gossip. I think she's seeing Bevins because she's hoping he'll tell her . . ." She glanced at the delicate crystal goblet in Rayven's hand. "You know."

"I see," Rayven remarked, and wondered why the possibility had not occurred to him sooner.

He placed the glass on the table, then leaned back, his elbows braced on the arms of the chair, his chin resting on his folded hands. He regarded Rhianna thoughtfully for a long moment. "What do you think I should do about it?"

"I don't know. Perhaps we should leave here."

"Do you want to leave?"

Rhianna shook her head. "No."

Her family was here, the only family she had. The only family she would ever have should Rayven let her stay on when their year was ended.

"And if Bevins should betray my trust, do you think your mother would believe him?"

A slight smile played over Rhianna's lips. "I think my mother would believe you were the very Devil himself, my lord husband."

"And what do you think, my sweet?"

The smile faded from Rhianna's lips. "What do you mean?"

He hated himself for asking, hated the doubts that continued to plague him. "You have lived with me here now for six months. I have taken your innocence, the very essence of your life. If I were to give you leave to go, would you take it?"

Slowly, she shook her head. "Do you still doubt me, my lord? Why can you not believe in my love, in me?"

A fleeting image of Rhianna and Montroy dancing together flashed through Rayven's mind, two mortals, vibrant with life, radiating health and youth and strength.

He lowered his arms, his hands clenching and unclenching in his lap as he imagined his bride and the viscount together, hating the idea even as he admitted that they looked as though they belonged together. Montroy loved Rhianna. He could give her everything she wanted and needed, everything she deserved. A home, a family, and a title all wrapped up in wealth and respectability.

Rhianna watched the emotions that flickered over Rayven's usually impassive face. She saw the doubts that continued to plague him. She had loved him without reservation, had offered him her heart and soul, the very blood that flowed through her veins, and it wasn't enough. How could they ever have a life together if he refused to accept the love she offered?

Rising, she tossed her napkin on the table and ran out of the room, out of the castle.

Outside, she stared into the darkness, then ran down the garden path that led to the maze.

He would never believe she loved him, never believe that he was worthy of her affection. When the time came, he would send her away. She had hoped to make him love her so deeply that he would let her stay with him as long as she lived. Only now did she realize how foolish that hope was. Why would he want to watch her grow old and bent? Her skin would wrinkle, her hair would turn gray, yet he would remain forever as he was, young and virile, with a young man's desires.

She was breathless when she reached the heart of the maze. There was a burning ache in her side. Gasping for air, she dropped down onto the stone bench and buried her face in her hands.

"Rhianna."

Her head jerked up, startled to find him standing before her, a tall silhouette clad in the darkness of the night. "How . . . how did you . . . get here so . . . fast?"

One dark brow rose in amusement. "How indeed?"

Of course, she thought. He was Vampyre. A child of the night. Able to travel with preternatural speed.

He knelt before her, his cloak fluttering as it

settled gracefully around him. "I love you, Rhianna," he said, taking her hands in his. "With every fiber of my being, every breath in my body, I love you."

"But you don't believe that I love you in return."

"I don't deserve your love."

"But you have it just the same."

"I know." He smiled, a sad smile touched with bitterness. "It's a heavy burden to bear."

"A burden?" The hurt in her eyes ripped his heart to shreds.

He nodded. "I should never have brought you here, never have touched you." He stroked her cheek, let his fingertips slide down the graceful curve of her throat. "It pains me to love you, to know that I will soon have to let you go." He took a deep breath. "To know that someday you will marry a man worthy of your love and bear his children."

Rhianna shook her head. "It doesn't have to be that way."

"Ah, but it does, my sweet. Your nearness sorely tempts me. It's wrong for me to keep you here, to make you live in shadow. You need to live as you were meant to live, and I . . ." He stared at the pulse throbbing in the hollow of her throat. "For too long I have denied what I am."

"Rayven, don't." She clasped his hands to her breast, frightened by the hopelessness she saw in his eyes, by the resignation in his voice.

She's mortal. Take her. Take what you want. What you need.

He drew back, fighting the hunger rising within him, fighting the longing to drink and drink and drink, until he was drunk with the taste of her, admitting, for the first time, that he had been playing a dangerous game. He had fooled himself into thinking he had conquered the hunger.

He had consumed the blood of sheep and told himself all was well.

He had bought young women and kept them in the castle, drinking from them while they slept, sending them away when he had taken all they could spare.

He had taken frugal sips of Rhianna's blood and applauded himself for his self-control.

And all the while he had been lying to himself, telling himself that he was no longer a monster because he no longer killed to survive.

He looked at Rhianna, burning like a flame in the darkness of his mind. Need and hunger rose up within him, hot and swift as lava exploding from a volcano. He tried to fight it, and knew that, this time, he was not strong enough. Knew if he took her now, he would destroy her and in so doing, destroy himself as well.

"My lord? Rayven? Are you well?"

"I need Bevins."

"My lord, are you ill?" She gazed into his face, alarmed by the feverish brightness of his eyes, the harsh rasp of his breathing, the taut line of his jaw.

"Bevins." Grimacing with pain, he rocked back on his heels, his fists tightly clenched. "Bevins!"

Rhianna stared at him, her heart pounding with fear. His cloak wrapped tightly around him, a cocoon of thick black velvet and silk. In the pale light cast by the moon, she could see that the material rippled gently over his back and shoulders, as though trying to comfort him.

Frightened by what she was seeing, she stood up. She whirled around at the sound of footsteps, breathed a sigh of relief when she saw Bevins running toward them.

"What's happened?" he asked.

Rhianna shook her head. "I don't know."

Bevins took one look at Rayven, then dropped to his knees beside him. "Go back to the house, milady," he said as he rolled up his sleeve. "Go. Now."

"No." She shook her head. "I want to help."

Bevins looked up and met her worried gaze. "It's what he wants," Bevins said quietly.

She wanted to argue, to beg Rayven to turn to her for help. If he needed nourishment, she wanted to be the one to provide it. She wanted to cry out at the unfairness of it all, at what he was.

"Rhi . . . anna. Go." His voice was raw, stretched thin with the pain knifing through him. "Please go."

"Yes, my lord." She turned away, her vision blurred by tears she had not realized she was shedding.

Bevins waited until Rhianna was out of sight, then he thrust his arm in front of Rayven, grimaced as he felt the sharp bite of the vampyre's fangs pierce the tender skin along his wrist. He clenched his fist, wondering, as he always did when the madness came on his master, if Rayven would be able to stop feeding before it was too late.

Catching a glimpse of the blood lust burning like perdition's flames in the vampyre's eyes, Bevins turned away, knowing his master did not like him to watch, did not like anyone to see him when the hunger was fast upon him, when the thin veneer of humanity shattered beneath a need too great to ignore, a craving too powerful to resist.

It was a look Tom Bevins had seen before, when he lay dying in a dark alley over fifty years before.

A look that, once seen, was never to be forgotten.

Chapter Twenty-three

Rhianna huddled under the covers, listening to the clock chime the hour. It was a quarter past four in the morning, and Rayven still hadn't come to bed.

At midnight, she had crept downstairs, hoping to find him sitting in the study, but the room had been dark and empty.

She had found Bevins in the kitchen. He had been sitting at the table, a heavy blanket draped over his shoulders, a large glass of brandy cradled between hands that trembled. Feeling her gaze, he had looked up, then glanced away. But that one haunted look had stilled the questions on her lips. It was the look of a man who had glimpsed the fathomless pits of hell, had stood close enough to feel the heat of the flames.

She had turned and run back to the tower. That had been hours ago.

Where was Rayven?

It would be dawn soon.

Why didn't he come to bed?

Rising, she wrapped a quilt around her shoulders and left the tower. The floor was cold beneath her bare feet as she made her way down the narrow winding staircase to the first floor.

No lights shone.

Drawing the blanket more closely around her shoulders, she walked slowly toward the study.

She knew he was inside as soon as she put her hand on the latch.

"My lord?" She opened the door and peered into the darkness. "Rayven?" She stepped into the room and closed the door behind her. "I know you're in here."

"Go back to bed, Rhianna."

"It's lonely there without you."

"I cannot come to you tonight."

"Are you ill, my lord?"

He laughed softly, bitterly. "I am never ill, my sweet. Only sick in mind and spirit."

She took another step toward him. "Let me help you."

"There is nothing you can do, Rhianna."

"But . . ."

"If you care for me as much as you say, you will go back to bed." He drew in a ragged breath and released it slowly. "Go now, while I am willing, and able, to let you go."

"Rayven, please . . ."

"Leave me."

He spoke from between clenched teeth, his voice harsh, resounding with the power he held tightly leashed within him.

With a strangled cry, she turned and fled the room.

His side of the bed was empty in the morning. Alarmed, she drew on her robe and hurried down the stairs. "Bevins! Bevins!"

"Yes, milady?" He stepped out of the kitchen, looking much improved from the night before.

"Where is he? He didn't come to bed. The sun . . ." She shook her head, her eyes wide with a fear she dared not voice aloud.

"He is well, milady."

"Where is he? He hasn't . . ." She took a deep breath. "He hasn't left the castle?" *He hasn't left me.* The words, unspoken, seemed to hover in the air between them.

"No, milady."

She frowned. "But if he's here, where is he?"

Bevins hesitated a minute, as though deciding whether he should tell her or not.

"Tell me."

"He's in the cellar."

"The cellar!"

Bevins's gaze slid away from hers. "He takes his rest there, on occasion."

"In the cellar? Why ever for?"

"I'm afraid only my Lord Rayven can tell you that."

She turned toward the door, felt Bevins's hand upon her arm. "He will not like it if you go there."

"I'm his wife and the mistress of this castle," Rhianna said, surprised by the faintly imperious tone of her voice. "I will permit no secrets between my lord Rayven and myself."

Bevins removed his hand from her arm, then

bowed. "As you wish, Lady Rhianna."

She met his gaze, an apology on the tip of her tongue. She had never treated Tom like a servant and was ashamed she had done so now.

Bevins shook his head. "You need not apologize, my lady." He pulled a long white candle from a drawer and lit it for her. "You'll have need of this." He reached into his pocket and withdrew a large brass key. "And this."

Taking both candle and key, Rhianna turned away, her heart hammering in her breast as she made her way toward the long narrow flight of stairs that led down to the cellar.

A wave of cold air met her as she opened the door. For a moment, she stood at the top of the steps, looking down into the darkness beyond. Why had he chosen to rest down there? What would she find?

Summoning her courage, reminding herself that he was her husband, she descended the steps. Holding the candle higher, she saw several well-stocked wine racks, dozens of barrels and boxes, an enormous trunk covered with dust.

Lifting the hem of her nightgown with her free hand, she made her way deeper into the cellar. The air was dank and musty. Dusty cobwebs hung from the corners of the ceiling. The floor of hard-packed earth was cold beneath her feet. Images of hairy spiders and rats flitted across her mind.

When she reached the far end of the room, she stopped. And then she saw it, a narrow iron-strapped door to her left.

He was there.

With a hand that trembled, she slid the key into the lock. Dropping the key into the pocket of her robe, she took a deep breath and opened the door.

Praying for courage, she crossed the threshold. The room was empty save for the coffin set against the far wall. A long black coffin, with the lid closed. And carved into the top of the lid was the image of a raven in flight.

Bile rose in her throat as she stared at the casket.

Aren't vampyres supposed to sleep in coffins? she had once asked.

And he had replied *I find them narrow and confining.*

Terror settled in her stomach like a chunk of winter ice. This was what he was. He had told her so plainly enough. He had let her see his face with the mask of humanity gone. And she still had not understood completely, nor, she realized, fully believed, until now.

With a determination she had never known she possessed, she forced herself to cross the floor, to lift the satin-smooth heavy lid, to look inside.

He lay on a bed of white velvet. His cloak was wrapped around him, the black of his cloak and hair a sharp contrast to the casket's lining.

Her husband. A vampyre.

He stirred, as though aware of her presence, and his cloak settled more firmly around him, as if to restrain him.

A look of pain crossed his face, and then a single word whispered past his lips.

"Rhianna."

Tears welled in her eyes and ran down her cheeks. Tears of sorrow and pity, tears of compassion and soul-deep anguish. Tears that fell faster and faster, wetting the robe she clutched to her breast, dripping onto Rayven's cloak. Tears that refused to stop. A river of silent tears that she feared would drown them both.

She had the feeling that he knew she was there. She could feel him struggling through layers of darkness, fighting to be free of the deathlike sleep that imprisoned him, and she knew she could not face him now.

And then Bevins was there beside her, offering her his arm, leading her away.

He woke with the setting of the sun, his nostrils filled with her scent. He vaulted from the casket, hands clenched in anger. She had been here. He had not dreamed her presence while he lay helpless in the dark, but then, he never dreamed. She had been there.

Bevins! Attend me! Now!

He paced the floor while he waited for his servant, the certainty of what he must do cutting through him like a knife. He whirled around as the door to the cellar opened.

Bevins eyed him warily. "My lord?"

"I'm leaving here. Tonight."

"I shall pack your things."

"No. I'm taking nothing with me." His gaze met Bevins's. "Nothing."

"Very well. I shall be ready."

Rayven shook his head. "No. I want you to stay here, with . . . with her." He couldn't say her name aloud, not now.

"I don't understand."

"I am not as other men, and I find I cannot pretend any longer."

"My lord, perhaps if you did not keep so much

to yourself. Perhaps if you went into the village of an evening and spent time with the people, let them see you. Perhaps if they knew you were the one providing funds for the shelter, it would help to dispel the rumors."

"No. It will be better for Rhianna, for all of us, if I leave." Rayven turned away, his arms folded over his chest. "I want you to stay with her as long as she needs you. When she's . . ." He took a deep breath. "When she's found someone else, you will come to me."

Someone else, he thought bitterly. Someone like Montroy.

"Yes, my lord." Tom Bevins cleared his throat. "Will you be telling her this yourself?"

"No." Rayven shook his head, despising himself for his cowardice. "I'll need paper and pen."

"Yes, my lord."

Rhianna looked up from the book she was reading, smiling expectantly, but it wasn't Rayven in the doorway. It was Bevins.

"What is it?" she asked, alarmed by the grim expression on Tom's face. "What's wrong?"

Bevins held out a sheet of paper. "This is for you, milady."

"A letter?" She stood up, the book in her lap tumbling to the floor, forgotten, as she took the missive from Bevins's hand. A letter at night could only be bad news.

She stared at it as if she had never seen a letter before, then slowly turned it over, her heart plummeting into her stomach when she saw Rayven's seal pressed into the wax.

With a bow, Bevins left the room.

Crossing the floor, Rhianna sat down on the edge of the bed, the bed she had shared with Rayven, and stared at the envelope, at the stark white paper, at the raven's head imprinted in the blood-red sealing wax.

Finally, with hands that trembled, she broke the seal.

Rhianna,

I cannot pretend any more. These past six months spent with you have been the happiest of my existence. You will never know the joy you have brought me, but I cannot stay with you longer. Your nearness soothes my soul even as it stirs the demon hunger within me, a hunger I fear I can no longer restrain.

The castle is yours. Do with it as you will. Bevins will stay with you as long as you need him. It is my wish that you forget me and find another. Montroy would make you a fine husband, one who can give you the kind of life you deserve.

Forgive me for telling you this in a letter, but, coward that I am, I could not tell you to your face for fear that you would convince me to stay. To do so might put your life, your very soul, in danger, and that is something I would never do.

Know that I shall cherish your memory and love you until my last breath.

Your obedient servant, Rayven

She stared at the words, words blurred by her tears, unable to believe that he had left her, that she would never see him again.

She didn't know how long she sat there, silent tears tracking her cheeks, staining the paper in her hands. He was gone.

"Milady?"

It was an effort to lift her head. Bevins stood in the doorway, his expression somber, his eyes filled with sympathy.

"Lord Montroy is downstairs, milady."

"I can't see him now."

"I'm afraid he's insisting."

"Send him away."

"He will not go." Bevins took a deep breath. "He says my lord Rayven bid him come."

Rayven! Perhaps Montroy would know where he had gone. "Very well."

She stood up, the letter clutched in one hand. She followed Bevins down the stairs, not caring that her eyes were red and swollen from her tears. She was beyond feeling, past caring what anyone else thought.

Montroy was in the front parlor, his back to the hearth. He swore under his breath when Rhianna entered the room, then swiftly crossed the floor and gathered her into his arms.

She didn't resist, simply stood there, forlorn as a lost child.

"Rhianna." Taking her by the hand, he led her toward the big overstuffed chair near the hearth. Knowing it was against propriety, he nevertheless sat down and drew her into his lap, holding her as if she were a babe in need of solace.

She snuggled against him, her face buried in the hollow of his shoulder.

Muffled sobs shook her slender frame; her tears soaked his coat. Murmuring to her softly, he stroked her back, quietly cursing Rayven for his cruel abandonment.

He had seen Rayven at Cotyer's earlier that evening.

"I am leaving Millbrae," Rayven had said without preamble. "I want you to look after Rhianna."

It had taken the viscount a moment to find his voice. "Where are you going?"

"It doesn't matter."

"When are you coming back?"

"I don't know. Perhaps never."

"I don't understand."

A trace of wry amusement had flickered in Rayven's eyes. "I cannot explain it to you, Montroy, but I want your word that you will look after her."

Dallon had stared into Rayven's eyes, those compelling black eyes that had, over the years, often made him uneasy. There was no hint of danger lurking in those eyes now, no arrogance, only a pain so deep it could not be concealed. "You know I will."

Rayven had nodded. "Be good to her," he had said, and then, his cape billowing behind him, he had left the room.

Disappeared, Dallon would have thought, if such a thing was possible.

"He's left me."

Rhianna's voice brought Montroy back to the present. "I know."

"Why?" She looked up at him, the pain in her eyes reminding him of the anguish he had seen in Rayven's.

"I don't know," Montroy replied softly. Taking a linen handkerchief from his coat pocket, he wiped the tears from her eyes, her cheeks.

"I thought he loved me." She looked at the letter still clutched in her hand. "He said he loved me."

"He does," Montroy said. "I'm sure of it."

She looked at him as if seeing him for the first time. "Why are you here?"

"Rayven asked me to come. He didn't want you to be alone."

"He sent you to me? You saw him?" Hope flared in her eyes. "When? Where? Where is he now?"

"He's gone, Rhianna. He wouldn't tell me where or why, only that he was going."

It hurt to watch the hope die in her eyes, to see the hopelessness settle over her once more. It hurt to know that she loved another.

"Rhianna, what can I do?"

"Do?" She stared at him blankly.

She shuddered in his arms as a fresh wave of tears filled her eyes. Helpless, he watched her cry, watched the silent tears flood her eyes and cascade down her cheeks.

After a while, she collapsed against him, and he held her tight, his hand stroking her hair, her back, wondering if she would ever smile again.

Standing outside in the shadows, Rayven peered in the window, watching. A pain as sharp as a stake pierced his heart as he listened to her tears and knew he was the cause.

"I love you, my sweet Rhianna," he murmured.

And it was that love that made him turn away, that sent him running through the night, away from the only woman he had ever loved.

Days passed, but Rhianna was hardly aware of them. She spent her mornings wandering through the gardens, remembering the nights she had spent walking in the moonlight with Rayven. She ate at Bevins's insistence, though she had no appetite for food. She took long naps and retired early to her bed because it was only there, in her dreams, that her husband came to her.

Montroy came to visit her each day, his concern evident in the look in his eyes, in his voice, the gentle touch of his hand. He didn't intrude on her grief, didn't tell her not to cry, not to grieve. He bowed to her wishes when she wanted to be alone, held her when she asked for comfort, dried her tears when she wept. And hoped that, one day, she would accept his love, prayed that one day she would grow to love him as deeply as she loved the dark lord of Castle Rayven.

And sometimes when she cried, when the pain in her eyes made his heart ache, he knew he would gladly see her reunited with Rayven if it would make her smile again.

Chapter Twenty-four

He hunted in the shadows of the night, venting his rage and his grief in the mindless shedding of blood. He stalked his prey relentlessly, feeding on their fear, letting his quarry see what he was, letting them see the bloodlust in his eyes, smiling as he bared his fangs. He was hurting, hurting as he had not hurt in four centuries, and he wanted to strike out in retaliation, hoping that by inflicting pain on others, he might ease his own.

He hunted prey as he had not hunted since he was first made Vampyre, hunted until the scent of blood and fear clung to his skin, his clothing, infiltrated every pore.

He had forgotten how intoxicating it was, to drink and drink and drink, until he was filled with the blood of life, until his heart beat in time with that of the unfortunate soul in his embrace, until his body swelled with the vitality of another's life force. Ah, to drink his fill, to drink in someone's life, their hopes and dreams and memories, their very essence.

He refused to consider the morality of it. What need had he of morals? He was not human, but Vampyre, a race apart. The laws of men meant nothing to him. Men preyed on helpless beasts for nourishment. Vampyres preyed on men. No one preyed on the Vampyre.

For too long he had denied what he was, denied the need that burned within him, denied the exquisite pleasure that could only be found in taking the blood of mortals. How close he felt to those he preyed upon as he cradled them in his dark embrace. How grateful he was for the swift surge of energy that flowed from their veins, filling him with vitality, making him feel like a young vampyre again, newly made.

And yet, for all that he drank his fill, he never drained his victims to the point of death. Strong as the desire was, he could not do it. Rhianna was to blame for that. She might understand his need for blood; she would never condone the taking of a life. And though he would never see her again, he could not be less than she thought him to be.

He reveled in the darkness that covered him, all his senses alert, hearing sounds in the night that mortals never heard—the soft splash of a single drop of rain falling on dew-damp grass, the sound of a mouse tiptoeing through the shadows. He saw the beauty hidden within the darkness of the night—the changing shapes and shadows of a world at sleep.

For weeks, he prowled the shadows of the

night, a silent phantom preying on those foolish enough to cross his path.

He was hunting now. Dark clouds covered the moon and stars, promising rain before dawn. There were but a few people on the streets—an elderly couple heading for home, a father and son huddled in a doorway, a young couple who walked hand in hand, staring into each other's eyes, blissfully unaware of the coming storm.

And then he saw her, a young girl running down a dark street, her hair blowing in the wind, the heels of her shoes clicking on the cobblestones.

He rode the wings of the night, silent as an owl stalking its prey, until he was beside her, his hand silencing her scream.

The scent of her fear mingled with the scent of her perfume. He could hear the frantic beat of her heart, hear the very blood that flowed through her veins.

He bent over her, his cloak enfolding them like the wings of a great black bird. And then he saw her eyes. Dark blue eyes filled with unspeakable terror. Eyes as blue as a summer sky, as blue as Rhianna's eyes . . .

With an oath, he reared back, shaken to the core of his being. He saw himself as Rhianna would see him, no better than a monster masquerading in human form, a wild beast unable to control the awful craving within him.

Filled with shame and self-loathing, he wiped his memory from the girl's mind, then vanished from her sight in a blur of swirling black velvet.

He hunted no more humans after that night. He took refuge in a crypt that held the lingering odor of moldering flesh and flowers long dead. Huddled in a corner, his cloak wrapped tightly around him, he stared into the darkness.

He was Vampyre. Undead. This was where he belonged.

The days passed in mindless sleep, the nights seemed longer than any he remembered. Nights when the hunger burned through his veins, when it clawed at his vitals, when, seeking relief, he gashed his own flesh looking for nourishment.

In the way of the world, time passed. Outside, the seasons were changing. Mortals were born. Mortals died. Yet he stayed ever the same.

Pain became his constant companion, striking deep, taunting him, urging him to go out and hunt. Phantoms took up residence in the tomb beside him—their cries of pain like knives cutting into his soul, their faces distorted with fear as they looked into his eyes and saw death there. So many ghosts come to haunt him, empty eyes filled with accusation. Had he truly killed so many in those days long past?

Individual faces had long ago been forgotten, all but the face of the first mortal he had killed. He had been a young vampyre then, ruled by the fierce hunger that refused to be satiated, ignorant in the ways of his kind. He had found the woman hurrying down a dark street. She had sensed his presence long before his hand closed around her arm. He would never forget the horror he saw in her eyes, or the sound of her voice, desperate with fear as she begged for her life. He had not wanted to hurt her, had not wanted to kill her, but the hunger had held him tight in its grasp, the pain more than he could bear. Clumsy in his haste, his fangs had ripped into the tender flesh of her throat. Her blood had gushed into his mouth, hot with life. And with that blood, he had tasted one of her tears. Horrified and ashamed, he had lowered her body to the ground. The look in her eyes had haunted him for more than a century.

He huddled deeper into the folds of his cloak, seeking escape, seeking solace. He cursed the hunger that licked at his vitals like the flames of Hell, cursed himself for what he was, cursed Rhianna for bewitching him, for giving him a taste of what he could never have. And, above all, he cursed Lysandra . . .

Lysandra!

All these years, she had kept a house but a league away. He had often sensed her presence but, like all vampyres, she was distrustful of others of her kind. She had never sought him out, nor had he gone looking for her, though, in the first days after he had been made, he had thought often of finding her, of destroying her for what she had done to him. Lysandra . . . She had made him what he was; if there was a cure, she would know it. If not, he would seek his destruction in the arms of the one who had made him.

Muttering an oath, he closed his eyes and sent his thoughts into the night.

"Rayven." Lysandra smiled warily, heartily surprised to find him waiting in her parlor when she arose that night. "Whatever brings you here?"

He felt a ripple in the air as she gathered her power close. "I mean you no harm."

Crossing the room, he took her hands in his. She was the oldest vampyre he had ever known, yet she looked exactly the same as she had when he had seen her last, her luxurious black hair arranged in thick curls atop her head, her eyes as black as pools of ebony beneath thick lashes, her alabaster skin aglow with a pearly translucence.

"Still beautiful," he murmured.

"As are you," she replied. She lifted one pale hand to his hair, smoothing it back from his brow. "But then, we never change, do we?"

"No," he said bitterly. "Never."

"And yet . . . You are thin, *mon petit*. What has happened to you?"

"Nothing." He shoved his hands deep into the pockets of his trousers. "I want to know if there's a cure for what we are."

"A cure?" She lifted one delicate brow. "You make it sound like some dreadful illness."

"It is the devil's own curse, and I wish to be free of it."

Lysandra frowned. "Whatever for? You look prosperous enough, though a trifle undernourished." Her eyes narrowed. "You've not fed recently, have you?"

"That's none of your concern," he said sharply. He took a deep breath. "Tell me," he said. "Is there a way to end it?"

"A walk in the sunlight, perhaps?" she suggested, the shadow of a smile teasing at her lips.

"Do not play games with me, Lysandra. I want an answer."

"I know of no cure."

His hands curled into tight fists as she spoke the words. "Then I want you to destroy me."

She trailed her finger over his cheek. "Has living become so unpleasant?"

"I can no longer abide what I am. It has cost me too much."

She regarded him through all-knowing eyes, and then smiled. "You've fallen in love with a mortal."

It was not a question, but a statement of fact, neither approving or condemning.

He did not bother to deny it. "Yes."

"There's no need to end your existence, Rayven. Simply bring her over."

"No."

"You would give up immortality for this woman?"

"Do not mock me, Lysandra. Have you never been in love?"

"You surprise me, Rayven. I did not think our kind was capable of such a human emotion."

"I wish that were true." He ran a hand through his hair. "I cannot bear it anymore. I want you to end it. Now."

"Why not stay here, with me instead?" she suggested. "We could hunt together." She placed her hands on his chest and looked up at him, her dark eyes alight. Her hands slid seductively down his chest, over his belly. "And play together."

Slowly, deliberately, he removed her hands from his body. "I did not come here looking for a hunting partner, nor a bed partner, only a way to end what I am."

He stared at her, watched the emotions chase across her face—disappointment that he would not hunt the night with her, anger because he had scorned her affection, a flicker of confusion because she could not understand his desire to end his existence.

And then he saw the blood lust rise in her eyes, quelling all other emotions. Her lips drew back in a feral smile, exposing her fangs.

He knew a moment of fear, a wave of gut-wrenching regret that he would never see Rhianna again, and then he bared his throat, wondering what it would be like to feel Lysandra's teeth tearing at his flesh again after so many years.

"No!" Rhianna woke, a scream on her lips. "Rayven, don't!"

Moments later, Bevins burst into the room, the candle in his hand sending a wash of yellow light over Rhianna's face. She had lost weight in the weeks since Rayven had left her. There were dark shadows beneath her eyes, eyes that were haunted with sadness. He feared for her health, yet nothing he did, nothing Montroy did, had been able to assuage her grief.

"What's wrong?" he asked, searching the shadows for the source of her distress.

"Rayven . . ." She stared at him through eyes wide with terror. "He's in danger."

Bevins set the candlestick on the table beside the bed. " 'Tis just a dream, milady."

"No." She shook her head. "No, it was real."

"There, there, milady. I'm sure he's fine."

"No." She shook her head again. "Can you not feel it?"

"Feel what?"

"He wants to die." She screamed Rayven's name aloud. "I will not live without him." She stared, unseeing, into the night, her hands clenched into tight fists. "Do you hear me, Rayven, I will not live without you!"

She sobbed his name one more time, then collapsed on the bed.

"Milady." Bevins bent over her, frightened by the sudden lack of color in her face, the slackness of her skin. He shook her slightly, shook her again when there was no response. "Rhianna!"

He shivered as a cold chill swept through the room and knew, in his heart, that she was right. Rayven was seeking to end his existence.

And Rhianna was going to meet him there.

"Not here," Lysandra said. She ran her nails down the length of his neck. "Come."

He followed Lysandra to her lair, stretched out on the red velvet settee that was the room's only furnishing save for a sleek mahogany coffin.

Lysandra sat beside him, her fangs bared, her breath coming hard and fast in anticipation. She would drink his blood, drain him to the point of death, and in so doing, she would gain the strength he had accumulated in the last four centuries. And then, when he was too weak to resist, she would carry him outside and leave him there. The sun would do the rest, burning away all evidence that he had ever existed.

He stared into Lysandra's face. Her black eyes burned with the hunger. His fists curled in the folds of his cloak as he felt Lysandra's hand move in his hair, lightly stroking, and he imagined it was another hand, Rhianna's hand.

Rhianna . . . Rhianna . . .

He felt the whisper of Lysandra's breath against his cheek, felt her lips, cool as a winter wind, brush his. Cold, he thought, when Rhianna's had ever been warm.

He flinched as Lysandra's hands folded over his shoulders, holding him in place. He had forgotten how strong she was.

Rhianna . . . Rhianna . . .

"Do it," he said, and closed his eyes.

He swallowed against the fear rising within him as he felt the prick of Lysandra's fangs against his throat. There was a sharp pain, the sensation of blood being drawn from his body. He forced himself to relax. This was what he wanted, an end to his wretched existence, the sweet oblivion of eternity.

He felt himself sinking into a swirling red mist, felt himself growing weak, weaker. Pleasure wrapped itself around the darkness, and he knew a moment of gratitude that she had decided to be kind and not cruel.

It was fitting, he mused, that he should find oblivion in the arms of the one who had made him.

Tremors wracked his body. Cold devoured him. *Rhianna . . . Rhianna . . .* He would never see her face again, never feel her warmth, see her smile. He began to struggle as his body's instinct for self-preservation took over. He felt Lysandra's hands tighten on his shoulders as he tried to escape her hold, felt his cloak gather around him, enfolding him, loving him, and he knew the end was near.

Rayven! Rayven! I will not live without you. Her voice, crying in his mind. *Rayven, come back to me.*

He tried to open his eyes, tried to fight his way through the smothering layers of darkness that dragged him toward eternity, but he lacked the strength. His heartbeat was slow and heavy in his chest. As from far away, he heard Lysandra's voice.

"I hope you find the peace you seek on the other side."

He wanted to speak to her, to tell her he had changed his mind, that Rhianna needed him, but he was empty, helpless. He had a sense of movement and knew Lysandra was carrying him outside. She carried him effortlessly, moving with preternatural speed through the dark streets.

He felt the wind upon his face, as cold and final as death itself, as she carried him away from her house, out of the city, into the middle of a graveyard that had been abandoned long ago. The sun would find him there, find him and destroy him, leaving no trace behind.

He was aware of Lysandra bending over him, felt the brush of her lips against his one last time. He could feel the vibration of her footsteps as she walked away, leaving him alone in the stillness of the night, alone to face the dawn.

Rhianna . . .

He was alone, weightless, helpless, floating in a sea of darkness that had no beginning and no end. The scent of damp earth and grass teased his nostrils, reminding him of the newness of life, of all that was forever lost to him.

Rayven! Come back to me. I will not live without you. . . .

Rhianna's voice echoed in his mind, over and over again, filling him with soul-deep regret and the knowledge that, in seeking to end his own life, he had failed her.

Hours passed. He began to shiver uncontrollably. He curled into a tight ball, drawing his cloak around him. Rhianna's voice pounded in his head, begging him not to leave her.

Rayven, don't leave me. . . . Please. . . . Come back to me. . . .

Her heartbeat echoed in his mind, growing ever weaker, until it beat in time with his, slow and heavy, and he knew that when death found him, it would find her, as well.

Rhianna . . . Rhianna . . . "Forgive me . . ."

Chapter Twenty-five

For a time, it seemed as though she would recover. Her appetite increased. She got out of bed for longer and longer periods of time; she asked Montroy to take her into the maze where she sat for over an hour, staring at the rosebushes, at the statues of the raven and the wolf.

She seemed at peace there, and for a time, Montroy hoped she had accepted the fact that Rayven was gone. *Now,* he thought, *now she'll turn to me and we can begin our life together.*

But it was not to be.

For no apparent reason, she went into a decline that came on rapidly, without warning. As the days passed, she grew ever weaker. Her mother and sisters came, bringing sweet treats to tempt her appetite, plying her with hot tea, smiling with forced gaiety as they told her of Aileen's pregnancy, hoping that the thought of a new life would bring her back from the depths of her despair.

But it was all in vain. She looked at them through eyes devoid of life even as she assured them she would be better soon.

Montroy summoned his family physician, but the man only shook his head, declaring there was nothing physically wrong with her.

Ada summoned the village priest, who laid his hands upon Rhianna's head, then turned away, promising he would light a candle and offer prayers for the welfare of her soul.

"She's willing herself to die." Ada stood beside her daughter's bed, staring down into Rhianna's pale face.

Montroy nodded. "I fear you are right, madam." He cursed softly, wondering if Rayven had foreseen such a thing happening when he took his leave.

"It's all that monster's fault," Ada said bitterly. "He's put a curse on her."

Montroy started to object. He didn't believe in magic, white or black. He thought of all the rumors he had heard about Rayven, the gossip, the speculation. Once, he had laughed it all aside. There were no such things as monsters who stalked the night, draining the life's blood out of others. But then he looked at Rhianna's pale face, at the dark shadows beneath her eyes, the hollows in her cheeks, and wondered if the rumors might not be true, after all.

He sat by her bed, holding her hand, while Ada McLeod urged her daughter to drink a little tea, felt his hatred grow until it became a living thing within him as he saw the empty look in Rhianna's once bright eyes. He heard her whisper Rayven's name, her voice barely audible, before she fell back on the pillows.

Stifling a sob, Ada turned away from the bed. Bevins materialized out of the shadows. For a moment, he watched her weep and then, needing to comfort her, he stepped forward and took Ada into his arms. For a moment, she stood stiff in his embrace, and then she collapsed against him. Feeling awkward, he stroked her hair and back, his gentle touch releasing the tears she had refused to shed.

Montroy felt his throat thicken as he listened to Ada McLeod weeping for her daughter.

He lifted Rhianna's hand to his lips and kissed her palm, afraid, deep in his heart, that she would never recover.

"Damn you, Rayven," he muttered. "I hope your soul is burning in Hell."

He woke with the setting sun. Staring into the crypt's darkness, he remembered how he had gone seeking death and how, when it had been within his grasp, he had discovered he wanted very much to live.

He had been hovering on the brink of oblivion when his skin began to tighten. Near the edge of eternity, he had smelled the coming dawn, had heard Rhianna's voice, growing ever weaker, echoing in his mind, begging him not to leave her, and he had known that, if he died, she would die, too. It was a burden too heavy to bear. He had been ready to end his own life, but he could not take hers, not when she had hardly lived at all.

With a strength of will he hadn't known he possessed, he had dragged himself toward the crypt in which he now lay. The door had been partly open, and he had squeezed in through the narrow crack. The rusty hinges had creaked loudly, shrieking like a soul in torment, as he pulled the door closed behind him and then, breathing heavily, his nostrils filling with the musty odor of old death, he had crawled into a corner and fallen into a deep, deep sleep.

How many suns had set since he took refuge here, he wondered. Ten? Twenty? He had lost count.

His stomach churned with disgust as he looked at the small furry bodies of mice and rats that littered the floor of the tomb. And yet their blood, repulsive though it might be, had kept him alive—that and his ever-growing need to see Rhianna again.

She was dying. He could feel her vitality ebbing along with her will to survive, and he knew that he was to blame. They were linked together by the blood they shared. But, unlike him, she was subject to the weakness of the flesh.

Salvatore, help me . . .

He closed his eyes, and the old Vampyre's image rose up in his mind. Salvatore. Slightly built, his black hair combed back, his dark brown eyes filled with the wisdom of the ages.

Rayven smiled faintly. Salvatore looked nothing like the Vampyres of legend. A dapper man, with a thin moustache and refined features. A man who knew what he was and accepted it.

To be Vampyre is not for the weak, Salvatore had once told him. *Eternity can be very tiring if one does not keep oneself amused. You must keep up with the world, or you will drown in the past. You can be a monster, preying off the life's blood of others, or not. The choice is up to you. . . .*

With an effort, he rose to his feet, ran a hand through his hair, settled his cloak around his shoulders.

Tonight, for the first time since he had sought death, he would hunt the streets of the city. And then he would go to her and beg her forgiveness.

If he was not too late.

Chapter Twenty-six

The spires of Castle Rayven loomed before him, shrouded, as always, in a thick, swirling gray mist. Dark clouds hung low in the sky, promising a storm before the night was through.

For a time, he rested in the changing shadows. Earlier, he had hunted the streets of the village, but in vain. For the first time in four hundred years, his powers had failed him. Desperate for sustenance, he had taken nourishment from a scrawny goat he had found tied behind one of the cottages.

Too weak to make use of his preternatural powers, he had made his way, step by slow step, up the long winding road to the top of Devil Tree Mountain, what little strength he had obtained from the goat expended by the time he reached the summit.

Closing his eyes, he rested his head against the

damp stone wall of the castle. For a moment, he contemplated going out into the fields and killing one of the sheep, but the urge to see Rhianna, to see for himself that she still lived, was more compelling than his hunger.

Pushing away from the wall, he made his way up the steps to the castle door. It opened at his touch.

He stood in the dark hallway, his senses probing the rooms. Bevins was in the kitchen. Rhianna was upstairs. He drew in a deep breath, and her scent wrapped around him, as warm and familiar and comforting as the folds of his cloak.

And then he heard voices. Montroy's. Ada's. A man's voice he did not recognize.

On silent feet, he climbed the stairs, padded noiselessly down the dimly lit corridor to the chamber Rhianna had used before she had moved into his tower room.

He paused outside the door. He felt a knifelike stab of disappointment that she no longer slept in his bed in the tower room, and with it a surge of gratitude that she had not revealed his resting place to others.

"She's not getting any better." It was Montroy's voice, filled with quiet despair.

"Perhaps we should take her to the hospital in London." Ada's voice was thick with tears.

"They can do no more for her there than we are doing here," said the unknown man. "It could be dangerous to move her, especially with the storm coming. If she's not better by tomorrow night, I'll bleed her again."

Bleed her! Muttering an oath, Rayven put his hand on the latch and opened the door.

All conversation came to an abrupt halt as he entered the chamber. He took it all in at a glance: Ada McLeod standing on one side of the bed, her fingers worrying her rosary beads; Montroy and a man Rayven assumed was a physician standing near the foot of the bed.

Rayven crossed the floor, his attention focused on Rhianna. The stink of garlic, believed to aid in healing and to ward off evil spirits, stung his nostrils as he drew near the bed. It was believed to ward off vampyres, too, he mused, but nothing would keep him from her side.

She lay as still as death, her face as pale as the linen beneath her head. Her hair was spread across the pillow like a splash of sunlight. There were purple shadows under her eyes; her cheeks looked hollow. A strong scent of blood rose from a covered bowl on the table beside the bed. Rhianna's blood, still warm. His stomach clenched in pain as the hunger rose within him.

"It's him!" Ada exclaimed, her voice filled with revulsion. "He's the one who's done this to her."

The physician placed his hand on Ada's shoulder. "Madam McLeod . . ."

"Sorcerer!" She shook off the doctor's hand and made the sign to ward off evil. "Spawn of Satan! Be gone from here!"

Too late, Rayven realized that Montroy had moved behind him. He started to turn, felt a crushing blow to the back of his skull as the viscount struck him over the head with the fireplace poker. He grunted as he fell to his knees.

Dropping the poker, Montroy rushed forward and wrestled him to the floor, holding him immobile with the doctor's aid.

Knowing it was futile, Rayven struggled against the viscount's grip. Lips drawn back in a feral snarl, he cursed viciously as his vision began to blur, then grow dim, until there was nothing but darkness, an endless swirling darkness that carried him away into oblivion.

He woke to blackness as endless as the grave. For a moment, he didn't know where he was, and then he realized he was lying in his coffin. His feeling of relief was quickly followed by a strong sense of dread as he tried to lift the lid, and failed. He pushed against the lid again, a sudden panic lending him strength, but the lid remained tightly closed. He wrinkled his nose against the overpowering scent of garlic.

Bevins! Come to me!

Alas, my lord, I cannot.

Explain.

They know what you are. During her illness, Lady Rhianna suffered a high fever. While she was unconscious, she spoke of you, of what you are. I tried to tell them it was nonsense, the babbling of a fevered mind, but Mistress McLeod believed her. She intends to have you destroyed on the morrow

What of Montroy? Rayven cursed under his breath, remembering how well the viscount had wielded the fireplace poker.

He does not appear to be altogether convinced.

Rhianna? Tell me of Rhianna.

They've not informed her of your return, my lord.

Is Montroy there, with you?

Yes, my lord.

You must convince him to release me. Tell him Rhianna will die without my help.

I will try, my lord. Are you well?

Rayven grunted softly. *I need nourishment rather badly,* he replied, thinking that was surely the understatement of the ages.

He severed the bond between them, then closed his eyes. He took several deep breaths, trying to stifle the panic rising within him. He had never liked small dark places; it was one of the reasons he did not take his rest in his casket. The thought that he might be forever trapped inside filled him with terror, and then he grinned ruefully. If Ada McLeod had her way, his forever would end with the coming of dawn on the morrow.

His eyes snapped open as he heard the sound of footsteps coming down the cellar stairs. Montroy! There was a pause at the door, the scrape of wood against stone as the door swung open.

"Rayven, can you hear me?"

"I hear you."

"Is it true?"

"What do you think?"

"I think it would explain much," Dallon said curtly.

"You must release me."

"I think not."

"Come, Dallon, you cannot seriously believe I am a vampyre." Rayven clenched his fists in an effort to keep his voice calm. "Surely, if I were the monster you believe, nothing you could do would hold me."

"I've never seen you eat," Montroy said. "Never seen you in the light of day."

"Easily explained."

"And this . . . ?" Montroy shuddered as he stared at the casket's gleaming black surface, at the life-sized raven carved into the wood. Was it his imagination, or were the bird's eyes following him? "Is this coffin also easily explained?"

"You must release me, Montroy. Rhianna needs me."

"The doctor says she's dying." The viscount's voice broke on the last word. "That she has lost the will to live."

"I can help her," Rayven said, his voice tinged with desperation. "But you must let me out of here. Now."

"How?" Dallon demanded. "How can you help her when my physician says it's hopeless?"

Rayven cursed the weakness that negated his powers. Had he been strong, he could have easily bent Montroy's will to his. But then, had he been strong, the man would not have been able to overpower him in the first place.

"Dallon, you must release me before it's too late." *Before the sun climbs over the horizon. Before Ada McLeod comes to take my head.* "Listen to me," he said, keeping tight rein on his impatience. "You've known me for years. You've spoken to Rhianna. Has she ever complained? Has she accused me of mistreating her? Have I ever said or done anything to make you think I would harm her, or anyone else?"

"No," Dallon replied slowly. "She has always spoken highly of you."

"She needs me," Rayven said, unable to disguise the urgency in his voice. "She needs to know that I am here."

He tensed as he heard Montroy cross the floor, hesitation evident in each faltering step.

"No one else can help her," Rayven said.

"Please, I'm begging you. You must let me out of here before it's too late."

He held his breath as he felt the touch of Montroy's hand on the lid of his coffin. *Yes,* he thought. *Do it, damn you!*

Dallon stared down at the casket. He was a well-educated man. There was no place in his life or his philosophy for that which could not be proven by fact or logically explained. He had never put any credence in the town's talk of vampyres, never believed in ghosts or goblins. He had, on occasion, felt a chill when he looked into Rayven's eyes, a sense of tightly controlled power, of danger waiting to be unleashed. But it had nothing to do with Rayven being a monster and everything to do with the fact that the master of Castle Rayven was a wealthy, powerful man, confident, arrogant, subservient to no one.

Dallon took a deep breath, willing to put his own safety at risk if there was a chance of saving Rhianna's life.

"I want your word, Rayven, your sworn oath that you will not harm her."

"You have it."

"Or anyone else."

Rayven hesitated only a moment. "I give you my word." He waited, hands clenching and unclenching, while Montroy made up his mind.

After what seemed hours but was no more than a moment or two, there was the unmistakable rattling of heavy chains, the screech of nails being drawn from wood.

They had secured his resting place well, Rayven mused. They had wrapped it with heavy chains, then nailed the lid shut. With silver nails, no doubt. He grinned wryly. Had they also sprinkled it with holy water?

Rayven squinted against the bright glare of a candle as Montroy lifted the lid.

Dallon swore softly, automatically crossing himself, as Rayven sat up.

Feeling as though he had been ransomed from the bowels of Hell, Rayven climbed out of the coffin.

He grunted softly as the stink of garlic filled his nostrils. Looking down, he saw the floor was strewn with the stuff.

Dallon Montroy backed away, felt the blood drain from his face as Rayven's black eyes met his.

"It's true," Montroy exclaimed, his hand tightening around the hammer in his hand. "All true."

"Indeed," Rayven agreed. He glanced at the thick gold cross hanging from a chain around Montroy's neck. "That will not protect you."

"You gave me your word."

"So I did." Rayven settled his cloak around his shoulders, then advanced on Montroy. He could hear the blood flowing in the man's veins, hear the frenzied beating of his heart.

He drew in a deep breath, drawing in the scent of blood, awakening the hunger.

Montroy backed up until he could go no further. "You gave me your word," he repeated, his pulse pounding wildly as he looked into Rayven's eyes. Eyes that glowed like twin coals in the very fires of Hell, burning into his mind, burning away his will to resist. He tried to look away, tried to raise his arm, to strike out with the hammer. But he could not draw his gaze away, could not summon the strength to lift his arm.

"Forgive me," Rayven murmured, and taking hold of Montroy's left arm, he sank his fangs into the tender flesh of the viscount's wrist.

Helpless, Montroy closed his eyes, surprised that there was hardly any pain. The hammer slid, unnoticed, from his grasp.

The hunger roared through Rayven, but he forced it back. Three long swallows, that was all, just enough to appease the hunger before he went to Rhianna.

He took a deep, calming breath as the hunger abated. After licking the wound in the viscount's wrist, and savoring the few extra drops of blood, he released Montroy's arm and turned away.

Taking the cellar stairs two at a time, he hurried to Rhianna's chamber.

Bevins was there, his arms and legs securely bound to a stout wooden chair. He grinned with rare good humor as Rayven swept into the room. "Good to see you, my lord."

"And you," Rayven replied curtly. With a flick of his wrist, he set Bevins free. "Get rid of Montroy, then bring me a glass of wine."

"Aye, my lord."

Lifting Rhianna into his arms, Rayven left the room, his steps carrying him swiftly up the stairs to the east tower. She was thin, he thought, so thin. Her heartbeat was slow, her pulse faint.

Inside the tower room, he closed the hidden portal, then gently lowered Rhianna to his bed. He drew the covers over her, his heart aching for the pain he had caused her, both mentally and physically.

"Rhianna? Rhianna!"

She moaned softly, then her eyelids fluttered open. "Rayven?"

"I'm here, beloved."

She tried to smile, but the effort was too great. "Stay . . . please . . ."

"I'll never leave you again. I swear it." Sitting on the edge of the bed, he lifted his wrist to his mouth, then opened the vein with his teeth. "Here, you must drink this."

She stared at him, uncomprehending.

Muttering an oath, he pressed his bleeding wrist to her mouth. "Drink, Rhianna."

Her eyes widened as she realized what he wanted, and then she shook her head.

"Drink, Rhianna. It is the only way."

His voice wrapped around her, soft as cotton wool, demanding her compliance. She didn't want to obey, but she was helpless against the dark power in his eyes. When he held his wrist to her lips again, she swallowed once, twice.

Just enough to restore her health, though he yearned to give her more, to bring her across the bridge from mortality to immortality, to keep her at his side forever. But even as he considered it, he knew she would hate him for it. And yet . . . He closed his eyes, feeling the warmth of her mouth on his flesh, the sensation of his blood flowing into her. What ecstasy it would be, to drink her to the point of death and have her drink from him in return, to know she would be his forever. With a harsh cry, he pulled his wrist away, ran his tongue over the ragged wound to close it. "Sleep now."

"No."

"I'll be here when you awake."

"You . . . promise?"

"I promise."

"Hold me."

With a strangled cry, he drew her into his arms and held her close. "Forgive me," he murmured. A single bloodred tear dripped onto her cheek, and he wiped it away, despising what he was, the pain he had caused her. "Please, beloved, forgive me."

When she was asleep, he settled her into bed once more, then spread his cloak over her.

Moments later, Bevins entered the room carrying a decanter and goblet. Wordlessly, he filled the glass and handed it to his master.

"Where's Montroy?" Rayven asked.

"I sent him home. He did not want to go."

"Is he all right?"

"He seemed a bit dazed."

Rayven nodded. "I shall deal with him later. Where's Ada?"

"She went home earlier this evening. She said she would be back tomorrow to, ah . . ." Bevins drew a finger across his throat. "I've secured the castle doors, my lord. No one will bother you."

"You've done well." Rayven took a sip from the goblet, stared into the glass, then took another swallow. "What is this?" he demanded.

Bevins cleared his throat, wondering if he had made a grave mistake. "A very little wine, my lord." He hesitated, his own blood running cold as he met his master's eyes. "Mixed with a great deal of blood."

"Whose blood?"

"Lady Rhianna's. The doctor bade me dispose of it."

Rayven stared into the goblet for a long moment and then, slowly, almost reverently, he drank the warm crimson liquid. He felt his strength returning, his power expanding, as her blood spread through him, filling him with a familiar warmth. But it was not enough to replace what weeks of starvation had cost him.

His gaze fixed on Bevins, Rayven set the goblet on the tray.

"My lord?"

"I'm sorry."

With a nod, Bevins rolled up his shirtsleeve and held out his arm.

She was dreaming, dreaming of Rayven. Dreaming that he was there beside her, holding her close. She could feel his breath fanning her cheek, hear his voice whispering that he loved her, begging for her forgiveness.

With a sigh, she snuggled deeper under the covers, hoping the dream would never end.

"Rhianna?"

She smiled as his voice caressed her. She had dreamed of him every night since he had left her, but never like this. It seemed so real.

She drew the blanket up over her head to block the light, frowned as her fingers closed over velvet and silk.

She gasped as her eyes flew open and she found herself staring into his face. "Rayven!"

He smiled at her, his beautiful dark eyes warm with love.

"You're here? You're really here?" Tentatively, she lifted a hand to his cheek. His skin was cool and smooth beneath her fingertips. "Tell me I'm not dreaming."

"You are not dreaming, my sweet." He captured her hand in his and lifted it to his lips.

"You were in danger." She clasped his hand in both of hers and pressed it to her heart. "I could feel it, in here. You wanted to die. You *were* dying."

"And you were determined to die with me."

Rhianna nodded. "I want no life without you, my lord husband."

He closed his eyes as though he were in pain.

"Rayven? What is it? What's wrong?"

"Nothing, my sweet. I intend to see that you have everything you desire, everything you deserve."

"My lord?" She gazed at him, wondering why his words of assurance made her suddenly uneasy.

"Go to sleep, Rhianna."

"Hold me?"

He swallowed against the pain knifing through him as he gathered her into his arms and held her close, certain that, before long, he would have to let her go.

In the last hour before dawn, Rayven made his way to Montroy's estate.

Thunder rolled across the heavens; the rain fell in a steady downpour. He drew his cloak more tightly around him, wishing he were back in his room, holding Rhianna in his arms. But there would be time enough for that when he had finished here.

Montroy's house was dark, all the doors and windows closed and locked.

"You'll not keep me out so easily," Rayven muttered. Grinning, he went to the back of the house where, with a wave of his hand, he unlocked the rear door.

On silent feet, he made his way up the stairs to Montroy's sleeping chamber and stepped inside.

For a moment, he gazed down at Montroy and then, gathering his power, he spoke softly to Dallon's mind, commanding him to forget all that had happened with Rhianna, to forget that Rayven had taken his blood, to forget that he had ever believed Rayven to be a vampyre.

Remember only that we are friends, and that I love Rhianna, Rayven commanded. *If anyone asks, you have seen me dine at your table, you have entertained me in your home, at your club, and found me no different from other men.*

He felt a moment of regret when he was certain he had erased all that was necessary from the viscount's mind, but there was no help for it. The other alternative was to destroy the man, and that he could not do.

He left Montroy's house as quietly as he had arrived. His next stop was Ada McLeod's. It was not so easy to manipulate Ada's mind. Her hatred and distrust posed a barrier that was difficult to breach, but, in the end, Rayven had his way, erasing her memory of her daughter's illness and her own intention to destroy him.

Satisfied that he had done all he could, he left the cottage and returned home.

He paused as he reached the top of the mountain. The castle rose from the ground in a graceful mass of dark gray stone and aged wood, the ever-present mist hovering over it like faerie breath, the moonlight limning the turrets with silver.

Safe within the hidden room in the east tower, he closed the portal, undressed, and slid into bed beside Rhianna. He drew her into his arms, a flood of emotion swelling in his heart as she murmured something unintelligible, then snuggled trustingly against him, the warmth of her body molding itself to his, chasing away the chill of the night.

Ah, Rhianna, he mused as he lightly stroked her hair. *Do you know how much I love you? How much I need you?*

He groaned low in his throat as she snuggled against him. Her nearness teased his desire, stirred his hunger, that damnable hunger that seemed ever closer to the surface since he had returned to her side. Was it because he had given her his blood, or was he losing control of the monster that resided in his soul?

He brushed a kiss across her cheek, felt his fangs lengthen. It would be so easy to take her while she slept, to drink and drink, to make her what he was. She would truly be his bride then, forever, for always.

No! He screamed the word in his mind. He would not, could not, condemn her to a life of darkness.

With an effort, he stilled the hunger, wondering, as he did so, how much longer he could keep it under control.

Chapter Twenty-seven

Rhianna woke slowly, a wondrous sense of well-being rising up within her when she opened her eyes and saw Rayven lying beside her. Once, the sight of him lying there, as still as death, had frightened her a little. But no more. He was not dead, only sleeping.

A smile warmed her heart as, ever so tenderly, she trailed her fingertips across his cheek, then bent and brushed his lips with hers. He was here, and that was all that mattered.

She studied him for a long pleasurable time, the sight of him filling her with inexpressible joy. She smoothed a lock of raven-hued hair from his forehead, traced the straight line of his brows, let her fingertip follow the faint white scar on his cheek.

He didn't stir, yet, in her heart, she knew he was aware of her touch, her presence.

"Sleep well, my lord husband," she whispered.

Rising, she pulled a robe over her gown and left the room, pausing to lock the outer door before she left the tower.

She found Bevins downstairs, sitting at the kitchen table, sipping a cup of tea.

"Milady!" Startled at being caught unaware, Bevins lurched to his feet. "I'm sorry, I didn't realize you were up. Shall I draw your bath?"

"Later. Please, sit down, Bevins. Do you mind if I join you?"

Bevins frowned. "It's not fitting, milady."

"Oh." Shoulders drooping, she turned away.

"Milady, wait!" Bevins pulled out a chair. "Please, join me. Would you care for a cup of tea? Some scones, perhaps?"

"Yes, thank you." She smiled as he poured her a cup of tea, added milk and sugar. "Tell me, Bevins, is all this formality between us really necessary?"

"I beg your pardon, milady?"

"Can't you just call me Rhianna?"

"I'm afraid it wouldn't be proper," Bevins replied, taking a seat across from her. "Lord Rayven . . ." He picked up his cup and stared into the contents. "I'm very much afraid he would not like it."

"Maybe you could call me Rhianna when we're alone."

"I think not, milady."

"All right, Tom. I wouldn't want you to be uncomfortable."

Rhianna finished her tea, then stood up. "Would you mind drawing my bath?"

"My pleasure, milady. Will you be wanting breakfast later?"

"Yes, thank you."

* * *

Later that day, Rhianna asked Bevins to take her to see her mother.

Ada met them at the door of the cottage. "Rhianna, how well you look," she said. She gave Rhianna a hug, smiled warmly at Bevins. "Come in, come in."

Rhianna looked at Bevins and frowned, mystified by her mother's lighthearted mood.

Ada led them into the parlor. "Sit down, both of you. Can I get you something to drink? Some lemonade, perhaps, or a cup of tea?"

"Lemonade would be nice, Mama. Where are the girls?"

"They've gone into the village to visit with Aileen. They'll be sorry they missed you. Mr. Bevins, can I get you something to drink?"

"Yes, thank you, Mistress McLeod. Lemonade would be fine."

"Can I help you, Mama?" Rhianna asked.

"No, daughter. It won't take but a minute."

Rhianna looked at Bevins and shook her head. "I thought she would be upset."

Bevins nodded. It was obvious that something strange was going on. And whenever there were strange happenings, Lord Rayven was usually behind them.

They spent an hour with Ada, chatting about the weather, Aileen's pregnancy, Lanna's new beau. Ada asked after Rayven, expressing her regret that he had been unable to accompany Rhianna, urging her to bring him along next time.

"I don't understand it," Rhianna remarked to Tom as they left for home. "She's never made any secret of the fact that she dislikes Rayven. What do you make of it?"

"I'm not sure, milady," Bevins replied. "Perhaps Lord Rayven will know."

"Why would he know?"

"Perhaps you should ask him."

"You've being very evasive, Tom."

"Yes, milady."

"What aren't you telling me?"

A pained expression crossed the man's face. "Milady, please."

"Oh, very well," Rhianna muttered, and then she cast Tom a sharp look. "He's done something to her, hasn't he?"

Bevins blew out a deep breath. "He has the power, milady."

"The power to do what?"

"I think perhaps Lord Rayven has erased certain things from your mother's memory."

Rhianna sat back, a little stunned. "He can do that?"

Bevins nodded. "Please don't tell him that I told you."

"I won't. Does he do that kind of thing often?"

"I'm sure I couldn't say, milady."

Rhianna sat back, lost in thought, until they reached home.

She changed into a dark green velvet gown for supper. It was one of her favorite frocks, with its deep vee neck and flared sleeves edged with Irish lace. The skirt was soft and full and swayed gracefully when she moved.

Going down to her own room, she stood in front of the mirror, studying her reflection. Her eyes sparkled in anticipation of seeing her husband, her cheeks rosy with a blush of excitement. She had left her hair unbound because Rayven had once said he preferred it that way.

Turning away from the looking glass, she hurried out of her room and up the tower stairs. He would be awakening in a moment, and she wanted to be there.

She fairly flew into his room. He was still asleep. Sitting on the edge of the bed, she took his hand in hers.

Her heartbeat quickened as the sun went down and she felt the life force flow through him, strong and sure as a river at flood tide. A moment later, his eyelids fluttered open.

Rhianna smiled at him. "Good evening, my lord husband," she murmured softly, and bent down to kiss him.

His hand curled around her nape, drawing her closer as he deepened the kiss. With a sigh, Rhianna melted against him, her hands sliding over his bare chest, down his belly, moving ever so slowly downward.

He gasped as her hand stroked him and then, without her quite knowing how he had managed it so quickly, she was lying naked beneath him, the sheets cool beneath her, his breath warm where it fanned her cheek.

"Rhianna . . . Rhianna . . ." He repeated her name over and over again, unable to stop, unable to resist the urge to bury himself deep within her silken flesh, to make her his. The scent of her blood called to him, igniting his hunger.

She moaned softly, her hands moving restlessly over his back and shoulders as he moved within her. She felt his lips caress her breasts, and then she felt the sharp prick of his teeth at her throat.

She experienced a rush of sensual pleasure and then, when he didn't stop, but drank and drank again, she went cold with fear.

"Rayven . . ."

"Rhianna, tell me to stop!"

He stared down at her, seeing her through a hazy red mist as hunger and desire melded into one, roaring through him like a raging inferno, threatening to devour everything in its path.

Rhianna looked back at him, helpless, vulnerable. His eyes, as black as midnight, burned into hers and she knew, in that moment, that she was looking death in the face.

"Rhianna!"

She heard the fear in his voice, the underlying pain as the hunger raged within him, threatening to consume them both. Fear for her own life receded in the face of his agony.

"Rhianna . . . help me!" He was breathing heavily now, terrified that the hunger would overcome him and that he would destroy her.

"I love you." She whispered the words over and over again, knowing she had never meant them more. Knowing he had never needed to hear them, to believe them, more than he did now.

With a hoarse cry, he pushed her from him, grabbed his cloak, and bolted from the room.

"Rayven!"

The sound of her voice followed him down the stairs, out of the castle. He paused to drape his cloak around his shoulders, and then he was running, faster than mortal eyes could see, running away from the only woman he had ever loved, from the scent of her blood, from the trust in her eyes.

"Fool!" He screamed the word into the wind that chased him through the night. "Fool!"

A fool to think he could have her, that he could take her blood, give her his in return, and forever deny what he was. What idiocy, to think he could live like a mortal man, that he could keep the hunger forever at bay. He was not a man, had not been a man for over four hundred years. He was a vampyre, and all the wishing in the world could not change that.

He knew now what he had to do. There was only one way to keep Rhianna safe from the monster. Only one way to protect her from what he was. He would rise early tomorrow night. He would feed well so that Rhianna's sweetness would not tempt him. He would erase his memory from her mind, and then he would go out to meet the sun. With nothing left to live for, he would welcome death.

He sought shelter in a cave cut deep into the side of Devil Tree Mountain. Shrouded in his cloak, he stared at nothingness. At dusk, he would seek out Rhianna. He would spend one last night in her presence, hold her in his arms one last time and then, while she slept, he would blot his memory from her mind. Montroy would provide her with all the comforts money could buy. He would cherish her and love her; in time, he would give her a child. The thought of Montroy caressing Rhianna sent a hot shaft of pain searing through his heart. But it was the only way to ensure that he did not destroy her. He no longer trusted himself to keep her safe, no longer believed himself strong enough to keep from forcing the Dark Gift upon her.

With the coming of dawn, he curled up on the damp earth, drew his cloak over his head, and waited for the darkness to overtake him one last time.

"Salvatore," he murmured as he slipped over the edge, "how did you survive so long without going mad?"

He woke an hour after the setting of the sun and knew immediately that he wasn't alone in the cave.

"I had not thought you to be a late riser."

The voice, so long unheard, so familiar, drifted over him. "Salvatore? Is that you?"

Soft laughter filled the cave. "Rayven, my friend, it has been too long."

Rayven sat up and drew his cloak over his nakedness. He could see the other vampyre now, leaning negligently against the wall of the cave, his arms crossed over his chest. "What brings you here?"

"You, of course. What else would bring me to this dreary place?"

"I don't understand."

"You called for me, did you not?"

Rayven frowned, then nodded.

"I would have been here sooner, but . . ." Salvatore shrugged emphatically. "I had been at rest when I heard your call." He smiled. "You understand, it took me some time to replenish my strength."

Rayven nodded. It was the way of the Old Ones, to go to ground every hundred years or so.

"So, my friend, tell me what it is that troubles you."

In short crisp sentences, Rayven told Salvatore about Rhianna, about his fears for her safety, the growing need to make her what he was, the sure knowledge that she would hate him for it.

"It is no longer safe for her to be with me." He turned tormented eyes on his friend. "And I have no desire to go on without her."

"So you intend to destroy yourself?"

"It is the only way."

"No," Salvatore replied softly. "There is another."

"Tell me!"

"You wish to renounce the Dark Gift, to be mortal again?"

Mortal again. Was it possible? Did he really want it? Would she still love him if he was mortal? He knew the allure of his vampyre blood, the underlying power that colored everything he did and said. "Is it possible?"

"If you truly wish it."

He thought of life without her, and then let himself think what it would be like to share her life, her whole life, each day, every day. "How? How is it done?"

"It is dangerous, my friend, and often fatal."

"It is a risk I am willing to take."

"You truly wish to give up your immortality for this woman?"

Rayven nodded. "Please, Salvatore, only tell me what I must do."

"First I would like to meet this woman."

"Salvatore . . ."

"It cannot be done now, my friend. We have time."

Rhianna ran down the stairs to meet him. Throwing herself into his arms, she held him close, oblivious to the presence of the other man.

"Where did you go? Where have you been? I've been so worried."

"I am fine, my sweet," Rayven assured her. He glanced over his shoulder at Salvatore. "Please, make yourself comfortable while I dress."

"Forgive me," Rhianna said, staring at the man standing in the shadows of the entryway. "I didn't see you there."

Salvatore bowed in her direction. "My lady."

"Rhianna, this is Salvatore. You remember I told you about him?"

She nodded, a sudden shiver rippling down her spine. Salvatore. Rayven had told her he was a vampyre, a very old, very powerful vampyre.

A faint smile played over Salvatore's lips. "Does my being here disturb you, my lady?"

"No." It was a lie, and they all knew it.

"Come with me, Rhianna," Rayven said. "Salvatore, we won't be long."

Rhianna followed her husband upstairs, a thousand questions chasing themselves through her mind.

She sat down on the edge of the bed, watching Rayven while he dressed. "Why is he here?"

"I need him." He dressed quickly, then knelt at her feet and took her hands in his. "Rhianna, would you love me as you do now if I were a mortal man?"

"What do you mean?"

"If I could be human again, would you still love me, still want to spend your life with me?"

"Of course." She frowned at him. "Why wouldn't I?"

"There's a certain intangible power inherent in vampyres. You may not be aware of it, but it's there. Some women are attracted by the *power*, but not the man himself."

"Rayven, what are you trying to say?"

"Salvatore told me there is a way for me to become mortal again."

She stared at him a moment, then threw her arms around him and hugged him tight. "That's wonderful! How is it done?"

"I don't know." He cupped her face in his hands and kissed her gently, felt the hunger stir to life. "Let's go find out."

"It is surprisingly simple, really," Salvatore said. "A few words, the shedding of blood . . ." His dark brown eyes bored into Rayven. "Faith that it will work."

"It sounds too easy."

"That's where faith comes in, my friend."

"We must do it now, tonight," Rayven said. He couldn't wait any longer. He didn't know why the hunger was riding him so hard. Was it because he had given Rhianna his blood? He had thought, after four hundred years, that he controlled the hunger, but he knew now it had never been true. The hunger would always be his master. It might rest, it might be appeased, but it would never be conquered.

"It must be done in a church as close to the rising of the sun as possible," Salvatore said.

Rayven nodded, though he could not help thinking a graveyard would be a more appropriate place to hold a ritual for the undead.

Salvatore placed his hand on Rayven's shoulder. "There are preparations I must make. Meet me in the chapel an hour before sunrise." He glanced at Rhianna. "You must come alone."

"No," Rhianna said. "I want to be there."

"I'm sorry, my lady, but no mortal may be present."

"But . . ."

"You might wish to spend these hours together."

"Last hours is what you mean, isn't it?"

"It is a possibility, my lady." Salvatore put his hand on her shoulder in a gesture of sympathy and affection, then looked at Rayven. "In the last hour before dawn, my friend. Do not be late."

"I'll be there."

Rhianna waited until they were alone, then she took Rayven's hand in both of hers. "Don't do this."

"I must."

"No. Make me what you are. Do it now."

"No, Rhianna. You don't want it, and you would hate me for it."

"Then let us go on as we are. Please, Rayven, I'm so afraid."

"We cannot go on as we are," Rayven said, the certainly building within him. "I cannot control the hunger any longer." Even now he could feel it swelling, building, surging within him, urging him to take her in his dark embrace, to drink her sweetness until he was glutted with it. He felt the beast writhing deep inside, felt its claws as it struggled for freedom.

"I won't let you do it," Rhianna said. "He said it was dangerous."

"You are the one in danger, Rhianna."

She stared up at him, at eyes that glowed with a hellish light. "I don't understand. What's done this to you?"

"This is what I am, Rhianna, what I have always been. I cannot fight it any longer."

"Rayven . . ."

He lifted her hand, brushed his lips across her palm. He had hoped to make love to her, but he dared not take the chance. The hunger was always aroused by passion.

"Find Bevins," he said, his voice gruff. "Stay with him. He will keep you safe."

"No. Please let me stay with you until it's time."

"Go, Rhianna. I beg of you, if you love me at all, leave me now."

"I do love you. I'll always love you," she cried.

"Go then. Please, Rhianna."

Hating herself for her cowardice, afraid of what might happen if she defied him, she ran out of the room.

Salvatore was waiting for him inside the chapel. He wore a long hooded cloak of dark blue wool. He held a small wooden cup in his hands.

"You must trust me in this," Salvatore said. "Any doubt on your part will be fatal."

Rayven nodded.

"Drink this, all of it."

"What is it?"

"An ancient mixture composed of a little garlic,

a little foxglove, a smidgen of mugwort, the dried petals of a white rose, yarrow and lavendar, a sprinkling of wolfsbane. And just enough red wine to make it palatable."

"You expect me to drink that?"

Salvatore nodded, his expression solemn.

Rayven took the cup, sniffed it, wrinkled his nose with distaste, and drank the contents down in one long swallow. "Is that it?"

"It is only the beginning. The potion is to purify your blood. Now comes the hard part. Remove your shirt, then lie down on the altar."

Heart pounding, Rayven did as bidden. The altar, of white marble, was cold beneath him. The words, as cold as the grave, hovered in the back of his mind.

With a blink of his eye, Salvatore lit every candle within the church. A faint rosy glow filled the room. Moonlight streamed through the stained-glass window over the altar, casting crimson highlights over Rayven's naked arms and chest.

Salvatore stood at the head of the altar. "You are sure this is what you wish to do?"

"Yes. No, wait!" Rayven sat up, his hands clutching Salvatore's robe. "I must see Rhianna, wipe my memory from her mind."

"If this succeeds, that will not be necessary. If it fails, I will see that she remembers nothing of you or this night."

With a nod, Rayven stretched out on the altar once more.

Reaching into the folds of his cloak, Salvatore withdrew a slender dagger. The hilt was made of wood, the solid silver blade gleamed in the flickering light of the candles.

Rayven stared at the dagger. "A blood sacrifice, old friend?"

"Of a sort. How do you feel?"

"Weak."

"It is the herbs. They are cleansing your blood."

Rayven stared at the knife, unable to take his gaze from the shimmering silver blade. Silver. Deadly to vampyres. A tremor of unease slithered down his spine. "You are going to cut me?"

"This is where your faith comes in. When the time is right, I am going to bleed you to the point of death, and then I am going to give your life, true life, back to you."

Rayven shook his head. He tried to rise, but his limbs felt heavy, weighted. "No . . ."

"You must trust me, my friend. The herbs are the first step. They will neutralize the vampyric agent in your blood and allow you to withstand the coming of dawn."

"You mentioned faith . . ."

"Indeed. If, deep in your heart, you truly wish to give up your immortality, you will rise with the dawn, a mortal man in every way. If there is any doubt, the sun will destroy you."

Questions flooded his mind, but he lacked the power to voice them aloud. His body was numb; he couldn't keep his eyes open. His blood slowed, feeling hot and heavy in his veins.

"Relax." Salvatore's voice. It seemed to come from a great distance.

He felt a sudden, sharp pain in his left wrist and knew that Salvatore had slit a vein. He could feel his life's blood flowing out of him, could hear the beat of his heart, beating fast in fear, slowing as more and more blood was drained from his body.

Rhianna . . .

Salvatore held a wooden cup to Rayven's lips, forced him to drink. He knew it was blood, his own blood, but it tasted like cool clear water. He drained the cup again and again, until nothingness overwhelmed him, smothering him in cloud-like layers of brilliant white light. He had expected to feel the fires of Hell, to be lost in darkness. The light burned his eyes and seared his soul.

This is what it feels like to be reborn, he thought. *Rhianna . . .*

Rhianna paced the floor, her gaze going to the door again and again. She looked at Bevins, but he only shook his head. And then she heard Rayven's voice calling her name. His voice, growing faint until it was gone.

With a cry, she ran out of the castle, down the path toward the chapel.

Sunlight fell over the building, limning it with silver and gold, turning it into a faerie place.

She came to an abrupt halt, fear making her heart pound and her mouth dry. She took a step forward, and then another. The door was open. Sunlight filtered through the stained-glass window, shining down on the body which lay, unmoving, on the altar. Streaks of red stained the white marble.

"Rayven . . ." His name whispered past her lips. "Oh, no . . ."

She didn't remember moving, but suddenly she was there, at his side. Her gaze skimmed his body. There was blood on the altar. It had to be his blood, but she could find no wound.

Lifting a shaking hand, she placed it on his

chest. His skin was smooth and cool. She could detect no heartbeat.

"Rayven! You promised you wouldn't leave me. You promised!"

She rested her head on his chest, tears burning her eyes. "You promised."

She wept, her tears falling on his chest, mingling with the blood on the altar. "Please don't leave me."

"Rhianna . . ."

His voice, echoing in her mind. But no, it was real. Slowly, she lifted her head, opened her eyes. "Rayven? You're alive!"

"So it would seem." He knew instantly that his powers were gone. Colors were less bright. He could hear nothing beyond the walls of the chapel. He took a deep breath, and his nostrils filled with the scent of candle wax and dew-damp grass and Rhianna's perfume. No trace of blood stirred his senses. The beat of her heart didn't thunder in his ears.

He sat up slowly. He felt strangely light, peaceful. And then he smiled. The hunger was gone. For the first time in over four hundred years, he was free . . . free of the darkness that had been his constant companion, free of the hunger that had plagued him. He looked at Rhianna. She was beautiful, the most beautiful sight he had ever seen. For the first time since he had met her, her blood did not call to him.

Rhianna was watching him carefully. "Are you all right?"

"I'm mortal again," he replied. "It seems I can't promise you forever anymore."

"I never wanted forever," she said, happiness

shining in her eyes. "Only a lifetime with the man I love."

"You shall have it, my sweet Rhianna." He glanced at the doorway, at the bright golden light beyond. The light beckoned him, tantalizing in its warmth, its purity. The world he had shut himself away from waited beyond that door. A world he could share with the woman he loved.

"Rayven . . ."

He drew her into his arms and kissed the tears from her eyes. "Ah, my sweet Rhianna, Salvatore will say it was the potion and my faith that worked the miracle, but I know better. It was your love that brought me through the darkness."

Happiness bubbled up inside him, and he kissed her again, exultantly, and then, rising to his feet, he took Rhianna by the hand and walked out into the sunlight of a new day, a new life.

Epilogue

Castle Rayven
One year later

He stood at the window, watching the sun come up. It was a sight he never tired of, a miracle he knew he would never take for granted.

In those first days after he had regained his humanity, he had spent hours basking in the sun, feeling its warmth upon his face as he walked through the gardens, or sat on the bench in the heart of the maze, reflecting on his past, looking forward to the future.

He watched the sky grow light as the sun chased away the night. The sun, so bright and beautiful. Its welcome heat had banished the last of the darkness from his soul.

Much had changed in the past year. Rhianna's sister, Aileen, had given birth to twin boys. Montroy had decided to take a trip around the world. Bevins had married Rhianna's mother and moved into her cottage.

A gentle cooing drew Rayven's attention from the brightening sky. Turning away from the window, he crossed the floor.

"Shh, little one. Your mama needs her sleep." He smiled as he lifted his four-day old daughter from her cradle. "How are you this morning, my beautiful Alisha? Did you sleep well?"

She was another miracle, he thought, his heart swelling with love as he cuddled the baby in his arms. He still could not believe that she was his, that after four hundred years of darkness, he had sired a strong, healthy child with hair like sunlight and eyes as blue as a midsummer sky.

So many miracles in his life, he mused. Indeed, his life was perhaps the biggest miracle of all. He remembered lying on the altar, drowning in darkness, hearing Rhianna's voice calling him back from the very edge of eternity, the feel of her tears like rain on his flesh.

The miracle of their love. It still amazed him that she could love the man he had become. He did not miss the darkness, but he occasionally missed the ability to read Rhianna's thoughts, to know what she was thinking. She was a mystery to him now, as every woman was a mystery to the man who loved her.

Rhianna. Her love for him was surely the greatest miracle of all.

With a smile, he placed his sleeping daughter back in her cradle, then picked up the book in which he had once recorded his dark thoughts. It was time for a new entry.

Redemption

aeons of darkness
shrouded my soul
I had forgotten
the warmth
and beauty
of the sun;

alone
lonely
I wandered the earth
hoping
yearning
dreaming
of redemption;

searching for an end
to the hunger
that
engulfed me
to the pain
that
tormented me;

for centuries
the night was
my day
the day
my night
there was no
color
in my world;

until you . . .

in your smile
I found hope
in your love
forgiveness
and now the light
once denied me
shines forever
in your eyes

Dear Reader:

I hope you enjoyed *A Darker Dream.* I always fall in love with my heroes, especially the dark brooding ones. I hope you do, too.

I want to take this opportunity to thank MICHAEL WHITNEY and REBECCA PAIVA for graciously letting me use their poetry. Rayven's poems are really theirs. "The Other Me" was written by Michael; "I Can Feel It Coming" was written by Rebecca. Thanks, you two! For those of you who surf the net, you might want to check out The Dark Poets Page. Lots of good stuff there.

I also want to thank MARY LOU VON METER for the use of her poem "Heart of Darkness." If you read my books, you've seen her work before. Thanks, Mary Lou.

I hope you're all having a wonderful summer, and that your days are filled with happiness and good books, and your "to be read" pile is filled with "keepers."

Love and hugs,
Amanda